HAWK'S QUEST

a Superior pursuit

NORTH SHORE AT LAKE SUPERIOR

HAWK'S QUEST

a Superior pursuit

ARVID LLOYD WILLIAMS

BONNIE SHALLBETTER

Beaver's Pond Press

HAWK'S QUEST

a Superior pursuit

Third in a Series

ISBN 10: 1-59298-211-5
ISBN 13: 978-1-59298-211-0

Library of Congress Control Number: 2007907605
Printed in the United States of America
First Printing, November 2007
11 10 09 08 07   6 5 4 3 2 1

Beaver's Pond Press is an imprint of
Beaver's Pond Group
7104 Ohms Lane, Suite 101
Edina, Minnesota, 55439-2129
www.beaverspondpress.com

ARVID LLOYD WILLIAMS

*This book is dedicated to my mother, Elsie Williams,
and my brothers and sisters, Audrey, Janet, Fran, Ken,
Bonnie, Raymond, Clyde, and Sharon, and especially to Janet,
Raymond, and Clyde, who have gone to the life beyond life.*

*I also dedicate this work to my children,
Steve, Sue, Mike, Kathy, and Maggie.*

*My thanks go to my writing partner, Bonnie Shallbetter,
for her part in this endeavor. This series would not have gone
as far as it has without her encouragement and support.
In addition, thanks and appreciation go to Bonnie's husband,
Steve Shallbetter, for his patience and understanding
while we worked on the series.*

*I thank Bonnie and Steve Just, owners of the
Just Up North gift shop in Outing, Minnesota,
for their support in the promotion of this series.*

*A great thank you to my daughter Sue and son-in-law
Chris Sullivan for getting us started on this journey.*

BONNIE SHALLBETTER

*I would like to dedicate HAWK'S QUEST, a Superior pursuit,
to my parents who lovingly guided me through life,
giving me encouragement and the freedom to express myself.
The book is a visible culmination of a lifetime of their support.*

BONNIE SHALLBETTER'S
ACKNOWLEDGEMENTS

I would like to personally thank the following people and organizations for their support and inspiration: The Duluth Public Library, The Grand Marais Public Library, The Grand Portage National Monument, Joni Carlstrom, Barb Retzlaff, Sheila MacDonald (my chronically silly friend), Marty Dehen, Steve Forsberg, (the music professor) Paul Forsberg, George Shallbetter, Steve Shallbetter, Erik and Matt Shallbetter.

My deep gratitude goes to Arvid, my writing partner, for the opportunity and privilege to share and create a story that has been a true adventure in every sense of the word.

A sincere thank you goes to Beaver's Pond Press, our publishers, for their dedication and support, and to all those involved in the process.

And heartfelt thanks go out to our reading audience for their continued support and patience.

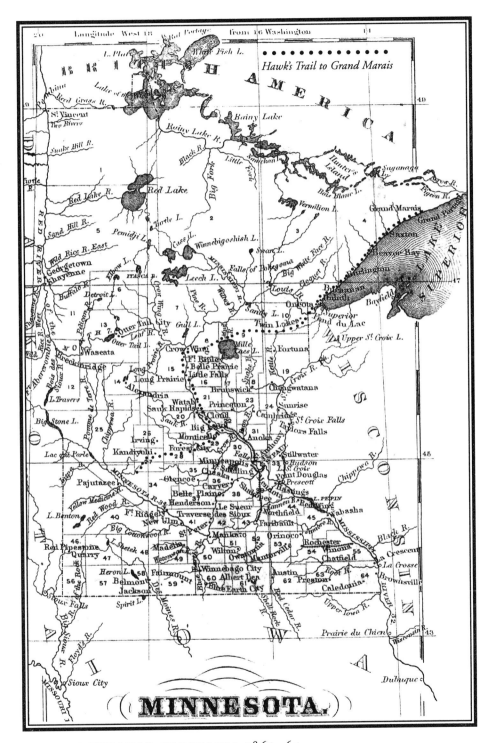

JOURNEY THROUGH MINNESOTA 1863–64

TABLE OF CONTENTS

A SOFT RAIN FELL ON THE MEN AND WOMEN STANDING SILENTLY AT THE FRESH GRAVE. Leaves fluttered down from the trees above them and a crow called as it flew overhead. Three Dakota Indians sat on horses away from the group. Their faces were painted black and hawk feathers stood in the black bands around their heads.

The mourners stood for long moments in silence. The men held umbrellas as women dabbed at tears flowing freely from their eyes. Reverend John Wakeman turned to Lorraine and took her hands in his. "Grandfather talked often about Hawk Owen. They could have been friends if things had been different."

"Little Crow and my father *were* friends," Lorraine said. "They were on opposite sides in the war, but that does not mean they could not be friends. They had a mutual respect, and that, Reverend, is as solid a foundation for friendship as could be asked for."

Journalist Return Holcomb stood with them and listened to the conversation.

"Let's go to the cabin," Lorraine said. "The ladies have prepared a luncheon and we wouldn't want it to get cold."

Reverend Wakeman shook hands with each member of the grieving party as they turned and walked to the log cabin thirty yards away. The Indians turned their horses and rode swiftly away from the private burial ground.

Return Holcomb walked with Lorraine Owen. "Miss Owen," he said. "Little Crow died a long time before Wakeman was born. How could he know his grandfather talked about Hawk Owen?"

"That, Mister Holcomb, is a part of the story that will not be told."

"Miss Owen, if you know something about Little Crow you must tell us.

The people of this state have a right to know." Lorraine ignored the reporter's statement and continued toward the house.

"You know," Holcomb said, "some people doubt that it was Little Crow who was killed that day."

Lorraine stopped, turned to Holcomb, and looked directly into his eyes. "Little Crow died in that berry patch seventy years ago and he will stay dead. That is the end of this conversation."

"You know, I find this such an interesting story and I want to get everything that's pertinent. Our readers will want to know, too. They have been patiently waiting."

Though Return Holcomb was ten years younger and four inches taller than Lorraine, he felt small and brittle under her challenging eyes. He smiled at her. "You have the same look in your eye your father had when he had his mind set. I won't bring it up again."

Lorraine turned once again, making her way toward the house. Holcomb fought the urge to run as he tried to keep up with her fast pace. "How is it that a beautiful woman like you never got married?" he asked between hard-won breaths.

"I have never found a man who could measure up."

"You mean you could never find a man who could keep up with you. Would you mind if we walked a little slower?"

Lorraine slowed her pace slightly and said, "I am the daughter of Hawk and Sophie Owen."

"Say no more," he said with a chuckle. "You told us there is more to tell about your mother and father. May we hear that story?"

"Come into the house and have a bite to eat. I'll tell you the entire story."

In a short while the mourners left and Lorraine took a chair with Mister Holcomb in front of the fireplace.

The room was silent except for the crackling of the fire and the steady ticking of the clock on the wall. Lorraine took a sip of tea, sat back in her chair, then began.

"In August of eighteen sixty-three, Sophie and Hawk were settled comfortably here in this house. The house was much smaller than it is now. There were just two rooms; the front room, where we are now, and the back bedroom. They had one hundred fifty acres of prime farmland with plenty of fresh water, grass, and forest, and Hawk Creek just behind the house.

"Minnesota had become a peaceful place to live since the war with the Sioux Indians had moved to the western plains. The Civil War continued in the South, but for Hawk Owen and his brother Jacob it was a far-away story and nothing that would change their lives in any way.

"President Lincoln was calling for more troops from Minnesota to fight in the war. In the spring of that year he signed into law the first national conscription law, which allowed the government to require young men to join the Union Army and fight the Confederates in the South. It was, in effect, the first selective service draft program in the United States.

"But there were provisions in the law that permitted a man to pay another man three hundred dollars to take his place in the draft. My father wrote a letter to President Lincoln complaining about the law, calling it an unfair way for the wealthy to keep their young men from having to go to war. It was called a rich man's war. Of course, he never got a response to the letter.

"Hawk and Jake had been wounded in the Sioux Conflict in the Minnesota Valley while fighting under General Henry H. Sibley and, therefore, were exempt from the draft. Hawk was appointed lieutenant of volunteers in the United States Army by General Sibley and served until the Indian wars were declared officially over, at which time he was discharged.

"Jake bought a farm northeast of Courtland, on the shores of Swan Lake, and worked hard to make it pay off. He was a year younger than Hawk and at the age of nineteen he had seen the horrors of battle and was considered an experienced Indian fighter of the first rate."

I

C H A P T E R   O N E

JAKE WAS ACCUSTOMED TO STOPPING at the Crow Bar Saloon in Courtland after a day's work.

He'd just come in from the fields where he'd spent the day planting corn. The corn would be sold to Walt Fraley who operated a moonshine still in a ravine near Swan Lake in south-central Minnesota.

Jake stood with one foot on the rail and his elbows resting on the bar. The bartender was polishing a glass at the far end of the bar while he talked to his waitress, Heidi.

Heidi, a girl of about twenty-one years, smiled and giggled as Tom talked his "stuff" to her. Tom was married but when he was in the bar that had little or no bearing on his behavior. His wife stayed in the back of the building keeping food hot for the farmers who came in for their daily feed and watering.

Jake was five feet ten and, according to some, was built like a freight wagon. His red hair hung out from under his floppy hat in curls to his shoulders. He wore baggy canvas pants held up by suspenders, a plaid shirt, and military-issue Brogans on his feet. His brown eyes stared unseeing at the bottles that lined the shelf behind the bar. His hat was tipped back showing the white forehead that contrasted sharply with the dark brown of his clean-shaven face. The tip of his nose was scabbed over from being burned daily by the springtime sun. His arms showed below the rolled up sleeves of the homespun cotton shirt his wife, Evangeline, had made for him.

Evangeline was a girl of twenty years. She was almost as tall as Jake, with wavy, dark brown hair and brown eyes. She kept herself and her house spotlessly clean. People who knew her said that she cleaned everything before it even had a chance to get dirty. She cleaned cooking pots and pans immediately after use, and the dishes were washed and put away before Jake got up from the table. In some mysterious way Jake could not understand, she still had time to sit and read the newspapers and books and go for long rides with him on horseback.

Jake liked to have a smoke of his pipe after meals, but Evangeline made it clear that she didn't like the smell in the house, so Jake did his smoking on the front porch swing.

Evangeline's mother named her after the character in Henry Wadsworth Longfellow's poem "Evangeline." Her mother and father called her Eve, and Jake found that name much easier to pronounce than Evangeline.

Eve was a direct descendant of the French Acadians who were removed from Nova Scotia in seventeen fifty-five. Her ancestors first located in New Orleans where Eve's great-grandmother married a French-Welsh farmer named Joshua Guillaume. From there the couple moved north to the farm country around Milwaukee, Wisconsin. Disillusioned by the high price of land, they moved on and eventually settled in the Minnesota Valley where Evangeline was born. The Sioux Conflict of eighteen sixty-two caused the family to return to Milwaukee where Joshua took a job in a factory building farm equipment. Eve stayed in Minnesota and worked as a housekeeper for the wealthy businessmen in Courtland and New Ulm.

Eve busied herself with keeping Jake's home neat and tidy, and when he came in from the fields or a visit to the Crow Bar, she always had a meal simmering on the stove.

Jake's visits to the Crow Bar were a bi-weekly business venture and Eve knew that he would drink a few glasses of beer and come home before dark. He talked with the farmers who came in about what they were planting, the weather, and what a dry spring it had been.

Jake wanted to plant wheat in the ten acres he'd plowed for the first time the previous fall. He needed to know how it was done, how much seed to buy—if he could get it—and when the best time was to plant. The Crow Bar was not only a place for a man to quench his thirst and get a home-cooked meal, but it was also an institute of higher learning for novice farmers like Jake. As it generally happened, each farmer he talked to knew everything there was to know about farming.

"You ought to be planting soybeans," Hank Winters offered.

"Barley, now that's the real cash crop these days," was the wisdom of Ed Schmidt.

"Me, I'm puttin' in oats, m'self," George Aldrich grumbled.

It was up to Jake to sift through the volumes of information and choose what sounded like the most sensible guess.

Jake liked to make his own beer and had a small crop of barley growing on his best ground just north of the house. Schell's beer was considered by the men in the area the best to be had. Jake knew that his beer was much better. One reason he stopped by the Crow Bar was to visit with people he didn't want coming around his farm looking for free beer.

A man sidled up to the bar next to him. "Are you Jacob Owen?"

Jake slowly recovered from his daydream and turned to the man. "Who's asking?"

"Do you own the old Emerson place out by Swan Lake?"

Jake turned away from the man and went back to his beer.

"I asked you a question, Mister Owen."

"I know, but you ain't answered my question yet."

"Excuse me," he said and put out his hand. "Robert Orley." He turned to his companions. "This is Mister Jardin and Mister Campbell. Now, I'd like to talk to you if you've got time."

Jake ignored the hand. "What's on yer mind?"

"They tell me you're the best Indian fighter in these parts."

"There ain't no Indians left that needs fightin'."

"You don't mind having those savages living in our country?"

Jake turned to Orley. "This ain't our country, Mister Orley. We stole it from the Indians."

"We didn't steal anything. We fought for it just like they fought each other to get it. Now it's ours."

"We didn't fight them for it, we starved and cheated them out of it, and this conversation is over. Go away." He turned back to his beer, and stared at the wall behind the bar ignoring Orley .

"Mister Owen, we fought for this land and some of us intend to keep it. Those Indians living up north have no right to live on land that belongs to the white men. We gave them land to live on; they belong up there."

Jake's face flushed red as he turned back to Orley. "How the hell can we give them land that's already theirs? The land they gave the Indians ain't fit for human beings to live on. It's nothing but swampland, and you know it."

"They wanted land and now they've got it. Let them go up there and live like the savages they are."

"Git away from me, Orley," Jake said and turned away from him once again.

Orley looked at Jake for a few seconds then said, "You ain't no Indian fighter. Yer a damn coward."

Still no comment came from Jake.

"I just called you a coward."

"You said your piece, now git away from me," Jake said without looking at the man.

The bartender came over still wiping a glass. "Mister, I think you've had enough. You'd better leave now. We don't want no trouble in here."

"There won't be any trouble. This Indian fighter doesn't have the guts to fight."

Jake studied the image of the man in the mirror behind the bar. Orley was an inch taller and about ten pounds leaner. His face was clean shaven and his hair cut short. He wore a white shirt with a necktie, and vest under a wool jacket. On his head was a black bowler with a silk band and a small feather tucked into the side.

Jake tipped his mug, swallowed the last of the beer, and started for the door.

Orley grabbed his shirt at the shoulder and spun him around. Instantly, Jake swung his fist, but the man ducked his swing and landed a fist on Jake's cheekbone. Another blow to the chin dazed Jake, and another fist to the cheekbone followed. Jake was stunned by the sudden attack but quickly regained his balance and swung at the man's face. Orley ducked the swing again, and Jake took another blow to his face. He stood upright with his fists clenched waiting for the next blow.

"Had enough, Injun fighter?" Orley said with a grin.

Like a flash of lightning Jake's left fist shot straight out and, two inches from the full extension of his arm, connected with Orley's nose. Orley's feet came off the floor and he landed on his back. Jake stepped up and stood over him with his feet apart about the width of his shoulders. "Git up. We ain't done yet."

Orley looked up at Jake, "My nose is busted."

"I know. I did that."

Orley rolled to the side and pushed himself to his feet. He brushed the dirt off his trousers, straightened his shirt, and pulled a white handkerchief from inside his coat. He tried to stop the blood flowing from his nose and said,

"You wadda bake sub extra buddy Bister Owed?"

"Ain't no such thing as extra money."

Orley lowered the now-bloody handkerchief. "We can pay you good money, you come in with us."

"Who's 'us'?"

"You wanna talk?"

"Nope; not interested in fightin' Indians."

"It's for a good cause."

"There's a doctor in Hutchinson who can fix that nose for you. He'll probably have some advice about getting into fights with better men than you." Jake turned for the door, climbed onto the bare back of his mule, and headed back to the farm.

"You're home early," Eve said without turning around. She sat at the table washing vegetables for their dinner. He walked up behind her, laid his hands on her shoulders, and kissed her on the side of the neck. She dried her hands on her apron, stood up, and turned to Jake. "What happened to your face?" she said calmly.

"Some guy wanted to fight and I didn't."

"A new man in town, apparently," she said in recognition of Jake's reputation as one with whom wise men did not quarrel.

"I don't know who he was, but he knew me."

"What was it all about?"

"I don't know. I didn't stick around to find out. I got all the trouble I need trying to keep this farm paying."

"Come over here. Let's clean that up a little." She took him by the arm and led him to the sink and pumped cold water into a basin.

"You and that brother of yours just seem to invite trouble," she said as she dabbed at the bruises on his cheekbone.

"We don't invite it, it just comes on its own."

"What was the fight about?"

"Not sure, but I think we've got some hotheads trying to stir up more trouble with the Indians up north."

"Jacob, I want you to stay out of that. We've had all we need of it."

He took her face in his hands and said, "Don't worry, I'm not going anywhere. I'm staying right here with you."

She kissed him on the lips, slapped his bottom, and said, "Go get yourself cleaned up. Dinner will be on the table in half an hour."

Later as they sat on the porch swing, Eve asked, "Why would any reasonable man want to start that awful war again?"

"What war?"

"With the Indians."

"Couldn't even make a guess about that."

"There's a chief up by Gull Lake who's causing mischief with the whites. Something about the traders stealing the money the Indians are supposed to be getting. A man named Hole-in-the-Day."

"How do you know about that?"

"See that stack of papers on the table over there? You should try reading them once in a while."

"Got no time for that. You do it."

"I do. Every time one comes out, I read it front to back. You'd be surprised at what you can learn from them. They say the store in town received a shipment of cotton fabric. Since the war between the states started, cotton is hard to find and I'd like to go get some."

"Do they tell how the white men are stealing from the Indians?"

"Well, no, but they do tell that the Indians, especially Hole-in-the-Day, are complaining about mistreatment by the white traders. There are government investigations going on about it."

"Yeah, well, we all know how those government investigations are handled."

"And how are they handled?"

"They're not."

Eve stood and said, "Let's go to bed before this turns into a serious discussion."

"Yeah, let's go to bed and turn this into something seriously disgusting."

"You're just like your brother," she said, snickering. "Come on."

"Yeah?" he asked as he raised himself off the swing. He stood in front of her and took her hands in his. "And what's my brother like?"

"Dragging Sophie off to bed, mostly."

"Seems to me Sophie's the one doing most of the dragging."

"I haven't heard him complaining."

"Ye blame him?"

"Not a bit. She's beautiful."

"Only one prettier," Jake said and kissed her on the nose.

He stopped the buggy and turned his head
to look at the naked couple.

2

CHAPTER TWO

HAWK HAD A PAIR OF MULES TO HELP WITH THE FARM. He'd found a cow wandering on the prairie that had been one of those captured, then abandoned, by the Sioux. Homeless livestock roamed the valley and the prairies and were free for the taking in Hawk's eyes. And feral pigs were fair game for his rifle.

Sophie once suggested they keep a sow and a boar and raise them for meat. "I ain't raising pigs," Hawk had said in response. "They stink to high heaven and they're a real problem when they get loose." To Hawk Owen that was enough excuse to keep from taking on another responsibility.

Sophie had rounded up a dozen chickens and fed them grain to keep them around the house. They supplied fresh eggs for the breakfast table and helped keep the wood ticks and other annoying critters out of the yard.

Hawk took particular delight in the occasional delicious Sunday dinner they provided. He would kill, scald, and pluck the chicken; then Sophie would roll the meat in corn flour and fry it in lard rendered from the wild hogs. Then she'd bake it in the wood-burning oven, basting it with wild honey and butter until the skin was crispy and just the right golden color. They liked red potatoes boiled with the skins on and covered with giblet gravy. The meal would not be complete without Sophie's cornmeal muffins fresh from the oven. In their own way of thinking they decided that twelve chickens in the yard was plenty. Any more that came around would only be in the way, so, as Hawk would say, "Oh darn. Chicken for dinner again?"

They had plowed ten acres for wheat and oats and another acre for a vegetable garden. They had once worked together in their garden, trying to keep the weeds from taking over but to Hawk it seemed a fruitless effort. So he left the garden work to Sophie.

Deer that came in at night and ate the tops off the vegetables were a problem for Sophie's garden, but they were a blessing to Hawk and his trusty rifle. They thought they had the deer problem solved by stringing a woven wire fence around the garden, but as any Minnesota gardener soon learned, a woven wire fence to a white tailed deer is simply something to step over when sweet, fresh greens are to be found on the other side.

Hawk considered the garden deer bait and kept their underground meat locker well stocked with fresh venison. They also had plenty of deerskins for clothing.

Hawk would stretch the skins on a rack, scrape them clean of the hair, fat, meat, and tallow and then tan them with the brains of the deer. The brain was mixed with two gallons of water, stirred into a slurry and heated. Then it was worked into the skin until it was well soaked. The skin was then stretched tightly inside a frame work of poles. He'd use the end of an axe handle to work the skin, pressing it into the wet hide, stretching it and softening it until it was completely dry. The buckskin he'd produce would be as white and soft as the finest cotton from the trader's stores.

He'd then smoke the buckskin over a willow fire to make it water repellant. Buckskin was more durable than fabric and they wore it to go about their daily chores around the farm or when hunting.

Every year he sold some of his buckskin leather for extra money, and with that money they were able to buy fabric clothing. Wool and cotton were much more comfortable in both warm and cold weather. But since cotton was hard to come by because of the war with the Confederate States, most of their clothing was made of buckskin. Hawk, of course, preferred hunting more than any of the other chores around the farm, and so he was usually in a worn buckskin shirt and pair of trousers. Sophie enjoyed the garden work and didn't seem to mind Hawk standing in the middle of the field one afternoon, leaning on the handle of his garden hoe seemingly enchanted by the distant woods and prairies. Sophie looked up from her work and smiled.

He felt a clod of dirt hit his back and turned toward Sophie.

"I'm talking to you," she said with a frown and that ever-present smile in her eyes.

"I'm sorry. What did you say?"

"You going to share your thoughts?"

"Just wondering how far that woods goes."

"Well, there's only one way to find out." She nodded her head toward The Brute, and said, "Get outta here."

"Naw, I'll stay and help." He took one more look toward the woods and turned to his hoe.

Sophie let her hoe drop to the ground. "Come on, you hitch the buggy an' I'll pack the lunch. Whad'ya say?"

"You really want to?"

"Sure. It'll be fun."

She took his arm and walked with him to the cabin. Hawk rounded up the mule and had her hitched to the buggy just as Sophie came out of the house, a woven basket hung on one arm and a blanket over the other. They climbed into the buggy, Hawk snapped the reins, and they were off. Hawk's black stallion, The Brute, and Sophie's chestnut mare, Gorgeous, whinnied from the corral and watched them drive away.

For almost a year they had never been more than a quick walk from their horses, and when they did leave, the horses whinnied and stomped, wanting to go along.

"When do you think you'll be able to ride?" Sophie asked.

"I'm not sure. I tried to get on The Brute a couple of days ago but couldn't get my foot high enough to hit the stirrup. That bullet knocked a piece out of my hipbone and I can't raise my leg far enough."

"You want to go see another doctor?"

"I'm thinking that same thing. We can go to Hutchinson; they must have a good doctor there."

"We can go right now if you want," Sophie said; "I don't like riding in this buggy. I want to be on my horse, and so do you."

"You're right about that; riding in this buggy is embarrassing."

"Not only that, but when we get on our horses, we don't have to stay on this road. We can go across the grass and ride through the woods to the other side. We'd see places only the Indians know about. Maybe we can find our own little hideaway where we can be alone, where no one will find us."

"We already have that. No one bothers us at home."

"I know that. But there we have things that need our attention—the fields, the garden, the horses, and the mules. It would be nice to have a place where there is nothing to do but each other."

"How far is Hutch from here?"

"Hey, you're the frontiersman, you tell me."

"There's a road up here that turns east that I think will take us there."

"Let's go first thing in the morning."

"What do you mean by first thing in the morning? I'm planning on being busy . . . how about you?"

"If it's gonna cost us another ten bucks for a bed frame . . ."

"Hungry?"

"Huh? Oh, yeah, I was just thinking . . . Aah, never mind. Bad timing."

He turned the mule off the road and into a grassy meadow on the bank of Hawk Creek about thirty yards across. It was surrounded by tall maples, basswoods, and oaks. A large tree had fallen that left an opening in the canopy allowing the sunlight to break through so that grasses and willows could take root and grow. Hawk unhitched and hobbled the mule to let her graze while Sophie cleared the ground, spread the blanket, and opened the basket. She took pewter plates and cups from the basket, then unpacked fried egg sandwiches, a wild raspberry pie, and a bottle of red wine.

After their lunch and a refreshing swim, they lay on the blanket and watched the white puffs of clouds float across the deep blue Minnesota sky.

A buggy drawn by a single white horse clattered on the road, and in the buggy seat was a long-limbed man with a black beard, protruding lower jaw, and thick eyebrows that met in the middle. He was dressed in a black frock coat and black hat with a rounded crown. The high white collar around his neck looked to Hawk like it would soon choke the life out of the man. The man stopped the buggy and turned his head to look at the naked couple on the blanket. Hawk sat up and looked back at the man. The preacher raised his hat and used it to swat at the flies circling his head. "Good day," he said with a sharp, cracking voice.

Sophie sat up and pulled a corner of the blanket up to cover herself. She positioned herself behind Hawk and laid her chin on his shoulder. "Good afternoon, Preacher," she said showing her white teeth in a first-class smile.

"I'm Reverend Diggs from Hutchinson. And you are Mister and Missus . . . ?" He switched the reins from hand to hand as he talked.

"I'm Sophie Boisvert and this is Hawk Owen."

He ran his finger around the inside of his collar, cleared his throat and said, "I'm pastor of the Good Samaritan Church in Hutchinson. Are you folks in need of my services?"

"We'll send for you if we need you," Sophie said. "We're pretty much committed the way it is, but thanks for the offer."

"Well then . . . I'll be expecting to see you there soon. Have a good day." He wiped a white handkerchief across his forehead, and snapped the reins. He glanced back at them one more time as he drove away.

Sophie rolled back on the blanket, laughing hard. "That poor man, he should find himself a wife."

"What do you mean?"

"Well, didn't you see how nervous he was, being so close to a naked woman?"

"He was thirty yards away from us."

"Yeah, but I'm sure that's closer than he's ever been."

Hawk lay on his back looking at the sky. "Gonna rain tomorrow."

"How do you know that?"

He pointed at the clouds. "Mare's tail clouds means rain coming tomorrow."

"You sure?"

"Not for sure, but the clouds say it's gonna rain."

"Are we going to let that stop us from going to Hutch?"

"Depends on how bad it is. You ready to go home?" Hawk asked.

"Yeah, the mosquitoes are coming out, and feeding them is not one of my greatest pleasures."

Morning thunder woke them from their sleep the next day. Sophie rolled over to face Hawk. "Guess what? It's raining. Looks like we'll have to stay here all day."

"Doesn't look too good for traveling, does it?"

He swung his legs off the edge of the bed and started to rise. He stumbled and fell against the table.

"What the hell was that all about?" Sophie said as she scrambled from the bed to help him to his feet.

"Damn hip gave out on me."

"I don't suppose sitting in that cold water yesterday did it much good."

"Soph, I gotta go see that doctor and get this fixed. I'm no damn good like this."

"You just sit still. I'll pack and hitch the mules to the wagon. We can stretch the canvas over the wagon seat so we're out of the rain."

"I can help, Soph; I ain't completely useless yet."

He stood and took a couple of steps and stumbled again. Sophie took his arm and sat him on the bed. "Dammit, I wish Jake was here."

Hawk stood and moved around the cabin, working his hip until the soreness eased and he was able to walk with the help of the cane he had gotten from the doctor at Fort Abercrombie.

Sophie turned as he stepped out the door. "Oh sure, all of a sudden you can walk, now that the work is done."

He smiled at her and hobbled over to the wagon. He tried to get a foot onto the spoke of the wheel but couldn't get it high enough.

"Go to the back and set your butt on the tail. I'll help you swing your legs up."

He did as she suggested and crawled from the back of the wagon to the seat and took the reins.

Thick underbrush and tall trees lined both sides of the trail through the woods. As they came out of the woods and out onto the road, Hawk pulled back hard on the reins. The wagon stopped alongside a man, a woman, and two small children. "Can we help you?" he asked.

The man slowly stepped to the side of the wagon, pulled his hat from his head, and held it with both hands. "Mister, it ain't my way to ask for handouts, but if youse have a bite to eat for my missus and the kids, I'd be more than willing to work for it."

The woman stood in the rain with a scarf pulled over her head and a rain-soaked shawl pulled around her shoulders. Her complexion was dark and her wet hair hung down the sides of her face in strings. Deep sorrow showed in her dark brown eyes as she looked up at Hawk. He was sure those were tears running down her face, not just rain.

A small, ragged, seven-year-old girl clutched at her mother's dress, her big blue eyes solidly fixed on Sophie and Hawk. A boy about ten years old stood behind his mother's wet dress peeking around at them. He had a well-defined scowl on his freckled face as he tried his best to look tough for the strangers.

"You folks climb in the back of the wagon. We'll fix you up."

"Thank you, mister," the man said and took the little girl in his arms and set her in the wagon. The boy scrambled up and moved to the front to make room for his mother. The father walked alongside.

Hawk turned the wagon around and went back to the cabin.

Once inside they invited the family to sit. Sophie and Hawk worked together to make a meal of fried potatoes, eggs, and venison chops. Sophie set the table and they sat down to eat.

"These are beautiful dishes," the lady said. "They're silver, aren't they?"

"No, they're just pewter. We can carry them around without having to worry about breaking them. I've got a whole set of them in the barn."

"That's why that trunk was so heavy. It's full of them tin dishes," Hawk said.

"They're kind of special," Sophie said. "They're the only things my father left me when I was put in the orphanage."

"Are you folks heading somewhere special?"

"We was trying to get to Sacred Heart," the man said. "Maybe find work in the gravel pits."

"It might be ten miles to Sacred Heart from here," Hawk added. "We'll fix you up with some grub and blankets and you can ride that far with us, if you want."

"I ain't got nothin' to pay youse for all that."

"No need to worry about that. You can bring the blankets back when you find work."

"Mister, if I find work it's going to be something that ain't gonna give me a chance to be comin' back here. All I ever did my whole life is farming and people ain't got money to pay farm hands. I'll be working in the gravel pits swingin' a pick and shovel for close to nothin'."

"I've got an offer for you," Hawk said as he pulled out a chair and sat down at the table. "We were on our way to Hutchinson when we found you. We're still going to Hutch and you . . ."

"We ain't goin to Hutchinson."

"That's not what I was saying. I'd like you and your family to stay here and watch the place while we're gone."

"Mister, youse haven't even asked my name. Why would youse trust me to stay here and not run off with all your stuff?"

"Look around you. Do you see anything worth stealing?"

The man looked around, smiled, and said, "I see what you mean. Youse folks live pretty simple, don't ya's?"

"Can't move around very easy with a heavy load on yer back."

"Youse don't sit still too much then?" he stated more than asked.

"Nope, and we sure could use someone to watch the place when we're out wandering around. We can't pay you but whatever you can pull out of this ground is yours."

"Mister, I ain't got no idea who you are but youse got yerself a farmhand."

Hawk stuck out his hand and said, "I'm Hawk Owen and this is Sophie."

The man took Hawk's hand and squinted. "Yer Hawk Owen?"

"Yeah, I'm Hawk Owen. Try not to stare."

The man wrapped both hands around Hawk's. "Mister Owen, it will be a pleasure to work your farm while youse are gone."

"And I should probably know your name," Hawk said.

"Oh yeah, Albert Stromberg. This here's my wife, Mildred." He put his hand on the little girl's shoulder. "And this is my little Maggie." Then he put his hand on the boy's head and mussed his hair. "The big guy here, that's Eli." Eli reached up and pushed his dad's hand away, shook his head, and gave Albert a threatening look.

Albert got on one knee, took the boy by the shoulders, and looked into his eyes. "Eli, this here is Hawk Owen. You heard of him. Him and his brother was the men who whipped the Injuns that took yer little sister."

"Mister Stromberg, it wasn't . . ."

Sophie interrupted him. "It's great to meet you folks."

Eli looked up at Hawk with his now familiar frown, then back to his dad. He shook his dad's hands from his shoulders, turned away, and took his position peeking at Hawk from behind his mother's dress.

"Sorry for the way the boy is," Al said. "He was one of the kids captured by the Indians during the war and he ain't been right since. Seems like he don't like strangers much and hasn't smiled once since he got away."

"Can I ask how he got away?"

"Don't guess he really got away, more like the Injuns forgot about him. They caught him out in the field playin' and threw him in the back of a wagon, then went up to the farm to do their killin' and stealin'. They left him in the back of the wagon when they went to the house and Eli ran when they weren't lookin'. The Injuns set the place on fire and shot all the people in the house, except one small girl they brought out and threw in the back of the wagon. They musta forgot about Eli 'cause they never went back for him and he got away."

"How is it that you know all of this?"

"It was my house they burnt and my daughter they took while we were away. My brother, Tom, and his wife were there because their house burnt down a few days before. That was just an accident, though—the Injuns didn't do that. Little Claire was only seven years old when they took her. Tom and Helen where staying at the farm while we were in Hutchinson getting supplies. Maggie was with us. She was only seven years old and Helen didn't want to watch her. We got back to the farm just in time to see what was going on and hid in the brush until it was over. Then we hightailed it out of the country."

"You didn't go after your daughter?"

"Mister, there was twenty or thirty Injuns in that party. What could I do? If I'da gone after them, they would have killed us all."

"Yeah, you're right about that."

"The Injuns weren't killing the girls they captured, just the boys, and we figured little Claire would be alright till we could find her."

"But you never did find her?"

"We went to see Sibley at Camp Release looking for her but she wasn't there. He said that one of the squaws might have adopted her and they're making an Injun out of her. I know he just said that to make us feel better, but we both know Claire is dead. She's probably better off dead than living with the Injuns anyway."

"Well, I don't know about that. Have you considered going looking for your daughter?"

"And where do we start looking? The Injuns have all moved out west and none of them are even with the bands they started with. It's hopeless, Mister Owen. We have fixed ourselves that Claire is dead and that's that."

"Call me Hawk."

"Youse can call me Al. We've been staying with Mildred's sister since that time. Her husband was killed by the Injuns, and Bernice—that's Mildred's sister, Bernice—she couldn't keep the farm. The county came and took it from her on account she couldn't pay what she owed on it and because she didn't have a man to work it. That put us all on the road. Bernice is in Saint Paul with the kids. We ain't got no idea how she's feeding them or what she's doing for work, but we figger she's a good-lookin' woman and she'll find someway to make a living, if ye know what I mean."

"Al, I can't ride right now, but if someday you'd like to go looking for your daughter, my brother Jake and me, and Sunkist will be glad to help all we can. If she's alive, we'll find her, and if she's dead, we'll find that out, too."

"I appreciate your offer, Hawk, and I'll keep it in mind. If you see her, you'll know it. Her hair is black like her ma and she's got a streak of white in it about an inch wide."

"That might help but we'd have to walk right up to her before we could see that." Hawk patted Al on the shoulder. "We'll do what we can. Now we've got to get to Hutchinson. You folks make this place your own and hopefully we'll be back in a couple of weeks."

"Mister Owen, I don't know the words to thank youse for this but youse can count on us being here and your farm in tiptop shape when youse get back. Looks to me like those fields and the garden need some lookin' after."

Little Eli had moved behind Hawk and was staring at the back of his shirt. Sophie leaned down and looked at the spot where the boy was staring. "What is it, Eli?"

"He ain't got no hole in his shirt," he said with a frown.

"Should he have a hole in his shirt?"

"If this here's Hawk, he should have a hole in his shirt and there ain't none."

"Oh, this is Hawk Owen alright," Sophie said. "He was wounded by the Sioux last year. Do you want to see the scar?"

"Soph . . ." Hawk said, his voice descending.

"Hawk," she said, "he wants to see." She lifted his shirt to show the scar from the Sioux bullet that sent Hawk to the doctor in Mankato, then to Sophie for recuperation. Eli looked at the six-inch scar across Hawk's back. He reached up and put his finger on the scar then backed away. He said nothing and ducked back behind his mother's dress and stared at Hawk.

"How'd he know about all that?" Hawk asked.

"There's stories around the valley about you and your brother that just keep getting bigger and bigger all the time. Looks to me like that one's true."

"Yeah well, most of 'em ain't true."

"I know that, but little boys know they are."

"We gotta go, Al. You make this your home, help yourself to what you find, and we'll be back in a couple of weeks."

They shook hands and Sophie led the way to the wagon. The rain continued as they drove off.

"Hawk," Sophie said, "when a boy Eli's age sees a man like you, he's seeing a hero. Let him see someone famous."

"But Soph, most of the things they say about us is bullshit. We're not indestructible heroes. We did what a thousand other men did. We just got more attention for it because of our red hair and because we took our women along."

"That's not what I'm talking about. I'm talking about Eli telling his friends that he knows Hawk Owen. I remember once when Alexander Ramsey came to the orphanage and talked with one of the girls. She talked about that forever. It made her feel important saying she knew someone famous."

Hawk sat quietly contemplating what Sophie had said. He decided that for now, it would be alright to be someone famous.

Sophie interrupted his delusions of grandeur. "Were you serious about going out looking for Mister Stromberg's daughter?"

"Huh? Oh . . . Yeah . . ." he said as he returned to the moment at hand. "Seems like the best fight going right now."

"I thought you said we were going to settle down and raise a family," she said with a sly smirk.

"I know I said that, but don't you think looking for Claire is a good cause?"

"Of course it is, and if you hadn't brought it up, I would have."

"I think we have some good people taking care of the farm. Want to go to Courtland and see Jake?" Hawk asked.

"Damn straight."

3

C H A P T E R   T H R E E

MORNING BROUGHT COOL AIR AND GRAY SKIES. Eve and Jake sat at the kitchen table sipping coffee. "Not much we can do today. Looks like rain."

"We need the rain," Eve said.

"Rain don't do much good if you don't have anything planted."

"It won't rain forever," she said. "Let's go to town."

"Can't you think of anything else to do on a rainy day?"

"Yes, but we can do that on any kind of day. I'd like to get some of that cotton fabric before it's all gone."

"What chuh gonna make?"

"Well, I'd really like to have a cotton nightgown to wear in bed."

"You gonna put fur around the bottom?"

"Why in the world would I want fur around the bottom?"

"To keep your neck warm at night."

"Get off that chair and let's go."

"What's your hurry?"

"I'm going to Milwaukee to see my mother, remember?"

"When are you leaving?"

"Next week. We talked about that."

"Yeah, I know."

"You don't want me to go, do you?" she said softly.

"Would it make a difference?"

"Of course it would."

"No, you go; you need to see your mother."

"Can you stay out of trouble while I'm gone?"

"I've got a farm to run. No time for getting in trouble."

Soon after arriving in town, they walked side by side down the main street of Courtland until they came to the general store. Eve turned and went into the store while Jake walked a few steps before he noticed the change in direction. Turning back and entering the store, he found Eve rummaging through the bolts of cotton fabric and stepped up behind her. He looked around the store for a few seconds and decided it was not the place he wanted to be. He walked outside to look over the new farm machinery on the grass next to the store. *I could really use one of those new plows sitting there,* he thought, but lack of funds prevented him from getting too serious about buying one. Behind the store was Otie Khecky's corral with a dozen head of horses and mules.

Otie was the town hostler and constable. Peace reigned supreme in Courtland since Otie took the job. Otie was well over six feet in height—taller than most of the men in Courtland. His hands and arms were powerful from working with the horses and mules. Everyone in town, young and old, respected him. Otie was just as likely to hold a scared kid's hand and walk him home as he was to take a mischievous boy over his knee and give him a good spanking. And Otie was just as willing to slap a feisty drunk down as he was to take him home and tuck him into bed.

Jake leaned on the rail fence for a few minutes daydreaming about a four-mule team that could pull a two-bottom plow. Again, lack of funds interrupted his dream. *Maybe someday,* he thought, *I'll be able to afford the fine, new machinery like George Aldrich has.*

Jake hated the word "someday." Someday seldom came. Someday was what people said when they didn't want to commit to something because something better might come along. Someday he was going to die. He hoped the other someday got there first.

He walked back into the store and found Eve at the counter with several pieces of fabric. "I'm going over to Tom's and have a brew." Then he saw a piece of fur lying next to the fabric. He flipped the fur with his fingertips, smiled at her, and kissed her on the neck and said, "Don't take too long in here."

"I'll meet you at Tom's as soon as I'm finished."

Crossing the dusty street, he walked into the saloon and stood at the bar.

"Howdy, Jake. Beer?"

"You know me too well."

"Not a good day for planting, is it?"

"Nice day if yer a frog."

Three farmers stood along the bar talking about what a wet spring it had been.

"How the hell we supposed to plant when all it does is rain?" George grumbled.

"Yesterday you were complaining about how dry it's been, George."

"One day it rains, the next day it's so damn hot ye can't get nothing done."

Jake chucked to himself and said, "You guys should find yourselves a woman so you got something to do on rainy days."

"Yeah, like goin' shoppin'," Ed laughed.

"She's shopping. I'm drinking beer."

"Don't drink too much. She's gonna need that money for pretty woman things."

"She's going to Milwaukee to see her mother next week. Guess she figured she needed new clothes."

"How long she gonna be gone?"

"Most of the summer, I guess. That's quite a ride down there."

"Ha!" Ed laughed and slapped his thigh. "Maybe we'll be seein' ol' Jake runnin' in and out of Kate's this summer."

"Ain't nothin' in Kate's place that interests me," Jake said.

"Mighty perty girls in there, Jake," Ernie said.

"Yeah, who'd know better'n you, Ernie?"

Ernie flipped his thumb. "George here might."

"George is too damn old to be goin' in that place."

"I been around a long time, Jake," George said, "but everything still works like it's supposed to."

"That's comforting to hear, George."

Jake turned at the sound of light footsteps on the wooden floor. Eve came up behind him, "Are you ready to go?" she asked.

"Not going to have a beer?"

"No, I'd rather just go home tonight."

"Did you spend all his money?" Ernie asked with a laugh.

"I left him enough for Kate's place while I'm gone."

Ernie laughed again and jabbed George in the ribs. George chuckled and looked across Ernie at Eve.

"Someone asked how long you're gonna be gone. I told them most of the summer. Was I right?"

"A couple of months, I'm sure. It's going to take a week just to get there."

"That's if the trains don't have trouble."

"I'm sure you'll be just fine without me, Jake."

The door opened and Robert Orley and two men walked in.

Eve turned toward the door as they came in. The blackened eyes, swollen nose, and yellow streaks running from the inside corners of his eyes and along his nose told who he might be. She turned to Jake. "Is that the man you fought yesterday?"

"That's him. Don't pay any attention to him."

"Looks like you hurt him pretty badly."

"I only had to hit him once. That stopped any fighting."

Orley walked by Jake, took one quick glance at him, then took a table and ordered a shot of brandy.

"Let's get out of here," Jake said. "I don't need anymore problems."

A few nights later they were on the porch reading the newspaper and chatting quietly as they often did. Jake asked Eve, "Did you get that nightgown done you were going to make?"

"Not quite," she responded. "But it'll be done soon."

"I'm anxious to see it."

"You'll see it someday. Are you going to plant tomorrow?" she asked.

"Na, that can wait," he said, a little disappointed that the conversation had taken a different track.

Jake had seen the finished nightgown hanging in her closet and couldn't help wondering why she hadn't worn it. *Maybe she's waiting for some special occasion,* he thought to himself.

The someday Eve was to leave came before the someday she was to wear the nightgown. They rode to town in the buggy to meet the stagecoach for Saint Paul. Once Eve's bags were thrown to the top of the coach and tied down, Jake held her hands in his and looked into her eyes. "You sure you wanna go?"

"I don't want to go, but I have to."

"I know. You have a good trip and hurry back."

They wrapped their arms around each other tightly and Jake held her like he thought he'd never see her again. His heart was telling him to cherish this moment for as long as he could. Moving his hands to her shoulders, he looked into her eyes. "God, you're beautiful," he whispered. Eve smiled and kissed him lightly on the lips. They broke apart and the driver helped Eve into the stagecoach. They left with a cloud of dust swirling behind them.

Jake stood and watched until the coach disappeared around the bend of the road, then turned to go back to the farm. He considered going to the saloon for a beer, but the thought of conversation with farmers didn't appeal to him at that time.

The next morning he was out of bed before the sun was up. He tossed a few sticks into the firebox in the kitchen stove and started to make coffee. But the stove took much too long to get hot, and the coffee pot refused to boil. He watched it as long as his patience would allow. He had become accustomed to Eve having coffee ready for him when he came out of the bedroom. Finding a cup of coffee that morning was not going to be an easy task. He then decided that after morning chores he'd go to the Crow Bar for breakfast. The Crow Bar was five miles away and his horse was somewhere in the pasture.

The farm needed his attention first, and he forced himself to go to the barn. He fed the pigs, milked the two cows, and fed the calf. Then he went to the chicken house to gather eggs. The rest of the day he spent in the fields not accomplishing much of anything but giving things a good looking over.

After the work was finished, he decided not to go to the Crow Bar. He spent the evening sitting on the porch with his pipe, a bottle of beer, and an old newspaper. The papers no longer interested him without Eve there to discuss the issues. He wasn't interested in politics, or the predicted grain prices for the fall harvest, or the ads for new clothing in the stores, or the fancy restaurants in Saint Paul. He tossed the paper to the floor and walked out into the yard. He pulled his hat from his head, shaded his eyes against the setting sun and watched a hawk circling overhead.

"That hawk up there got no farm, he's got no house, and he don't worry about where his next meal is coming from, just like Hawk. He don't worry about nothin' either. He probably should but he don't."

Then he saw himself in his mind's eye. Since Eve left, Jake had spent most of his days loafing. He wondered if he'd be just like Hawk if Eve wasn't there. Would he keep the farm up and running? Would he have painted the house? Would he have even bought the farm? Sometimes a man needs someone around to help him set goals and give him a reason to accomplish those goals. What were Jake's goals? Jake wanted to be happy in life; he wanted to live without worry. He wanted to be like that hawk up there— no one to impress, no one telling him what the word "success" means, and no one telling him what they think he should be. *It's easy for a man to please himself,* he thought. He doesn't need much to keep him happy. A fried egg for breakfast, if there hap-

H A W K ' S   Q U E S T

pens to be one around, will suit his needs. Last night's leftovers will keep body and soul united for another day. A blanket or two to sleep under at night, without sheets or pillow covers is perfectly good enough. *Without Eve I'd be just like that hawk up there. Maybe that's not such a bad thing.* He sat on a hard-backed chair and stared out the door across the field at the wide-open spaces.

The house needed cleaning but since Eve was not around, it would wait. He went into the bedroom and stood by the bed. Slowly he turned his eyes toward the closet where Eve kept her clothes. He opened the closet door and found it nearly empty. He smiled to himself, thinking how she had taken enough clothing to be gone for a year. *But why didn't I see her pack it or carry it to the stagecoach?* He knew that trying to understand women was a fruitless effort, so he shook the thought from his head and went into the kitchen for a bedtime snack.

One evening when he came in from the field, he found an envelope on his front door. The envelope was addressed to him from Saint Paul. Jake was not a good reader but he slowly worked out the words on the paper.

> Dear Jacob,
>
> I regret to inform you that I have left you and I'm going back to Milwaukee with a dear friend. I simply cannot live the life you expect me to live. I am not a farm girl and I am not an Indian fighter. I want a normal life without having to worry about you coming home dead from some pointless barroom brawl. That last fight you were in was the end of it. I can't take it anymore. I will always love you and will never forget you. If you love me, you will understand why I chose to be with a man like Edward. He is a very successful attorney and I am looking forward to a happy future with him. Best regards to you and your brother.
>
> Evangeline

Jake sat at the kitchen table and studied the letter hoping to find something he'd misread. "I'll take it to Heidi at the Crow Bar in the morning and have her read it. She'll know what it says," he said out loud.

The evening passed slowly. He ran the past two years through his mind over and over trying to figure out where he'd gone wrong. The trip to Dakota Territory the year before ended with no one being killed. The farm was doing well. She was allowed all the freedom she needed. Maybe that was it. Maybe she didn't get the attention she needed. It always bothered him when they were out that she spent more time with other men than she did with him. But that was the way Eve was. She gave Ernie more attention than he deserved, hanging on to his arm and laying her head on his shoulder when he made her laugh. It was alright. Ernie was more fun than Jake and he knew it, so he just smiled and tried to ignore it. She was outgoing and fun to be around; Jake was quiet and didn't talk much. And Eve loved the attention she got by being part of the Pa Hin Sa.

He tried to tell himself it was better that she was gone, but that didn't help. She'd become part of his life, and now she is gone—part of his life was gone. He wanted to cry, but he had cried all his tears out after loosing his mother and his Sioux girl, Sisoka. He'd lost too many friends and loved ones.

Could Jake drink enough to forget that Eve was gone? Slowly he turned his head back to the bedroom and the closet. Maybe her new nightgown was there. It would make him feel better to know it was there and to think she might come back for it. He opened the closet door and pushed aside the few remaining garments. He stopped and looked back and forth across the bar that held the clothes. The gown wasn't there.

Silence . . . silence like the grave.

He stared into the closet while in his imagination he saw her wearing the gown with the fur around the bottom for another man. He felt pressure building in his head. His throat caught and his breathing became deep.

Suddenly, he grabbed the few dresses hanging on the bar and threw them out of the closet into the middle of the bedroom floor. Then he ripped the bar from the wall and pitched it across the room. "Goddamn that . . . goddamn that . . . goddamn . . . !"

He couldn't bring himself to say it. He loved Eve no matter what she might have done. A lump formed in his throat that almost forced him to cry. He turned, kicked the pile of clothes out of his way, and went out the door without bothering to close it. He threw himself up onto his bareback mule and walked him to town.

"Beer?" Tom asked.

"Give me a brandy," Jake responded, his voice deeper than usual.

Tom looked at him for a moment. "Whatever you say, Jake. Brandy, comin' up."

"Send Heidi over will ye, Tom?"

HAWK'S QUEST

"She ain't here right now, Jake. She'll be here in half an hour."

Jake stood up from his stool and walked over to a table at the back of the room. He sat quietly and watched the door. People came and went. Ernie came to his table and started to pull out a chair. Jake put his hand on the chair stopping him.

"Rather be left alone, Ernie."

Ernie stopped and looked at Jake. "Yeah, sure, Jake. Whatever you say. Everything alright?"

"Yeah, everything is great. I just need to be alone."

"Missin' the missus, huh?"

Jake looked up and said, "Ernie . . . scram!"

"Yeah, sure, Jake. I, ah . . ." Ernie turned and walked to his place at the bar.

"What's eatin' him?" he asked Tom.

"Probably like you said, he's missin' Eve."

"Maybe we should arrange a visit to Kate's for 'im."

"Appreciate the offer, boys," Jake said from his table, "but if you got money for that, Ernie, you use it."

Ernie turned back to Tom. "He's got better ears than I figgered."

Jake was left alone until Heidi came through the door.

"Hey, Jake!" she shouted as she walked in.

Ernie turned quickly and stopped her from walking to Jake's table. "Better leave 'im be. He ain't in too good a mood right now."

"Heidi," Jake said. "Come over here, will ye?"

"Sure, Jake." Heidi walked to his table and he pushed a chair out for her with his foot. She sat down. "Something wrong?"

"Can you keep your mouth shut if I show you something private?"

"I know more damn secrets in this town than the priest."

"I want you to read this letter for me. But do it quiet so they can't hear what it says."

Heidi took the letter and read it to herself. Her face lost most of its color and she put her hand over her mouth and looked up at Jake. "Oh, my God, Jake." She looked quickly around the room. "Oh, God, are you alright?"

"So it says what I thought it said, right?"

"Yes, but . . . why? Why would she do that? I mean, why would she do that to you?"

"She says it all right there in that letter."

"Oh, God, Jake, I'm so sorry."

"Ain't nothin' for you to be sorry about. I'm the one to blame."

"No, she's the . . ."

"Heidi, get me another brandy, will you?"

"Sure, Jake." Heidi went to the bar. Ernie looked at Jake, then at Heidi. She put her hand up, palm forward, toward Ernie. "I don't know nothin'."

"You alright, Jake?" she asked as she sat the drink in front of him.

"Yeah, I'll be headin' home when I get this down."

"You know that guy Orley has been coming in pretty regular, don't you?"

"I'll be out of here before he gets here."

"Probably a good idea."

Jake drank his brandy slowly and ordered another. The Crow Bar was quiet that evening. People knew something was bothering Jake and they left him alone.

George Aldrich walked in and pulled up a stool. "Orley's on his way," he said.

"Dammit!" Tom said from behind the bar. He turned to Heidi. "Go get Otie. Hurry up."

Heidi walked quickly out the door just as Orley walked in. He stepped to the bar and ordered whiskey, then turned halfway around, leaned one elbow on the bar, and looked toward Jake. "Ev'nin', Jake."

Jake didn't respond.

"Something bothering you, Owen? I said 'good evening'."

Tom came to Orley. "Leave him alone, Mister Orley."

"Yeah?" He turned toward Jake. "Got troubles, Owen? What's botherin' you? Your wife cut you off?"

Jake looked up at Orley then turned his head back to his brandy. Orley stepped away from the bar and started toward Jake's table.

"Mister Orley!" Tom said. "Otie's on his way over. I think you should sit down or, better yet, just leave."

Orley ignored the suggestion and stepped up to Jake's table. "Mind if I sit?" he asked as he pulled out a chair and started to sit down.

"Git the hell away from me, Orley," Jake said slowly and quietly.

"Now that's no way to talk to an old friend."

Jake looked directly into Orley's eyes. "I'm gonna say it one more time and if you don't go away I'm going to stomp your head into this floor. Now git the hell away from me."

"Oh." Orley leaned back in his chair. Looking around the bar, he said, "The Indian fighter's feeling feisty tonight."

Suddenly, Jake threw the table aside, came off his chair, and slammed a fist into the middle of Orley's chest. Orley tumbled backward onto the floor. Jake was on him in an instant, lifting him to his feet and smashing his fist into Orley's face. He swung his left hand around and caught Orley in the ribs. Everyone heard the sound of bones breaking. One of Orley's men came to help, but Jake whirled and slammed a hard fist to the center of the man's chest stopping him mid-stride. The man stumbled back and leaned on the bar trying to suck the wind back into his lungs. Orley was trying to get to his feet when Jake pulled him up. He held onto his shirt and slapped him with his open hand across the side of his head. Orley let out a short cry of pain as his knees buckled and he crumpled to the floor. He lay on his side groaning, one hand covering his left ear.

Jake turned and glared at Orley's other friends. Intense rage showed in his eyes as he started toward the man. "Come here, you son of a bitch," he said.

The man turned and quickly walked out the door.

Constable Khecky had walked in just before the last slap ended the scrap. "Jake, you'd better go home," he said as he pushed Jake away from Orley. "Everyone here knows this man has been looking for trouble with you and no charges will be brought against you. Now go home."

"Get up on the table and remove your trousers."

C H A P T E R   F O U R

Sophie and Hawk rode through the day in the rain with two mules pulling the wagon and two horses walking behind. At sundown they rolled out their blankets in the back of the wagon, hobbled the mules and horses, and tried to go to sleep. Hawk tossed and turned trying to get away from the pain in his left hip that kept them both awake for the better part of the night.

In the morning the sun came up to a bright blue, cloudless sky. They made a small fire, cooked coffee, and fried venison for their breakfast, then started moving. They soon passed another wagon going the opposite way.

Hawk pulled back on the reins. "How far to Hutchinson?" he asked the man in the wagon.

"About twenty mile down the road," he answered without stopping.

Sophie turned around on the seat and yelled through the wagon cover. "Excuse me! Could you pass the word that Hawk Owen wants to meet Sunkist at Courtland?"

The man waved a hand without turning around and kept moving.

"Maybe we won't have to go looking for that renegade and he'll come and find us," she said.

About sundown they saw the city. They stopped in a small grove of trees and set up a camp.

The next morning they were in Hutchinson looking for the doctor. They went into a store and asked the man behind the counter where to find him.

"Yep," he said, "Doc Bernier. Got his shingle hangin' out in front of his office just down the road. Just walk in, he ain't doin' much these days but sittin' around that jug readin' doctor books."

They found the doctor's office and Hawk walked in with his cane and an exaggerated limp.

The doctor looked up from his book. "Something I can do for you?"

Hawk was surprised to see the doctor sitting behind an oak desk wearing a buckskin shirt, a wide-brimmed hat with a wolverine tail dangling down the back, and spectacles pulled down on his nose.

"You any relation to Lorraine Bernier?" Hawk asked.

"I've heard the name but have yet to meet the lady. What can I do for you?"

"Well, I've got this sore hip," Hawk said.

"And?"

"What can I do about it?"

"Limp."

Hawk turned to Sophie. "He's got a good sense of humor, I'll say that for him."

Sophie leaned over the desk and said softly, "Limp has been one of the major problems, Doc."

"I see . . ." Doctor Bernier said. "What's wrong with your hip?"

"That's what I came here to find out."

"Did you have an accident?"

"No, it's from a bullet."

"Indian wars?"

"Yeah, a couple of months ago."

"Is the bullet still in there?"

"No, the doctor at Fort Abercrombie dug it out."

"And that was during the fighting, right?"

"No, about three days after I got hit."

"Well, lie down on that table and let's have a look."

Hawk painfully climbed onto the table. The doctor sprang from his chair and with quick, short steps made it to the table. He pushed the glasses up on his nose. "What's yer name?"

Hawk looked at Sophie.

"He's Hawk Owen, Doctor."

"That's what I thought. The Thief shot you, right?"

"Yeah."

"Heard all about it. Folks are saying you were a damn fool going in those woods after The Thief."

"Doctor, I'm not interested in what people are saying about me. I had good reason to go in that woods and we'll say no more about it."

"You're going to have to remove those pants if I'm going to look at your wound."

"Remove my pants?"

"Just pull them down so I can see the wound."

"I can help if you want, Hawk," Sophie said.

"You just stay over there. I've got enough problems without you crawlin' all over me."

Sophie grinned and turned to sit on the chair in the corner of the room.

The doctor poked around the wound feeling under the skin. "Umm-hmm, umm-hmm, umm-hmm," he mumbled after each poke. He raised Hawk's leg and flexed the hip joint. "Ah," he said as he looked over the top of his glasses at Hawk, "Was the bullet in one piece when they took it out?"

"Yes, I think so. Why?"

"Well, you have something in there that's interfering with the movement of your hip. If the bullet wasn't broken up it's probably a bone splinter."

"Can you get it out?"

"I would suggest you go to see Doctor Mayo in New Ulm. He's the best medical man in Minnesota right now."

"So you're telling me you can't do it?"

"Oh, I can do the surgery alright. I'm just saying that Doctor Mayo would be much better at it than I am. He gained a lot of experience treating wounds during the Sioux Conflict."

"Well, Doc, I want it done now. Not next week sometime."

"Very well, Mister Owen, let me do some reading and we'll do it tomorrow."

"Reading? What kind of reading?"

"Just to brush up on the procedure. I could do it right now as you lie there, but I think you would want me to do it without guesswork. Go find a place to spend the night and come back first thing in the morning. We'll have you on your feet by noon."

"Works for me." Hawk pulled his trousers up and he and Sophie started out the door. The doctor rushed to his bookshelf, quickly pulled a thick book out, and in a wink was back in his chair. From under the desk he pulled a stoneware jug, the cork coming out with a squeak and a thump. He tipped the jug up and took a swig. After a long sigh and a stifled belch, he said, "Good for cleaning wounds, too." He then reached out to turn the flame up in the coal-oil lantern and began flipping through the book's pages.

Sophie and Hawk got into their wagon and headed out of town. They pulled into a clearing, picketed the animals, and set up their canvas tent.

In the morning Hawk was wide-awake as the sun started to lighten the eastern sky. Sophie lay with the blankets pulled up to her neck. He looked at her as she slept and stopped himself from leaning down to kiss her; he didn't want to wake her. He slipped out from under the blanket and started to get up. His hip collapsed and he fell to the side nearly landing on top of her.

She awoke with a start. "Well, hello! There's really no need to get rough. Just put the blankets back when you're done."

Hawk was embarrassed. "My leg gave out, again."

"I know, Hawk. Let's get to town and get that thing taken care of."

They packed their camp, loaded the wagon, and went to town. Pulling up in front of the doctor's office, they went inside.

"Well, Mister Owen, are you ready?"

"Ready when you are, Doc."

"Now, we've got a couple of ways to put you to sleep while I do the surgery." He picked up a wooden mallet and said, "This method is called impact anesthesia. The other uses ether. Which would you prefer?"

"Can I administer the impact anesthesia?" Sophie asked with a grin.

"Before we let her do that—and I do have a choice—what's ether?"

"Ether will put you to sleep for a while and when you wake up, the surgery will be done."

Hawk glanced at Sophie. "I'll choose the ether."

"Alright, ether it is, and if all goes as planned, you can be on your way by lunchtime."

"What do you mean, 'if all goes as planned'?"

"I plan on opening the wound to see what's giving you the pain. When I manipulate the joint of your hip, I can feel something that doesn't belong there. It may be a bone fragment interfering with the movement of your hip. If I'm right, it will be a simple matter of finding it and removing it."

"Sounds like something Sophie could do."

"Well, there's a little more to it than that, but making the incision and removing the splinter is certainly quite simple."

"Alright, Doc, let's get on with it."

"Get up on the table and remove your trousers."

Hawk climbed up and started to open the front of his trousers.

The doctor took a copper container from the tray next to the table. It was about the size and shape of a hip flask with two tubes coming from the top. He put the tubes under Hawk's nostrils. Hawk jumped and pushed the container away.

"Phew! That stuff stinks!"

"This is the ether. Be thankful it's not chloroform, Mister Owen. We need to do this if we're to do the surgery."

"Sorry, Doc. You just surprised me."

"Good night, Hawk," Doctor Bernier said.

Hawk awoke from his sleep, seeing nothing but the ceiling. After a few minutes, he regained his awareness and turned his head toward the doctor. "Didn't work, huh?"

"Yes, Mister Owen. I got the splinter out and just as I thought, it was in the cartilage in the socket of your hip. In two or three days you'll be up and running around like a kid again."

"How soon can I ride?"

"If you mean on a horse, you can hop on right now without hurting anything, but I doubt if the pain will allow it. Give the incision a few days to heal before you do anything too strenuous.

Hawk was having trouble keeping his eyes open, but wanted to get off the table. He started to swing his leg over the edge but found the pain too much and lay back down.

"Here, let me help you," the doctor said. "The incision will be sore for a while but don't baby it. It is very important that you keep the wound clean. We don't want the fever to get in there and undo everything we've accomplished. Keep that hip moving as much as you can so it doesn't stiffen up. You'll be fine in a week."

"Thanks, Doc. How much do I owe you for this?"

Doc Bernier stretched out his hand, palm up. "Fifty bucks."

"I don't have fifty bucks with me."

"I was just kidding. Thank God you didn't bring any chickens or cranberry pie. How does ten dollars sound?"

"Kinda steep, but if it works, it's worth it."

"Hawk, if you don't have the money just give me what you can afford."

"I've got the money and I was just kidding about it being too much. I appreciate you taking the time to do it."

"There is something you should know. That injury will probably be a problem for you for the rest of your life. The bone has been injured. It will heal itself, but it's all too common for rheumatism to set in at the sight of an injury of this sort. The best thing to do is to keep it moving. Don't let it stop you."

"Nothing can be done about that, Doc?"

"No, they know too little about rheumatism to even make guesses about it."

Hawk took Sophie's arm and they walked out the door just as the clock in Doctor Bernier's office chimed noon.

"How ye feeling, Hawk?"

"Sleepy, but I can walk."

"You lay down in the back of the wagon and I'll do the driving."

"Where we going from here?"

"Courtland."

"You know the way?"

"About thirty miles straight down this road."

"Let's go."

Hawk slept for the first couple of miles of the trip. He awoke and crawled forward to kneel behind the seat and looked over Sophie's shoulder at the road.

"How are you feeling?" she asked.

"Great. Think I'll get out and walk a little."

"Do you think that's a good idea?"

"Well, stop this wagon and let's find out."

Sophie stopped and Hawk squirmed his way out the back of the wagon. "My leg hurts a little but it moves."

"Want to walk for a ways?"

"Well, maybe later."

"That's what I figured."

He climbed up onto the seat next to Sophie. "Let's call it a day and stop for some rest and food."

Sophie steered the wagon off the road and into a small woods. They set up a camp and spent the night out of the tent, under the blankets, looking at the stars.

Hawk dozed off while Sophie studied the sky watching the clouds move in and cover the stars. A drop of rain hit Hawk's forehead and woke him. Sophie was on her side facing him, her face cradled in her hand. "It's raining," she whispered.

"I noticed."

"Might be a good idea to go in the tent now."

"Ye think?"

"Ever made love in the rain?" she asked softly.

"You'd know it if I did."

Sophie leaned over and kissed him on the lips. "Me either. Maybe some other time." Hawk's arms went around her and pulled her tightly to him.

"Can you get up and go in the tent, or should I move the tent over here?"

"I can get up," he said with a groan. "I think." He reached and took Sophie's hand and she helped him to his feet. They made the short walk to the tent and went inside. Sophie helped him lie down and lay next to him.

"Really hurts, huh?"

"Not so much right now, but I can't touch it."

"Well, you try to get some sleep and we'll get going first thing in the morning."

Hawk rolled to his right side—the side that didn't hurt—and Sophie climbed over him to lie down facing him. They looked into each other's eyes until they drifted off to sleep.

He wanted to roll over and sleep on his other side but the pain wouldn't allow it. So he suffered another restless night. Sleeping on one side, without being able to roll over, caused him to have strange and frightening dreams. He dreamed of buffalo stampeding over him, and lynx and bobcat stalking him in the night. That night, the soft whisper of the breeze in the treetops, usually a comforting sound, was a terrifying phantom bringing terrible storms with wind, rain, and hail. He lay on his right side, then on his back, and again on his side. Sophie cuddled close when she could, just to let him know she cared.

Light rain tapped on the top of the tent throughout the night, and in the morning heavy drops from the trees above woke him from his fitful sleep.

The sun was up and shining brightly through the canvas when Hawk awoke, warming the tent to insufferable levels. Flies buzzed around inside the tent and landed on Hawk's face, and when he brushed them away, they just circled around and landed again.

When he'd finally had enough of fighting the pesky flies, he threw the covers off and sat up. "Don't flies ever sleep?"

Sophie was not beside him and he could smell the aroma of fresh brewed coffee. He forced himself to his feet and stumbled out of the tent.

"Good morning, sleepyhead. How ye feeling?"

"Feel like I've been shot at and missed, and shit at and hit."

"You'll feel better after you have some of my special coffee."

"What makes it special?"

"I'm putting brandy in it."

"Sounds interesting."

"It wakes you up but you don't really care if you get anything done."

"Where'd you get the brandy?"

"While you were having your surgery I went to the store and picked up a pint. Doc says it will do you more good than harm."

Hawk turned and walked around in a circle to try out his hip. The incision hurt some but the bones worked just fine.

They each had two cups of brandied coffee, along with flapjacks with raspberry syrup. When they finished breakfast, they loaded the wagon and set off once again to Courtland. By noon they were tied in front of the Crow Bar saloon. They walked inside and found Jake sitting at a table.

5

C H A P T E R   F I V E

"WELL," HE SAID. "LOOK WHO'S HERE."

"Hey, Jake," Hawk said. "We came in to see if anyone knew where you live. Guess we found out."

"Yeah, I prob'ly spend more time here than I should. Hey, Soph."

"Hey, Jake." She gave him a hug. "Where's Eve?"

"She ain't here," Jake said.

"She's alright, isn't she?" Sophie asked.

"Yeah, she's doin' just fine, I guess. What's with the cane, Hawk?"

"Aw, it ain't nothin', just that bullet The Thief put in me."

"It's a little more than that, Jake," Sophie said. "He just had the doctor in Hutchinson dig some bone splinters out of him. He's sore as hell but too stubborn to admit it."

"Got that from his dad. Whenever we got hurt, Robert would tell us to pretend it didn't hurt. 'Don't baby it,' he'd say. 'It'll just get worse.'"

"Well, he's not babying it. I wish he would a little." She looked at Hawk, her head tilted to the side and one eyebrow raised.

"It'll heal," he said.

"You let me know when you're ready to give it the stress test."

Jake pulled out his pipe, tobacco pouch, and a sulphur match. They all stopped talking, knowing that when Jake lit his pipe, his attention was on the pipe and the pipe only. He pulled a proper measure of tobacco from the pouch and tamped it into the bowl. Then he struck the match on the tabletop and held it to the pipe. He kept an eye focused on the bowl as he drew on the pipe, puffing clouds of blue smoke out the side of his mouth. When he had the tobacco glowing properly, he leaned back on his chair, drew in a generous helping of smoke, took a quick glance at the door, then looked up at Hawk. "So," he said around the pipe stem. He paused for a couple more puffs of smoke then raised one eyebrow and rolled his eyes toward Hawk. "What brings you down so far?"

Hawk and Sophie watched the lighting of the pipe as if it were some sort of religious ceremony. "Mmm," Sophie said smiling. "I like the smell of a pipe."

"I did too, at first," Heidi said from behind the bar. "But after a while it gets stale in the bar and STINKS!" She snapped the last word at Jake.

He pointed the stem of his pipe over his shoulder at Heidi. "Kinda per-tic'lar about things . . . So, what's up?"

"We got a couple looking after the farm while we're gone," Hawk said. "One of their little girls was captured by the Sioux and they don't know if she's dead or alive."

"The father didn't go after her?"

"He's a farmer, not an Indian fighter," Hawk said. "If he'd gone after the girl the whole family would be dead. They don't have a thing left in this world. I think we can find the girl. Whad'ye say?"

Jake blew smoke down onto the tabletop. "Where do we start looking?"

Sophie fanned the smoke away from her face and said, "Lots of children were left without mothers and fathers because of the war. I think the best place to start looking is the orphanages and the churches."

"Any idea where Sunkist is holed up?" Jake asked. "He's gonna want to be in on this."

"He's up the valley somewhere around Sacred Heart Creek. I'm not sure exactly where, but he has to come down from his perch once in a while. We'll put word out and he'll come a-runnin'."

"So where to first?" Sophie asked.

"They have an orphanage at the Good Samaritan Church in Hutch," Jake said. "We could start there."

"We know the preacher at that church," Sophie said with a smirk. "He might know something."

"You know Preacher Diggs?" Jake said.

"Well, sort of. We met him a couple of days ago."

"Don't tell me you two went and got . . ."

"No, Jake," Sophie said, "we didn't get married." She turned to Hawk. "Since this is a saloon, do you suppose we could get a beer? I'm parched."

Jake raised his hand and turned towards the bartender. "Greg, four beers."

"Make that five beers and a sasparilly," a gruff voice said from the doorway. They all turned to see Sunkist standing there, a grin barely showing through his beard. Standing behind him was his Cherokee wife, Posey.

"Heard you animals was squeezin' up 'roun' cheer. Figgered we'd come and join the fun."

The bartender brought their drinks and sat them down on the table. Posey pushed the glass away. Sunkist pushed it back and said, "Sasparilly."

Posey picked it up, tasted it, smacked her lips, then tipped the mug up and drank it down.

"Well," Sophie said. "Here's to the Pa Hin Sa, all together again."

All glasses went into the air and clinked together. A substantial amount of beer slopped onto the table.

"Hey!" Sophie said. "Let's save our strength; we may need it later. No sense in wasting beer."

"Jake," Sunkist said. "Word is you got some problems with some galoot from out east."

"Na, that's all taken care of. He won't be comin' back here till he heals up."

"Folks got it in their heads that when the Owen boys got troubles, something's gonna make the papers. What's going on?"

"Nothing that's gonna make the papers," Hawk said. "We're gonna find a little girl who was captured during the war."

"How about we go to my place," Jake said, "I've got beer there and we can talk about this girl we're going after."

Hawk turned to Sophie. "You got any of that brandy with you? I like that a lot better than beer."

"Sure, and we can probably get more from Greg."

"Well, let's get some. For medicinal purposes, you understand."

"Of course, I understand," Sophie said.

Jake led the way and in an hour they were sitting on chairs on the porch of a log house with a flower garden along the whitewashed picket fence that surrounded the yard. The porch was painted white, and had a lattice-work rail around the front and four pillars holding up the roof. Wilted, dried up plants drooped out of flower pots that were suspended above the rail.

Inside the house the floors were covered with wool carpeting as thick as the floor of a pine forest, and the walls had been smoothed with plaster and painted white. A sofa sat against the wall, and soft, stuffed chairs stood in two corners. Each of the chairs had an article or two of clothing thrown over it. Pictures hung at preposterous angles on the walls, and dust covered the fine china figurines that stood on shelves around the room. In one corner was a bookcase with more books on it than Sophie had seen since she attended school at the orphanage.

When they walked in, they smelled the wood-burning cook-stove, along with the slight scent of baked bread, butter-fried onions, and the strong smell of pipe tobacco.

"Go ahead and look around," Jake said.

Sophie and Posey walked through the house. The bedroom carpet was littered with dried grass that had been tracked in. The bed had not been made. On one side of the bed was a pile of dirty clothes that left barely enough room on the other side for one body to sleep. On each side of the bed stood a small table with an oil lamp topped with smoked glass chimneys.

Jake, Hawk and Sunkist walked to the back of the yard to the well where Jake kept his beer and meat cold. The backyard was surrounded with the same white picket fence as the front yard. There was a garden in the corner with perfectly straight rows of green weeds, and a small patch of sweet corn.

"Weeds got kinda out of hand there, Jake?"

"Yeah, Eve took care of . . ." Jake stopped at the well. "I'll get the beer," he said. He pulled a leaky tin bucket up from the well and took out five bottles of beer then dropped the bucket back to the bottom. They walked around to the porch and took their chairs with the rest, then pulled the corks from the bottles and tipped them up.

"Well? How do you like it?" Jake said.

"Like heaven in a bottle," Sophie said.

"I make it myself. I got the recipe from a guy who got fired from the Schell's Brewery in New Ulm. It's easy to make. Timing's the secret."

Sophie raised the bottle in front of her eyes. "Hawk, we'll be making more trips down here to visit your brother."

"Just make sure you bring some of this brandy with you." Hawk said with a laugh.

"What's he drinking?" Sunkist asked.

"Brandy mixed with cider."

"Can he handle that stuff?" Jake asked.

"Probably not," Sophie said, "but we'll see . . . Hawk?"

"Yeah?" he answered with a wide grin on his face and half-open eyes.

"How's your hip?"

"Whad 'ip?" he said, and laughed out loud.

Sophie smiled and turned to Jake. She raised her bottle and clicked his. "I don't think he's gonna be feeling anymore pain in that hip tonight."

"Yeah, well, we'll see what tomorrow brings."

"Tomorrow will be just another today," Hawk said a little too loudly. "Only different."

"And how is it going to be different?" Sunkist asked.

"Well, listen, Sunshine—um, kist. Today we're sitting here drinking booze, and tomorrow we'll be out looking for that kid. Little, um . . ." He stopped and looked at Sophie through blurry eyes. He lowered his eyebrows and looked at her. "What's that kid's name?"

"Claire."

"Right!" he said with a forced nod of his head. "I knew that. I was just seeing if you did."

"Want another brandy, Hawk?" Jake asked.

"Sure, what the hell. Might as well make this a party."

Jake went to the kitchen and brought another brandy.

Hawk took it, brought it to his lips, but lowered it before taking a sip.

"Zoph? Can you stop this porch from spinning around?"

"Sorry, nothing I can do about that. Maybe another brandy is not a good idea right now."

"I gotta go water the trees." He started to stand and dropped back into the chair. He looked up at Sophie with a pleading look in his hazy eyes.

"Come on, Hawk, I think it's time to find you a nice comfy place to sleep." She pulled him up from the chair and he started to fall. Jake jumped up and took him by the arm. They walked him off the porch and out into the yard.

"Jake? Where's she taking us?"

"We're going to bed in the house," Sophie said. "You're going to bed in the barn."

"How come I gotta sleep in the barn?" he asked everyone in the county.

"You'll learn the answer to that one in a few minutes."

They took him to the barn, laid a blanket on the hay, and lowered him onto the blanket. He closed his eyes and immediately opened them wide. "Whoa! Stop this barn and let me out!"

"Hawk, lay down and go to sleep," Jake said. "You'll be alright in the morning."

Jake and Sophie walked back to the house and left Hawk to his spinning world.

Suddenly, from the barn came the anguished sounds of a man throwing his evening's entertainment into the hay.

The night and the barn got quiet. "Spose he's alright in there?" Jake asked.

"Hail, he's been through worse than that," Sunkist said.

A buggy pulled by a single horse came into the yard.

"Here's Heidi," Jake said.

Sophie looked at Jake curiously.

"She comes to help out once in a while," Jake said.

Sophie laid her hand on Jake's arm. "Jake, if something's troubling you, you know you can tell any one of us."

"She don't live here anymore. She ain't dead. She's just gone, and that's that." He stood and walked off the porch toward the barn.

Heidi touched Sophie's arm and said softly, "He's hurting right now. He'll talk about it when he's ready."

Jake heard the sounds of agony coming once again from the barn and turned back toward the porch.

"Why doesn't someone go help that poor man?" Heidi said.

"Help him?" Jake said. "And just what is it you think we can do for him?"

"Well, can't you just go out there and be with him?"

"If you want to go out there and watch a man puke his guts out, you go right ahead. I'm staying here. He'll be alright in a couple of days. Think of it as doing him a favor."

"Making him sick is doing him a favor? You're going to have to explain that one, Jake."

"Well, look at it this way. His hip ain't hurtin' him right now."

"Well, that is true. We'll offer him more pain medicine in the morning. Maybe he'd like a little in his coffee."

"If you don't mind, Jake," Heidi said, "I'll stay here tonight. I'll sleep in the back bedroom."

"You don't snore, do you?"

"No one's ever complained about it."

The next morning Sophie was up early and went to the barn. Hawk lay on the hay, next to the blanket, snoring loudly. She smiled and turned back to the house. Heidi brought coffee from the kitchen.

"How's the patient?" she asked.

"Sleeping. We'll let him wake up on his own."

Jake came out of the bedroom fully clothed. His clothing was wrinkled and sweaty as if he'd slept in them. He took a chair at the table. "Coffee," he said from deep in his throat.

Heidi brought him a cup and set it in front of him. He took a sip. "Mmm, mornin'." He paused for another sip. He stood and walked to the door and stared through the screen with his coffee cup in hand. "Ever'one make it through the night?"

"So far, so good." Sophie said. "We haven't heard from the barn yet. But I saw him breathing, so he's still alive."

"His guts still where they belong?"

"As far as I can tell."

Jake turned and went back to the table just as the front door flew open and slammed against the wall. Hawk stumbled in. His eyes were red and his face was as white as the driven snow. He wore only stockings on his feet and his shirt hung out of his pants on one side. His fly was unbuttoned revealing his faded red underwear. His curly red hair was plastered to the side of his head and soaked with sweat. No one talked or even looked up when he walked into the room . He stood in the doorway staring at the group of people at the table.

After long moments of silence, Jake looked up and said, "Well, look what the cat puked up."

"Soph?"

"Yes, Hawk?"

"How far is it to that doctor in Hutchinson?"

"Hawk, you're not sick, you're just hung over."

"I know that," he said with his eyes fixed on Sophie, his right hand wrapped around the doorknob for balance and his left arm hanging limp at his side.

"Then, what do you want with the doctor?"

"I want to ask him if he can remove my head."

"How's your hip?"

He raised his eyebrows then lowered them and slowly looked down at his hip. He looked at it for a few seconds, raised his head, squinting from the pain and said, "It don't hurt anywhere near like my head."

Sunkist and Posey came through the door. Sunkist put his elbow on Hawk's shoulder and nudged him aside. Hawk stumbled and caught himself on the back of a chair, almost turning it over. He then slowly turned to Sunkist and greeted him with a low grunt that sounded like, "Hey."

"Hey."

Posey looked at Hawk then at Sunkist. She said something in Cherokee and Sunkist shook his head. "No."

She tilted her head slightly to the side and looked into his eyes. Again he shook his head and said with more force, "No."

Heidi got up from the table and went into the kitchen.

"Hawk," Sophie said, "you better sit down and have some coffee. It'll make you feel better."

"I don't think my stomach can handle anything right now."

She poured him a cup of coffee and slid it over to him. "Here, try it, you might be surprised."

He stuck one finger in the handle of the cup and lifted it from the table. The cup started to slip from his grip and Sophie casually put a finger under it to stabilize it. Using both hands to get it to his mouth, he took a sip and jerked his head back. "Youch! Hot." He winced at the pain the sudden movement caused his head.

Sophie watched him with an elbow on the table and her face cradled in her hand. "Watch out . . . it might be hot," she said lethargically.

"Thanks for tellin' me." He set the coffee on the table and cupped his face in his hands with his elbows on the table. "Jake, if I ever take another drink of brandy, I want you to kick my ass up around my throat so I can't swallow."

"Don't worry, big brother, I don't think you'll be tempted again any time soon." Jake's eyes showed sympathy for his big brother. He'd had the same experience a few times recently and knew the misery.

Sunkist looked at Posey and nodded. She got up from the table and went out the front door. The screen door slammed and Hawk nearly jumped off his chair. He grabbed his head and groaned loudly.

Suddenly, the aroma of potatoes and eggs frying in bacon grease filled the room. "Breakfast will be ready in a minute!" Heidi shouted from the kitchen.

Hawk's head came up and he jumped from his chair, knocking it to the floor behind him and ran out the front door.

Sophie started to get up but Sunkist put his hand on her arm.

"He'll be alright. Posey's gonna fix him up. He's jiss gotta git some of that poison out of his innards. She's got more medicines in that bag than any white doctor . . . He'll be hisself rot quick."

Posey came to Hawk on the porch and said, "You drink, you get better."

He looked up at her and took the cup from her hand.

"You drink."

He knew the healing power of her medicine and without hesitation put the cup to his lips and turned it up.

Posey patted him on the shoulder and said, "You be better rot quick."

He sat on the porch while the rest had their breakfasts. In half an hour he stood and walked into the house.

"I guess I could handle some of that bacon and a couple of fried eggs now."

Sophie looked at Sunkist. He shrugged one shoulder. "Got me a damn good woman there."

Sophie got up from her chair and walked to the kitchen. "You want help with the dishes, Heidi?"

"I'm not doing these dishes. I'll cook for the guy once in a while when he's got company, but I don't clean his house."

Sophie glanced toward the door then turned to Heidi. "Heidi, do you have any idea what's going on with Eve?"

"Eve left him for some lawyer in Milwaukee. That's all I know."

"Sophie!" Jake yelled from the living room. "C'mon out here. We gotta talk about finding that girl."

They gathered on the front porch, sitting in the chairs they had occupied the night before. Sophie sat next to Hawk and kept a hand on his leg.

Heidi harnessed up the buggy and drove out of the yard.

"So, what's the girl's name?" Jake began.

"Claire Stromberg."

"Where and when was she taken?"

Hawk looked at Sophie. "Guess we never did find that out. They were on a farm when they were attacked. Not sure when either."

"Maybe that wouldn't be any help anyway. None of these orphans are anywhere close to home."

"Where should we start looking?" Sophie asked.

"We could ask at the Catholic church in Hutchinson," Jake said. "And like I said before, there's the Good Samaritan we could check out."

"Right, Preacher Diggs's church," Sophie said. "Do you know exactly where it is?"

"Right in the middle of town. You probably drove right by it on your way here."

"We'll go down and visit the Indians and see if they can tell us anything," Sunkist said.

"Then I'll start at Saint Peter," Jake said.

"I'll saddle the horses," Hawk replied.

"I thought the doctor recommended giving it another week before you ride."

"Soph, I can ride. It's just the cut the doc made that hurts now."

"That's a two-day ride back to Hutchinson, you know."

"We'll take our time and if it gets uncomfortable we can stop and rest."

Sophie stood and started for the house. Hawk leaned forward, started to rise from his chair, and promptly fell to the floor.

"Dammit!" he said as he rolled to his side. He used the rail of the porch to help himself to his feet. "We'll take the wagon and tie the horses to the back," he said.

"You okay, Hawk?" Jake asked.

Hawk held the rail while he swung his left leg forward and back trying to limber it up. "This hip seems to work right, but the meat around it is swollen. That's what's giving me the trouble."

"Remember what Uncle Robert used to say? 'Just pretend it don't hurt.'"

"I remember," Hawk said with an air of sarcasm.

"Hawk, this time he's wrong. You keep bangin' that thing up, and you ain't never gonna heal. When you get out of a chair or off the ground, don't just jump up, 'cause yer gonna fall down. We know it hurts and we ain't gonna laugh at you for doin' things slow. We need you healed up. Ain't no tellin' what we're gonna run into with this chase."

"I'll go hitch up the mules," Sophie said. "You bring the horses and tie them to the wagon."

They climbed into the wagon. Hawk turned and said, "See you here in one week."

"Good luck."

They left Jake's farm and headed back to Hutchinson following a wagon trail straight north out of Courtland until they came to the main road.

Hawk turned to Sophie. "What's the deal with Eve? Do you know?"

"I guess Eve walked out on Jake. Heidi told me she left him for some lawyer in Milwaukee."

"What the hell'd she do that for?"

"My guess is that she was just not cut out for the life Jake lives. Running around the country getting shot at isn't for everyone."

"Yeah, I s'pose yer right."

They passed through a settlement called Eagle City.

"Wanna go in and have a brandy?" Sophie asked without looking at him.

"You wanna git out and walk?" he replied without looking at her.

Sophie smiled. "How ye feelin'?"

"I don't ever want to taste that stuff again. I feel like I got no guts, and my head is ready to explode."

Sophie handed him the water jug. "Here, drink all the water you can hold. It'll help."

Hawk turned the jug up and drank most of the gallon.

"How about stopping for the night?" she asked.

They pulled off the road into a patch of woods and settled in.

In the morning they were up and moving by the time the sun topped the trees. The sky was deep blue and the temperature was rising quickly.

Sophie looked up and, more to herself than to Hawk, she said, "I love the morning light; it brings life to everything. But my favorite light, as you know, is that soft orange light that makes the world glow for just a few moments before it fades to evening."

"I think this is going to be a hot one," Hawk said.

The air was already hot on their skin. The only breeze they felt was filled with the dust that rose from the feet of the mule. By midday they were covered with a heavy coat of brown dust that mixed with sweat and turned to clay on their clothing. Flies buzzed around their heads and gnats landed on them and bit into their skin, leaving welts that burned and itched.

The air was hot and still and seemed to be singing a high-pitched whine. Not a bird or animal moved. The only sounds were the feet of the mules and horses, and the clatter of the iron-rimmed wagon wheels as they struck rocks or dropped into holes in the road, stirring more dust into the air. In the distance they saw dust devils playing across the fields of prairie grass, picking up straw, leaves, and dust, carrying it all upward, and dropping it as the whirlwind disappeared in the hot afternoon air.

Above them soared a bald eagle, riding the hot thermals. They watched it climb higher and higher, soaring effortlessly, playing on the wind with its eight-foot wingspan.

"Suppose he's watching us sweat down here?" Sophie asked.

"Yeah, and probably laughing at us," Hawk responded.

The wagon crossed another road going east and west, and three miles further the road curved around a lake. The water glistened and shimmered as bright sunlight played on the ripples. Clouds of flying insects formed twirling columns over the weeds and grass along the shore, and the air was heavy with the pungent smell of the lake.

Suddenly, Sophie turned and grabbed Hawk by the front of his sweat-soaked shirt. She pulled him toward her and put her face directly in front of his.

With her face inches from his, Sophie growled, "What say we stop and cool off in the lake?"

Hawk pulled his head back, surprised by the sudden attack. "What the hell was that all about?"

"Well?" she said with a grin. "Wanna go for a swim?"

"I don't know. Is it safe?

"Guess you'll have to find that out for yourself."

He turned the mules off the road towards the water. Sophie jumped out of the wagon and ran to the water, stripping her clothes and dropping them as she ran. Twenty feet into the lake, she dove head-first into the water, leaving a cloud of brown dust from her hair in the water behind her.

Hawk walked into the water until it covered his lower legs then let himself drop backwards and float on his back.

"Damn," he said with his eyes closed and a big smile on his face, "that brandy finally killed me and I've gone to heaven."

"You're not in heaven—yet," Sophie said, as she laid her hand on his chest and pushed him under. He scrambled up blowing lake water from his mouth, got his feet under him, and took off after her. She laughed and headed out to deeper water. She stretched out and began swimming away from him. She stopped, turned around, and bounced off the bottom. "You want me, Hawk? Come and get me!"

Hawk laid himself out on the water, started a strong overhand stroke, and caught her. He put his hand on the back of her head and pushed her under the water. He was bouncing on his toes, barely able to keep his head out of the water, when suddenly he felt a pain on his back end. He jumped up, turned himself around, and dove down to find his assailant. Under the water he could see Sophie's legs scissoring and her arms pushing water as she swam away from him. Her auburn hair drifting in the clear water was like a golden cloud, and her movement was as graceful as a fish swimming leisurely through the water.

His longer arms and stronger muscles made it easy for him to catch her, and he took hold of one ankle and pulled her backward to him. He was just about to sink his teeth into her butt when she suddenly flipped over and he found himself between her thighs. Sophie stopped thrashing and lay still on her back in the water with her legs on either side of Hawk's face. He stopped and ran his hands up her legs, feeling the perfect roundness of her thighs and her cold skin on his face. Then he realized he was under water and running out of air. He came up with a splash and a gasp. He pushed her legs up and she somersaulted backwards. He was now in water shallow enough to stand in, his chest out of the water. Sophie came up in front of him and wrapped her arms around his neck and her legs around his middle.

She pulled her face away and looked into his eyes. "Hawk?"

"Yes, Sophie?"

"Turn around."

He held her with his hands on her backside and slowly turned around. His gaze fell on a black buggy with a white horse in front of it. A thin man with a black beard and eyebrows that met between his eyes sat on the seat.

Hawk stood for a few long seconds looking at the preacher. Sophie hung on tight and turned her head around. Her dripping hair hung down her face past her shoulders. She looked through the strands with her devilish blue eyes and said, "Good afternoon, Reverend Diggs."

"Good afternoon," the reverend said. "Beautiful day for a swim."

"That's about all this afternoon is good for. It's too hot for anything else."

"It seems the two of you have found activities suitable for such a warm day," he said, a slight smile showing on a face that surely seldom, if ever, enjoyed a smile.

"We were on our way to see you, Reverend," Sophie said.

"I will leave you, then, and go to the church and make preparations for your visit."

"You do that, Reverend," Sophie said. "Enjoy the day!"

The buggy clattered away and out of sight. Sophie threw her arms up and laughed out loud, dropping backward into the water but keeping her grip on Hawk's waist with her legs. He reached out and took her hands, pulling her out of the water.

"How's the hip?"

"Doesn't seem to be bothering me anymore."

"Want to get back on the road?"

"How about we set up a camp and stay here for the night?"

"Ready for that stress test?"

"I'm willing to give it a try."

Hawk's hip hurt him like the fires of hell but Sophie's love made it easy to ignore.

They lay with their heads under the blankets to ward off the hoards of mosquitoes buzzing around them. But it was hot under the blankets and sleep was hard to come by. Eventually the night cooled down and the mosquitoes stopped their torturous attacks.

"Hawk, look at the sky!"

He looked up and saw lights glowing in the northern sky. "Northern lights. I haven't seen them since I was back in Ottertail County."

The lights danced and grew until they covered the entire northern sky. Close to the horizon they appeared as bright silk curtains blowing in a soft breeze. Straight above, the lights slithered to and fro like a burning cloud, shooting streaks of light across the sky, then disappearing only to send another streak out in a different direction.

A shooting star passed across the sky. Hawk started to make a wish but his wish was already lying next to him.

"What do you think causes the northern lights?" Sophie asked softly.

"Some say it's the sun shining on the snow on the North Pole and they dance like that because the wind is blowing the snow around. But Lorraine says it's the light from the sun making the air over the North Pole glow. Something like lightning, I guess."

"In other words, you don't know."

"Right."

The next morning a fly walking across Hawk's face woke him from his sleep. The sun was up and the sky was as clear and blue as it had been the day before. The horses and mules had pulled their ropes loose from the tree and were grazing in the meadow of green grass a hundred feet away.

Sophie opened her eyes and peeked from under the blanket. "Morning," she said.

"Yeah, I know."

"Want to get going?"

"No."

Sophie threw the blankets off and jumped up. "Come on, Hawk. Let's take a dip in the lake before we go see the reverend."

6

C H A P T E R   S I X

THEY ARRIVED IN HUTCHINSON ABOUT NOON and drove slowly down the main street until they came to the wooden sign in front of the church. They got down from the wagon and stood at the foot of the steps leading to the door. Hawk looked at Sophie. "What are you gonna tell him?"

"Me? I'm not telling him anything. You're the guy with the questions."

"I don't mean about the girl. I mean what are you—ah, we—going to tell him about getting married?"

"Oh, that. Well, if you're asking for my opinion, I think things are fine just as they are. A piece of paper isn't going to change the way I feel about you."

He smiled, kissed her on the nose, and said, "Let's go in."

They climbed the steps to the door. "Do we knock?" Hawk asked.

"I've heard doors to God's house are always open."

Hawk took hold of the doorknob, turned it, and pulled. It didn't open. "Guess we knock."

He knocked on the hardwood door three times and dropped his hand to his side, flexing his bruised knuckles. They waited for a few minutes before he knocked again, this time with his open palm. From behind them they heard Reverend Diggs's voice.

"Good morning, my friends. May I assume you have come for the matrimonial observance?"

"Let's not assume anything," Hawk said. "I thought the doors to the church were always open."

"There has been an amendment to the commandments. God said, 'Remember the Sabbath, but lock your doors when you go to church.'"

"We're here to talk to you about a little girl who was taken by the Indians.

Do you know anything about a girl about nine years old named Claire Stromberg?"

"I'm sorry, I didn't get your names," Reverend Diggs said.

Hawk walked down the steps trying hard not to let his limp show. He stuck out his hand. "I'm Harlan Owen and this is Sophie."

Diggs put out his hand. "How do you do." He took off his hat and bowed slightly at the waist. "Charmed, Missus Owen."

"Reverend Diggs, we're looking for the little girl of some friends of ours. They were attacked by the Indians and the girl was stolen. Do you take in orphans?" Sophie asked.

"We have only two children living here, and the parents of both of them are known to be dead. Their bodies have been found and buried where they were killed. I know of no others in this town. The church down the street has none, and no families here have any orphans. Have you talked to the military? They may know something."

"The girl's father talked to Henry Sibley at Camp Release and he was no help. He told them their daughter might have been taken by the Indians out to the plains. Personally, I think that was an easy way out for Sibley."

"Mister Owen, General Sibley did a wonderful thing by taking on the fight against the Indians. He deserves more credit than you give him."

"Henry Sibley's part in that war is not what I came here to talk about. Do you know anymore about where we might look for Claire?"

"Yes, you might try the agency schools. There are a number of children there both Indian and white. That would be the best place to start."

"Thank you, Reverend. We'll go there."

"Mister Owen, my housekeeper will have dinner on in a few minutes and I would enjoy having company for a change."

"Soph?"

"We would be delighted, Reverend," Sophie said.

Reverend Diggs pulled a large key from his coat pocket and unlocked the door. It opened with a shrill squeal and he stepped back to let the couple walk in ahead of him. Sophie walked in first and Hawk watched as the preacher's eyes moved down Sophie's back to her bottom. The reverend saw that he'd been caught and looked at Hawk, grinning slightly and tipping his head a little to the side apologetically. Men looking at Sophie didn't bother Hawk. She was a beautiful woman and men were going to look as they would look at any work of art. He raised his eyebrows at the reverend and grinned back. Diggs patted Hawk firmly on the back and followed him into the church.

He led them to the back of the building into a parlor. "Please," he said. "Make yourselves comfortable. I'll tell my housekeeper we have company."

Centered in the room was a large oak table with carved lions-foot legs and six matching chairs around it. Reverend Diggs pulled a chair out for Sophie. She thanked him and sat down. The table was covered with a white linen table-cloth. There were six place settings with polished silverware neatly laid out on white linen napkins. Fine china plates, a stemmed wine glass, and a glass tumbler adorned each setting. A pair of silver candelabra stood in the middle of the table with four tall beeswax candles burning brightly in each of them.

Reverend Diggs came into the room.

"I'm sorry. Were you expecting company, Reverend?" Sophie asked.

"Oh no, we keep the table set for unexpected guests."

Sophie and Hawk sat side by side close enough that their knees touched under the table. Reverend Diggs sat across from them.

A woman came through the door with a glass pitcher on a silver serving platter. She silently moved around the table pouring freshly squeezed lemonade into each glass before them.

Sophie looked at Hawk and he looked back, knowing that she was silently commenting on the extravagance of the table.

"Mister Owen," Diggs said, "may I introduce my housekeeper, Miss Erickson."

"Miss Erickson, this is Mister Owen and his lovely wife, Sophia."

"Reverend," Sophie said. "My name is Sophie, if you please."

"Sophie—yes, of course, forgive me." He looked at Miss Erickson, gestured with his palm up and his fingers pointing to Sophie. "Sophie Owen."

Miss Erickson was short and as round as a washtub. A white lace apron covered the front of the light blue dress that draped to the floor. Her large breasts spilled out around the sides of the bib of the apron. The collar of the dress was tied tightly with a dark blue ribbon, and the fat around her neck squeezed out above the collar.

Her gray hair was pulled in to a bun behind her head, and a lace doily was fastened atop her head with a long hat pin. The tip of her nose to her throat ran in a straight line; there was no chin. Hawk looked at her, thinking she looked awfully familiar. He was reminded of the weasel that lived in their woodpile, the one that Sophie thought was so cute.

"How d'ye dew?" she said with a strong Scandinavian accent.

Hawk nearly spit out his lemonade when he heard the accent. "Your name is Erickson?"

"Ya. Do yew know someone by dat name?"

"We met a man in Brown's Valley last fall by the name of Erickson. Lloyd Erickson, I think his name was."

"Ooooh, yew know my brodder Lloyd, den?"

"Oh yes, we know him. We stayed in his cabins for a night."

"Vell, I vos youst dare a couple of monts ago and he iss doing youst fine."

"We weren't there long; just one night. He probably wouldn't remember us."

"He vos a little upset about some people by da name off Owen hew came trew dare last fall. Dat ruffian Hawk Owen and hiss brodder, Yake." She leaned over the table at Hawk, shook her finger at him, and said with a teasing smile. "Dat vosn't yew, vos it?"

"I never considered myself a ruffian, Miss Erickson."

"Vell dats gyude, 'cause if it vos yew, I would heff tew collect dat fifty dollars he said dat hyooligan owes him."

"Fifty dollars?" Hawk blurted out. "Last I heard it was two dollars and six bits, and we paid him that."

Sophie put her hand on Hawk's arm.

"Um, just the stories I've heard," he said softly.

Miss Erickson looked hard at Hawk. "Yumpin' yimminy, yer him, aren't yew?"

"Yes, Miss Erickson, I'm Hawk Owen."

"I knew it," she said, holding the coffee tray against her belly and tucked under her oversized breasts. "Yew heff da look of a ruffian," she said angrily. "Your narrow eyes and your long hair and dat mean look on your face!" She half turned toward the kitchen, looked over her shoulder, and added, "Yew shoult be ashamed off yourself beating up on an olt man like dat!" The glass pitcher rattled on the tray as she spoke.

"I didn't beat up on him! Who the hell told you that?"

"Mister Owen!" she shouted. "Dare iss no call to use dat kind off language in da house off da Lord."

"I'm sorry, Miss Erickson, but I did not beat up on your brodder—brother. And I do not owe him fifty dollars."

"Reverend Diggs," Miss Erickson said, "da Bible says 'Thou shalt not suffer a murderer in dine house.' You should trow dees people out right diss instant!"

"Now, now, Miss Erickson, the Bible also says, 'Judge not, that ye shalt not be judged.' Matthew, chapter seven, verse one."

"I can name a few people who should try to remember that," Sophie said.

"Diss man iss a murderer!" Miss Erickson shouted. "I vill not heff him in diss house!" She was angry and her voice split the air like a meat cleaver.

Hawk stood and said, "Miss Erickson, I am not a murderer. I fought in the Indian wars like almost every man in this state. I killed no one who was not trying to kill me or someone else. If you don't want to be near me then you leave. I'm staying."

Reverend Diggs stood, walked around the table, and put his hand on Hawk's shoulder. "Here now," he said calmly, "let's stop this bickering and get down to dinner. We can talk about this another time."

"I've said all I have to say," Hawk said. "I'm not explaining myself to her or anyone else."

"Miss Erickson," Reverend Diggs said as he jingled a small glass bell. "Please? Dinner? And, Ester, please be your gracious self."

She started to speak but Reverend Diggs put a finger to her lips and pointed to the door to the kitchen. "Dinner."

She sniffed, threw her nose in the air, and walked out of the room. Her robust backside shifted from side to side as she moved.

"I must apologize for her. She can be a bit cantankerous. I find myself walking on the edge of disaster much of the time."

"No need for apologies, Reverend." Hawk said.

Miss Erickson came back into the room pushing a cart loaded with roast beef, boiled red potatoes with the skins on, sweet corn roasted on the cob, a large pitcher of milk, and baked apples swimming in brown sugar and butter, each in its own silver serving bowl.

"It all looks so delicious," Sophie said with a smile. Miss Erickson looked at her, turned, and walked out of the room without responding.

Hawk and Sophie picked up their forks. Reverend Diggs folded his hands on the table, lowered his head, and silently said a prayer of thanks. Hawk and Sophie quickly put their forks down, glanced at each other, and joined him.

Each of them took what they wanted from the tray of food and began eating quietly. When they were about half finished, Diggs picked up and rang the glass bell. Miss Erickson came in with a decanter of red wine and began serving each of them in turn. When she got to Hawk she picked the glass from the table and stepped back to pour it.

"Miss Erickson," Sophie said, "did you see the northern lights last night?"

"Missus Owen, da Lord gave us da night to rest. I go to bed ven the sun goess down and rise ven da sun comes up. Dat iss according tew da vishes of da Lord."

"I'm sure that works nicely for you, Miss Erickson. I have always been fond of the night. There is something so magical and mysterious about the northern lights, and I feel blessed whenever I see them. The northern lights are some of God's finest work, and to ignore them, I think, would be an insult to his efforts."

Hawk looked up from his plate just in time to see Miss Erickson's lower jaw snap shut with an exaggerated "Humph!" She turned and stomped out of the room.

Hawk picked up his wine glass, looked at for a few seconds, and drank it down. "Hmmm, not bad."

Sophie tasted the wine, raised an eyebrow, then set the glass down.

"It's not to your liking, Mrs. Owen?"

"It's delightful," she replied with a smile.

Hawk gave Sophie a quick, confused glance, and said, "Right."

Diggs looked across the table at Sophie and raised his glass. "In honor of the lady," he said with a smile and a nod toward Sophie. He finished his wine, pushed his chair back, and stood. "Shall we adjourn to the library?"

They got up from their chairs and the preacher led them across the hall to the library. The room was only four steps from one end to the other. The walls were lined with maple bookcases filled with hundreds of books of all shapes, fashions, colors, and kinds. A small maple table sat in the center of the room surrounded by four stuffed chairs with carved maple backs and legs. Each chair was covered in red velvet. On the table was the latest edition of the Saint Paul *Pioneer Press*, a small wooden box, a large glass ashtray, and another small glass bell. The library smelled strongly of cigar smoke.

Sophie walked over and looked back and forth, up and down at the books on the shelves, tilting her head to read the titles. Reverend Diggs and Hawk each found a chair and sat down. Sophie stopped and pulled one of the books back to look at the title then let it go back to rest on the shelf.

"Do you read, Mrs. Owen?"

"Oh, I love books."

Diggs's face turned red and he said, "Please come and join us."

Diggs leaned over and opened the lid on the box and said, "Would you like a cigar, Mister Owen?"

"No. No thank you. I don't much care for cigars."

"Reverend Diggs," Sophie said, "where are the two children you say you have here. We'd like to see them, if you don't mind."

"The children stay in the cottage behind the church. They're well cared for and they've been fed and put to their beds for the night."

"Do you ever have them sit with you at dinner?"

"Oh heavens, no. Those children would have no idea of table manners, and they are not used to rich foods such as we enjoy. Their tastes are much simpler."

Sophie and Hawk exchanged a glance and let the subject drop. Hawk saw a change come over Sophie's face that told him she was not comfortable with what she had just heard, but chose to let it go for the moment.

Reverend Diggs rang the small bell. Instantly, the door swung open and Miss Erickson stepped in.

"Yes, Reverend?"

"Miss Erickson, would you bring the brandy?"

"Preacher," Hawk said, "I don't need any brandy either."

Sophie turned and said, "I might like a sip of brandy, Reverend."

Diggs looked at her curiously. "Mrs. Owen?"

"If you don't mind, sir," she said with a smile.

"Uh, well, yes, of course, it's just that . . ."

"If there's a problem, Reverend . . ."

"Well, no, of course not. It's just that . . . Well, I have never seen a woman take brandy."

She leaned over the table and looked into his sunken eyes. "Some women even smoke cigars."

Suddenly, the door burst open. Miss Erickson stepped in and shouted, "DAT ISS KVITE ENOUGH!" She stomped across the room toward Sophie, shaking her finger.

"Yew tew come in here tinking yew can take over dis house vit your foul talk about killing Indyuns, and vimmin drinking vhiskey and smoking dem ceegarss. Yew are notting but a coupla sinners and I em telling yew to leaf diss house diss instant." Her face was red and her breath came in gasps.

Sophie stood straight and looked into her eyes. "Miss Erickson," she said calmly. "Hawk has taken on the job of finding a lost child for some people he doesn't even know, and he's not asking to be paid for it. You have no right calling him a sinner."

"Now yew youst vait a minute!"

Without comment, Sophie continued her direct stare. Hawk put his hand on her arm. She continued, "There are starving children by the hundreds on the reservations and you have chosen to live in your fancy home, with your fine china and expensive silverware, and let the children starve." Her voice softened and she gestured with a sweeping motion of her arm. "Wouldn't it be better to share some of this with them?"

"Reverend," Miss Erickson started, "are yew youst going tew sit der and let her talk . . . ?"

"Reverend," Sophie interrupted, "what about those two children in that cottage? Don't they have the right to enjoy some of these pleasures you have in this house?"

"Please, Missus Owen, those children are being well cared for, I assure you."

"May we see them?"

"I'm afraid that won't be possible. They have been put to their beds for the night."

"Are you ready to go, Hawk?" she asked.

"I'm ready when you are."

They turned toward the door. Miss Erickson stood in their path. Sophie stopped in front of her, inhaled deeply, squared her shoulders, then directed her gaze toward the door. "Excuse me, we're leaving."

They left Miss Erickson standing with her mouth moving but making no sound. She looked at Diggs with fury in her eyes, pointing her shaking finger at the closing door.

They climbed into the buggy and Hawk snapped the reins.

"Hawk, I'm worried about those children they have there."

"What do you mean?"

"I don't think they're being cared for as well as Diggs said they are."

"Want to go back and check on them?"

"Not right now. They'd never let us get close to them. We'll go back later."

"What do you mean by later?"

"Tonight, after dark. Think you can ride yet?"

"I think I can, and I also think this would be a good time to try."

They rode out of town and set up a small camp. The night fell quickly and the sky clouded over.

"Hawk, one of the books on the shelf in that library was a book about a prostitute in France. It's called Fanny Hill. It gets real explicit about the things people do in brothels."

"You saw that on his bookshelf?"

"Yes, I saw it. It wasn't hard to pick out. It looked like it was the most used book there."

"How do you know about that book?"

"When I was married to Robert we did a lot of entertaining for his lumber business. The men would often excuse themselves and go to another room to smoke. Once I walked in while he was reading that book to his business associates."

"Looks like our Reverend Diggs has a hidden side to him."

"Another thing, I didn't see one Bible on that shelf."

Sophie rose up on her elbow and put her face in her hand. "You ready to ride?"

"Ready when you are."

They saddled their horses and made for town.

Lightning flashed in the west, illuminating a bank of storm clouds on the horizon. Slowly and quietly they rode past the church and tied their horses to the rail a block down the street. They walked back and went behind the church to the small log cabin set fifty feet from it. A large padlock hung from the hasp on the door. It was no difficult task to pull the screws from the half-rotted wood of the doorframe and open it.

Moonlight streamed through the open door onto two small bodies lying on a wooden pallet on the dirt floor. Two small girls sharing one pillow slept under a single blanket.

On the floor of the cabin sat two wooden bowls with a spoon in each, and a chamber pot sat in the corner. Sophie picked up one of the bowls, held it up to the moonlight, and examined the remaining contents. She looked up at Hawk. "Cornmeal. Hawk, this is what I was worried about," Sophie whispered. "These children are not being cared for. I don't know why they're here, but it's pretty evident those people in that house do not care one bit about these children or what happens to them."

"Let's take them out of here."

"Believe me, Hawk, I would like nothing more, but that would be kidnapping."

"We'll go to the county sheriff and report this," Hawk said. "Maybe he can do something about it."

One of the little girls rolled over and looked at the two people standing in the half-light. She elbowed the other girl and said, "Erica, we have to get up."

Erica rolled over and started to cry.

Sophie knelt down next to her, smoothed her hair, and said softly, "No, Erica, it's not time to get up. You just go back to sleep and we'll be back in the morning to get you out of here."

"Where are we going?" the little girl asked rubbing her eyes.

"We don't know yet, but we'll find you a much nicer place to live than this. What's your name, sweetheart?"

"Katie," the little girl said with a sob.

"How old are you, Katie?"

"I'm nine and Erica here is eight."

"Alright, Katie, you curl up with Erica and we'll be back in a jiffy."

Sophie stood and turned to Hawk. "Let's go see the sheriff."

Fifty yards ahead a single light shone through a window illuminating a sign that read, 'Police.'

Silent lightning flashed in the distance as they walked their horses along the street. They tied the horses to the rail and stepped onto the boardwalk. Hawk turned to look at the approaching rain clouds, then knocked twice on the door and walked in.

Inside they found a man half-asleep tipped back in a chair with his feet propped up on the desk. He opened his eyes and looked at them briefly. "Oh," he said with a start. "Hello there," he quickly pulled his feet off the desk and jumped up. "Can I help you?" he asked as he tried to straighten his clothes. He felt for the short-barreled Colt pistol in a holster high on his belt and arranged it so it was properly aligned with his shooting hand. "I was just . . ." he started, but stopped and quickly grabbed his hat from the desk and straightened it on his head.

"Are you the sheriff?" Hawk asked.

"No, um . . . No, I'm just a constable here, but I can help you just the same—I guess."

"Constable, I'm not sure if this is something you can help with or not," Sophie said, "but we have to tell someone about it."

The constable grabbed his hat from his head and dropped it on the desk. He nodded quickly to Sophie and said, "Howdy ma'am. Um, tell someone about what?"

"Are you aware of the two children at the Good Samaritan Church?"

"Hold on a minute," he said. "Let me get a grip on myself here."

He sat down, leaned his elbows on the desk, and vigorously scratched the top of his head. "Yes," he said, "they were orphaned in the Indian wars. Preacher Diggs is taking care of them, and he's doing all he can to find them a home."

"How long has he had them?"

"Just a few days, as far as I know."

"Constable, those children are not being properly cared for. They're sleeping in a shed and being fed cornmeal mush and sleeping on board pallets with only one blanket over them. They're not even allowed in the house at mealtime."

"I didn't get your names," the constable said.

"I'm Sophie Boisvert and this is Hawk Owen. We would appreciate someone looking into the state of affairs at the church."

"Well folks," the constable said, "you have come to the right man. I don't like those people over there, and it will be my pleasure to come with you to look at things." He pushed himself out of the chair with a groan and walked around the desk. "They're the wealthiest people in town and are forever hounding the parishioners for more money. Lead the way."

Rain had started to fall, and they stepped into it as they walked off the boardwalk into the street. A few distant lights reflected in the mud forming along the street. They walked the block and a half to the back of the churchyard. Hawk opened the door and they moved into the dark shed slowly. The constable struck a match and found a candle on the wall. The two little girls, shivering from cold, sat up in their bed and started to cry.

Sophie knelt down in front of them, put her arms around them, and pulled them close. "Don't cry. Things are going to be alright now. Come with us and we'll find you some nice soft beds and some good food. Would you like that?"

All of a sudden Miss Erickson's voice split the night air. "Vhat iss going on out here? Hew are yew people, and vhat are yew doing in diss cabin?" She held an oil lantern above her head as she came in.

"Hello, Miss Erickson," Sophie said.

"Oh, it's yew!" she barked, pointing her finger at Sophie. "I might heff known it voult be yew tew. Yew heff caused enough trouble around here today. Yew tew go avay or by God I'll call da police!"

"The police are already here," the constable said.

Miss Erickson turned and looked at him. "Vhat are yew doing here?"

Reverend Diggs came in the door. "What's all the commotion?"

"Reverend, we've come to rescue these children from your care. We're going to find them a decent home where people will take good care of them, unlike what they are receiving here."

"These children are cared for as well as they are accustomed to living," Reverend Diggs said.

"They might be accustomed to living this way but that doesn't make it right. They have the right to good food and proper sleeping facilities, just as much as you do."

"You vill not take dees children," Miss Erickson shouted. "Day belong to us."

"They BELONG to you?" Sophie burst out. Her face flushed and her eyes burned with rage. "They belong with their families. They are not slaves! They are their own people just as your God made them!"

The constable interrupted. "Diggs, you'd better back off. There are some serious charges to be brought against you. I'd recommend that you go back to your house and let us take these girls without anymore fuss."

Miss Erickson was furious. "Yew cannot take dees girls from us!"

Reverend Diggs put the back of his hand in front of her face. "Ester, be quiet. We'll deal with this in the morning. There is obviously nothing we can do about it now. Go back inside."

"I'll be seeing you in the morning, Diggs," the constable said. "Consider yourself and Miss Erickson under arrest and don't leave town."

"Arrest? Arrest for what?" Diggs asked.

"We'll start with unlawful confinement and go from there all the way up to kidnapping," the constable answered.

"Vee are people of God," Miss Erickson burst out. "Yew cannot arrest us!"

Sophie lowered her voice, "I know of no God who would condone what you have done to these innocent children."

Diggs took Miss Erickson by the arm. "Come, Ester. We'll talk about this inside."

As they started towards the door, they stopped and turned around as Sophie interjected, "Oh, just a little advice for the two of you. Don't go around telling people that you are people of God. That would be an insult to your God. Hawk, let's go, I can't stomach this any longer."

Miss Erickson threw her noise in the air. "Humph!" she snuffed and continued out the door.

"Where will you take the girls, Constable?" Sophie asked.

"We'll take them to my wife. We've got extra beds, and we'll feed them and find them decent clothes. We've got a daughter about their age. We'll take care of them until we can find them a proper home. Rachel will enjoy having a playmate."

"Thank you. May I ask your name?"

"Yes, I'm Officer Paul Pinsonnault. My wife's name is Katherine."

"And Rachel is your daughter?"

"Yes."

"Well, we can't thank you enough for what you've done. May we come back and see the girls?"

"Of course. Anytime you're around the country just stop at the office. There's always someone there. In fact, you might be required to come back if charges are brought against the preacher."

"Anything we can do to put those two hypocrites in jail, we'll do gladly," Sophie said. "If there's one thing I cannot tolerate, it's people mistreating children. I've seen too damn much of it."

Hawk and Sophie stepped out into the rainy night.

7

C H A P T E R   S E V E N

THREE DAYS LATER THEY SAT ON CHAIRS on Jake's front porch. There was no one else around, so Hawk walked to the backyard to get two cold beers from the well while Sophie carried their bags to the house. When Hawk returned to the porch, Sophie was sitting with a cotton dress pulled halfway up her thighs and the top three buttons at her neck undone and pulled open. Hawk watched as a single bead of sweat trickled down between her breasts. He envied the journey. One thing he admired was the fact that she could be so damn feminine and, at the same time, could shoot the hair off a flea.

She slouched back with her legs spread slightly and stretched out in front of her, allowing the cool air to circulate over her body. "I know this isn't very lady-like, but it's a lot cooler than those wool pants."

"Wanna get naked?" Hawk asked. "That would be even cooler."

"That would be fine with me, but it might raise an eyebrow when Jake gets here."

"Jake ain't here."

"He soon will be," she said, pointing over his shoulder toward the road.

Hawk looked and saw Jake coming through the gate. "Great timing."

Jake rode up, swung his leg over his horse, and hopped down with his rifle in hand. "Heard anything from Sunkist?" he asked as he leaned the rifle against the side of the house.

"Not a word," Hawk said.

"Might as well wait here. No point trying to find that outlaw. He might be anywhere in this valley."

Jake walked to the backyard for a bottle of beer. "Horses coming," he said as he rounded the corner of the house.

Sunkist and Posey came through the gate and into the yard to the porch. "Well?" Hawk said.

"We talked to the agent at Red Wood. He said the best place to go would be Yellow Medicine. They got the best records about orphans. We figgered, bein' it's a haul up there, we'd come back here and go as a group. Sophie, you seem to be the ramrod in this track, so you can do the talking."

"I'm no ramrod, that would be him," she said with a quick glance and a smile at Hawk. "But I'll do the talking if that's what you want."

"It's still early, wanna get moving now?" Hawk said.

"Let's wait till tomorrow," Sunkist said. "We've been on these critters all night. Ye got another one of them there beers? My throat feels like I bin chewin' sawdust."

"I'll get you the first one, then yer on yer own."

Jake stood and walked to the well. When he came back he said, "Last one. We might have to run to town to quench anymore dry throats."

"Reckon Tom's got all the beer we need," Sunkist said.

"How far is it to the Crow Bar?"

"It's about five miles down the road."

It wasn't long before the group walked into the bar. It took a minute for their eyes to adjust to the darkness. The place smelled of smoke, mainly from the fat cigar hanging from the corner of the piano player's mouth.

The bartender watched as the group made their way to the bar. "What can I get fer ye? Howdy there, ma'am." He nodded to both Posey and Sophie.

"Beer!"

The bartender counted with a nod of his head at each of them. "Six beers, coming up."

"Make that five beers and a sasparilly," Sunkist said.

Posey stepped next to him. "I have beer."

"You sure?"

"I have beer, like Soapy."

"You got it," Sunkist said. "Make that six beers, bar-keep."

Sunkist looked at the bartender. "Hey, Bubbles," Sunkist said. "This beer is kinda piddlin'. You got anything with some bite?"

Bubbles came to Sunkist, looked back at Sophie, and pointed his thumb towards her. "I like her. She's cute."

"I noticed," Sunkist said. "You got anything good back there?"

"We got whiskey."

"Gimme some of that."

Bubbles turned to Heidi. "Bring the man some whiskey."

She brought the glass to Sunkist. He tasted it and said, "Got anythin' with some bite?"

Bubbles leaned over the bar. "I got some homemade hooch a guy outside of town makes. Damn near pure alcohol."

"Now yer talkin'. Gimme some of that."

Bubbles walked to the backroom and came out with a pint jar filled with liquid as clear as spring water. Sunkist took it, unscrewed the lid, and took a small sip. He swished it around in his mouth before swallowing it. His face turned red and a shiver went through him. His chin dropped to his chest and he shook his head violently. He drew in a breath that sounded more like a braying mule, then let it out. "Whew! Now that's what I was lookin' fer." He took another sip. This time it went down more smoothly but still sent a shiver through him. "How much fer the jar?"

"Take it with you. Ain't no one around here can drink that shit. Yer the first."

"Son, this is a taste of heaven in a jar."

Sunkist drank slowly from his jar of heaven and got more mellow as the evening wore on. The crowd inside the bar had grown until there was hardly room to walk around. Hawk watched Sunkist enjoy his new-found beverage and get quieter and quieter.

"Hey, Bubbles," Sunkist yelled. "Ye gotteny more of this hooch?"

Bubbles quickly disappeared to the backroom and came out with another jar of liquid heaven. "Here ye go. This is the last one I've got, but I can tell you where you can get more."

"Where's this guy live?"

"I ain't s'pose to say, but considering, I guess it'd be okay." Bubbles leaned over the bar and whispered to Sunkist. "His name is Walt Fraley. He lives over by Swan Lake. Got him a still in the woods down in a ravine."

Sunkist sat up straight and yelled. "Well, I'll be dipped in shit and called a petunia. Hey, Jake, you picked some mighty fine neighbors!"

"Yeah, I know the old buzzard."

"Ye know 'im?"

"Yup."

"Where's he live?"

"Half his life is spent watching my cornfield, the other half is down by the lake making whiskey."

"Ye gonna innerduce me?"

"Be glad to."

Hawk leaned close to Sunkist. "I think it's time to get back to the farm."

"Yup," Sunkist said, "ain't no excitement in here enna way. Might jiss as well go home."

Sunkist rode behind the pack with Posey at his side, sipping from his jar and singing songs no one recognized.

"Hey, Hawk!" he yelled. "You know any of them there Frenchy songs?"

"Just the one my ma used to sing. '*A La Claire Fontaine.*'"

"Well, git back here and sing with me!"

"Sorry, old friend, I don't know the words."

"I do," Sophie said.

Hawk looked at her. "You do?"

Sophie started to sing. *"Lui y a longtemps que je t'aime, jamais je ne t'oublierai."*

Sunkist laughed and slapped his knee. "Woo-hoo!" he shouted. "Hot damn! Come on back here, li'l gurl. Let's wail!" The next three miles they rode to the sounds of Sophie and Sunkist stumbling over the words to the French voyageur tune. Posey chimed in as best she could with a wide smile on her face and the stars twinkling in her black eyes. She wasn't singing the words, but shouting the melody at the top of her lungs.

Sophie smiled and her white teeth shown in the starlight. She leaned over and said, "Posey, you have a perfectly beautiful smile." Posey glanced at her and continued her song. To a sober ear, the group might have sounded like a pack of baying coyotes. From somewhere in the distance, a dog joined the chorus.

Sunrise found the Pa Hin Sa sitting at Jake's kitchen table, silent and sober. The dinner mess from the previous day and the breakfast mess still sat in the sink.

"Anyone feel like riding today?" Jake asked.

Sunkist answered first. "I wanna go find that galoot Walt Fraley."

"How are you feeling, Hawk?" Sophie asked.

"I'm fine. I didn't drink much. Beer just don't sit right in my guts."

"Jake?"

"No problems here. I can ride when you're ready."

"How about you, Sunkist? You wanna ride?"

"You folks go ahead on," Sunkist said. "We'll catch up."

They turned their horses to the trail and rode through Courtland, passed the Crow Bar, then turned north. They camped for the night beside Eight Mile Creek, then traveled along the rim of the valley to Fort Ridgely. The fort was crowded with wagons and people. Tents of all shapes were set up around the fort, and people scurried around like ants on a sugar cube. Buggies and wagons crowded the fort so tightly they couldn't find a path through. A hundred wagons loaded with furniture, barrels, sacks, and kids crowded the square in the middle of the fort. Hawk walked his horse up to a man carrying a load of supplies on his back. "What's going on here?"

Without stopping the man said, "Goin' to the gold fields in Montana. Gonna be rich by this time next year, you watch."

"There ain't no gold in Montana."

"Like hell there ain't. People been scoopin' it up in buckets. I seen it."

"You seen it? You've been there?"

"Nope, ain't been there, but a feller name of Fisk had a sack full of the shiny stuff and said it come from the gold fields in Montana 'n Idaho. That's all I need to see. I'm goin'."

"Well, good luck." Hawk said as the man disappeared into the crowd.

"Maybe I should consider going out to Montana," Jake said.

"You just stick around," Hawk said. "We got work to do."

Jake looked at Hawk for a moment then said, "Wanna buy a farm?"

"Nope. I got a farm of my own I can't take care of. I don't need another one." He turned and said, "Let's move on."

They turned their horses and rode out of the fort and headed northwest. After traveling for two days, Hawk turned his horse north, up Hawk Creek. They rode for five miles and pulled up in front of his cabin. He looked at the garden and saw the clean rows of vegetables free of weeds, and the yard around the house was cut short to keep the bugs out. The fields of wheat and oats were ripe and ready for harvesting. A new log building stood half-finished just to the north of the house, and the boards were cut and stickled in neat layers next to it, ready to be nailed to the roof.

Albert Stromberg came out of the house. "Well, you're back. Youse was gone longer than we figgered you'd be. I think you'll find everything in good shape."

"Hello, Al. Yeah, it took a little longer than we thought it would."

"Ye git all fixed up?"

"Healthy as the horse I'm sittin' on."

"Mister Owen?" he said, with expectation in his eyes. "When can we go looking for Claire?"

"That's where we're going now, to Yellow Medicine Agency and ask some questions."

"Youse want me to come along?"

"No, Al; we'll be gone for who knows how long, and you should stay with your family."

"Ye mean youse ain't stayin'?"

"No, the place is yours till we get back. If you want to stay, that is."

Al looked back at his wife and kids. Mildred smiled back. Al said, "Looks like we stay if that's what youse really want, Mister Owen."

"I need someone to take care of the place, and by the looks of things, you're doing a hell of a lot better job of it than I did, so I guess you stay."

Missus Stromberg said, "Please come in and have some coffee. I have fresh baked bread and sweet rolls."

"Can't pass that up can we?" Jake said.

They climbed off their horses and made their way to the house.

"It seems kinda funny being invited into our own house," Sophie said, amused.

The house was clean and smelled of freshly baked bread. They each took a chair at the table and Mildred brought the coffee pot and poured each of them a cup.

Hawk looked in his cup for a few seconds before raising it to his lips.

"If you're wondering what that is in your cup, it's egg," Al said. "Mildred always boils an egg in the coffee. It takes the bite out of it."

"Never heard of that before," Hawk said quietly.

"Mister Owen? How long do youse think it will be before youse find Claire?"

"No way to even guess at that. As I said, we're on our way to the Yellow Medicine Agency right now to check with the mission up there and see if they know anything."

"We was up there and they couldn't tell us nothin'. The lady we met was kinda hard to talk to. She made us feel like we was in her way. She sent us to some guy who looked through a pile of papers for Claire's name, but he never found it." Al's face was somber and he fought back tears as he talked.

"Mister Stromberg, we'll find her if Clair is dead or alive."

"We've been praying every night that you find her," Mildred said. "God will find a way."

"Mildred, we will find Claire, don't you worry. We just have to be patient."

"Hawk?" Al said. "What happens to us when youse get back?"

"When you find time, I want you to build another cabin next to the woods. That way when we come back we'll have a place to stay."

"But this is your house. You should be staying here."

"When you get the crops in, you take them to town and sell them. Keep the money you get and save it."

"But . . ."

"Al, we don't need much," Sophie said. "We probably won't be staying around here much anyway. You've done a great job of taking care of this place, and it would be a shame to come in and take it all away from you. Now no more discussion. The place is yours as long as you need it."

"But . . ."

"Al, where would you go? To the quarries? You're a farmer, and apparently a darn good one. You belong on the farm. Consider yourself our employees, and anything you make on this farm will be your wages."

"Well," Al said with a sheepish look on his face, "I hope you don't mind, Hawk, but I've been doing some carpenter work in your barn, using your tools and stuff. I been making furniture and fixing things for folks around here. It brings in a little money."

"Good for you, Al," Hawk interrupted. "Like I said, treat this place like it's yours. Those tools were here when we moved in so they're not really mine, and the guy they belonged to doesn't need them anymore. I'm sure he'd be glad to see them being used."

"Hawk, can I ask you something?" Al asked.

"Sure, anything."

"Where did youse folks come from? We ain't never been treated like this before. People are all the time trying to take things away from us, now youse come along and try to give us things. I think God has already answered our prayers." He walked to the stove and picked up the coffee pot, then turned to Sophie. "Youse gonna stay the night?"

"Might just as well, we won't be traveling anymore today," Sophie said.

"Youse take the bed, we'll sleep in the shed out back. The kids can sleep in the loft."

"Loft?" Hawk said.

Al pointed his finger up and Hawk followed it to the loft that wasn't there when he left a few weeks before.

He looked at Al, smiled, and shook his head slowly from side to side.

Al smiled back. "Pretty good with building things, I guess."

"Pretty good? Al, I think you missed your calling. You should have been a house builder."

"I'll get started on that cabin right away."

After a couple of hours of talk, they all retired to their places for the night. Hawk and Sophie went to their bed in the back of the cabin. Jake disappeared into the night and Sunkist and Posey found their comfort under the stars.

HAWK'S QUEST

"We did not make her lonely,
loneliness has always been there."

 CHAPTER EIGHT

SUNRISE FOUND THEM AT THE TABLE in the center of the room having eggs and fried venison chops.

"Well, Al, I guess it's time we move along. We've got some of God's work to do."

"Thank youse for stopping. And thank youse for all youse are doing for us."

"Al," Sophie said, "you are doing for us, too. Remember that."

As they walked out the door, Hawk turned around and said, "Oh, Al, ye might want to go in there and fix that bed. Seems it had a rotten board or something."

"Rotten board, my ass," Sunkist said quietly. "Youse two need a cast iron bed set on a concrete slab."

They moved north, following the rim of the Minnesota Valley, then crossed the river a few miles north of the cabin and turned south toward the Yellow Medicine Agency. Along the way they passed an Indian village made up of sod and bark shanties. The Indians watched as they passed and made no attempt to communicate. Old men sat quietly smoking their pipes, and the women sat on the ground mending torn clothing or scraping hides. A dozen children ran and played behind the small circle of shelters. They seemed unaware of the miserable living conditions forced on their people by the white men.

"I wish there was something we could do for them," Sophie said.

"They must be some of the friendly Indians who were allowed to stay after the war."

"If they were friendly to the whites, why are they still left to live like this?"

ARVID LLOYD WILLIAMS
BONNIE SHALLBETTER

83

"The white man won't give up his money to help them. His money is more precious to him than people's lives."

Sophie slipped down from her horse and untied the strings that held her blanket behind her saddle. She walked over to a very old woman sitting on the ground next to a bark hut. The woman had a tattered shawl wrapped around her shoulders and a scarf pulled over her head and tied under her chin. Eyes that were once alive with pride and confidence were now lifeless and pale as they followed Sophie's approaching feet. Her head slowly turned up toward Sophie. The old, brown, deeply wrinkled face showed the sadness brought on by the war. The fear of the white people who'd brought them to this end had diminished to absolute indifference towards life. Her weary eyes traced up Sophie's body as far as her waist. Then they closed and she turned to stare silently at the ground.

Sophie wrapped her blanket around the old woman and got down on one knee in front of her. The woman sat silently, without moving, as Sophie pulled the blanket snuggly around the old woman's boney shoulders. She reached out and gently touched the woman's face with the back of her fingers. The woman's lips trembled slightly. Sophie stood and walked back to her horse. She swung up onto Gorgeous and touched her ribs.

Hawk had stopped abruptly, turning The Brute around. He held his horse in the middle of the road looking back at the Indian camp as Sophie rode up.

"What is it?" she asked.

"I don't know. Something I saw in that camp, but I don't know what it was."

"What did you see?"

"That's what I don't know." He looked into Sophie's eyes. "Something in that camp caught my eye, but I'm not sure what."

Jake and Sunkist came up. "What's goin' on?"

"I saw something in that camp."

"Trouble?" Sunkist asked.

"No, it's not trouble," Hawk said. "I don't know what it was." He turned The Brute around. "Come on," he said. "If it's important, it'll come to me."

They rode into the agency and saw the burned-out buildings and the graves of the people who died there during the Indian attacks.

A man came up to them. "How can I help you?"

He wore a black suit and hat. His sagging cheeks and the loose skin hanging from his neck jiggled as he talked. The buttons on his vest strained hard to contain the belly that forced the front of his coat wide open. Both hands held a black, leather-bound Bible on top of his belly.

"We're looking for a little girl named Claire Stromberg," Hawk said. "Some friends of ours lost her during the war and don't know if she's dead or alive."

"We have some orphans here but they're all Indian children. They're in school right now and you're welcome to go and have a look." He put out his chubby hand and said, "I'm Francis Franzen. I'm one of the sub-administrators here at the school." He glanced toward a brick building to his left. "The chief administrator keeps reminding me that I am just a subordinate here."

They walked to the brick schoolhouse on the west end of the compound. The sides of the building above the windows and the door were still scarred with smoke stains. The roof had been repaired and new glass put in the windows.

Mister Franzen knocked softly on the door before lifting the latch and walking in. Six children turned their heads to watch them enter.

"Please continue with your lessons, Miss Westman. We are just here to observe."

Miss Westman was a young woman, barely five feet tall, with blond hair that fell in soft waves to her shoulders. She wore a light blue dress that covered her from her neck to her feet.

She opened her book and looked at the class. "Winnnnter," she said slowly and clearly.

The children responded in unison. "Winnnnter!"

"Snoooow," she said and raised her hand then lowered it slowly while wiggling her fingers.

"Snoooow," the children responded with the same hand gesture.

"Miss Westman is teaching the children the English they will need when they grow to adults and go out into the civilized world."

"She ain't no taller than some of the kids," Hawk said.

"Win-n-n-n-n-d . . ." said Miss Westman, waving her hands to the side.

"They will be retaining their own language, I hope," Sophie said.

"Yes; our superintendent has specifically ordered that the children will not be required to give up their language or their culture. They will be instructed to observe all of the cultural heritage of their ancestors."

"I'm glad to hear that," Sophie said. "Most of the schools won't allow the children to speak their language. They want to make white men of them."

"Missus Owen, if it were my choice they would be restricted from any of the heathen ways of the Indians. They would be taught to live the life of civilized, white Christians."

Sophie looked straight into his eyes. "Mister Franzen, trying to turn these children into white men is like trying to hitch a white-tailed deer to a plow. A deer is as much of the make up of the world as a horse, and the Indians are as much of the make up of the world as a white man."

"That may be true, Missus Owen, but the religion of the Indians is a pagan religion. It is made up of stories fabricated by ignorant men and women who had no concept of Christianity."

"If you read the Bible, Mister Franzen, you will find stories that were made up by ignorant men who themselves had no concept of Christianity . . . because it didn't exist when the Bible was written. If you were an Indian and heard the story of the creation, you'd see it as ridiculous and laugh at anyone who believed it."

"Missus Owen . . ." Franzen started.

"Mister Franzen," Sophie interrupted, "are you doing anything to help those people living down by the rapids?"

"Those people are perfectly capable of working, if they would just rise up and find work."

"Don't you have work for them here, just enough work for them to earn their meals?"

Franzen cleared his throat and said, "I would not have an Indian working for me under any circumstances."

Sophie looked hard at Franzen. Her eyes narrowed and her breath quickened. "If white men won't hire Indians, how the hell . . . ?" She stopped in mid-sentence and turned to Hawk. "Let's go look for Claire before I do something I'll regret."

Hawk turned to Franzen who was watching from the doorway of the school. "Where can we find the superintendent of this school?"

"Her office is in the next building. But I warn you, she is not one with whom to banter words."

"We're not here to banter words," Sophie said coldly.

Hawk, Sophie, Sunkist, Posey, and Jake all started toward a building with a sign over the door that read, 'Administration.'

The building was newly built of yellow brick with oak doors hung on heavy hinges and an iron latch. Hawk lifted the latch and walked in.

Without looking up, the woman at the desk said, "I have asked you to knock before you come in."

Hawk looked at the woman leaning over her books then at Sophie. He returned his attention to the lady, smiled, and said, "It ain't my way to knock on a friend's door."

The woman looked up. "Hawk! My stars, what are you doing here?"

Lorraine showed no signs of the time she'd spent in captivity with the Indians. Her face had come back to the soft, dark complexion of a Métis woman. Her hair was as black, shiny, and wavy as it had been when they traveled with the Métis to Saint Paul three years before. Her eyes beamed as she scurried around her desk to throw her arms around him. "It's so good to see you," she said.

"Hey, Lorraine," Hawk said, grinning wide.

Then she turned to Sophie and hugged her, then to Sunkist, Posey, and Jake.

"What brings you back here?"

"We're looking for a girl named Claire Stromberg. Have you heard the name?"

"Yes, I have. There was a man here a few months ago looking for her. We have no one here by that name, and other than the children of the people who live here, no white children at all. She might have been taken by the Sioux out to Dakota Territory, and if that is the case, you may never find her. Quite frankly, I don't think you're going to find her alive."

"Oh, we'll find her," Sunkist said.

"I would like to go to the school and talk with some of the children," Sophie said. "We might learn something about Claire."

"There are no white children in that classroom, Sophie, but we can if you want."

A man walked into the room. He wore short pants that came to his knees, and were held up by white suspenders. White stockings covered his skinny lower legs. The shirt under his dark blue, pin-striped coat was ruffled down the front and around the cuffs. He wore a bow tie and his hair was slicked back and tied in a queue behind his neck. His black shoes were shined to a gloss and sported leather bows across the tops.

"Miss Bernier," he said, "I am finished with this ledger. Where would you like me to put it?"

His high-pitched voice came through his nose and it sounded as if he struggled to speak.

Lorraine paused a few seconds, contemplating her response. Finally she answered, "Oh, just put it on the desk, Abernathy. I'll look at it later."

Then she turned to Sophie and said softly, "Sometimes I think I am just too decent." Then turning to Hawk, she said, "Hawk Owen, this is my secretary, Abernathy Wayne. Abernathy, this is Hawk Owen and his friend Sophie. His brother Jake, Sunkist, and his wife, Posey."

Abernathy was as tall as Lorraine but as thin as a willow switch.

Hawk put his hand out. Abernathy looked at him through thick, wire-framed glasses. "I am delighted to meet you, Mister Owen. I have heard so much of your adventures in our beautiful valley."

Hawk's big hand engulfed Abernathy's thin, soft one. Hawk was reminded of his mother's wet dishrag. He let go of the scrawny hand and wiped his own across the front of his shirt.

Abernathy turned to Sunkist and pushed his glasses up the bridge of his nose with his middle finger. "Now, don't tell me, let me guess. This is the big, red-headed Sunkist." His hands clapped in front of his chin and he snapped his hand out. "Am I right?"

"Um, yeah. I guess."

"I have heard so many exciting stories about you, sir."

Sunkist took one step back and looked curiously at the thin man. "Um, yeah, nice to meet ye." He turned to Hawk and whispered in his ear, "Do I say 'sir' or 'ma'am'?"

"Oh, I assure you, Mister Sunkist," Abernathy said with a smile, "I am quite masculine. You will please disregard my appearance, as I prefer to present myself in this fashion. It is so much more dignified than . . ." He paused and glanced briefly at Sunkist's greasy buckskin garb. "Well, I do hope you will not judge me by my attire. After all," he said with a little giggle and a shake of his finger, "one cannot judge a horse by its color, now, can one?"

Sunkist put his palms forward and said, "Hey, you dress the way you want. Don't make me no never-mind." He turned and took two steps toward the door, stopping next to Jake. He then turned to keep an eye on Abernathy.

"Abernathy, don't you have work to finish?" Lorraine asked.

"Yes, Miss Bernier. It is just such a delight to finally meet the people of whom you have spoken so eloquently."

"Abernathy!" Lorraine said sharply.

Abernathy jumped. "Yes, Miss Bernier," he said and quickly turned to walk to the backroom. His tiny behind swung from side to side as he moved with quick, short steps.

"Situpsa," Hawk said softly.

"What was that?" Lorraine asked.

"Situpsa," Hawk said. "The name Little Crow gave Sophie. It means wagtail."

Lorraine raised one eyebrow. "I see," she said, glancing down Sophie's body. "Let's go to the school."

They walked into the schoolhouse, and again the children turned to see who was coming in. Sophie looked across the classroom for a few moments and said, "Does anyone here know a girl named Claire?"

A little girl turned around and looked at Sophie.

Lorraine looked toward the little girl, then at Sophie. "She was found alone on the prairie. Her parents were most likely killed in the war and she was abandoned by the rest of the band."

"Maybe she knows someone named Claire."

Sophie knelt down before the little girl, who was dressed in a white cotton dress that covered her from her neck to her leather shoes. Her black hair was brushed to a fine gloss and shimmered in the sunlight that streamed through the window.

"Do you know someone named Claire?" Sophie asked the girl.

The little girl looked wide-eyed at Sophie and said, *"Wong ye Cha."* She then reached up and tugged at Sophie's hair.

Sophie looked up at Jake.

"It means lightning bug," he said.

Lorraine smiled. "She likes your hair. She compares it to the lightning bug, I suppose, because it is a lighter color than she is used to seeing."

Sophie reached up and smoothed the girl's hair and said, "You have beautiful hair, too. It's so soft and shiny."

The little girl reached for her own hair and pulled a tuft of it away and said, *"Wong ye Cha."*

Hawk took Sophie by the arm and urged her to her feet. "Sophie! I know where Claire is. Come on; we gotta get back to that Indian camp."

"But Hawk, we saw the children in that camp, none of them were white."

Hawk tugged gently and said, "Come on; we have to get over there right now." The group, including Lorraine, ran to their horses and rode at a canter to the Indian camp. When they arrived, Hawk dismounted and ran to the place they'd seen the children playing.

He stopped and watched the children run and laugh as they kicked a leather-covered ball around the meadow.

"Hawk, will you please tell me what's going on?"

"Hold on," he said and cupped his hands around his mouth. "CLAIRE!" he shouted.

The children stopped and looked their way then resumed their game.

"Claire!" Hawk called again.

He turned to Jake. "What was that name that girl used?"

"Lightning Bug?"

"Yeah, the Indian word."

"I thought you knew Dakota."

"Jake, what the hell's that name?"

"Wong ye Cha. What the hell's going on?"

Hawk turned and called to the children, "Wong ye Cha!"

The children stopped and turned toward him. A boy about ten years old walked slowly towards them. He pointed to the west and said, "Wong ye Cha."

"She's gone?"

The boy only looked at him.

"Where'd she go?" Hawk asked.

"The child doesn't speak English," Lorraine said. She knelt down to the boy and spoke in Dakota. The boy answered.

Lorraine stood and said, "He says Wong ye Cha has gone away with her mother."

"Where? Where did she go?"

"He doesn't know. He said her mother took her away."

Hawk looked out toward the north. "We have to go and find that girl."

"I don't understand. Why do we need to find this Wong ye Cha?"

"Lightning Bug. That girl in the school was telling us a girl with a white streak in her hair is called Lightning Bug. Claire has a white streak in her hair. Her father told us that when we talked to him."

"I've seen that child," Lorraine said, "but she is not white, Hawk, she is Indian."

"How many Indian children have you seen with a white streak in their hair?"

"Well, just this one, but . . ."

"We'd better find her and make sure," Sophie said. "The boy said she was here just an hour ago, so she can't be far." She turned to Hawk. "Can you track well enough to find them?"

"If I can't, Posey can."

Lorraine bent down to the Sioux boy and spoke to him. He turned and ran toward the woods just to the west of the camp. He stopped and pointed to the ground. There Hawk found where someone had pushed through the tall grass and moved into the woods.

"Come on," he said. Sophie followed him as he slowly picked his way through the grass.

Posey came from behind and pushed Hawk aside, running ahead through the grass, following the trail. The rest of the group followed through the thick brush. Suddenly, they heard the sounds of someone running through the woods. Hawk, Jake, and Sunkist ran ahead toward the sound.

They ran for about a hundred yards when Hawk stopped and held his hands out to his sides. The rest stopped and found themselves standing before an elderly woman sitting on the ground holding a girl tightly to her.

Sophie moved close to the girl. She reached out and lifted a streak of white hair on the girl's head then turned to look up at Hawk. He smiled down at her and nodded.

Sophie turned back to the girl. "Claire?"

The girl looked at the woman holding her, then back to Sophie.

"Claire?" Sophie said again.

The girl started to back away.

"Wong ye Cha."

The girl stopped and Sophie said quietly, "I'm Sophie."

The girl pointed at Jake. "Pa Hin Sa!" she said angrily, then made a motion with both hands out from her body and quickly downward to her side.

"No, Claire," she said and glanced quickly at Jake, then back to the little girl. "Jake is a good man. He will not harm you."

The girl looked at Sophie. "Mi ye, Wong ye Cha!" she said in a loud voice.

"Do you know someone named Claire?"

The child turned to walk away but Sophie took her by the arm and gently held her back. The girl turned and scowled at Sophie, and the old woman made a hissing sound from her throat and reached out to stop Sophie. Sophie was startled by the sudden threat and took one step back. Posey stepped in front of Sophie and faced the woman. The old woman sat back against a tree, staring up at Posey.

With Indian sign, Posey told the woman to stay down, then knelt down to the girl. "You Claire," she said.

The girl softened and responded with a very slight nod.

"Can you tell us where we can find Claire?"

The girl nodded then looked toward the old woman then at Sophie and whispered, "Wa-ung Claire."

"She says she is Claire, but she is not a white girl," Lorraine said with a shake of her head.

"Do you know Maggie and Eli?" Sophie asked.

The girl's eyes got wide as she looked up at Sophie, then at Posey. She turned and looked over her shoulder toward the Indian woman. Then her eyes started to tear and, as she focused on Sophie, she began crying hard.

She threw her arms around Sophie. "Ho. Mi-tang-ka, a sung-ka." She hugged Sophie tightly around the neck.

Sophie looked up at Lorraine for translation.

"Sister and brother . . . I'm a bit embarrassed that we didn't discover this sooner," Lorraine said. "I see no reason to doubt that you have found Claire. This girl came in after Mister Stromberg was here and we saw no reason to believe she was white. I hope you understand."

"There is no need to explain, Lorraine. We can well understand."

Sophie held the girl by the shoulders and asked, "Would you like to go and see your sister and brother?"

Claire held tight to Sophie and nodded her head slowly.

The old Indian woman reached for Claire and screamed loudly. Claire left Sophie's embrace and turned toward the woman. She spoke to her in Dakota and the old woman stared at her a moment, then let out a low growl. Claire went to hug the woman but was pushed away. The girl turned and took Sophie by the hand.

"May we take her to her mother and father?"

"Yes, of course. Come to the office. We have papers for you to fill out, then you can take her home."

"How did you know she was here?" Lorraine asked.

"The girl in the school wasn't referring to *Sophie's* hair. She was referring to the white in Claire's hair. Her father had told us about the white streak. On the way here we stopped at an Indian village so Sophie could help an old woman. There were children playing in the field."

Hawk lifted the tuft of white in the midst of Claire's black hair. "I caught a glimpse of this white streak on one of the children. I didn't put it together until I saw the sunshine coming through the window in the school, reflecting off a little girl's hair."

"So, the name Lightning Bug refers to the white streak," Sophie said.

"Lightning Bug is kind of a cute name for a little girl with a streak of white in her hair," Hawk said. "Don't you think?"

"Somehow," Jake said, looking out across the field at the children playing, "I don't think Claire would have suffered too much living with the Indians. She seemed to be having a pretty good time playing ball with them."

"When white children are captured by the Indians at an early age," Lorraine said, "they are often adopted by the tribe, and their new mothers love them as much as their own children. White people will rarely allow Indian people to live anywhere near them, and they will never accept them as part of the community. Many white children convert to the Indian ways so completely that they do not want to go back to their white families. After a very short time, they completely forget about their birth parents and consider their adoptive parents their families. I think it was very fortunate for Claire that you found her before she became completely Indianized, as it is called by some people."

"You mean if we hadn't found her she would have been just as happy living with the Indians as she would have been with her birth parents?"

"She would have been much happier with the Indians . . . That is, until she was rescued. Then the white men would kill all the new relatives and friends and she'd be an orphan again."

"What about the old woman who had her?" Sophie asked.

"She will be lonely and probably adopt another child to replace Claire. Or she will die of a broken heart. It's not unusual."

"Can't we do something for her?"

"I'm afraid that is not possible. She will morn for Claire as if she were dead. There is nothing we can do, short of leaving Claire here."

Sophie turned to the woman. "Would you like to come with us?"

The Indian woman looked sadly at Sophie, then turned and disappeared into the forest.

"Sophie," Lorraine said, "that woman has known since she first adopted Claire that she would some day have to let her go."

"Such loneliness," Sophie said.

"We did not make her lonely, loneliness has always been there. It has simply moved from one mother to the other. That is the way it must be for an Indian woman."

Back at the agency, they entered the office and Lorraine rang a small bell that sat on her desk. Abernathy came in. "Yes, Miss Bernier?"

"Abernathy, please bring release papers. We have a child to send home to her family."

"Yes, Miss Bernier." He turned and smiled at Sunkist briefly, then disappeared into the back room. They heard the shuffling of papers from the next room, then the door flew open and Abernathy came scurrying in clutching a folder to his chest. Lorraine dictated the name of the girl and her parents while Abernathy scratched across the paper with a quill pen.

Hawk and Sophie signed the papers, thanked Lorraine, and started toward the door.

Lorraine stopped them. "Hawk? Will you be coming back through here?"

"Yeah, I suppose we will from time to time."

"We have a lot of homeless children here and at the other posts. We could use your help finding their parents."

Sophie looked at Hawk. "Feel like taking on another assignment?"

"Sounds interesting. Let's get Claire home and we'll talk about it. Let's go."

They left Lorraine and started their trek back to Hawk Creek. Claire rode with one or another while they were on the road and slept in Sunkist and Posey's tent that night. Sunkist held her most of the day, and Posey seemed to have taken Claire as her own. They took their time on the road, stopping several times for a quick lunch or a wade in a stream. Posey washed and brushed Claire's hair till it shimmered in the sunlight. She braided the white streak and tied a hawk feather to the end of it. Little Claire never went hungry or thirsty or got too cold or too warm. Claire took to Posey like a child to her mother. She followed Posey wherever she went and held her hand as they walked through the groves of trees looking at the different plants and animals.

Two days later they arrived at the farm. When they walked their horses into the yard, the door of the cabin burst open and Missus Stromberg came running out to meet them.

"Oh, my God, my little girl!" she screamed and reached up and pulled Claire from Sunkist's arms and held her tightly. She cried loudly, tears flowing from her eyes. Al Stromberg came running from the building he was working on and flew across the yard with his arms open wide. He ran to his wife and daughter and wrapped his arms around both of them and cried. Eli came out from the new building and walked slowly to the scene with little Maggie right behind him.

He looked up at Hawk. "You are Hawk."

"Yes," Sophie said, "he is Hawk Owen."

All of the people in the group had tears in their eyes. Mildred set Claire on the ground and knelt down to hug her one more time. Then she stood and put her arms up to Hawk. Hawk climbed down from his horse and Mildred threw her arms around him and kissed him on the cheek. "My God," she said, "how can we ever thank you?"

"You just did, ma'am."

Mildred then went to the others, hugging and kissing each one.

She slowly turned to Sophie. "Sophie, there is no way in the world to tell you how thankful we are that you came into our lives." She put her arms around her and hugged her tightly. "Thank you."

Mister Stromberg picked up Claire and said, "Come to the house and tell us how youse found Claire."

They went into the house and sat around the table. Missus Stromberg made egg coffee and brought out a spice cake with brown sugar frosting.

"Now, how did youse guys do it?"

"Well, it wasn't that tough. We found her living with a family of Indians over by Yellow Medicine."

"We were there. They told us that they didn't have any white girls there."

"Al, they thought Claire was Indian."

"Why would they think that?"

"I thought she was, too, when we first saw her," Sophie said. "She could easily be mistaken for an Indian."

"I suppose so," Al said. "She gets it from her mother."

"Is her mother Indian?"

"Oh no. She's full-blooded French."

"French," Hawk said. "Where'd she get the dark eyes and black hair?"

"I think there was an Indian in the woodshed," Al said with a grin.

Missus Stromberg elbowed him and laughed. "He's been saying that since we met."

Al got a somber look on his face. "So, what happens now? Are youse staying?"

Hawk looked at Sophie. "I guess so. I don't have any plans, do you?"

"Well, we could go back to Lorraine and see what she's thinking about finding homes for more orphan children."

"I guess that means we're going to have to make our way to Sacred Heart and find work," Al said.

"Not on your life," Sophie said. "You can stay right here, if you'd like. You've done such a great job taking care of this farm."

"Missus Owen, we can't just take over this place like we own it. This is your place."

"But Al, we are extending the offer to take care of our farm until you can get settled in a place of your own."

"Where was your farm?" Hawk asked.

"We can't go back there. It'd be too hard with all the bad memories."

"Don't you have any good memories about that place?" Sophie asked.

"Oh sure, lots of them. That's where all our kids was born. We built that house ourselves and lived in it for twelve years before the Indians burned it down."

Sophie looked at Al. "I'll bet you had a swing in the tree in the backyard for the kids, didn't you?"

"Yeah, I did," Al said. "And I built them a tree house in the big cotton-wood down by the crick, too."

"And I'll bet you cleared the rocks from the bottom of the creek for them to swim in."

"Yeah, how'd you know that?"

"Al, any man who loves his children as much as you do does those things for them."

"Where is the farm, Al?" Hawk asked.

"Over on Buffalo Creek. About halfway to Hutchinson from here."

"What say tomorrow we go over there and see what's left of it?"

"Al," Mildred said, "let's go look at it. Maybe there's enough left to salvage." She had a tear in her eye as she spoke.

Al looked at her. "Do you really want to, Mildred?"

"Yes, Al. That's our home and there are too many good memories. Let's not let the bad ones spoil it."

He placed his large, roughened hand over hers. "Okay, tomorrow we'll go take a look."

Jake stood and walked outside. Sophie watched as he slowly opened the door and stepped out. She walked out behind him and found him sitting in a chair on the porch. "Are you alright, Jake?" she asked.

"Just gettin' some air."

"Is there anything I can do for you?"

"I'd just like to be alone."

"I'll be around if you need anything."

"Thanks, Soph. I'll be fine."

In the morning Jake came in from the barn where he'd spent the night. He sat quietly at the table sipping his coffee, looking around at the people sitting there. "I'm going home," he said. "I've got my own farm to worry about."

"Yeah," Hawk said. "I figured ye might do that. Anything you need, just holler and we'll be there."

"I know that." He slapped his hands on his knees. "Well, no sense sittin' here jawin' about it. I'll be headin' out."

"See ye down the road," Sunkist said. Sophie gave him a hug before he walked out the door.

The rest had their breakfast and set off to the Stromberg's home.

9

C H A P T E R   N I N E

JAKE RODE THE TRAIL HE TOOK WHEN HE CAME TO THE VALLEY. He passed through the meadow where he had thought about setting up his farm and stopped to look up the bluff toward the cave where he lived when Sisoka was his woman. The trail was no longer a trail but a road for wagons and horses. He passed the spot where the Grenges boys killed Sisoka. He glanced toward the spot where he knew her body still lay as it had for over two years. His heart left his chest, and he felt a loneliness that caught in his throat and brought tears to his eyes.

He quickly wiped a tear from his cheek then kicked his horse to a full gallop. Below the Lower Sioux Agency, he stopped to look over the sight of the Redwood Ferry battle. Depressions in the ground showed where he'd helped bury the dead soldiers; the bodies had been removed and taken to the cemetery at Fort Ridgely for reburial. He passed the fort without stopping. Around every turn lurked reminders of the past three years.

As he walked his horse through Courtland toward his farm, he sensed something wasn't right. He stopped and looked over the farm a half-mile away. Suddenly, he knew. There was no barn. He kicked the horse to a gallop as memories raced through his mind, memories of the time back in Ottertail County when he rode into his father's farm and found the house burned to the ground . . . and his mother dead.

He brought his horse to a stop and stepped down. All that was left of his barn was a pile of burned timbers and boards. Feeling helpless and alone, he went into the house and poured himself a full glass of brandy. He was feeling the effects of the brandy when he fell asleep in his easy chair.

The next morning he was awakened by the sounds of wagons coming up his road. He jumped up and went to the door. There were three wagons with two men in each of them.

"What the hell happened, Jake?"

"My barn burnt down."

"We know that. How'd it happen?"

"I don't know. I didn't leave the lantern in there and the animals were all out in the pasture. I don't know what happened."

"Wasn't lighting, was it?"

"There was no lightning that night, Ed," George said.

"I know, but sometimes . . ."

"It wasn't lightning, Ed."

"Yer gonna need some help puttin' 'er back up, Jake," Henry Miller said. "I got lumber in the yard. You can have all you need and pay me when ye can."

Henry Miller ran the local lumber yard. He was usually tight about giving credit, but he made Jake the offer just the same.

"Thanks, Henry. I might have to take you up on that."

"Well, let's get busy and clean up this mess."

"Let it be for now," Jake said. "You guys got crops to take care of and so do I."

"When you're ready, just give a holler and we'll come a-runnin'," Ed said.

"Hold on a minute, I'll come to town with you. We'll do some dealing on lumber." He got his horse from the pasture, saddled him, and they went to town.

He hadn't named his horse; he figured naming him would make him more of a pet than a ride. He just called him Horse.

In the Crow Bar saloon they sat around a table talking about the barn. Each of them had a different guess about how it caught fire until Jake finally broke the conversation and said, "It don't matter how it got started. I need to get it rebuilt so I can get back to farming."

"Heard you've got some problems, Mister Owen," Orley said as he walked in the front door with two men behind him.

"Git away from me, Orley," Jake said without looking up.

"We could help out if you're interested in rebuilding it."

"You've been trying to get me into something to make easy money since you showed up. And I've been tryin' to tell you, I ain't interested."

"If you want to talk, I can come out to your place tomorrow and tell you all about it."

"You could tell me right here and now if it's something legitimate."

"I'd prefer a private meeting, if it's all the same to you."

"Well, it's not all the same to me. Not interested. Go away."

"Sorry you feel that way, Mister Owen. You could make enough money to build a new barn. If you change your mind, I'll be around."

Orley and the two men walked out of the saloon.

"What's that all about, Jake?"

"Wish I knew."

"Well, meet up with him and find out."

"Ed, I've got too many things goin' on right now to get into anything else. Just drop it."

"Ye don't suppose Orley had anything to do with your barn burning down, do you?" Ed asked.

"No way to know that, and I can't be blaming anyone till I know fer sure."

"The lumber is still there when you're ready Jake," Miller said.

"Thanks, Hank. I'll let you know. I gotta clean up what's left of the ashes before I get started on the barn."

Jake went back to his farm late that night feeling the beer he'd had. Sleep came with no problem and he dreamed of Eve coming in the front door walking by him, smiling over her shoulder. Her face was tipped down a little as she smiled and she looked at him from the corner of her eye, the way she did when things were about to get interesting. She had a way of looking at him that made him feel like he was melting from the inside out. Her deep brown eyes and full lips made Jake's heart flutter each time she did that to him. She knew how her flirtatious ways affected him and she enjoyed the game. Sometimes the flirting went for an entire weekend until she knew Jake was about to explode. Then it was anything-goes lovemaking.

Jake spent the next three days cleaning up what was left of the barn. He gathered up the wood that was still useable and broke the rest up for firewood for the next winter.

When the mess was cleaned up, he went to town to talk to Henry Miller about buying wood for the new barn and to recruit help for the raising. He knew he had to get the barn built before winter set in. He made a deal for the lumber and started toward home.

When he walked in the door of his house, he tripped over a rope that had been stretched across the bottom of the frame. Two men jumped on his back and held him down. They pulled his arms behind his back and tied them tightly with rope. Then they pulled him to his feet, spun him around, and stood him in front of Robert Orley. Jake instantly kicked out at Orley and caught him on the left shin.

Orley jumped back. "You just don't quit, do you, Owen." He hit Jake in the center of his face and said, "That's for the broken nose."

"What the hell is this all about?" Jake demanded.

"Settle down and I'll tell you all about it."

"Get these goddamn ropes off me!"

"No, Jake, that won't be possible. Maybe after we have a little talk we'll take them off."

Jake was ushered backward to a chair and pushed down into it. Orley came and stood before him. "Do you recognize this?" he asked as he pulled a hank of brown hair from his jacket pocket.

"What the hell is that?"

"Your wife left for Milwaukee a couple of weeks ago, right?"

Jake started to get out of the chair but one of the men pushed him down with the butt end of his rifle.

"Your wife didn't get there."

"What the hell are you talkin' about?"

"Oh, don't worry, Jake, she's being well cared for." He chuckled and said, "She's in good hands, I assure you."

"My wife," Jake started, then decided to be quiet and hear what Orley had to say. He sat back in the chair. "Alright, what's this all about?"

"You know this is just between us and no one else can hear about it. Remember, Mister Owen, we have your wife, and if anyone hears about this, she and you will be eliminated."

"What do you want from me?"

Orley walked around behind Jake. "You're aware of the troubles around Crow Wing County, I'm sure."

"I don't know anything about it, and I like it that way."

"There's a man up there we need to talk to. He's got a war party with him wherever he goes and we haven't been able to get close to him."

"Who's this man you're looking for?"

"That's where you come in. We need your help to find him—just to talk with him. You'll be paid enough to get your farm back on its feet and money left over for beer. What do you say?"

"Who's the man you're looking for?"

"A chief called Hole-in-the-Day."

"Not interested."

Orley ran the hank of hair under Jakes nose and said, "You might want to reconsider, Mister Owen."

Jake smelled Eve's favorite perfume in the hair. He scowled up at Orley, "You dirty son of a bitch. How the hell did you stay alive this long?"

"By taking care of myself, Jake, and not worrying about other people. You'll come with us then?"

"I don't have much choice, but any killing that's done, you'll do it."

"No one said anything about killing anyone. You're coming as a guide and for no other reason."

"When do we start this assassination project?"

"You'll have time to get your barn built and get your crops in. We'll let you know when we're ready. We'll give you time to make your arrangements in town and find someone to take care of your place while you're gone. But remember, if we hear anything about it from anyone, no matter who it is, your life will become unbearable." Orley tossed the hair at Jake's feet and turned to leave. "We'll contact you when we're ready."

When the men left, Jake found a knife in the kitchen drawer to cut the ropes. He walked around the house for a few minutes to gather his thoughts. He picked up the hair from the floor and smelled it. It smelled like Eve's perfume, but the texture was too coarse. He knew then that Orley was lying.

He sat in his chair and thought about the situation. *Orley's lying about going to Crow Wing to 'talk' to Hole-in-the-Day. He's going there to kill him.* The thought of a cold-hearted assassination sat heavy on Jake's mind. He stood up abruptly, slamming his fist on the table. "I can't let that happen."

He took his Henry rifle from the wall and loaded it, then strapped his dragoon to his belt and went out and saddled his horse. He rode into Courtland slowly, watching between the buildings and down the alleys. His rifle lay across his lap and his hat was pulled low on his forehead.

A figure stepped into his path. "What's up, Jake? Why the guns?" Jake walked his horse around the man without responding.

As Jake walked into the Crow Bar, the bartender said, "Jake, you know we don't allow guns in here."

"Gimme a cup a coffee."

Tom saw that this was not a good time to be telling Jake what he could and couldn't do, so he brought the cup of coffee. "No beer today, Jake?"

"Has Ernie been in?"

"Yeah, he's across the street spending money. He should be back anytime. Goin' hunting?"

"Yeah, goin' hunting."

Tom looked deeply into Jake's eyes and saw nothing but trouble. "Is anything wrong, Jake? If you need anything, I'd be glad to help."

"Nope, everything's just fine, Tom. Just need some meat."

Tom knew there was no meat to be found in the Minnesota Valley at that time. All the deer had been killed off or driven out by settlers. He also knew that Jake didn't need to eat venison, since he raised his own pork and beef. Tom was troubled as he slowly stepped away from Jake to stand next to Heidi.

"Something's got Jake in a bad way," he said to her.

"Want me to talk to him?" she asked.

"No, I think this would be a good time to leave him alone. I just hope that Orley feller doesn't come in right now."

"What if he does?"

"Jake's got that look he had when he was fightin' Indians. I think someone's gonna be in trouble when he finds them."

Tom and Heidi watched Jake from the corner of their eyes. His hand gripped the coffee cup as if he were about to lose it. His eyes stared at the back wall as his right foot tapped on the rail. He dribbled coffee down his shirt and brushed it off.

Heidi moved over to him. "Anything I can help with, Jake?" she asked.

Jake slowly turned his attention to her. "No, I'm just tired."

"You've got a lot of work to get your barn built. Maybe you should go and do it. I could come out and cook for you and take care of your house."

"Thanks for the offer, Heidi, but I'll manage."

"There's other things I could help with, too . . . if you need it."

"Heidi, I'm fine. It's alright, I'll manage. Guess I'll do like you said and get back to the farm."

"Ernie will be back in a few minutes if you want to talk with him."

"I'll catch him later."

Just then the door flew open and Ernie walked in with a wide grin on his face. Ernie was almost six feet tall and wore thick glasses and a heavy black mustache. He never wore a hat unless he was working in the fields. Ernie was a bird hunter. He liked double-barreled shotguns and often came to Jake's house to show off his latest purchase. One wall in his small log house was lined with all makes of shotguns, some of them old and worn out and some of them new. When he'd find a shotgun for sale, he'd buy it, no matter what shape it was in or whether he needed it or not.

His main source of income was buying and rebuilding houses in town and selling them for a small profit. Each house he worked on was done with the most expert care, but the house he lived in was in worse shape than any he bought. He walked to the bar, glanced at Jake, and said with a laugh, "Well, look what the cat dragged in." Tom reached over the bar toward Ernie to get his attention. Ernie stopped and looked at Jake. "What's goin' on with him?"

"He's in a bad way. He's looking to talk with you."

"Gawd, I hope he ain't mad at me for nothin'."

"G'wan over and talk. I doubt if it's about you."

Ernie walked over to Jake. "Hey, Jake. Heard you was looking to have a talk. What's up?"

"Let's go over to the table," Jake said.

After they sat down, Heidi brought more coffee and a mug of beer for Ernie.

"Coffee? You must have some ugliness going on in your life."

"Ernie, I'm going to be gone for a while. Can you watch my place for me?"

"Well sure, Jake. Can I ask where yer goin'?

"Going up north for a while. Don't know how long, maybe a month or better. I'll pay you when I get back."

"No worry about payin' me, I got nothing to do once I get the Schmitt house done. Want me to work on your barn?"

"Naw, you won't have time for that. You got your own place to take care of."

"My place is small. The garden is all in and now all I do is sit and watch the grasshoppers get fat."

"Walt will be there now and then to keep an eye on the corn, so you won't have to worry about that."

"That ol' coot's perty anxious to get his hands on that corn, huh?"

"He pays well for it. I gotta go talk to him, too, before I leave. You take care and stay away from Kate's."

"I'll take care of your place but I ain't stayin' away from Kate's. One of the girls over there kinda likes me."

"She likes your money, Ernie, that's all. See you in a couple of months then."

"You gonna be alright, Jake?"

"I'll be back."

Jake went to the door and stuck his head out, looking up and down the street before leaving. Two men standing next to the general store watched him go. He climbed onto his horse and kicked him hard in the ribs, leaving behind anyone who might follow, then went directly to Walt Fraley's place.

"Damn," Walt said as Jake stepped down. "What's the big rush? That corn ain't even growed yet."

"Just giving the horse a good run. Say, Walt, I'm gonna be gone for a month or so. Could you keep an eye on my place?"

"Been watchin' that corn ever' day since ye planted it. Recon I could give the rest of the place a look-see at the same tom. Where y'off to?"

"Got some business up by Crow Wing. I'll be back in a month or two."

"Crow Wing, eh? I knowed a gal up there. Got herself a saloon. Recollect her name was Kather'n er somethin' lock thet. If ye should happen tuh run acrost her, tell 'er I said howdy."

"I'll do that. I don't think I'll have a lot of time for gettin' to know folks up there, though. I gotta go, Walt. I'll see you before I leave."

Jake was back at his house before dark. Being in the house and in the back bedroom where Orley's men would expect to find him, made him feel vulnerable. He grabbed a blanket and slept under the big oak tree in the backyard.

When the crows woke him, he went into the house to make his breakfast. The smell of the stove starting up and the bacon frying in the pan brought memories of Eve. He could see her in his imagination, standing by the stove in her apron humming while she cooked.

Two days went by without hearing from Orley, and he began to think the deal was off when a rider came into the yard. "Got a letter for you, Jake," he said from atop his horse. Jake's hand shook as he took the letter and opened it. He was praying that it was from Eve saying that she was coming back, but his heart dropped into his stomach when he saw it was signed by Robert Orley.

Dear Mister Owen. Meet us at the church in Belle Prairie in five days. Do not be late and come alone.
R. Orley.

Jake was angry as he saddled his horse. He was being manipulated and that didn't set right in his life. He had been his own boss since he left the family farm in eighteen sixty-one. He'd fought Indians and white men, and now he was being forced to do something that would take him away from his home and fight for someone he didn't know. He would go along with them as long as he could, but the first chance he got, he knew he'd kill Orley. He had no plan about how he would do it, but he knew the time would come.

He went into the house, gathered a small camp and all of his extra ammunition, packed it all on his horse, and left without looking back. His Henry rifle lay across his lap and the dragoon pistol was strapped to his belt. He wore moccasins rather than his heavy work boots and had donned his buckskins in preference to the wool work clothing he'd worn on the farm.

10 CHAPTER TEN

THE PA HIN SA ARRIVED LATE IN THE AFTERNOON and rode into Al Stromberg's yard. Hawk looked at Sophie. "We buried the bodies of the people who were killed here when I rode with Grant on the burial detail," he said solemnly. "That's when we got attacked at Birch Coolie."

"You were at Birch Coolie?" Al said.

"Yeah—we were there."

"That's just west of here. We heard the shooting."

"Where are the bodies buried?" Mildred asked.

"Right out in the front yard."

"Can you find them?"

"I think so."

In the front yard they found four patches in the sod that showed signs of having been disturbed.

"I don't remember who was buried here but if I'm not wrong there was a man, a woman, and two youngsters."

"The man would have been Al's brother and the woman would be his wife. I don't know who the other two are."

The house was still standing but part of the roof had been burned off. The barn was intact but was pocked with numerous bullet holes.

For the next two weeks they put their hands to work rebuilding the house and putting up a new roof. Hawk, Sunkist, and Al worked together on the repairs, and the women worked on getting the house back in shape. The kids did their part by keeping the water buckets full, tending to the animals, and generally staying out of the way.

Mildred gathered rocks and laid them over each of the graves in the front yard and Al built a rail fence around them.

By the end of the two weeks the weather had turned cold. Sunkist sat on the new front porch with a pint of his *heaven in a jar*, sipping and grinning and bringing up an occasional satisfied belch.

"Hey, Al?" Sophie said. "They got a saloon around here?"

Al leaned forward on his chair. "That reminds me," he said.

"What?"

"Be right back."

In about five minutes, Al came around the side of the house with a big grin on his face.

"I forgot all about this." He held up a burlap sack, set it down, opened it, and drew out a bottle of beer.

"Well, Al, you crafty old dodger, you," Sophie said with a wide, toothy grin. "Where'd you get that?"

"I had it in the well out back. Good thing the Injuns didn't find it."

"Well, wha'd'ya waitin' for? Pop those corks and let's have one," Sophie said.

Al pulled the cork from the first bottle and foam spilled out and ran down his hand.

"How long has this stuff been down there?" Hawk asked.

"About three years, I guess."

"That's long enough." Sophie reached for the bottle and tipped it up. She looked at it for a few seconds while she swished the beer around in her mouth then swallowed.

"Well," she said, "it's not quite Schell's beer, but it's wet."

"That's what it is, Schell's."

Sunkist sat quietly, focused on his jar.

"What's that ye got there, Sunkist?" Al asked.

Sunkist looked at his jar and smiled. "Heaven in a jorrrrre," he growled.

"Mind if I have a taste?"

Sunkist handed it to Al. "Good luck."

Al took a mouthful and drank it down.

"Whoooa, holt on thar!" Sunkist said, reaching for his jar. "That there ain't yer rag'lar wha'd'ya-call-em lemonade ye got there."

Al's mouth dropped open and his eyes bugged out, his face turned red and tears rolled from his eyes. He tried to take a breath but each time he tried to draw in air, the fumes corked his throat shut. He stood that way for half a minute before Sophie handed him a beer bottle. He turned it up, took a mouthful, and spit it out on the grass.

"Good Gawd," he croaked, "that hasta be some of Walt Fraley's grizzly-piss."

"Right you are," Sunkist said as he looked affectionately at his jar. "I figger he's got the recipe down to ab'slute perrrfection."

"That stuff should be outlawed."

"I'm afraid if it ain't now, it will be soon. Nothin' this good can last fer-ever."

"It'll last as long as ol' Walt Fraley's around."

Hawk and Sophie and the rest headed back to their homes.

A week later, they sat together on the porch in front of their house. "Kinda quiet around here," Sophie said.

"I hate to say this, but my feet are getting itchy already."

The pistol went off at the same time Jake's did.

CHAPTER ELEVEN

JAKE HEADED STRAIGHT NORTH TOWARD SAINT CLOUD. Fort Ripley was one hundred forty miles away and Jake had only five days to get there. He knew his animal could do it, but he chose to take his time and let Orley wait. *After all,* he thought to himself. *What's he gonna do if I get there late?*

As he rode, his anger built, as did his hatred for Robert Orley. He'd been on the road for five days and was anxious to find Orley when he came to Belle Prairie. Jake knew that the most likely place to find him would be the local saloon, the middle building on the west side of the main street. He went inside and stepped up to the bar. The bar was made from a great pine log that had been split lengthwise and polished to a fine gloss. On the wall behind the bar was a mural of a woman reclining on a couch scantily dressed in a flimsy red gown. Eight stools lined the bar. Two men stood together talking at the far end of the bar, and four men were sitting at a table playing poker.

"Howdy, stranger," the bartender said. "What can I get ye?"

"Glass of beer, if you got it."

"Comin' right up."

The bartender set the mug in front of Jake.

"You seen a man named Orley around here?" Jake asked.

The bartender thought for a moment and said, "Nope, no one around here by that name. Not that I know of, anyway."

"Any other new people been through?"

"There's new people coming through here every day. Mostly men lookin' for work cutting trees. Had a big brawl in here a couple of nights back. Lumber men got drunked up and picked a fight with the soldiers from the fort."

"This man Orley is a prize fighter. S'pose he was one of them?"

"Don't know. I got the hell out of here. Don't need to get all busted up over nothing."

The bartender moved down the bar to talk with the two other men. Jake finished his beer and walked out. He looked up and down the street, hoping to see Orley, but only saw a wagon and a few people walking. At the end of the street stood Father Pierz's church. Jake thought about going in and saying a couple of prayers, but since he didn't know exactly how that was done, he dismissed the thought from his mind.

What the hell do I do now? he thought to himself. *Stay in Belle Prairie and hope Orley shows up or ride to Crow Wing looking for him? Orley did say to meet him at the church.* He looked at the silent church for a few seconds and started in that direction. Next to the church stood a small log house with a cross carved into the door, which he walked past to the door of the church. He took hold of the door knob and turned it, but the door didn't open. He knocked. There was no answer.

"May I be of service?" he heard a woman's voice say from behind him. He turned and saw a nun standing by the open door of the small house.

"I'm looking for a man named Robert Orley."

"Are you Jacob Owen?"

"Yes."

"I have a letter for you from Mister Orley. I will get it."

Jake walked to the door and waited for her to return. The door opened just far enough for a hand to reach out. He was handed the letter, then the hand drew back into the house and the door closed. He heard the lock slide into place. Opening the envelope, he read the message.

> *Mister Owen, we will meet you at the church in Crow Wing. Come immediately.*
> R. Orley.

Jake mounted his horse and headed up the road toward Crow Wing, keeping an eye on his back trail. He passed wagons loaded with lumber, and some with people and their family belongings. Men on horseback nodded as he passed. When he arrived at Fort Ripley, it was teaming with people— some white and some Indian. He came next to a wagon carrying a man, a woman and three children. "What's all the excitement at the fort?" he asked the man.

"Hole-in-the-Day is threatening to attack the settlers. The army called everyone to the fort for protection."

"I thought all that trouble was over."

"It was until that so-called chief got things fired up again."

Jake rode next to the wagon as they talked. "What's he so all-fired up about now?"

"The last treaty he signed said the Indians were gonna be sent to White Earth to live. Day doesn't like the land they got, so he's refusing to move his people. He says it's nothing but swamp. In that treaty he was supposed to get farms for all his people, and mules and plows, and even white men to teach the Indians how to farm. Black smiths, too."

"You seen the land the Indians are going to?" Jake asked.

"Nope. I got no idea what's up there."

"From what I've seen with the Sioux, I'd bet Hole-in-the-Day is right about it being just swamp."

"He shouldn't have singed the treaty, then."

"Maybe he hadn't seen the land either."

"Hell, that man knows every square inch of this country. He knew what was there when he signed the treaty."

As they approached the fort, Jake stopped his horse and looked inside. *Too many people*, he thought to himself and rode on. There were no Indians to be seen along the road, but there were plenty of wagons and horses. To him it didn't seem like an emergency that would cause such a rush for protection. But then, Jake had seen the flocks of people come into Fort Ridgely two years before when the Dakota war began, and this didn't match up.

Jake rode on, his mind on Eve and his hand on his pistol. He crossed the river on the ferry and took the road into Crow Wing City. The streets here were also busy with people and wagons moving in all directions. He heard the sound of hammers somewhere in town and the whine of a sawmill coming from the river. On the hill overlooking the town stood a church. He became anxious and turned his horse up the hill. He stopped briefly and took a deep breath before getting down from his horse.

"Mister Owen," he heard from behind. He turned to see a man dressed in clean, pressed trousers, a silk shirt and necktie, and a wool coat. A bowler sat squarely on his head. "You won't be needing those guns," he said. "You can leave them in the saloon."

"I'll be keeping the guns," Jake said.

The man walked up to Jake. "Mister Orley said you should leave the guns in the saloon."

Jake looked down at the ground, took a deep breath, then looked into the man's eyes. "I guess you didn't hear me. I'll be keeping my guns."

The man reached out for Jake's guns and caught a left fist on the end of his nose. He wobbled a little and started to swing, but another fist caught him on the cheekbone. He staggered back and came at Jake again. This time Jake put his full power into the swing and hit the man on the side of his face with his open hand. The man made a half-turn to the right and fell to the ground. He reached into his coat but stopped when he saw Jake's pistol an inch from his nose.

"You hearing a little better now?" Jake asked. "Listen to me. I'll be keeping these guns in my hands."

The man nodded. "If I was you, Owen, I'd watch my back, real good."

"I'll keep that in mind. Where's Orley?"

"I'm gonna take you to him."

"Git up. Let's go."

Jake led his horse as they walked down the street to the hotel. They climbed the stairs to the second floor and the man knocked on the door.

"Come on in, Jack."

Orley sat on a stuffed chair smoking a pipe. "Bring your pipe, Jake?" he asked.

"I got my own tobacco. What do you want from me?"

"Jack," Orley said, "I told you to be careful with Mister Owen. Obviously, you didn't hear me."

Jake looked at Jack, then at Orley. "Jack has a hearing problem."

Orley chuckled and waved Jack to the corner of the room. "Mister Owen, as Jack told you, you will not be needing those guns. You can leave them here or wherever you wish."

"Mister Orley," Jake said. "Like I told Jack, I'll be keeping my guns in my hands."

"Very well, just remember," he said as he pointed at the two men standing in two opposite corners of the room, "we have insurance against your doing anything foolish."

"Where's Eve?"

"We have people taking care of her. No harm will come to her as long as you do as we tell you."

"Alright, tell me what you want."

"I want you to find Hole-in-the-Day. With your reputation with the Sioux down south, and you being a friend of Little Crow, you are almost assured safe passage through Chippewa country."

"The Chippewa hate the Sioux. Why would Day let me into his world?"

"Hole-in-the-Day and Little Crow were allies in that uprising. They planned the entire war. Little Crow was going to attack every town west of the Mississippi, and Day was to wipe out every white man east of the Mississippi. Didn't you know that?"

"That's bullshit. That was rumors started by some panicky major at the fort."

"No, Jake, I know it was true. Hole-in-the-Day is a very dangerous man and has to be eliminated."

Orley snapped his fingers at Jack. Jack got up from his chair and brought a cotton bag and handed it to Jake.

"Open it up, Mister Owen. I think you'll recognize the article inside." He waved a finger at the two men and they came and stood next to Jake. One put his pistol against Jake's head and slowly urged the rifle from Jake's hand.

"Go ahead and open it," Orley said with a depraved smile.

Jake untied the cord that was holding the bag closed and tossed it at Orley. He reached inside and drew out a nightgown like the one Eve had made. Blood throbbed in his temples and his face turned red. The metallic sound of a pistol being cocked against his head was like the sound of thunder. He stared silently at Orley, feeling his pulse in his neck and below his ears.

Orley smiled at him. "Well? Do we have a deal?"

"We have a deal," Jake said quietly.

Orley slapped his hands on the arms of the chair and started to get up.

Suddenly, Jake exploded. He flipped the nightgown at Orley, his arm coming up and wrapping around the arm of the man holding the pistol to his head. He turned the arm elbow-down, turned himself around and broke the man's elbow over his shoulder with a resounding pop. The man screamed in pain and dropped his pistol. In a simultaneous move, Jake pulled his own pistol from his belt and shot the other man, then turned the pistol down and shot the man lying on the floor. Orley was about to turn when Jake slammed the muzzle of his dragoon into Orley's forehead, right above his nose. "You blink— just goddamn blink—and I'll blow your fuckin' brains all over this room." Jake started to back away.

Orley's face showed none of the confidence he had displayed when Jake came into the room. Now he was scared and trembling.

"What's the matter, tough guy? Yer body guards ain't here to protect you?

Ye look like a goddamn weasel standing there shaking like that."

"Don't kill me, Jake. Please don't kill me."

"Yer as good as dead already, Orley."

"If you kill me, Jake, you will never see your wife alive again. I can get her free for you."

"How did you get that nightgown?" Jake asked pointing to the garment on the floor. It was then that he realized the gown had no fur around the bottom. It was not Eve's.

Jake looked down and shook his head. "Orley, you are pathetic. Not only are you a chicken-shit coward, you're a piss-poor liar, too."

Orley just stared at Jake.

"The gown you showed me was not Eve's gown. And the hair you showed me was not Eve's hair."

Orley was quiet as he gazed into Jake's eyes, then he said, "Why did you come with us then if you knew we didn't have your wife?"

"To stop you from killing a man and starting that stupid war with the Indians again."

"I am not the one who wants Day dead," Orley said. "There are a number of men, important men, who are tired of his trouble-making."

"You mean they're tired of Hole-in-the-Day out-smarting them."

"Whatever the reason, they will keep after him until he's dead."

"Come on," Jake said. "Yer going to the county sheriff."

"Let me get my coat." Orley said as he reached toward the coat hanging on the back of his chair. "My tobacco," he said with a smile. "You understand."

He lifted the coat from the chair and turned quickly with a pistol in his hand. The pistol went off at the same time Jake's did. Jake felt the bullet dig into his side as he saw Orley crumple to the floor. His short-barreled, thirty-six caliber Colt pistol clattered to the floor.

Jake stood over him with his pistol pointed at his head. "Ye should'a come with me peacefully, Orley. I had nothing to throw you in jail for." The words went unheard. Orley was dead.

Jake's side was burning where the bullet hit. He opened his shirt and looked down at the wound. The bullet had gone through the flesh of his side without doing any serious damage.

"Damn!" he groaned as pain gripped his side. *I wish Posey was here. She could fix me up with some of her herbs and Indian medicines,* he thought to himself. He pulled the handkerchief from Orley's jacket pocket, pressed it over the wound, and then pulled his belt in tightly to hold it in place. Then a thought of Heidi passed quickly through his mind. He pictured her standing by his bed changing his bandages. The thought disappeared as quickly as it came.

He opened the door and stepped into the hallway. Three people stood there trying to peer into the room. They looked at Jake as he walked out. He stopped and said, "Looks like they fought it out and killed each other."

The people turned to one another repeating the story. Jake shrugged his shoulder and turned to walk away.

He walked onto the street and looked up and down. He had no idea where to find Hole-in-the-Day, but he knew where to go looking. He put his coat over his shirt to cover the blood stains, climbed onto his horse, and rode south out of Crow Wing toward Fort Ripley.

Jake rode directly to the commandant's quarters, walked in without knocking, and strode over to the desk where the colonel sat studying papers.

"It's customary to knock before you enter," the colonel said without looking up.

"The last door I knocked on no one answered."

"Where was that?"

"The church . . . I need to find Hole-in-the-Day."

"I wish I had a hole in my day. These Indians are working me day in and day out," he said as he stood from his chair. He put his hand out and said, "Colonel Thomas. May I ask who you are?"

"Jacob Owen, Courtland, down by Fort Ridgely.

"I know the town. You know where the Crow Bar is then, right?"

"I know the place. Where can I find Hole-in-the-Day?"

"Why do you need to find him so bad?"

"Got a message for him."

"You can give me the message, I'll see that he gets it."

"Alright. Tell him someone's trying to kill him."

"Really," the commander said sarcastically. "Damn near every white person in this country and the whole damn Pillager Band wants Hole-in-the-Day dead. If you want my opinion . . ."

"I don't. You wanna give him the message?"

"No, I think I'll let you handle that one."

"I gotta find him. It might be important to the safety of your people."

"All you gotta do is find yourself an Indian and tell him you're looking for Hole-in-the-Day. He'll get the word."

"And where do I find this Indian?"

The commander pointed past Jake. He turned around and saw sixteen Indians standing outside the door behind him.

"Do you have any food for them, Mister Owen?"

Jake turned around and said in a loud voice, "Tell Hole-in-the-Day the Pa Hin Sa wishes to speak with him."

The Indians murmured amongst themselves as Jake walked through the crowd.

He turned back and called to the colonel, "Any idea where he lives?"

"Sure. He's got one of the nicest houses in these parts. It's six miles up toward Gull Lake. You won't get close to him, though, and even if you do, you won't find him there."

"Where is he?"

"Who the hell knows? He doesn't sit still very long and he's got warriors with him wherever he goes. If Hole-in-the-Day doesn't want to be found, the Good Lord himself can't flush him out."

Jake walked into the street. He was alone again. He wanted someone to talk to. Heidi passed through his mind. Heidi was fun to be around and willing to take care of Jake's house, and Jake, too. She was single and making her own way through the world. And she was good looking. Jake started thinking a lot about having her around.

He stood outside the door of the commandant's office for a moment, straightened his hat, and started toward his horse.

"Oh, Mister Owen," he heard from inside. Jake stopped, turned around, and walked back into the office.

"If you want to find Hole-in-the-Day, you might try the saloon a mile up the road. John Camels runs it. He's a bigger problem to us than the Indians. He'll know better than anyone where Hole-in-the-Day is."

"Exactly where is this saloon?"

"Just follow the road north, you'll see it. It's a rundown shack with a bunch of drunken soldiers puking all over the place and Indians carving each other up with hunting knives."

"Thanks. I'll give it a shot."

Jake mounted his horse and headed out of the fort and up the road. He came to a shack with a tepee fifty feet behind it. Thinking it would be best to ask an Indian about finding another Indian, he headed for the tepee.

An Indian woman came out of the tepee screaming, followed by a man yelling and shaking his fist. "You goddamn bitch squaw. I'll stomp your head open for that!" he yelled. The woman picked up an ax from the woodpile and swung it at the man. He warded off the blow and hit her with his fist, knocking her to the ground. He then kicked her in the ribs and then in the face.

Jake jumped off his horse and grabbed the man. "That ain't no way to treat a lady."

"That goddamn bitch . . ." he started, but was quieted by a set of hard knuckles smashing into his mouth. He fell to the ground and lay there looking up at Jake's calm face staring down at him.

"What the hell's it to you?" the man hollered. "Ain't none of your damn business what I do to this squaw!"

Jake stood over him with his feet next to the man's neck. "Touch her again and yer gonna get your own head stomped open."

The man got up from the ground and went into the saloon. Another Indian woman came and helped the injured woman to her feet and took her into the tepee. Jake turned and walked to the saloon and up to the bar. Three men in army uniforms stood at the bar paying no attention to the excitement outside. The bartender was the man he'd just knocked down. He came to Jake, wiping his split lower lip with the bar towel. "What'll ye have?"

Jake looked out the door then back to the bartender. "Beer."

"Comin' right up."

"Wha'd she do, you had to beat her like that?" Jake said.

"The bitch bit me."

"Ye hadn't outta to be slappin' women around like that."

"Sometimes, mister, they just got it comin'."

"You know anything about Hole-in-the-Day?"

"What d'ya want with that outlaw?"

"Just need to talk to him."

"Ye can't talk with Hole-in-the-Day. He does all the talkin'."

"Where can I find him?"

"You'll find him in hell someday, just like all these damn soldiers and Injuns."

"Jacob Owen." Jake heard in a soft voice from a table behind him. Jake stopped, turned his eyes, and then cautiously turned his head toward the sound. His muscles tensed and his hand went to rest on the pistol at his belt. He turned his body around slowly and focused on an Indian sitting alone at a table.

"That's Dead Crow," the bartender said softly.

"You know me?" Jake asked the Indian. The Indian's face was painted black on one side and red on the other. He wore a floppy hat and faded calico shirt with a yellow ribbon tied around his collar.

"Come. Sit with me."

Jake walked slowly to the table and the man pushed a chair out for him with his foot. He motioned with his glass for Jake to sit.

Jake looked into the man's eyes thinking he recognized him from another time. "You know me?"

"You are the Pa Hin Sa."

"Do you know where I can find Hole-in-the-Day?"

"I can take you to him."

"Who are you?"

"I am Dead Crow Walks Alone."

"I don't know anyone by that name."

"You knew me when you were in Dakota."

Jake turned and looked around the room. The bartender was busy drying glasses and the men at the bar were talking softly among themselves.

He turned to the Indian. "Little Crow?

"Little Crow is dead. I am Dead Crow Walks Alone."

Jake was silent for a moment. "Then Hawk was right," he said softly. "You ain't dead."

"Why do you look for Hole-in-the-Day?"

"I know of a plan to kill him."

"Many men would kill him."

"These men were hired to kill him. The trader Beaulieu is the one who hired them."

"Do you know these men?"

"Yes. They tried to get me to take them to Hole-in-the-Day. Those men are dead."

"You killed them?"

"Yes."

"If they are dead they cannot kill Hole-in-the-Day."

"They were hired by other men to do it."

"Did you kill the trader Beaulieu?"

"I don't know. I only knew the names of two of the men who were killed. A man named Orley and one named Jack. Beaulieu might have been one of them, I don't know."

Dead Crow sat quietly contemplating what Jake had said. He took a sip from his glass. "How do I know you do not want to kill Hole-in-the-Day?" he asked without taking his eyes off the table in front of him.

"I'm here to keep him from being killed."

"You say that, but how do I know you are not lying. All white men tell lies."

"Not all men tell lies, Dead Crow. Some of us are not in this world to get rich. We are happy with what we have. Money brings nothing but greed and more lies. If a man has enough to feed himself and those who depend on him, why does he need more? More money than you need is nothing but something else to worry about."

"You have money, Jacob Owen?"

"I have enough to keep my farm producing enough food to feed me and anyone who cannot feed himself."

"If a man is hungry, you will feed him?"

"Yes."

"What if a man is too lazy to feed himself?"

"Then he can go hungry. And I'd better not catch him in my potato patch."

"I will take you to Hole-in-the-Day."

Jake started to push his chair back to stand.

"Not today. He is away."

He sat back down. "When will he be back?"

"I do not know. He will come back when he is ready."

"Well, I ain't sittin' around here waiting for him. I've got a farm to run."

"Do you have a woman, Jacob Owen?"

Jake got quiet and Dead Crow saw loneliness on his face. "She is dead?"

"No, she's not dead. She left me for another man."

"Then you must kill him."

"No. It's not his fault. It ain't no one's fault. She just found happiness with someone better than me."

"That is not true, Jacob. She is happier with that person because he can give her things you cannot. You are not a farmer, you are a warrior, and women do not want a man who may be dead the next time she sees him."

"I suppose yer right about that. But I ain't no warrior. I hate fighting."

"Then ask yourself why you are up here looking for Hole-in-the-Day when you know you will have to fight."

"Well, I . . ."

"Do not answer me. Answer yourself. You are the only person you have to answer to. Go back to your farm and forget about Hole-in-the-Day. He will be killed. You cannot stop it, and I cannot stop it. He knows this as well as we do."

Dead Crow pushed his chair back and stood. "It is good to see you are not killed, Jacob Owen." With that he turned and walked out the door.

Jake mounted his horse and rode back toward the fort. He stood on the east side of the Mississippi and looked at the bustle inside the walls. "Can't think of any good reason to go back in there," he said to his horse. "Let's go home." He touched the horse's ribs and started down the road.

When he arrived at his farm he stepped down from his horse and walked to the house. Inside he stood in the middle of the kitchen wondering silently what to do with himself. *Having a house and a farm is a good thing if you have someone to share it with,* he thought. His mind went back to Heidi. *She'd be good to have around . . . Am I trying to replace Eve with someone else? Would just about any woman do?* He didn't know any other women who were available.

He slept deep that night and in the morning got out of bed and had a small breakfast. His thoughts of Heidi through the night were forcing him to go to town and see her.

He walked into the Crow Bar and took his usual stool.

"Welcome home, Jake," Tom said. "Coffee?"

"Yeah, coffee. Put a shot of brandy in it."

"Kinda early to start drinking."

"Where does it say when to start drinking?"

"Guess it don't say it anywhere. I'll have one with ye."

"Heidi been in?"

"She should be here any time now," Tom said as he glanced at the clock on the back bar. "Farmers will be in for their morning feed pretty soon. Most of 'em have been in the fields for hours already. How come you ain't?"

"Corn can grow without me."

Heidi walked in the door with a big, wide smile on her face. "Hi, Jake, welcome home."

"Hello, Heidi. How's life treating you?"

"Jake, I have the most wonderful news. Bruce Aldrich asked me to marry him."

Jake's heart fell into his stomach. He stared at Heidi for a while before finding the nerve to say, "That's great, Heidi. Did you accept?"

"Of course I did. He is just so wonderful. We'll be married in one month. Isn't that wonderful?"

Jake was trying hard to keep his hands from shaking. His voice wouldn't come and his mind was whirling like a beehive. "That's great, Heidi," he said as he turned toward the bar.

"I have to go, Tom. I'll be seeing you later." He reached out and touched Heidi's shoulder. "Congratulations, Heidi. I wish you all the happiness in the world."

"Thanks, Jake. We'll send you an invitation to the wedding."

He walked out the door, mounted his horse, and rode down the street to the land office.

"Howdy, Jake. Can I help you? Wanna buy some land?"

"No, I want to sell the farm."

"You're going to sell your farm?"

"You heard me right. I'm gettin' out of here."

"Well, you came to the right place. What are you asking for it?"

"I don't care. Just sell it."

"Well, George Aldrich is looking for farmland for his kid. Maybe he'd be interested. You sure you want to sell?"

Jake said nothing.

"Alright, if that's what you want." The agent reached into his file cabinet, pulled out papers, and laid them in front of Jake.

"Just fill these out and we'll get going on it."

"How long will it take?" Jake asked.

"Can't very well tell. This is a bad time to be selling land. All the farmers have their money tied up in seed. You go back and make yourself ready and I'll let you know when I have a buyer. How much did you have in mind?"

"Just put a fair price on it, sell it, and give me the money."

Jake went back to his farm and sat on the porch. *Looks like Heidi will be living in my house after all,* he thought to himself.

Summer turned to fall. Walt Fraley came and harvested his corn. The rest of the crops dried and withered.

The season turned from fall to winter. Ernie and Jake stood on the ice on Swan Lake staring down the hole they had chopped.

"How stupid is this?" Ernie said in a low voice.

"What's that?"

"Standing here freezing our asses off, waiting for a fish to swim by."

"Just think about how good a mess of sunfish is gonna taste when we get home."

"I'm thinking about how good it's gonna feel to crawl betwixt the sheets over at Kate's."

Jake was silent.

"Maybe you should break down and sneak over to Kate's just once, Jake. Do ye more good than harm."

"Been thinking about that." He paused. "But I just can't do it. I just ain't ready."

"What d'ya mean you 'ain't ready'? Still missin' Eve?"

"Eve ain't comin' back, Ernie."

"Ain't comin' back? What are you talkin' about, 'ain't comin' back'?"

"This is just between you and me, Ernie."

"Whatever you say, Jake." Ernie looked anxiously at his friend.

Jake's eyes were blank as he looked at Ernie.

"Well?" Ernie said impatiently.

"Eve left me for some lawyer in Milwaukee."

"Damn, Jake. We know she's been gone a long time, but we never figured . . ." Ernie stared at him for a moment and said, "That why you was carryin' guns that day in the bar? You was gonna kill 'im, right?"

"No, I wasn't gonna kill anyone. That was a different matter altogether."

"You should'a killed the bastard. No one would'a blamed you."

"It wasn't his fault, Ern. Any man who didn't want Eve has got something wrong with him."

"You sayin' it was her fault?"

"No. It wasn't nobody's fault. I just couldn't give her what she needed. It's not a fault, it's just a matter of I couldn't. Not that I wouldn't—I couldn't."

Ernie looked at Jake for a long moment. Then said, "Ye mean you couldn't . . ." He looked Jake up and down and pointed below Jake's belt. "Ye mean you couldn't?" he said again.

"No, ye dumb ass. I didn't have no problem with that. It was the tenderness women need. I just ain't got it."

Ernie contemplated that thought for a moment then said, "Well, hell, Jake. You had the farm all to yourself. No one to make excuses to, no one to explain yourself to. Hell, you had everything goin' for you."

"Yeah, everything going for me except someone to enjoy it with."

"Can't ye find someone else?"

"Don't want no one else, Ernie. I don't want to get involved again. Too damn much pain."

"Whoop! Whoop!" Ernie suddenly hollered, pulling his fishing line out of the water. "Got me a good one! Yee-ha! Feels like a big ol' walleye."

In Minnesota the numeric temperature reading
has little to do with scheduling your everyday activities.

12

CHAPTER   TWELVE

Soon after the oats and wheat had been harvested, the yard around Sophie and Hawk's house was covered with a thick blanket of fallen leaves. The air was filled with the sweet aroma of birch, poplar, elm and oak.

Sophie raised her nose to the air and inhaled. "I love that smell."

"Reminds me of a place south of the farm back home. I used to go there and just sit in the leaves and listen to the crows." Hawk got a far away look on his face. "Like to go back to the spot some day," he said softly.

"If you want to go, then let's go. I'd like to see where you grew up."

He laughed. "You always wanna go somewhere. Maybe someday," he said and kissed her on the forehead.

They went into the cabin and to the bedroom. They lay down side by side and drifted off to sleep.

In the morning they sat quietly while they ate their breakfasts. Once a day, even as the air grew colder, they saddled their horses and went for a ride through the countryside. A month passed and then another. Life at the Owen home was becoming monotonous for the couple.

Winter eventually set in hard, and Hawk had a tough time keeping the snow cleared from the path that led to the barn. The animals stayed in the barn for the most part and Hawk threw down hay for them daily.

One day, sitting in front of the fire and armed with a couple of beers, Sophie turned to Hawk and asked, "Have you ever tried snowshoeing?"

"Yeah, Robert had a pair he used when he was hunting sometimes. I tried them a few times but figured they're more work than I cared to do."

On the wall were two pairs of snowshoes that had been left by the previous owners of the house.

"How about skiing?"

"Nope, never tried that."

"Ye wanna?"

"I'm game if you are."

"Good. I saw two pairs of skis in the barn—I'll go get 'em." Sophie slammed down her beer then jumped off the bed. "Let's go. Whad'ya waiting for?"

Hawk smiled, "Right behind ye."

They donned their heavy winter clothes, went outside, and grabbed the skis. They fastened them to their feet and Hawk promptly fell onto his backside.

"This ain't gonna be easy," he said.

Sophie helped him to his feet and he leaned on the ski poles.

"Ready?" she asked.

"I guess."

Sophie started to move forward and Hawk fell on his butt.

"Little balance problem there, partner?"

"I'll get this."

On his feet again, he slid one foot forward and then the other. He was moving but not getting anywhere.

"Use the poles to push forward and to help balance yourself."

"Good idea. Wish I'da thought of that."

Soon he was moving along with Sophie. His skis slid sideways several times, but for the most part he was able to stay upright. After an hour of work and practice he was able to keep up with Sophie, as long as they stayed on flat ground. The downhill slides were a different story. He stopped at the top of a small rise and looked down the slope about seventy-five yards to the bottom.

"Keep your knees bent and your weight slightly forward," Sophie said. "You'll make it." Then she pushed off with her poles and went sailing down the hill as gracefully as an otter slipping into the water.

Hawk pushed himself off the top of the hill, concentrating on her instructions. By some primal instinct for balance and self-preservation he managed to keep the skis under him as he picked up speed. The deep snow helped to keep some of the speed manageable. He kept his eyes on his skis to make sure they stayed parallel to one another. He thought he heard Sophie yelling something and he looked up just in time to see a big elm tree directly in his path.

Sophie hadn't covered this kind of emergency in her instructions. *Stopping,* he thought to himself, *would have been a subject on which a novice skier should have had extensive coaching.* With no time to waste thinking, he tipped himself sideways and dropped to the ground just as his right ski caught the tree. It sent him into a spin on his back, down the hill and over a large bump. He was catapulted into a head-over-heels roll. He saw his skis above him and then below him, and in his mind's eye he could see them twisting his legs like a piece of cheap rope. He heard loud grunts coming from inside him each time he hit the ground. He tumbled down the slope—crashing through the brush like a runaway boulder—flying through the air, landing and sliding to a stop on his belly just beyond Sophie.

"You alright?" she asked as she stifled a laugh.

"I saw my ass pass me a couple'a times," he said as he rolled to his side. "Better check on that first."

Knowing Hawk was still breathing and able to speak, she let go a laugh and reached for his hand.

"Here, let me help you up and let's make sure it's still there."

"Is this really a good way to get around in the winter?"

"They've been doing it for hundreds of years, so there must be something good about it. I love it. It's a great way to enjoy the winter months."

"Sorry, but I can't share in your enthusiasm right now. Let's get back to the house; my toes are about to freeze off. Where'd my skis end up?"

Going back to the house on skis was a whole new game for Hawk. Getting down the hills was easy enough. But going uphill on skis was nearly impossible. Sophie tried to teach him to side-step up the hill, but the skis kept slipping out from under him. He finally had to take them off and trudge through the knee-deep snow to the top.

In the cabin they sat on chairs with their feet propped up on stools close to the potbelly stove. Sophie heated apple cider and slipped a shot of brandy, along with a pat of butter, in each cup.

A warm glow came over them as they sipped on the hot cider. After two drinks each, they put on their coats and went outside to enjoy the cold December air.

It was early evening and the world was shrouded in deep blue. The trees were covered with a frost that seemed to make them glow. The night came on quickly. The moon showed itself as a bright patch in the thin clouds, and the countryside was as bright as day. Everything was still and silent. A light, glistening snow began to fall straight down.

Sophie sighed, "It's beautiful, isn't it? I love this time of night. It's the best part of the day, especially cold, clear evenings like this."

They talked quietly so they wouldn't disturb the silence. Sophie took Hawk's hand and they walked to the woods. On the floor of the woods they saw mouse tracks and deer tracks, and here and there a brown leaf that had just fallen, lying on top of the fresh snow. The branches of the trees stayed motionless.

"So absolutely silent," Sophie whispered. "It's the type of silence that almost hurts your ears."

They lay down on the snow and looked up at the trees without talking. Nuthatches and chickadees flitted from tree to tree, pecking at the bark, then quickly flew away with an audible flutter of wings. Their quiet "chip-chip-chip" somehow made the forest even more still for the pair of nature lovers lying in the snow.

An unexpected shiver went through Hawk.

"Cold?" Sophie whispered.

"Yeah."

"Me, too. Wanna go back?"

"I don't want to, but I don't want to freeze to death, either."

Back in the cabin, Hawk threw a couple of sticks in the stove, closing the damper to keep the fire from burning too fast and using up the wood before morning. Sophie brought blankets and draped them over chairs close to the stove to warm them. She then made them each another hot cider and they sat together on the floor.

"Hawk, we have to get something straight between us."

"Yeah? What's that?"

"Follow me." She grabbed the warm blankets and they went to the bedroom and slipped under the covers.

Morning came and Hawk climbed out of bed. He went to the stove, tossed a log on the glowing embers, opened the damper, and went to make coffee. The water bucket was frozen over and he had to break the ice to pour water into the coffee pot.

The potbelly stove began to warm the house and the coffee started steaming but was taking too damn long. So Hawk crawled back into bed next to Sophie.

She jumped when his cold skin touched hers. "Good God! Put something on before I get frostbite!"

"Oops. Sorry."

She wrapped her arms around him and threw a leg over him. "Come here, snowman, I'll melt that frost off your hide."

After a good morning, they climbed out of bed to find the coffee pot had boiled over, the grounds splattered over the top of the stove. The smell of burnt coffee stung their noses and Hawk went to open the door to let fresh air in. A blast of icy wind blew a cloud of snow into the house and he had to lean into it to close the door.

"Damn blizzard blowing out there," he said.

"Didn't you hear the wind?"

"A man can't hear the wind with a pair of thighs covering his ears."

The wind shook the shutters and door, and small drifts formed on the floor where the cracks allowed the snow to blow in. The stove popped and fluttered as wind blew over and down the tin stovepipe. The small stove did little to warm the house and they were forced to sit close to keep warm.

"Guess I'd better go out and check on the animals."

Sophie moved closer to the stove. "I'm sure I'll hear all about it when you get back."

He opened the door and, once again, the cold wind brought snow in, dumping it on the floor. He stepped up onto the snow and pulled the door shut. The wind was fierce and stung his face as he made his way to the barn. The horses whinnied and blew.

"Yeah, yeah, I'm coming."

He forked a large pile of hay in front of each of them and did the same for the mules who had followed him in. The barn was left open and the animals could come and go as they pleased. The snow had packed over the grass, and the creek was frozen to the bottom. The animals could eat snow for their water, but Hawk melted it for them over the stove each day.

"Soph," he said as he came back into the house, "you know we're snowbound, don't you?"

"It's getting that deep?"

"Can't even see where the road runs. The snow is too deep for the horses, and I can't even reach the ground when I step in it."

"Snowshoes?"

"If we plan on going anywhere, it will be on snowshoes or skis."

"Well, I don't have anywhere I have to go right now, do you?"

"Yeah, I gotta go under that blanket. Move over."

The wind blew and the windows rattled. Sophie and Hawk huddled together under a woolen blanket sipping hot apple cider and chewing on buffalo jerky.

"Do we have enough food to make it through the winter?" Sophie asked.

"The cow is still out there somewhere."

"Fresh beef would taste good right now."

"I'd better go out and dig out the root cellar. No telling how deep this will get before it's over."

Once again Hawk donned his bearskin coat and mittens and went out into the freezing wind. He took a long pole and poked through the snow until he found the hole in the ground where their meat and potatoes were stored. He dug with his shovel so deep into the snow that he had to toss it up and over the pile that was growing around the hole. Sophie came out and looked down the hole.

"You alright down there?"

"Working up a sweat, but I'm hittin' dirt now."

He began tossing bundles of meat out of the hole. Sophie gathered them and carried them to the house. When all the meat was in, they opened one bundle and set it on the stove to thaw. The rest they put close to the door, knowing the wind blowing underneath would keep it frozen.

"Looks like we live on venison for a while," Hawk said.

"Potatoes frozen?"

"Yup."

"Wonder how Sunkist and Posey are doing."

"He probably doesn't know there's a blizzard going on."

The storm raged for two days, and then the wind died down and the air turned bitter cold.

In Minnesota the numeric temperature reading is only a point for curiosity and has little to do with scheduling your everyday activities. A person has to do what he has to do, regardless of the weather. But that day it was cold enough to make Hawk curious.

"You shouldn't look at the thermometer when it gets cold," Sophie said. "It just puts value to your misery."

By the time she'd said that, he had his thermometer and was holding it to the candle. It read forty-five degrees in the house.

"Heck, that ain't bad."

Then he took it outside and laid it on a board for a few minutes. He picked it up and looked. "Holy cow! It says it's thirty-eight below zero."

HAWK'S QUEST

"Throw another log on the fire, will you, Hawk?"

"Damn. Gonna have to go out again and bring in more wood."

"I'm coming with."

They each carried wood in until their faces and hands were nearly frozen, then went inside. They brushed the snow from their clothing and stamped it off their feet and hurried to the stove. They sat for a while and had hot cider then went for more wood. Hawk shoveled snow from the woodpile and they both carried armfuls into the house. By the end of the day they had wood piled to the ceiling at one end of the room.

"We'll try to keep the fire low and wrap up in blankets to keep warm. I don't know if we can get in the woods to do anymore cutting," Hawk said.

"Do you have any idea what day this is?" Sophie asked.

He looked at Sophie for a few seconds and said, "No, come to think of it, I don't."

"For all we know, Christmas might have come and gone."

A week passed and the weather warmed for a few days, then turned cold again. One night they heard gunfire from the south, then loud explosions and more gunfire.

"Let's start counting days," Sophie said.

"What for?"

"It's New Year's Eve."

"Well, I'll be darned. Guess you're right. Wanna go celebrate?"

Sophie jumped from her chair and headed for the bed. "How about a few fireworks of our own?"

The next morning as they lay in bed Sophie turned to Hawk. "Let's go for a walk in the cold."

"Yeah, I like it when it gets real cold."

They put on their snowshoes and bundled up in coats, sweaters, scarves, hats, and mittens and stepped out into the cold. The wind blew, cutting through their coats and sweaters. Hawk's breath froze on his mustache and Sophie had ice on the scarf around her face, and her eyelashes were coated with frost. The snow was packed hard and their snowshoes hardly made tracks. Snow blew across the ground and swirled around them as they walked a mile from the house, then turned back.

"What the hell are we doing out in this?" Hawk said.

"You can't talk about it if you haven't experienced it."

"So who wants to talk about it?"

"You will. Someday you'll tell people about walking around in a blizzard like a damned fool."

On the way back they heard a loud pop, like gunfire. "That musta been a tree that froze so hard, it split."

"Never heard of that happening."

"We could go and try to find it if you want."

"I'll take your word for it. Let's get back to the stove."

So went the winter of eighteen sixty-three and four at the log cabin on Hawk Creek.

One sunny day as Sophie stood close to the creek, she saw bubbles moving under the ice.

"Hawk," she called out to him. "The creek is flowing!"

He came and stood next to her. "Pretty soon we can jump in there and take a swim."

"It doesn't look too inviting right now."

"Yeah, with all this cold we've had, ye wonder if it'll ever warm up."

Another month went by and the creek opened up and turned peaceful Hawk Creek into a raging river. Ice flows crunched against one another on their way to the Minnesota River five miles downstream. Uprooted trees and broken branches tumbled in the fast moving water.

Green grass began to show through the brown grass from the previous summer and the horses and mules spent the days munching on the sweet, new bill of fare. They became shaggy as they shed their winter coats, and they raced around the pasture getting their muscles and hooves back in shape for traveling.

"You going to put in crops?" Sophie asked.

"Been thinking about that. I think I'll ask Al if he wants to put something in the fields."

"That's what I thought. You need to be up and moving around, getting into trouble."

"Don't really need the trouble, but the moving sounds good."

"Let's go down and see how Sunkist and Posey are doing. We can stop at Al's and talk to him about planting crops."

"When do you want to go?"

"Anything wrong with right now?"

"Not that I can think of. Well, there is one problem. We don't know where Sunkist lives."

"He told me it was down by Sacred Heart Creek."

"That's a lot of territory."

"Well, let's go see Al, anyway—maybe he knows."

"Okay, let's go in the morning."

The next day they were at Al's farm drinking beer on the front porch.

"So, Al, how would you like to put some oats in my fields?"

"I'm going to put some corn and wheat in and maybe if youse is serious, I'll put some in over to your place, too."

"Oh, we're serious, alright. I'm no farmer and I won't be planting anything. You go ahead and use the ground and watch over the place while we're gone. That'll be your rent for the fields."

"Youse don't need any money for the rent? I could pay you some, but not a lot."

"Al," Sophie said, "we have everything we need. You go ahead and use the fields while we're gone."

"Youse going somewhere special?"

"We'll be gone for a couple of days but after that we don't know," Hawk said. "We've been cooped up in that house all winter and we're getting itchy feet."

"If that's what youse want, youse got yerself a deal."

Hawk put his hand out. Al took it and they shook. "Deal."

"You got any idea where Sunkist is holed up?"

"Somewhere between Sacred Heart Creek and Beaver Creek is all I know."

"Well, we're going over there to see if we can find him."

Once they prepared for their departure, they climbed aboard their horses and headed west toward the Minnesota Valley. They'd been traveling for half a day when they met a buggy pulled by a scruffy, old jenny mule.

The man in the buggy pulled the reins and hollered, "Y'all know where I mawt find a galoot nime'a Sunkist?"

"We were going to ask you the same thing," Sophie said.

"I recon he wants tuh see me powerful bad."

"Why would he want to see you so bad?"

"Got me a deelivery fer 'im."

"What kind of delivery?"

He got a serious look in his eye. "Druther nawt sigh."

Sophie looked at Hawk, a slight smile on her face. She turned to the ragged man in the buggy and said, "Are you Walt Fraley?"

He turned his head slightly to the side, squinting at her out the corner of his eye. "Who's askin'?"

"This is Hawk Owen and I'm Sophie."

Walt jumped up in the wagon, pulled his worn out hat from his head, and slapped it across his knee. "Well, I'll be hung like a stud mule. Ain't this sumthin', meetin' up witch y'all out cheer in the middle of nowhere's like theeus. Sunkist done tole me you was the most undisciplinated herd o' rebels he ever did meet."

"Well, I don't think we're quite that bad," Sophie said. "Come on, let's go find that old scoundrel."

"Where ye figger on looking? I bin all 'round this here motherland and ain't seen hide nor hair of 'im."

"All we have to do is be around. He'll come sooner or later."

"Yeah, thet maught be true, but I got tuh git back tuh my place and git cookin. Uh cain't wait around ferever."

"Somehow Sunkist knows when we're around. He won't be long finding us."

"Ye wanna hunker down 'n wait rot cheer?"

"No, I think it would be better to move on down toward the river."

"Well, spank them ponies an' let's git tuh movin'."

They walked the animals down the road until the sun was low in the west, then pulled into a clearing in the woods. Walt jumped from his buggy. "This ol' mule has seen better dies."

The mule stood with her head hung close to the ground and her ears drooped in front of her eyes. Walt was dressed in baggy pants three sizes too big for him and the bottoms of the legs were rolled up, showing his dirty ankles. He wore a plaid shirt that hung outside his britches, and the tag end of his wide leather belt hung two inches out of the bottom of his shirt, causing Sophie a fleeting moment of distress. A worn-out hat sat precariously on his head and he wore no stockings inside his shoes. His pants were mud-stained from the bottoms halfway to his knees.

"This here mule is the third one I've had since I left home four years ago," he said as he unhitched the mule. "Gotta keep tradin' 'em off when they git tard." Hawk and Sophie smiled as they listened to the man talk and work.

He pulled the harness off the mule and started toward the back of his buggy. With a grunt he threw it into the wagon and said, "Y'all got inny vittles a man could purchase off'n ye?"

He tied ropes around the mule's front feet and slapped her on the rump. Her rear end jumped a little and she walked off to graze with the horses.

"We have food, but you don't have to buy it."

"Nope, by crackey, I ain't one tuh take handouts. Awl go shoot me a squirrel afore I'll take anything from ye fer free." He bent his head low searching the ground, kicking sticks and leaves around.

"Walt," Sophie said, "we're not giving you a handout; we're sharing what we have."

He stopped, turned, and looked at her curiously. "It ain't no handout?"

"Nope. It's sharing."

"Well, since ye put it that-a-way, ah thank-ee. Don't much cotton tuh squirrel meat, enna ways." He bent down and picked a stick from the ground.

"Sometimes we have to eat whatever comes along, Walter."

"Miss Sowphie, plys don't be a-callin' me Walter. Uh cain't stand that nime." He squatted down and sat on his heels, flatfooted on the ground. "Cain't figger how a momma could name her baby Walter," he said softly. "Sounds like thuh name of some dumb mud-grubber down in Chicken Creek Holler."

"Isn't that your real name?"

"Well, shore it is, but uh don't heff tuh lock it."

He turned his stick over and around in his hands and said as if to himself, "Down where I come from we only shoot the female squirrels." He reached into his pocket and brought out a folding knife. "Bucks is too tough tuh chew. Uh ain't got no teeth, ye know." He cut shavings from the stick with quick flicks of his pocketknife.

"Where do you come from, Walt?"

"Wess, bah Gawd, Virginny. Logan County, Wess Virginny. It wasn't no state win I left, but it is now. Had me a place down there in the mountains till the army come and busted up muh kitchen. Guess they didn't take kindly to me sellin' whiskey to the sowl'jers."

"What brings you to Minnesota?"

"Did'n wanna come up here at first—too Gawd-almighty cold. But then I heard they was a passel a ground a feller could squat fer free, so I figgered it cain't be owl bayud."

Hawk built a fire and Sophie got out the fry pan. She cut venison into small bits and stirred in wild onions and turnips.

"Smails almighty app'tizin', Miss Sowphie," he said without looking up from his whittling. "Beats squirrel meat by a long shot, ah'm here tuh tail ye."

"Walt," Hawk said. "What's it like down in West Virginia?"

"Perdiest country ye ever laid eyes on. Mountains thet reach on up through the clouds all covered with pine trees, and clear cricks runnin' with all kinda fish. And more squirrels than ye kin shake a stick at. And they's big, like a faux. We call em faux squirrels down there." He looked down at his whittling and said quietly. "Cain't eat them bucks though." He shook his head. "Nope. Too tough."

"I think Walt has a passion for squirrels," Sophie said with a smile.

"Does it get as cold down there as it does here?" Hawk asked.

"Gits Gawd-almighty cold in the mountains, but down on the flats it's plumb tol'able. Man cain't hunt in the mountains in the winner tom, onna conna the snow gits too deep. Ain't nothin' up there innaways. The deer all move down to where they kin git at the grass'n setch. Only thang yer gonna find in them mountains in the winner is squirrels, and yer perty lucky tuh fine you a doe. They's usually hidin', getting ready tuh have bybies."

They finished their dinner and Hawk set up the small tent. Walt went to his buggy and rolled out his bedroll in the back. "Well, y'all have a good noght."

"Hey, Walt!" Hawk said, "I been wondering."

"Yeah? Uhm goin tuh bayud. What is it?"

"How do you tell a male squirrel from a female when they're in the trees?"

"That's easy. Ye jiss grab the tree and shake it. If ye hear his nuts a-ratt'lin', then it's a buck. G'noght y'all."

Hawk stood with his mouth open thinking about what Walt had just said.

"You just had to ask, didn't you?" Sophie said.

"He set me up," Hawk said pointing at Walt.

"Yup, saw it right off."

"Why didn't you say something?"

"And spoil Walt's fun? Not a chance."

Morning came with a bright blue sky. Hawk heard voices outside the tent and peeked out to see who was there. Walt sat next to the fire talking to Sunkist. Posey stood behind Sunkist with her eyes fixed on Walt.

"Soph, wake up. Sunkist is here."

"So whad'ya want me to do about it?" she said without opening her eyes.

Hawk thought for a second. "Nothing. Go back to sleep." He slipped out of the tent and walked slowly to the fire.

"Sun's already up," Sunkist said. "Figgered you two was gonna sleep all day."

The air was cold and Hawk wrapped his coat around himself and squatted by the fire with his cup in his hand. Sunkist tipped the coffee pot up and filled Hawk's cup. Steam rose from it and disappeared in the morning air. He sipped a taste and made a sour face.

"Gawd, who made the coffee?"

"Ah deeyud," Walt said with his strong West Virginia accent. "What's wrong with it?"

"Too strong. Ye shouldn't use so much coffee. Coffee don't grow on trees ye know."

"It don't? What does it grow on then?"

After a moment of deep thought Hawk said, "I guess I don't know."

"Well then, don't be a-makin' talk about things ye don't know nothin' about."

Sophie came out of the tent. "Hey, Sunkist. Hey, Posey. Glad to see you. Morning, Walt."

"Mornin', mayum. Roght purdy die, ain't it."

"Yes, it's beautiful," she said, as she looked up letting the sun warm her face. She sat on a folding chair next to the fire, wrapped in her long woolen capote with the hood over her head and her hands wrapped around her warm cup. Hawk sat cross-legged on the ground next to her sipping his coffee.

"So what brings you two down here?" Sunkist asked. "Something going on I should know about?"

"Nothing going on. We just had to get out of that cabin. Looks like you and Posey came through the winter alright."

"Huh? What winter?"

"Never mind."

Walt began hitching his mule to the buggy.

"Where ye going, Walt?" Sunkist asked.

"Gotta git back to muh kitchen. Got me some sour mash I gotta git cookin'."

Sunkist turned to the others. "Anyone fer a trip down to Courtland?"

Everyone responded in the affirmative.

"Hey, Sophie," Sunkist said, "got a surprise fer ye."

"Oh good. I love surprises."

"Brought Dan along."

Sophie moved in front of Sunkist and looked up into his eyes. "Does Dan still have both his hams?"

"Yes, li'l gurl. Dan's still got both his hams. Figgered him to be too good a horse to be pickin' pieces off'n 'im. Besides, that little scratch that bullet put in me healed up jist fine without any horse meat to help it along."

Sophie stretched up and gave Sunkist a kiss on the cheek. "I knew you wouldn't eat horse meat."

"Well," Sunkist said looking into Sophie's eyes. "I done it few times back in muh trappin' days. But that was when there warn't nothin' else around tuh eat. We hadda eat our beaver skins one winter. Ye kin eat beaver, ye know."

"I know," Sophie said, "but a man cain't live on it."

"Be a hell of a way to die of starvation," Hawk said.

"Well," Sophie said, "as long as Dan's alright."

"Yeah, he's jiss fit as a fiddle. After my horse went down I figgered on git-tin' me a new one, but Dan is such a smooth ride I figgered I'd ride him. He ain't as fast as muh other one but he's a damn good horse, and carryin' me ain't no trouble fer 'im a'tall."

Sophie asked, "Who wants to go to Hutchinson?"

"What's in Hutchinson?" Sunkist asked.

"I'd like to go and see how the two girls are."

"Good idea," Hawk said. "I'd like to see what happened to Reverend Diggs and his lady friend."

"She was no lady."

"Well, whatever she was, I hope she doesn't have those kids."

Around midday they rode into Hutchinson. They passed the Good Samaritan Church and saw a sign on the door that read, 'Closed,' so they went on to the sheriff's office.

They walked in, and a man sitting at the desk said, "Can I help you?"

"We're looking for Officer Pinsonnault."

"He don't come on till midnight. Anything I can help you with?"

"We were wondering what happened to the two girls that were at the church."

"Oh, you must be Hawk and Sophie Owen."

"Can you tell us anything about the girls?"

"Yes, we put out circulars and the parents came and took them home."

"That easy?"

"Yup. They live down in New Ulm. They came right up and got the kids. They told me to thank you for finding them and if there's anything they can ever do for you to let them know."

"And what about the preacher and his housekeeper?"

"We've got warrants out for their arrest. They skipped the country the night you came and took the kids."

"Where'd they go?"

"We're not sure, but they were seen in Saint Paul last winter and they went through Elk River sometime in the spring."

"They get around, don't they? Why didn't you arrest them there?"

"We only heard they were there. We couldn't find them."

The sheriff slid his chair back and opened the desk drawer. He pulled out a folded paper. "Mister Owen, we have a letter for you from the Yellow Medicine Agency. It came last February. We didn't know where to find you, but Pinsonnault said you might be showing up here and we should hang onto it till you do."

"You couldn't have gotten through the snow up there, anyway."

"Yup, I know what you're saying. One of the worst winters we've ever had. They tell me the temperature dropped to sixty-two below in Pembina. In Minneapolis it hit twenty-five below."

"Thirty-eight below where we live," Hawk said.

The sheriff handed the letter to Hawk. He opened it and handed it to Sophie.

Jan. 1, 1864

Dear Hawk and company,

First, let me take this opportunity to thank you for finding Claire's parents and bringing them together.

We would like to hire you and your friends to help find and reunite families of both white and Indian children who have been separated as a result of the conflict of eighteen sixty-two. You will be paid for your services out of funds provided by the State Government at a rate of one dollar per man per day, two dollars per horse per day, and three dollars per wagon per day. Rations will be provided as needed by the state militia.

If these arrangements are satisfactory, please contact me as soon as possible.

Sincerely, Lorraine Bernier

Sophie folded the letter and handed it to Hawk. "What do you think?"

Hawk opened the letter and looked at it for a moment. "She needs to work on her handwriting."

"Let's go talk to the others and see what they want to do."

"Mister Owen," the sheriff said, "I also have a proposition for you that might be of greater importance."

Hawk turned and looked at the sheriff.

"We think there is more going on with these children than meets the eye. We need to find Diggs and his woman and talk to them. Would you consider going to Fort Ripley to investigate their disappearance?"

Hawk looked at Sophie.

"Don't look at me," she said, "you're the ringleader here. Your decision."

"Sheriff," he said, "we'll do it."

"Good. We can make you the same offer Miss Bernier made. Local law enforcement agencies at Saint Cloud and the commanding officer at Fort Ripley have been notified that you are coming, and you will be supplied with everything you'll need."

"You already told them we're coming?"

"Your reputation precedes you, Mister Owen. You will be sworn in as a deputy marshal before you leave today."

"Tell us more."

"Diggs is traveling slowly because of the woman he has with him. If he knows he's being chased, he'll drop the woman and take off like a scared rabbit. If that happens, he'll be out of reach long before you can get close to him."

"How many people know we're coming?"

"For particular reasons we won't go into here, we've been very careful to keep this as quiet as we can. Only certain law offices and the military at Fort Ripley know about it."

"Do we get to know the reason?"

"You will know everything when the arrest is made, Mister Owen."

"Ye wanna call me Hawk? I don't much care for being called 'mister'."

"Of course, and please call me Sheriff. I worked hard to get that title."

The sheriff stood, leaned over the desk, and put out his hand. "Erik Shallington here."

Hawk shook his hand. "Pleased to meet you."

A man in stocking feet walked in from the backroom. He stretched and yawned, tucking some of his shirt-tail into his trousers. "What's all the chatter out here?" he asked as he adjusted his suspenders.

"Hawk, this is my brother, Matt, one of my deputies. Matt, I want you to meet Hawk and Sophie Owen."

Matt looked at Sophie. "Do I know you from somewhere?"

"Hmm . . . you *do* look familiar," she said.

He shook his head and walked to the coffeepot on the stove.

"So," Hawk said, "we start by going to Fort Ripley?"

"That would be your best bet."

"Do you want us to grab him when we find him?"

"Yes, arrest him on suspicion of murder."

"Murder?"

"Yes, murder. He's been connected with a series of murders in Saint Paul and other places. You'll be familiarized with the details when you get to Saint Cloud."

"We'll have to get my brother Jake in on this."

"Your brother has been notified and we're waiting for his response."

Hawk looked quizzically at Sophie.

"Yup," she said, "you're that predictable."

"Hawk," Erik said, "it's imperative that you leave as soon as possible. If Diggs is up there, he won't stay long. We think he may be going farther north. Probably to Grand Marais."

"Why Grand Marais?"

"In his sermons he talked about Grand Marais quite often. That's where he comes from, and we suspect that's where he'll go. We also think he spent the winter in Saint Paul, but that's just a guess. He would not have traveled in the winter. Saint Paul would be the only place he could stay without worrying about being recognized."

"No idea who he stayed with?"

"Don't know. He could have stayed in any of the hotels down there under an assumed name and no one would have questioned him."

"Why would he go to Ripley and not take the road from Saint Paul to Superior?"

"He'll be going through Indian country. The Indians up there consider him a friend and will protect him where they can."

"That's gonna make it tough to get to him."

"That, Mister Owen, is why we are offering you the job. You know Indians and how to handle them. Also, you know Mister Diggs. You'll take the job, then?"

"Yup."

The sheriff swore Hawk in as a deputy state marshal and handed him an envelope of money. "There's one hundred dollars in here. That should take you to Fort Ripley. If you need more just tell the commanding officer and he'll give you another advance on your wages."

"Wages? I never thought I'd be working for wages."

"Call it earnings, then. You might as well take it now while you can. The state has a way of running out of money at convenient times."

When Sophie and Hawk left the sheriff's office, Deputy Matt looked at his brother. "She reminds me of Ma."

"Yeah, I thought the same thing."

"Can't get there from here."

13

CHAPTER THIRTEEN

THEY STEPPED ONTO THE BOARDWALK and started toward the horses. A buggy coming down the street made them step back to avoid being splashed with mud. The horse's powerful legs pounded the sodden, rutted road, and with each step its feet made loud sucking sounds. The main street of Hutchinson was bustling in spite of the rain-soaked road.

The only ones who did not seem to mind the rain were the horses. The activity on the muddy street provided a certain amount of entertainment for onlookers—in particular, the sheriff. He leaned on one foot against the wall outside his office, chewing on a blade of new spring grass. His black hat rested over his face and covered his dark brown eyes, eyes so dark that when he was a baby, his mother told him that he looked as though he had no pupils at all. He pushed his hat up with the knuckle of his index finger and watched a buggy plodding through the mud. It stopped in front of him.

The woman in the front seat wore a gold and silver broad-striped satin dress and a large-brimmed hat with delicate spring flowers around the crown that fastened with a wide ribbon tied softly under her chin. The hat shaded her face but could not hide her beautiful, sparkling blue eyes. She held an infant on her lap, and seated next to her was a gentleman in a dark brown suit and hat.

Behind them was a young boy about ten years of age sitting straight up, studying his new surroundings. He was dressed in a dark blue suit with a matching hat. Next to him sat a girl who appeared to be half his age. Her hair was the color of the yellow dress she wore. She had her mother's blue eyes.

"Excuse me, sir," the woman smiled, "are you the sheriff?"

The sheriff took off his hat, "Yes, ma'am," he said and extended his hand toward her. "That's what people keep callin' me. The name's Erik, Erik Shallington."

ARVID LLOYD WILLIAMS
BONNIE SHALLBETTER

143

"Pleased to make your acquaintance, Mister Shallington. I am Virginia Forsberg, and this is my husband, Bill."

They shook hands. Bill continued with the introductions. "These are our children, Steve, Bonnie, and our newest addition here is Paul."

"Cute little fellow. Now, what can I do for you folks today?"

"We were wondering where we might find the Andersen residence. I'm the new schoolteacher, and we have made arrangements with them for a place to stay. Can you tell me where they live?"

"If you follow the road and take the first right, you'll find a small house with a white fence and a large pine in the front yard; that's it." Erik looked at Steve. "Well, Steve, welcome to our town. You'll find plenty of kids here to play with."

"Are you really a sheriff? I've read stories about you in school!"

Erik laughed, "I see that you like to read. What book do you have there?"

Steve held the book out in front of him with both hands, "It's called *Gulliver's Travels*. It's by a man named Jonathan Swift. It has swell pictures!"

Virginia, who had been listening to the conversation, turned around. "And do you remember what a person is called who writes books?"

"Of course . . . he's an author."

Bonnie instantly chimed in. "My book is about make-believe. I like make-believe. I know what it is called, but I can't really read yet, I just know."

"It's called, *Fairy Tales*, by Hans Christian Andersen," Steve said confidently.

"I was going to tell him the name!"

"I think we need to let Sheriff Shallington get back to work. We have taken enough of his time. Thank you, and please stop by the schoolhouse. Perhaps you'll be our guest and tell the kids just what a sheriff does."

"Yeah, that would be fun!"

"Count on it, and if there is anything else I can do for you, please let me know." Erik said as they pulled away. He could hear Steve playing a harmonica as they drove off. *Hmm, nice family,* he thought to himself.

Just then the door opened and his deputy, Matt, stepped out onto the front porch of the office. Before the door closed completely, a streak of black darted out. Without looking down, Erik reached out and patted the muscular black and white dog, "Hi, Domino."

The tail swished faster, and he cocked his head at hearing his name.

Matt looked at his brother. "You look like you're lost in thought. Am I interrupting anything?

"That woman I just saw . . ."

"Well, if you need advice about the ladies, I'm the man." He displayed his characteristic charming smile.

Erik looked up at Matt, "This lady was beautiful—and old enough to be your mother. It's just that she looked so familiar, but I just can't place her."

"Well, when you find one that's not too old, I'll find a place for her," he laughed as he leaped off the boardwalk with Domino bouncing around him, happy to be at his side.

"Sometimes I wonder where he ends and the dog starts." Erik said aloud.

Hawk led the group south out of town. He told them about the plan and they all agreed to go.

"If y'all are a-goin' lookin' fer Jake, I'll foller along. Got me a delivery tuh make," Walt said.

They rode into Jake's farm. George Aldrich came out of the house. "If yer lookin' for Jake, he ain't here. This is my place now."

"Your place? Jake sold his farm?"

"Yup, Jake's living in Ernie's house till he can find a place to go."

"Who's Ernie?"

"Worthless vagabond lives outside of Courtland."

"How do we find his place?"

"Go into town, turn south off the main street at the bank, and head down into the valley about a mile. Ye can't miss it. It looks like a cyclone went through it."

It didn't take them long to find the place. They rode into the yard around piles of boards, an old broken-down buggy, a stack of assorted junk, and up to the front door.

"Anyone home in there?" Hawk shouted.

They heard a voice from behind the house and Jake walked into view carrying his bow and a handful of arrows. "Just doing a little target practice," he said. "What are you guys doing here already?"

"Jake, what's going on?" Sophie asked. "Why did you sell the farm and move in here?"

"Long story, Soph."

"Well, if it's a long story," Hawk said, "you can fill us in on the way to Fort Ripley."

"I can't go right now. I got things I have to take care of first. Sold the farm, ye know."

"Yeah, we know. The sheriff wants us to leave right away."

"You guys go on ahead, I'll catch up with you at Ripley."

"We cain't go nowhere anymore today," Sunkist said. "It's gittin' too late."

"We'll have to go and talk with Lorraine before we leave, too."

"Me and Posey'll go talk with her," Sunkist said. "You two go on up. I don't think there'll be any trouble you can't handle between here and there."

"Jake," Hawk said, "ye gotteny beer?"

"Yeah, Ernie keeps his beer down the well. Who wants beer?"

Sophie looked at Sunkist. "I never thought I'd ever hear Jake ask a stupid question."

"Guess you're right. That was a stupid question. Wait here."

"So, Jake," Sophie said, "where is this Ernie?"

"Well, he's either working on some ramshackle house in town, or working on some ramshackle whore at Kate's."

"Hmm, sounds busy."

"I'll get the beer."

Jake came with a bucket filled with beer bottles and passed them around.

Walt went to his buggy and brought a jar of *heaven in a jar* and handed it to Jake. "Thought I fergot, din ye?"

"I'll get your money," Jake said. "Later."

They sat on the porch talking and soon the conversation came around to a Minnesota man's favorite subject—deer hunting.

"Lemme tale y'all bout the tom we was at the huntin' shack in the hills back in Wess Virginny," Walt said.

Sophie looked at Hawk. "Don't ask any questions."

"Don't worry."

"It was the liest die of the hunt an' we hadn't shot nothin'. I jiss crawled outta muh bayud and was goin' out the dower in response to Mother Nycher's deemands. When ah opened up the dower there was the biggest whot tyle doe I ever did see, roght thar a-lookin' at me. Well, uh course she took off—and me in muh long johns, and barefoot, took off aifter her. Uh didn't even think tuh grab muh gun. I jiss took off a-runnin' behind her. Thet doe run me up the hills and down, and through the swamps and thuh hollers. Through the braars and acrost the cricks fer dang near a hour. We musta ran twinny mall 'roun' them there heals. Mah lowng johns was dang near ripped tuh shreds and muh feet was a-bleedin'." He paused and squinted his eyes at Sophie and pointed his index finger at her. "An' ye know, perty soon I was jist clost enough

HAWK'S QUEST

tuh git the tip of mah finger in her ass."

Sophie sighed and grinned at Hawk. "Here it comes."

"Now jist wait a minute," he said, holding a hand up to Sophie. "Theeun, it wasn't but another hunnert yords till ah could gain on her enough tuh crook that fanger."

Sophie laughed. She pointed at his beer and made a quick slicing motion across her throat. "Cut him off."

"Moght be best anyway. Beer don't sit too good on ma innards. Mought hev me a sip uh Sunny's jore, thou."

Sunkist cradled his jar in his arms and looked at Walt. "You don't git none of my *heaven in a jore.*"

"And why in tarnation naught?"

"'Cause you called me 'Sunny.'"

"Okay, Mister Sunkeeust. May ah plies have a sip of yore *heaven in a jore?*"

"No. Go git yer own damn jore, Wal-l-l-l-ter-r-r-r. I paid for this and it's mine."

"Tightfisted old codger, ain't he."

They stayed the night with Jake and in the morning Sunkist and Posey rode out toward Yellow Medicine. Walt went back to his still by the lake and Hawk and Sophie went back to their cabin on Hawk Creek. They stopped at Stromberg's farm and told Al that they would be gone for the summer and their place was his to watch over and make prosperous.

They spent the night at their home and in the morning loaded two mules with their shelter and what food stores they had, then headed north before the sun topped the trees.

For three days they followed the course of Hawk Creek and the Chetomba River to the marshland where the river commenced its journey to the Minnesota River, sixty miles to the southwest.

They passed a sign next to the road that read, 'Whitefield Pop 9.'

The town was composed of three log buildings, one of which was a saloon.

"Wanna go in and see if they have beer?" Sophie asked.

"Sure. We can ask about getting to Fort Ripley, too."

The room was lit by two oil lanterns hung from the ceiling. Two tables with four chairs each crowded the bar. Three men at one of the tables turned to watch them come in.

"Well, looky here," one of them said, "ain't she a perty one?"

Hawk glanced over at the man and continued to the bar.

The man behind the bar came slowly to them wiping the inside of a glass mug with a dirty towel. He looked at them without speaking.

The man at the table pushed his chair back, stood up, and walked over to stand next to Sophie. He was a bit taller than Hawk and wore dirty overalls and a brown coat, which hung open showing a dirty wool shirt with stains down the front. His cheek bulged from a large wad of tobacco in his mouth.

"You got any beer?" Hawk asked the bartender.

"Course he's got beer," the man said, "this is a saloon." He tilted his head back a little as he talked to keep the tobacco spit from running out of his mouth.

Hawk took Sophie's arm and led her to the other side of him to place himself between the two.

"We'll each have a beer," he said to the bartender.

The barkeep turned the handle of the spigot on a wooden barrel and filled two mugs. Foam spilled over his hand and dribbled to the floor as he turned and set them on the bar.

"Two bits," he said as he dried his hands on his apron.

The man standing alongside Hawk leaned to the left and spit at—but not into—the cuspidor on the floor. He lifted his collar and wiped the drool from his chin and said, "Where youse two headed?"

"Fort Ripley," Hawk said.

"Can't get there from here," he said looking directly at Hawk.

Hawk looked at him for a few seconds. "What do you mean by that?"

"Ye have to go through me to get there."

Hawk looked him up and down and said, "That doesn't look like a big problem."

The man looked surprised as he pondered Hawk's response then laughed and slapped him on the shoulder. "I was just kidding," he said. "Jiss follow the road east otta here. It'll take you to Monticello. When youse get there just turn north and follow the river. If youse stay with the river, ye can't miss it."

"Thanks. We'll finish our beer and be on our way."

"I'm ready when you are," Sophie said.

"Not going to finish your beer?"

"No, I'm ready to go."

They walked out of the saloon and climbed onto their horses.

"Good thing we didn't drink the whole thing, we'd be spending the night down by the crick, puking."

They rode slowly up the road until they came to Forest City. There they found what was left of the stockade the people had built in eighteen sixty-two to protect them from roving bands of hostile Indians. It was a fair sized town with shops and stores and, of course, a saloon.

"Still want that beer?" Hawk asked.

They went into the saloon and ordered a glass of beer each and sat at a table by the window. People came and went and no one bothered the couple. After two glasses of beer and a beefsteak dinner, they walked out of the saloon and got on their horses. Two more days of travel brought them to Monticello, and the next day they were on main street in Saint Cloud.

14

C H A P T E R   F O U R T E E N

SUNKIST AND POSEY SET OUT FOR THE YELLOW MEDICINE AGENCY. They traveled from sunup until sundown and covered the ninety-five miles in two-and-a-half days. Posey kept them fed with the supplies she had in her saddle bags and fresh spring greens that grew along the roadways and forests. They rode quietly, neither of them having anything they thought worth saying.

They rode into the agency and directly to the superintendent's office. When they knocked, Lorraine looked up from her work. "Well, good afternoon."

"Hey, Lorraine."

"Is Hawk going to take me up on my offer?"

"He's on his way to Ripley right now. He said you wanted to talk about this. We're here to hear what you got to say."

"What I have to say is, I'm coming along."

"You know where we're going?"

"Yes. We will be going to Fort Ripley. I know about Reverend Diggs and I am just as anxious to find him as the sheriff is. We think he may be helpful in finding homes for the children."

Sunkist looked directly at her. "You know he's wanted for murder, don't ye?"

"I know that, but he may also know the answers to some of my questions. Can you be ready in the morning?"

"Ma'am, I was born ready. We're gonna set up a camp and stay the night. We gotta rest the horses and get some shuteye ourselves."

"I've been ready to go since I sent that letter to Hawk. So, when you're ready, just come and get me."

Abernathy Wayne came in from the back of the building with a wide grin on his skeletal face. "Well, bless my heart! It's my dear friend Sunkist." He clapped his hands in front of his chest. "Oh, how won-n-n-n-derful."

"I ain't your dear friend," Sunkist said with a growl.

"That is just a figure of speech, Mister Sunkist."

"And quit calling me mister. Gawd, I hate that."

"Very well then, may I call you Sunkist?"

"I'd prefer you didn't call me a'tall," Sunkist grumbled.

"Abernathy, do you have the papers ready for the trip?" Lorraine asked.

"Yes, Miss Bernier, I have them ready and in your satchel."

"Good. Go tell the hostler to have my horse ready in the morning."

Abernathy looked down at the floor and said softly, "Miss Bernier, have you any foresight as to the duration of your journey?"

"No, Abernathy. We will probably be gone through the summer and into fall."

"I see," he said and walked slowly out of the room.

"What's eatin' him?" Sunkist asked.

"I don't really know," Lorraine said as she looked at the closing door.

"Figger maybe he wants to come along?"

"Yes, I'm afraid that's what's on his mind."

"Lorraine?" Sunkist said with a teasing look from the corner of his eye. "Figger he's sweet on ye?"

"Oh, don't be ridiculous. Abernathy?" She glanced at the door. "Never."

"Well, you ain't such a bad lookin' woman, ye know."

"That will be enough of that kind of talk, Sunkist. Abernathy has no desires whatsoever toward me."

"Why not bring him? Might be we could make a man out of him."

"Sunkist, Abernathy is quite masculine in spite of his appearance."

"Well, bring 'im along then."

Lorraine looked back toward the door. "Abernathy!" she said sharply.

The door swung open instantly. "Yes, Miss Bernier?" he said with a slight smile in his eyes.

"Have the hostler have your horse ready, too."

"My horse?"

"Yes, Abernathy, your horse. You're coming with us."

Abernathy clapped his hands and turned in a circle and said, "Oh, my dear God! Do you really mean it? I'm coming with you?"

"Settle down, Abernathy. Yes, you will be coming along."

"Oh, Miss Bernier! I could just kiss you."

"ABERNATHY!"

Abernathy stopped and stood straight. "Yes, Miss Bernier," he said, looking at her and trying hard to hide the smile in his eyes.

Sunkist watched the display. "I think I opened my mouth at the wrong time."

"Will we be leaving in the morning then?" Abernathy asked.

"Yeah, we'll be here at *sunrise*."

"Oh, this is so exciting." Abernathy said with his hands folded over his chest. "Imagine that. Me riding with Sunkist and Hawk and Jake. Why it's like a dream come . . ."

"ABERNATHY!"

"Yes, Miss Bernier."

"Go and make yourself ready."

"Yes, Miss Bernier. We'll see y'all in the mornin'," Abernathy said, mimicking what he considered a American frontier accent. He laughed as he turned to leave the room.

"Are you sure you want him along, Sunkist?"

"Is it too late to change muh mind?"

"I'm afraid so."

Sunkist started toward the door, stopped, turned, and looked at Lorraine. He started to speak but thought better of it and walked out.

"That man is different from others," Posey said.

"Boy, I'll say." Sunkist looked backward over his shoulder and then at Posey. "It's kinda scary. A man cain't tell if he's a buck or a doe."

"There are those in the Tsalagi nation also. The Tsalagi have much respect for them because the Great Spirit has made them different from the rest. They are both man and woman."

"Yeah, that might be so, but I'm gonna keep an eye on him just the same."

They rode north out of the agency for a quarter of a mile and set their camp in a grove of cottonwoods.

"Sunkist," Posey said, "you must try to understand the man Ab'nath Wayne. He is a man the same as you."

"He ain't just like me."

"He chooses to dress the way he does because that is what he is. He is a gentle man, but he will show that he is very much a man."

"Posey, it don't make no difference to me what he is. He's just a little different. Ye kin figger most men out and ye know how to handle 'em, but I ain't never seen the likes of that one." He nodded and grinned at Posey. "I'll wait till I know him better before I hate him."

"You are afraid of him?"

"Afraid's got nothin' to do with it. A man has to be watchful of the things he don't understand. Jist like when we met John Owen a couple of years back. I didn't know the man and didn't think him to be dangerous, but we both kept an eye on him on account we didn't know what he was gonna do."

"Yes. He was a bad man."

"And now yer tellin' me Abernathy Wayne is a good man?"

"Yes, my husband. Ab'nath Wayne is a good man." She placed her hand on his. "You sleep now and tomorrow you will see."

Morning came bright and warm. Sunkist and Posey packed their camp and headed back to the agency. Abernathy was busy saddling his horse. The horse was unlike anything Sunkist had ever seen. He was pure white with long, well-shaped legs, a perfectly rounded barrel, and powerful muscles on his shoulders and rump. His neck was beautifully arched and his eyes were wide and alert. He stood perfectly still while Abernathy saddled him. The saddle was also something the likes of which Sunkist had never seen.

"What the hell kinda saddle is that? You cain't ride a horse on that thing, It ain't got no horn on it."

Abernathy Wayne turned to Sunkist. "This, my dear friend, is an English riding saddle. It's much better suited to comfort than that heavy saddle you have there, especially for the horse."

"We'll see about getting you a real saddle when we get to town."

"That is very thoughtful of you, Sunkist, but this saddle will do nicely, thank you."

"Well, when you git blisters on yer butt don't come cryin' to me."

"Mister Sunkist, this saddle is no different than the one you have there. The lack of a horn, as you call it, is not a problem. I will not be roping cattle or chasing buffalo across the plains."

"Well, excuse me all to hell. You jist go ahead and ride whatever you want."

"Thank you, sir."

"Sir. Yeah, I like that. You can call me 'sir'."

"That, my friend, is a figure of speech. It denotes respect, which, like it or not, I do have for you . . . In very limited measure, however."

Lorraine came out of the office wearing cotton pants, a wool shirt, a wide-brimmed hat, and high riding boots. Their pack mule was loaded and ready.

"Are we ready to ride?" Abernathy asked.

"Git on that cayuse and let's git movin'."

Abernathy wore black buckskin trousers without fringing, a white shirt covered with a dark blue vest, and a derby hat. Shiny black boots covered his lower legs to just below his knees. He swung himself up onto the horse and sat tall and straight. Without an obvious command, the horse backed away from the hitching rail and turned his head to the north. Sunkist pulled back on the reins, pulled Dan to the left, and kicked him in the ribs. "Gid-app."

Lorraine followed and they set out along the road to the Minnesota River crossing. Sunkist watched Abernathy closely and saw that he was obviously comfortable on a horse.

The butt end of a rifle showed from a scabbard under his leg.

"What's that rifle yer packin', Abby?"

"Mister Sunkist, please do not call me Abby."

"Well, I ain't gonna be callin' you Abernathy Wayne all the way to Ripley."

"Then I would prefer you don't call me at all."

Then, without a noticeable command, Abernathy's horse took off at a cantor ahead of Sunkist.

Sunkist looked at Lorraine. "Kinda touchy about that name, huh?"

"Apparently."

They rode until the sun was low in the west and set up a camp close to Chetomba Creek.

Lorraine and Abernathy set up two small tents, one for each of them. Abernathy pulled the rifle out of the scabbard, sat on a small folding chair, and began to wipe it down with a soft cloth.

"Mister Wayne?" Sunkist said.

"I will be addressed as Abernathy."

"Hey! What the hell's put a burr in yer britches?"

"I do not have a burr in my britches, as you so delicately put it. I have my preferences, just as you do, and if you continue to address me by any name other than Abernathy, I shall call you Jim."

"Don't you be callin' me Jim," Sunkist said with a threatening look from under his eyebrows.

"And I will not be intimidated by your threatening stare. Furthermore, if you intend to persist in this conduct, please remove yourself from my presence."

"Look, you little . . ."

Lorraine stepped between them. "Is this going to go on through the entire trip?"

"No, it ain't," Sunkist said. "I'm gonna stuff that little weasel in the next hollow tree I see."

"You may find that a challenge far greater than you anticipate." Abernathy said without looking up from his work.

Sunkist stepped back and looked at Abernathy then at Lorraine. "This guy is agger'vatin' like a boil on yer ass. What the hell's wrong with him?"

"Sunkist!" Lorraine said.

"Umm, sorry fer the rotten language, ma'am, I . . ."

"Oh, never mind that. Come with me." She took his arm and led him away. "I think you should go easy on Abernathy. He is having a wonderful time being what he thinks you would want him to be."

Sunkist ran his fingers over his beard and looked toward Abernathy. "Ye think that's what he's a-doin'?"

"It could also be that you do not intimidate him."

Sunkist's face softened as he looked over at Abernathy. "Yeah, guess he knows I wouldn't never hurt a little feller like that."

"Yes, let's assume that."

The next day they passed the sign that read, 'Whitefield Pop 9.'

"Let's go in and see if they've seen Hawk and Sophie," Lorraine said.

A man standing by the bar turned to Sunkist and said, "Yer new in town."

"I already know that," Sunkist answered.

"Kinda touchy today? Been a long trail?"

"Git away from me," Sunkist said, "you stink."

"Leo!" a man at a table said loudly.

The man at the bar looked up and down Posey's body. With an arrogant smirk on his face he looked around the bar then turned to Sunkist. "How much fer the squaw?"

Sunkist jerked his rifle up and slammed it on top of the bar. Instantly, both fists flashed out and caught the man on both sides of his chest just below the shoulders. The wind came out of the man and his feet came off the floor. He flew onto the table behind him, breaking the legs off one side. The table crashed to the floor, sending the man end-over-end to land on his stomach. Two men who'd been sitting at the table scrambled away as the man rolled by them.

A man rushed to the one on the floor, slapped him lightly on his cheeks, and said, "You alright, Leo? I tried tuh tell ye. That there's Sunkist Whistler. Ye hadn't aught'a riled him."

Leo rolled to his side and looked up at Sunkist. "Hell, Sunkist, I didn't know it was you."

"You ever say something stupid like that tuh me agin, you'll be lookin' up at the sod in the mornin'. Which way to Ripley?"

"Jist follow the road east and it'll take ye to Monticello. Then follow the river upstream. It'll take youse right to it."

"You seen a redhead go through here with a woman?"

"Yeah, he was looking for Ripley, too. Week or so back. You know him?"

"Yeah, that was Hawk Owen."

Leo's friend knelt next to him and said, "Leo, I think you better be careful who you pick on."

Sunkist turned to the bartender. "Fergit that beer. We'll be movin' on."

"One on the house, Mister Sunkist?"

"No."

They left the saloon and took the road east.

"Sunkist," Lorraine said, "there was no call for violence in there."

"He was a-callin' fer it."

"He was just giving you a bad time. I do not think he was looking for a fight."

"I don't like people givin' me a bad time."

As afternoon grew old, they made camp for the night on the north side of Forest City. Abernathy pulled the rifle from the scabbard and began cleaning it.

"That a Sharps ye got there, Abby?"

Abernathy continued cleaning the rifle without response.

"You gone deaf, Abby?"

Abernathy ignored him.

"Abernathy!" Sunkist barked. "I'm talking to you."

"Oh, hello there, Sunkist. I thought you were addressing someone named Abby."

"I was talking to you, ye little . . . Aw hail, what's that rifle ye got there, *A-ber-na-thy*?"

"This, my dear friend, is a Sharps rifle. It was made specifically for target competition. Hence, the heavy barrel."

"Kin ye hit enna thin' with it?"

"I have been known to strike the center of the target quite effectively."

"Looks kinda heavy to be packin' around in the field."

"It is not designed to be packed around in the field. It is strictly for target shooting."

"I kin shoot better'n you."

"I never boast of my shooting abilities. There will always be someone who is better than me."

"Yup, and you met him today."

"Well, I'll just take your word for that," Abernathy said with a cold tone that bordered on sarcasm.

"What d'ye mean by that?"

"It means, I believe you when you say you can shoot better than me."

"Well?"

Abernathy looked up at Sunkist, raised his eyebrows, paused momentarily, and tipped his head slightly to the side. "Well what, Sunkist?"

"Well, don't ye wanna try and beat me?"

"Oh! May I assume you wish to engage in a competition?"

"That's what I was trying to get through that thick scull of yers."

"There is no need for insults. If you wish to shoot against me, just say so. I would be delighted to accommodate you."

"Well, let's stop a-jawin' an' git goin'."

"Perhaps another time, my friend. This bright sun has my eyes a bit weary. Tomorrow perhaps."

"Yer jist afraid yer gonna git beat."

"I am never afraid of being defeated. If I am defeated in competition, it is because the opposition is more advanced in the sport than I, and it puts forward the incentive to become more proficient at my game."

"Huh?"

"I simply said, I have been defeated before and I still enjoy a good shooting match."

"Okay, tomorrow we'll see who's best. Bring yer cryin' towel."

"Yes, I will do that and you do the same."

Morning came and found Sunkist sitting cross-legged on the ground, wiping the bore of his Springfield rifle. He looked up and saw Abernathy loading his pack mule and saddling his horse.

"I thought we was gonna shoot."

"Sunkist, the sky is overcast and it is probably going to rain. Haven't you noticed?"

"Yer scared."

"I am not scared. I only wish both of us to have every advantage to do our very best."

"When you get in a scrap with Injuns ye don't check the weather before ye shoot."

"That would be an entirely different state of affairs, Sunkist. This will be a contest of skill, not of survival."

"Git yer skinny ass up on that horse afore I kick it up there."

"Oh, Sunkist. Another thing," Abernathy said as he mounted his horse. "Whut?"

"My pony can run faster than yours."

"Why ain't I surprised at that?"

"Catch me if you can!" With that, Abernathy's horse took off at a full gallop down the road. Abernathy sat straight up on the saddle with both hands holding the reins lightly in front of him. Sunkist watched him disappear over the hill.

"I ain't gonna chase him. It'd be alright with me if he stayed away out in front of us all the way to Ripley."

"Abernathy seems to have a well-developed love for competition," Lorraine said with a smile. "Let's not let him get too far ahead."

In three days they were in sight of Saint Cloud. They set up a camp at the fringe of the town and settled in for the night.

"We have reason to believe that he is connected
with some murders at Grand Marais."

15   CHAPTER FIFTEEN

Sophie and Hawk found the streets of Saint Cloud muddy from the rain shower that had gone through that morning. Wagons and buggies lined the sides of the roads, and people scurried about in every direction doing their business. No one paid any attention to them as they walked their horses through the busy street.

"I ain't stayin' here long," Hawk said.

A wagon rumbled by them and splashed mud up the horse's legs. The driver didn't seem to notice and drove on without looking. People stepped off the boardwalks directly into their path, causing them to rein back the horses for fear of running someone down.

On the corner they saw a three-story frame building with a sign that read, 'Stearns House'. The building was painted white and had a front porch surrounded by double wooden pillars, and above that, another deck with tables and chairs.

"Do you suppose they have bathtubs in there?" Sophie asked.

"Probably. Let's go in and see."

They tied their mounts to the rail alongside the building and climbed the four steps to the door. A man in a suit and top hat stepped in front of them. "May I help you?"

"Do you have a bathtub in here?"

He looked her up and down and said. "We have bathing facilities, but unfortunately they are reserved for our guests."

"Do you have a room available for a night?"

He cleared his throat and said, "I'm sorry, but our rooms are quite costly. May I suggest the hotel down the street? Their accommodations may be more suitable for your needs."

She looked at the man quizzically. "And what, may I ask, are more suitable accommodations for us?"

"Madam, please. Our establishment caters to people of influence and capital."

Sophie turned to Hawk. "Hey, Hawk, do we have *capital*?"

"Well, I . . ."

"The room will cost you eleven dollars per night."

"Yeah, we can do that."

"Sir," the man said, "we have prominent guests staying in this hotel and, quite frankly, you do not appear to be, well, shall we say, dressed for the occasion?"

The atmosphere was suddenly drenched in silence. Sophie looked at the man for a short moment and said dryly, "No, what you mean is, that in your opinion, we are not affluent enough to warrant our staying here, is this not correct?"

"Madam, I am sorry, but we do have our standards."

She turned to Hawk. "Come on, let's go."

They turned and walked down the steps to the street.

"Where we goin'?"

"Let's go down to the river and wash up. It's open twenty-four hours a day, and no one cares what you look like or what you smell like."

When they finished bathing they walked back to town. Strolling down the boardwalk they passed a mercantile with a mannequin in the window. She was wearing an exquisite rose-colored evening dress with delicate flowers around both the collar and bottom of the dress. Sophie stopped, backed up a few steps, and stood there a moment. "Hawk, we're going in."

"We are?" He looked at her expression and knew something was happening he could not even try to anticipate. He realized he never really knew what went on in a woman's mind, especially when they were after something. "Why do I have this weird feeling in my stomach?"

"Come on. This will be fun."

"That's funny, my kind of fun don't involve no clothes at all."

A man came to them with his hands folded in front of him. "May I be of service?"

"I would like to try on the dress in the window," Sophie said. "And we'll need a suit for him."

The man snapped his finger to a young lady working on the racks of women's clothing and told her to get the dress from the mannequin.

He turned to Hawk. "Come with me." Hawk followed the man to a rack of men's suits."

"What size do you wear, sir?"

"Size? Size of what? That ain't none of your damn business."

"Well now, let's try on some garments and we'll fix you up nicely."

He pulled a suit from the rack and handed it to Hawk.

He looked over at Sophie and she nodded. He looked back at the salesman, "Now what?"

"Take it behind that screen and try it on."

"Change clothes in *here?*"

"Sir, that is the only way you will know if the suit will fit you."

"But . . ."

Sophie came over and ushered him behind the screen. He went behind the curtain and came out wearing a pair of trousers that were a little too long and a little too big around the waist. He was given another pair and another before they found trousers that fit. The clerk fit him with a new derby hat and black shoes. When they were finished dressing the poor man, he stood in front of a full-length mirror and wondered who the man looking back at him was.

While Hawk was being fitted for the suit, Sophie had been trying on the dress and shoes. She came out from behind the curtain wearing the dress and a wide-brimmed hat, and carrying a lace parasol.

Hawk's mouth dropped open and he let out a gasp. "Soph?"

She made a slow turn with the open parasol over her head. "You like?"

"My God, Sophie, you're beautiful," he said.

"You're not too bad yourself, stranger."

They paid the clerk for the clothing, bundled up their old clothes, and walked out arm in arm.

Sophie looked at Hawk and smiled. "I never thought I'd ever see you in a suit."

"Well, don't get used to it." He ran his finger around the collar and said, "How long do I have to wear this?"

Suddenly, Sophie turned and went into a store leaving Hawk alone on the sidewalk. She came out in a few minutes with a straight cane with a polished knob and handed it to Hawk. "*Voila*—the outfit is complete."

"I don't need this thing anymore."

"It's just for looks, Hawk."

"Is that all this is for? Looks?"

"Yup. Sometimes a woman just likes to get dressed up and do something different."

"If it makes you happy, Soph, it's alright with me." He got a grin on his face, straightened himself, and swung his cane in a circle as the heels of his new shoes popped on the boardwalk. "Ye know something? Being dressed in fine clothes and walking with the prettiest woman in Minnesota kinda makes a man feel down right important."

"And the handsomest man in the whole damn country."

"Soph, ye really want to have some fun?"

"What did you have in mind, handsome?"

"Follow me."

They walked back the Stearns house and climbed the stairs. Sophie was about to say something but changed her mind and followed him, her curiosity piqued.

The man behind the desk stood tall and straight and said, "Would you like to register?"

"May we inquire as to your nightly rates?" Sophie asked pleasantly.

"One room for one night is six dollars, ma'am."

Suddenly, Sophie slammed the palm of her hand on the desk. "My gracious!" she said loudly. "How disgusting!" She wiped her handkerchief across her hand as if removing some sort of repulsive matter.

"Harlan, this will nevah do. I will naught stay in a dilapidated establishment such as this for even another moment. I would be afraid of these cockroaches coming into the bed as we slept. Harlan, take me from this, this, this *wallow*, immediateleh!"

"Yes. Come, my dear," Hawk said as he took Sophie's arm. "We shall find more suitable accommodations elsewhere."

Sophie raised her nose to the air, spun around, and walked quickly toward the door with her handkerchief over her nose. Hawk threw his chest out and walked beside her making sure his heels and cane thumped loudly on the carpeting. He stopped abruptly and slammed the tip of his cane on the floor. "Boy Jove, I got the bloody little bawst'd," he said smartly and smiled at Sophie.

Sophie stopped and turned to the desk. "Sir!" she shouted, "you would do well to have your domestic clean up these mouse droppings along the wall!"

They walked out the door and down the steps to the street. Hawk led them a few steps down the walk and stopped. They broke out laughing.

"That made this all worth it. I'd even do it again!" Hawk said through his laughter. Then he added in his mock British accent, "I believe all of this non-sense has given me an appetite. Shall we?"

"Let's go," Sophie said and put her arm through his.

"Where did you learn to talk like that?"

"Like what?"

"Like you did when you pretended to kill that roach."

"I traveled with Joe Rolette a couple of years ago. He always said that when he'd shoot a squirrel or something. "By Jove, I got the bloody little baw-st'd!" Hawk repeated.

"Hawk, would you take the horses to the stable? I have something I have to take care of."

"Sure. Meet you right here in half an hour?"

"I'll be back," she said.

Hawk picked up their horses and mule and walked them to the stables. He paid the man for boarding the animals and storing their possessions, then went back to the street to find Sophie.

Horses and wagons rushed by him and people walked quickly in every direction. He was uncomfortable with so many people around and so close, and found himself dodging them and stepping out of the way. It seemed he couldn't move three paces without someone getting in his way or him getting in someone else's way. No one seemed to notice him as he snaked his way through the crowds. He wondered why *he* was the one who moved out of the way of on-coming people. *What would happen if I didn't move out of the way?* he wondered to himself. *Would they walk right into me, or would they turn and move around me?* He tried to pretend he didn't see a lady walking directly toward him, but at the last instant he turned his body to get out of her way. He still didn't know whether she would have bumped into him or not.

The incessant noise of chattering people and the sound of horses, wagons, mules, and the squeal from the axels of an oxcart burned his ears. A man shouted from across the street to another man.

Why does he have to shout? Hawk thought to himself. *Why doesn't he go over and talk to him?*

He jumped onto the boardwalk to keep from being splashed with mud from the wheels of a large freight wagon passing by.

"Hey, handsome!" he heard from behind. "Busy tonight?"

He turned to see Sophie in a one-horse buggy and a man in the driver's seat wearing a top hat and black suit.

"Well, come on, get in. Important people like us shouldn't have to walk around town."

Hawk looked around to make sure it was him who was being addressed, then climbed into the buggy.

"Hit it, driver!" Sophie said, obviously enjoying this new adventure.

The driver turned halfway around. He was a tall man in a black suit and top hat which sat on a head of wavy gray hair. A pipe rested in the corner of his mouth and sent an occasional billow of blue smoke into the air.

"Vhere vould yew like to go, madam?"

Hawk looked at her, "Madam? Never thought of you that way." That earned him an elbow to the ribs.

"Well, that depends. Where would you suggest, Mister . . . ?"

"Yew can call me Helmar. It means helmeted warrior." He nodded his head upwards towards the top hat, "Some helmet. Vell, I vould eat at da Stearns House. Dey heff gyud food. Da viffe and I like tew go dere sometimes."

She looked at Hawk and raised an eyebrow, "Thank you, but we are actually in the mood for something . . . different."

He rubbed his chin in thought, "Vell, if yew are really in da mood for someting different, dat vould definitely be da African Saloon and Barbershop. It yust opened tree years ago. Upstairs, dey even heff a room where yew can get shaved, shorn, or shampooed. And all da vay downstairs, dere is Professor R. Cromwell who is a genuine African who can whip you up a cold lunch, and darn qvik, tew! Dey heff da roast beef, veal cutlets, or, hmmm, dere is one more, oh yeah, da mutton. Da viffe and I don't care much for da stuff. Ooff da! But people seem to take to it. Both da ladies and gents are velcome dere. Den on da tird floor landing, dere is a nice, small, secluded table dat overlooks da flower gardens."

"Sounds perfect."

"Dey grow all dere own flowers for da tables, don't ya know. Not many people know about dat table. Yew yust tell 'em dat ol' Helmar told yew about it. Dey vill take gud care uff yew tew."

Hawk rubbed his hand over his cheek, "Might even get a shave to go with this fancy gitup, but the shampoo thing is overdoing it—waste of soap."

At this, the driver let out a hearty laugh. Then they heard the whistle of a bullwhip and a sharp crack over the heads of the horses.

"Driver!" Sophie said. "Must you use that whip?"

"Oh, no! I youst make the vhip crack for show. Dose people from down sout, day tink it iss exciting. Don't vorry. Dere's no extra charge for it."

In a few minutes, the carriage stopped in front of the African Saloon and Barbershop.

"Vell, yew tew heff a gud time and remember to tell them Helmar sent yew."

"Thank you. We'll make sure we do that." Sophie handed him a tip. "Helmar, do you think you could come back here in a couple hours?"

"Ya sure, I ken dew dat."

"By the way, this is Hawk Owen and I'm Sophie Boisvert."

"Pleased to heff met you tew. Gyud bye fer now." He tipped his hat and was off with a crack of the whip.

"Likes to talk, don't he?"

"Yeah, but look where we are because of it. I'm starved, let's go in."

"A couple hours? In there? In this outfit? Guess I've been through worse. It don't really take that long to slam some fancy food down, does it?"

"I think this is going to be an experience you won't forget."

"That's what I'm afraid of."

As they entered, a man in a black suit with a red carnation in his lapel, approached them. "May I help you?"

"Yes, we're here for dinner."

"Do you have reservations?"

"I'm afraid not. Helmar brought us, but he didn't say anything about reservations."

"Oh, Helmar . . . Of course. Very well, then."

"Is the table overlooking the flower garden available?" Sophie asked.

"Yes, you have come early enough. Please, follow me."

They climbed the last stairs leading to a small landing. The maître d' opened the long lace curtain, revealing tall, bowed windows behind a small, round table with white linen, fresh flowers, and a candle. He pulled a chair out for Sophie.

"Thank you."

The maître d' raised an eyebrow.

"I will have your waiter bring menus and something to get you started."

Soon a waiter approached their table. "Good evening. My name is Edward, and I will be your server this evening. Is there something I can start you off with? A beverage, perhaps?"

"Bring us your best champagne," Hawk said confidently.

"We have several, sir. What do you prefer?"

"Uhh, whatever's the best."

Edward gave a slight bow and descended the stairs.

"Nice recovery." She turned toward the windows. "Look at this view, I bet these flowers are from the garden below."

Hawk reached over and picked a flower from the vase. "For you."

"Thank you. I've always loved pansies."

Soon the waiter showed up with the champagne. He presented the bottle to Hawk. "This happens to be my favorite—Dom Perignon."

"Mine, too," Hawk quickly added.

Edward uncorked the bottle and filled their glasses and laid menus on the table. "Our specials this evening are roast turkey with wild rice and mushrooms, and ham timbales with potato balls. All of the entrees are served with a lovely, fresh, spring green salad, and your choice of either peas with mushrooms and pearl onions, or carrots in a dill cream sauce. You also have a choice of either our very popular, and may I add, delicious, cream of asparagus soup or a nice beet soup."

Hawk looked up at Edward, "Just like mom used to make."

"Yes, I'm sure. I'll give you some time to look over the menu."

"Thank you."

Hawk raised his glass, "Lead the way, partner, I have no idea what the hell I'm doing in here."

"Just pick something off the menu and tell the waiter."

Hawk open the menu and ran his eyes down the page. He folded it shut and dropped it on the table. "I have no idea what this menu says."

Sophie laughed, "Would you like me to read some of the other items on the menu for you?"

"How about you do the ordering? Ya know . . . this champagne ain't bad. Kinda tickles when you get your nose right in the glass."

"Well, I'm glad you're enjoying yourself. Everything looks good on the menu. I think I'll have the fish with gruyere."

"What's that?"

"It's a type of cheese."

"Then why don't they just call it cheese?"

"Drink up, Hawk. It may be a long night."

Edward came back and they gave him their order, then finished the bottle.

A man approached their table. "Excuse me," he said. "I'm Sheriff Beaupre. Are you Hawk Owen?"

He was a tall, well-built man with a handlebar mustache, dark blue pin-striped suit, and a string tie around his neck. He held his black hat in his hand.

"Yes, I'm Hawk Owen."

"May I sit?" Beaupre said as he pulled a chair to the table.

"How'd you know who I am?"

"I asked the buggy driver. I saw you come into town and thought maybe it was you, but I had to be sure. You raised quite a stink at the Stearns," he said with a slight smile.

"You gonna arrest us?"

"No, of course not. That place could use some livening up."

"Then tell me why you're so interested in us."

"You're on your way to Fort Ripley, correct?"

"Right."

"May I ask who sent you?"

"Sheriff Shallington down in Hutchinson."

"And his brother's name?"

"Sheriff, I don't like question-and-answer games. You're interrupting a good meal, so come out and say what's on your mind or leave."

"Never mind. I just have to be sure who I'm talking to."

"And your reason for being here?"

"We have been informed that you are looking for a man named Diggs who claims to be a preacher. Am I right?"

"Do you know where to find him?" Hawk asked.

"We could find him quite easily. He's not that good at hiding, but due to the war in the South, we don't have the manpower to go get him."

"Why are you looking for him?"

"We have reason to believe that he is connected with some murders and disappearances around the state and at Grand Marais."

"He's the killer?" Hawk asked.

"We're not sure. All we know is that his name can be traced in a round-about way to each of the dead people. He may have known them personally or knows someone who does."

"Well, why don't you just arrest him if you know he's involved?"

"We have to know what he's guilty of before we can arrest him."

"Isn't mistreatment of children enough to put him in jail?" Sophie asked.

"Missus Owen, the laws pertaining to the proper treatment of children are so vague and incomplete, especially regarding orphan children, that it's nearly impossible to prosecute on any basis of law."

"Well, Sheriff, there's no excuse for that kind of injustice. Something needs to be done."

"I agree," Hawk said. "When did all this with Diggs start?"

"The first one killed was a man in Iowa by the name of Greenwood. He was hogtied and shot in the back of the head—an assassination style killing. That was a number of years ago."

"And he was from Grand Marais?" Hawk asked.

"Yes. He was involved with some mining interests after the Hudson's Bay Company and the American Fur Company moved to Canada. There were a lot of crooked dealings involved in that move, and a lot of people went broke."

"And how about the law up there?"

"There is no law in that region, and it should not be our concern, but the murders have happened as far south as Saint Paul and Iowa. A man who came from Grand Marais was murdered in Saint Paul just last spring, and another in Mankato this past winter. Both of them knew Reverend Diggs. We know there are more, but we don't know who or when."

"Why doesn't the state do something about it?" Sophie asked.

"The state *is* doing something about it. They have hired you and your party to investigate the situation."

"Why us?" Hawk asked.

"Because you and your brother are the most capable men we could find, and with so many of the Minnesota boys going to the war in the South, you are the most available. Now, Mister Owen, we have made arrangements for you and Missus Owen to stay at the Stearns House. You may stay as long as you wish, but I would recommend that you don't wait around too long. We need to get to the bottom of this before any more people die."

Hawk turned to Sophie. "You want to stay at the Stearns?"

"I think we could make it a memorable experience," she said.

"When you finish your meal," Sheriff Beaupre said, "meet me at the Stearns House, and we'll get you set up."

Sheriff Beaupre stood and reached across the table to shake Hawk's hand, then tipped his hat to Sophie and left.

When they finished their meals, Hawk pushed his chair back. "I'm not sure where all this is going, but I'm ready for some dessert if they have any, or should we just get some more champagne?"

"I'm having dessert," Sophie said. "*Mousse au chocolat.*"

"Sounds like something you should shoot and put out of its misery. If they have ice cream, I'll have vanilla, and one of those fancy cakes I saw on our way to the table. And some coffee."

"Coffee does sound good."

They finished their desserts and the evening light had dimmed when Edward came back to their table. "Pardon me. I am to inform you that Helmar is outside waiting to take you back to wherever you came from. Will there be anything else I can do for you?"

"No, thank you, just the bill." Sophie said. "The asparagus soup was very good. In fact, everything was quite delicious, especially the chocolate mousse."

Hawk looked up at the man with slightly unfocused eyes, "I'll bet it was hard to find a chocolate moose around here."

"Yes, sir," the waiter said as he started picking up their dishes. "It kept me out the better part of the night." He turned and started walking down the stairs. "Do come back. Tuesdays would be good. It's my day off."

On the street, Helmar sat patiently waiting. "To the Stearns House!" Hawk shouted with a wave of his arm.

Sheriff Beaupre met them at the front door and escorted them inside.

"Good evening, madam," the man at the desk said with a distinct frost in his tone. "Your behavior has gotten you in trouble with the law, I see."

"This is Hawk and Sophie Owen," the sheriff said. "We have a room reserved for them for an indefinite stay."

"Oh, I beg your pardon, Mister and Missus Owen. I had no idea who you were when you came in earlier," he said as he quickly flipped through the register. "Yes, yes, here it is. Please forgive us," he said with a slight bow. "We have your room prepared and you may take it when you're ready. Do you have luggage?"

"Luggage?" Hawk said.

"Yes. Your bags and suitcases."

"Oh. We'll have to go and get them from the stables."

"The stables?"

"They're over there with the horses."

"I see," the clerk said dryly. "Would you like us to send someone to fetch them for you?"

"No. We can handle that."

The man handed the keys to the bellboy who escorted them up a flight of stairs to their accommodations.

Once in the room, Sophie looked at the chandelier hanging from the ceiling, the large brass framed bed in the center of the room, and the gas lamps on the wall above each side of the bed. The floor was covered with carpeting and the walls with flower patterned paper, and light blue draperies hung over the windows. A china wash basin with a matching pitcher sat on a table, and a dressing screen was folded tightly in the corner of the room.

"Will there be anything else?" the bellboy asked.

"No, that will be all, thank you," Sophie said. The man stood and looked at them for a few moments, shrugged his shoulders, and turned to walk out the door.

"This looks like the rooms at Linda's *dance studio*," Sophie said with a grin.

"Kinda fancy for us," Hawk said.

"You'll be much too busy to even notice," she said with mischief in her eyes.

Sophie sat on the edge of the bed. "Come over here and let's talk about it, shall we?"

"We'll get these fancy clothes all messed up."

"You worried about it?"

Hawk jumped onto the bed, "Nope," he said in mid-air and lay back on the bed, listening to the sounds of people and wagons on the street below the window.

"What are you thinking about?" Sophie said as she played with the knot of his tie.

"Just wondering what Diggs could have been mixed up in to cause this much trouble."

She pulled the tie from his neck and started to undo the buttons of his shirt. "You think there's more to this than what they're telling us?"

"They're going through a lot of trouble if there isn't."

"One thing I do know is . . . these clothes gotta go."

"I can help with that."

The next thing Hawk knew, his belt was being loosened and pulled from around his waist. Sophie gave it a unceremonious toss across the room.

"Nice move."

"I have more if you're interested."

"I'm interested."

She pulled his shirt out of his trousers and finished unbuttoning it.

"Ah, that feels good. I'm not used to all these clothes."

"I can help with that, too."

"Looks like I came to the right place then."

She unbuttoned his pants and pulled them down his legs to his feet and he gave a quick kick, sending them flying though the air and landing on the bedpost.

"Nice move." Sophie crooned, looking at him from the corner of her eye, the hint of a smile on her lips.

"I have more if you're interested."

"I'm interested."

Later, as Hawk lay on his back, his body wet with sweat, he said, "Do you suppose Sunkist and Jake are on their way?"

"Sunkist is, but I don't know about Jake."

CHAPTER SIXTEEN

A FEW DAYS EARLIER, JAKE SAT ALONE at the dinner table and stared at the empty chair across from him. He didn't eat all that he'd prepared for himself. He stood, picked up the plate and callously tossed it into the sink, then walked out the front door.

He packed a mule with provisions, mounted his horse, and headed north, following the government road along the rim of the valley. He passed below Fort Ridgely not wanting to see anyone or talk to anyone, then made a wide circle around the lower Sioux Agency. In two days he pulled into Hawk's yard and spent the night in the house. The next day he followed Chetomba Creek to Whitefield.

He pulled up in front of the saloon and walked in. "How far to Fort Ripley?" he asked the bartender. Leo stepped up to him. "Ye can't git there from here."

"What's that supposed to mean?" Jake asked without looking up.

"It means you have to go through me to get there," Leo said.

"Okay," Jake said as his fist came up and smashed Leo's nose. Leo started to fall backwards, and in a desperate attempt to keep his feet under himself, ran backwards out through the bat-wing doors. Jake walked out directly after him and looked down at the man.

"You broke by goddab dose!" the man shouted.

"You seen a big red-headed man go through here?"

Leo looked up at him with blood pouring from his nose. "Ye bead Sudkist Whistler?"

"That's him. Ye seen him?"

"Yeah, he was through here a couple days ago. Who's askin'?"

"Jacob Owen."

"Dabbit, I should'a dowed it," he grumbled and spat blood into the mud.

A man walked out the door. "Leo, you alright?"

"Yeah, I'll live," Leo said, holding his bent nose.

"Not if you keep pissin' people off you won't."

"You gonna tell me you knew that was Jake Owen?"

"Sure I knew it. You should'a knew it, too. They was at the fort when the Injuns attacked. Don't chuh remember?"

"Hell, I was idd duh barracks. How the hell did I doe who was dere?"

Jake climbed onto his horse and rode north out of town.

"About time you got here," Sunkist said as Jake rode into camp.

"Seen anything of Hawk?"

"Nope. Figger he's up to Ripley by now."

Jake looked toward the town. "You been in town yet?"

"I ain't goin' in there."

About that time Abernathy came out of the alder grove fastening the buttons on the front of his trousers. "Well, if it isn't my dear friend Jake Owen! How delightful."

Jake looked at Abernathy, then at Sunkist. "What the hell's he doing here?"

"Agger'vatin' me, mostly."

"Traveling through our beautiful state with Sunkist and Posey and Miss Lorraine has been such an exhilarating experience. And now we have . . ."

"Lorraine, too?"

"Yup, her, too."

"Where is she?"

"She went into town to see if Hawk has been there."

"When did she leave?"

"Early this morning. She should be back any time now."

"Hey there, Posey," Jake said as he walked to the kettle hanging over the fire. He dipped some of the soup into his bowl. "Ye mind?"

Posey nodded her head.

"Didn't figger you to show up for a couple'a weeks," Sunkist said.

"Nothin' to keep me down there. Prob'ly never go back."

They stayed in camp until late afternoon when Lorraine rode in.

"See anything of Hawk?" Jake asked.

"They left here two days ago. They should be at Fort Ripley by now. I had lunch with Sheriff Beaupre at a wonderful restaurant. You should have come along; the pork steak was wonderful."

"Too damn many wagons and horses runnin' up and down this road fer me," Sunkist said. "Ye won't catch me in there."

"I would have loved having lunch with you, Miss Bernier."

"Maybe next time, Abernathy." She tipped her head slightly to the side as she looked at him.

Abernathy's face had lost the pasty-white pallor it'd had at the start of the trip. The sun had darkened his skin, and his eyes had a faint squint from the bright sun. His three days growth of beard had grown out dark brown.

She looked at him for a long moment. "Where are your spectacles?"

"I don't seem to need them. Perhaps working on the papers in that *very dimly lit office* where you had me confined had my eyes weary and caused me to need the corrective lenses."

"That office was perfectly adequate for the work you were doing."

"Perfectly adequate?" Abernathy said sarcastically. "That is quite a mix of words, Miss Lorraine. You might have said perfectly good enough. That office was a dungeon and you know it—that is why you had *me* in there instead of yourself."

Lorraine was startled by his retort. Abernathy had never before addressed her by her given name. Her dominant character called for swift and severe reprimand. But a hint of a smile appeared on her face as she became aware of Abernathy's changing countenance. She turned and walked away.

Sunkist began splitting wood to feed the fire during the night. Abernathy walked quickly to him and asked, "Chopping wood?"

"No. This piece of wood had a itch. I was just scratching it fer 'im."

"Oh, how clever. I suppose that *was* a silly question."

Sunkist glanced at him and continued chopping wood.

"Sunkist, I have never had the pleasure of chopping firewood. May I do that?"

"Ye ain't never split wood afore?"

"No, sir."

Sunkist handed him the axe. "Well, have at it."

Abernathy swung the axe and it glanced off the block of oak and buried itself in the dirt.

"Better let me do that, son." Sunkist said, reaching for the ax. "We don't need you hobblin' around here with a split foot like a cow."

"Oh, no, I took this job and I will continue until we have enough wood for the night."

"Well, ye gotta swing that ax. Ye cain't split wood bumpin' it off'n the block like that."

"I shall become skilled at this chore if it takes me all night." He raised the axe and swung again. This time it stuck in the wood. Sunkist showed him how to split thin slabs from the sides of the block rather than trying to split the whole thing in two. Soon, Abernathy was splitting wood like he knew what he was doing.

After a while, Sunkist stopped him. "Ye kin stop now. We got enough wood for the next three days."

He took his spot by the fire. "The boy takes after wood like a hungry beaver after a popple tree."

Morning came and they crawled out of their shelters and mounted the horses. They followed the road through Saint Cloud then forded the river at the old oxcart crossing.

"I can take care of myself. You just go."

17 CHAPTER SEVENTEEN

"YOU WANNA GET GOING TO RIPLEY?" Hawk asked as he rolled out of bed.

"Yes, I think I've seen enough of this town." They got into their riding clothes and went down the stairs to the dining room for breakfast.

"Watch their faces when we walk in," Sophie said.

When they entered the dining room a few faces turned to look at them, then a few more, and soon the entire room was staring.

"Good morning, everyone," Sophie said with a big smile. No one responded. She and Hawk were ushered to a table in the back of the room where they ordered their breakfast. A large woman who sat at a close table turned and greeted them. "Good mawnin', I understand that y'all are Mister and Missus Owen," she said with a southern drawl.

"You're close," Sophie said, "I'm Sophie Boisvert and this is Hawk Owen. But we're not married."

"Y'all are not married?" the lady said. "But didn't you just sleep in the same . . ." She turned and went back to her meal. A hush came over the gathering. Then the soft mumble became clear. Heads turned their way and eyes glared at them. Sophie looked up from her plate, stabbed some eggs with her fork, and held it up in front of her with a big smile. Then in a loud voice she said, "These here are some mighty tasty vittles. Hey, waiter! Got any beer to wash this slop down with?"

Hawk leaned close to her. "What was that all about?"

"They can't stand the thought of two unmarried people sleeping in the same bed in their swanky hotel."

The waiter came to their table. "Madam, we do not serve alcoholic beverages in this hotel."

"What, no beer? That's inhumane."

"Madam," the embarrassed waiter said as he looked around the room, "I could bring you a mint julep if you would like." He leaned close. "Our mint juleps are made with ingredients that are rather pleasing to the pallet—if you know what I mean." He winked at her slyly.

She smiled at him and said in a loud voice, "Well, that's different. Bring me a tall mint julep and one for Hawk."

"As you wish, madam."

After breakfast they picked up their horses and mule and headed north along the river. After the first day riding, they camped on the banks of the Mississippi River outside of Little Falls, and the next day they rode out onto the flat prairie, staying on the west side of the river. The ground was flat and unremarkable for five miles on either side of the river. They rode past a church and through a small settlement called Elk City and one called Belle Prairie.

The weather was warm and Fort Ripley was quiet as they rode in. The fort consisted of several one-story buildings situated to form three sides of a square. The forth side of the square was open to the Mississippi River, and two unmanned cannon stood facing the river. There were block houses on two opposite corners of the fort from which cannon could command the four sides. On the east side of the fort stood a stockade made of up-ended logs. Between the buildings forming the square were openings, and through one of these Hawk and Sophie entered the fort.

They rode up to a man walking with the help of a single crutch. "Where can we find the commander of this fort?"

"We ain't got a commander. The company left for Dakota just last month. All we got here is cripples and sick men that can't fight."

"Who's in charge?"

"Lieutenant Holister. You might find him in that building." He pointed to a large frame structure on the northeast corner of the fort.

They rode to the building and knocked on the door. The door of the next building came open. "Can I help you?"

"Yeah, I'm Hawk Owen."

"Oh, come in. We've been expecting you, Marshal." He put out his hand, "I'm Lieutenant Holister. Welcome to our fort. Where is the rest of your company?"

"They're on their way. They should be here in a week or so."

"Well, we have plenty of room for you. All the able troops have been ordered to Dakota to fight the Sioux."

"You know about the Reverend Diggs deal?" Hawk asked.

"I know as much as I've been told, and that's not a lot. All I know is that you are looking for him."

"Do you know if he's been through here?"

"We think he has. A man and a woman who fit the description traveled through a week ago."

"Why didn't you grab him?"

"Didn't know he was here till he was gone. They had a wagon filled with household goods and were heading north like a thousand other people since the road was built, if you want to call it a road. There's nothing north of Crow Wing but Indians and wild country. The road is more like a mud bath through the heaviest forest in the state, and just around the next turn you'll find the wettest, flattest land you'll ever want to see. Most of it is sand and pines, but in the hardwoods it's mud that doesn't dry all summer. The trees keep it wet. And the mosquitoes and flies will drive you crazy. Plenty of deer up there to feed on, though."

"Tell me what you know about Diggs."

"I just did."

"Are there any other strangers in the fort?"

"Some pass through and some stay for a day or two, but no one has taken up residency." He raised his finger and pointed at Hawk. "Well, there is that old Frenchman who showed up a few days ago. He don't say much, just hangs around dirtying up the place. There's settlers coming in trying to get in on the land around the reserve. But the government backed out on the sales, and now they're all mad because they have to give up their places and go start again somewhere else."

"Is there any place close where we might find a cold beer?" Sophie asked.

"Beer and whiskey are not allowed on the reserve, but there are plenty of saloons in Crow Wing. John Camel's got a saloon a mile up the road, but you don't want to go there. Then there's Kathleen's place in Crow Wing where you could get one. Irish woman runs the place. Hard woman she is, too, as coarse as any of the soldiers around this fort. Damn good-lookin' woman, she is."

"Did you say you have a place we can stay?"

"Sure. You can stay in the officer's quarters next door if you want."

"How about the one closest to the stables?"

"Go right ahead. Make yourselves at home. Straight across the parade. Take any one you like."

As they left the lieutenant, they passed a dirty man standing close to the officer's quarters. Hawk nodded at him and he nodded back. The man was short and heavily built. His hair and beard were long and black, and he wore a faded red stocking cap on his head with the tassel hanging down the right side of his face, a long shirt of course wool, and a red bandana around his neck. He wore drop-front trousers that came to just below his knees, and striped stockings covered his lower legs. He followed them with black eyes that were barely visible under his eyebrows.

"Must be that old Frenchman the sergeant mentioned," Sophie said.

"He must think you're pretty good to look at the way he was eyeing you."

"I have a feeling any woman he sees is pretty good to look at."

They had stayed in the fort for two days waiting for the rest of the group to show up when Lieutenant Holister came to Hawk. "Some of the boys saw a feral boar out there in the pines. You wanna go hunting?"

"Well, hell yeah. I ain't been on a boar hunt in three years. When do we go?"

"Git yer stuff. We'll go right now while he's still in the area. These boys have been eating army rations and a good feed on fresh pig meat might do them some good."

"You coming along, Soph?"

"No, you two go ahead. I'm going to stay here and enjoy some peace and quiet."

"Suit yourself, but we'll probably be gone through the night."

"I can take care of myself. You just go."

Hawk was visibly excited about the prospect of hunting wild boar again and gathered his sleeping blanket and rifle.

Lieutenant Holister and Hawk walked out of the compound and across the prairie to the tall pines to the east. The forest floor was covered with a thick layer of pine needles, and their footsteps were practically silent. They knew, however, that the floor was even more silencing for the feet of the boar. Among the trees they found places where the boar had been rooting in the ground, perhaps for a ground squirrel or gopher or some succulent root that he'd sniffed out. They stayed in the woods through the night, hoping to get a shot at the boar when it started its daily search for breakfast.

Not long after Hawk and Holister had left, Sophie sat outside the cabin and watched the sun set behind the tall pines to the west of the fort. A few soldiers walked by, nodded, and wished her a goodnight. The fort got quiet as the men retired to their bunks. When the mosquitoes began to be bothersome she reluctantly went inside and got ready for bed.

She had just gotten into bed and was about half asleep when she heard her horse, Gorgeous, start to act up. She knew their horses were the only ones in the stable, and if someone was trying to steal horses, they'd go after the ones in the pasture.

Gorgeous kept up the noise. Sophie rolled to her other side and moaned in her half dream state, "Gorgeous, hush up!" and started to drift off again, but the horse continued making sounds of alarm. Sophie sat up in bed and yelled into the air, "It's the middle of the night, for God's sake, go back to sleep!"

Wide awake now, she sat up in bed and decided to check on Gorgeous. The mosquitoes had nearly eaten her alive when she came from the mess hall earlier, so she grabbed her buckskins for protection, slipped on her boots, and headed for the door. Once outside, she looked up at an incredibly bright sea of stars. The Milky Way appeared more like clouds stretching from one horizon to the other. She realized she should have been sleeping outside . . . but those damn mosquitoes!

Suddenly, a hand came from behind, cupping her mouth tightly, while a second pair of hands quickly tied a blindfold over her eyes. She felt a cloth being jerked through her teeth and tied behind her head. Then her feet were kicked out from under her and she fell hard to the ground, hitting her face and chin. Searing pain shot through her nose and she felt a warm stream of blood running toward her mouth. As she lay on the ground, someone grabbed her feet and tied them together at the ankles. *Well hell*, she thought, *I may not be able to see, but I can still use my legs to kick out and hopefully connect with at least one of them.*

It was the only action she could think of. She knew it wouldn't do any serious damage, but anger and panic had taken over rational thought. To her surprise, she managed to connect with something solid. She was stopped short by a hard kick to her back. Then she heard a man saying, "*Sacrebleu, méchante!* That hurt. That is my shin you kick!"

She smiled to herself despite the fact that she felt like throwing up from the pain. She could smell his foul breath as he took her face in his hand and brought his close. "You juss make it hard for yourself!" he said and sharply pushed her face away.

"Get your hands off her," she heard a voice say softly but very firmly. "We need her alive. Now get her out of here." She heard the sound of footsteps quickly retreating, then the sound of a horse galloping away.

Her assailant continued, "If you stop this foolish fighting, it will make things easier. I have no time to waste!"

She did not recognize the voice, but he spoke with a French accent. In a desperate attempt to increase any chance of escape, she tried to scream through her gag to get someone's attention. Her assailant grabbed her by the hair and jerked her head back. Again, she could smell his foul breath in her face.

She heard him laugh to himself. In a particularly wicked tone he said, "Dey tell me you are dee spirited one," he said. "I tell them it is nothing Jerard needs to worry for."

He put his weight on her as he tied a rope around her chest and under her arms, then he walked away. She thought he had left when she heard a sharp slap and the sound of hooves hitting the ground. An unexpected jerk ripped through her body and she realized she was being dragged behind a horse.

That bastard has no idea what kind of trouble he was getting into, she thought. She had an impulsive urge to laugh out loud, but the pain of being dragged on the ground by a horse at full speed kept her mind focused on the immediate situation. The sound of horse's hooves echoed behind her head and she could feel the earth as it came flying at her. She thought she might die from being kicked in the head by the horse, and she wondered how that would read on her tombstone.

She tried digging her boot heels into the ground to relieve some of the friction, but it required too much effort. In the back of her mind she knew Hawk would pick up the tracks.

She had no idea where the Frenchman was taking her, or *why* she was being taken. The feeling of not being in control was one she did not particularly care for.

The rope bit into her chest; her back hurt from the constant jolting; her wrists burned from being bound; her backside hurt from the friction between it and the ground. Her face throbbed from when she had fallen, and she could still taste blood. She was glad, though, they were staying on the grass rather than the road. The rope that tied her to the horse was short enough that it held her back and shoulders up and only her backside and legs dragged on the ground.

Sophie had never felt this sort of rage toward anyone. She tried to think of anything she might have that she could use as a weapon. At the time it happened she thought she was merely checking on a skittish horse, therefore there was no reason to bring weapons.

After what seemed an eternity, they came to an abrupt halt. She was not sorry they stopped, but she did wonder where they were and, more importantly, what was to follow. The man pulled her blindfold off. She could make out in the darkness that he was holding a knife and figured he was either going to slit her throat or cut her ropes.

As he bent down to do whatever he was going to do, Sophie started screaming through the gag, calling him a coward and a sawed-off son of a bitch. She thrashed with her feet, making it difficult for him to get near her. He backed away to avoid getting kicked and slowly said, "Hush, hush. It is true, my spirited little *fille,* that there were other ways to get you from dee fort. This was dee quickest and dee most fun for Jerard. You would not like to take all of Jerard's fun away, eh? I like my woman broke in, it makes for better— how you say—cooperation, no?"

He laughed at his humor, obviously pleased with how clever he was and how well the abduction was going.

She remembered her other abductor saying, "We need her alive." She wondered who the second person was, why he had left when he did, and where he was going. None of this made any sense to her.

The man knelt down in front of her, putting his weight on her lower legs, and cut the rope that was binding her ankles and chest, leaving her hands tied.

He said, "You will help now. I do not wish to carry you." He reached around and tugged at the knot at the back of her neck. "*Non,*" he said, "de gag, she stay."

She tried to ignore the pain and stiffness that was settling into her muscles and focus on the surroundings. They had come to the Mississippi, about two hundred yards north of the fort. All she could think of was that he was going to throw her in the river and hold her head under and watch her drown. She was frantically searching her mind for different ways to escape, and started making loud sniffing noises to get his attention. He tried to ignore her at first, but she kept it up until he stopped what he was doing, pointed his finger at her, and said, "Quiet. You do not want me to loose my temper, eh?"

He stepped toward her and she sniffed loudly again. He reached for the bandana around his neck and put it to her nose, "Blow that damn nose of yours. I do not want to hear anymore from you."

She managed to muster a good blow into the bandana and winced at the pain. He smiled at her and said, "You see? Jerard can be nice, if he wants." He looked at the bandana he was holding then quickly shoved it down the front of her shirt. "Here, you keep. A small gift from Jerard." He laughed as though he had made a good joke. "Do not ever say that Jerard give you nothing. You will owe me for dees." At this, Sophie realized that this man might be strong, but the vacancy sign on his forehead was possibly her ticket out.

He continued, saying, "And do not get any wrong ideas." His hand went to his side, fingering a long blade that hung from his belt. "I will not hesitate to use dees if I have to."

He slid the knife from the sheath and walked over to her, putting the point to her throat, and asked if she understood what he was saying. Looking directly at him, she nodded her head.

"*Bon*. Jerard would hate to have to use this on such a pretty face. Now we get in canoe; ferry no run at night."

The only light came from the canopy of stars, but this did not slow the Frenchman down. He moved with an aptness that comes naturally to those who spend most of their lives in the wild.

He told her with a quick motion of his knife to move in front of him and they walked a short distance to a small canoe. He picked the canoe up with little effort and placed it on the water's edge, making her climb in and move toward the bow. Keeping her center of balance as low as possible was challenging without the use of her hands. As she got in, the Frenchman walked back to where the canoe had been and picked up a gun. He then moved toward his horse and grabbed the reins leading it back to the canoe. He climbed in and tied the lead rope around the stern.

"Remember my friend?" he asked and touched the knife at his side. "It is no problem adding to its history. A little more blood will only give it more character." He stroked the barrel of the gun on his lap and said, "The same goes for Jerard's other friend." Then he laughed his wicked laugh.

She knew his were idle threats, since she'd heard the other man say he wanted her alive, and so she was determined to make this as unpleasant for him as she could.

The night was silent except for the sounds of the paddle as it entered the water and the horse swimming behind them. She thought about adding the sound of a canoe being tipped over, but decided against it, knowing that she wouldn't get far with her hands still tied.

To the left, she saw the Nokasippi River flowing into the Mississippi just a few yards away. They soon crossed to the opposite shore and climbed out of the canoe, the man quickly cut the ropes that bound her hands. She felt her arms and shoulders instantly relax. She thought about Posey's pine-pitch ointment and how good it would feel to have it rubbed into her sore muscles. She wondered if her body would ever be the same.

He pulled the gag off and said, "You scream or try to get away, you die." As he was leading his horse to shore, she slowly backed toward a small shrub just a few feet away, all the while facing him. She reached inside her shirt to get the bandana he had so graciously given her. Little did he know that one nice gift deserves another. The Frenchman's gift would be one red-headed, six foot Welshman with an attitude. When she reached the shrub she hung the bandana on one of the branches.

Watching her captor ready his horse made her think of Gorgeous and how she missed the mare. She imagined herself riding at full gallop across the prairie. She could almost feel the wind in her hair and breathe in the smell of the grasses. Then she became aware of Jerard's voice telling her to get on. When she approached his horse, he reached down and grabbed her arm, hoisting her up in front of him.

"Take it easy, damn it!" she said and pulled her arm away from him. She couldn't imagine being any sorer than she already was. When they started to move, she had to lean over the horse's mane to alleviate the pain in her backside. She tried not to fall asleep, but her eyes were not cooperating. Finally, consciousness slipped away.

Dawn was breaking when she opened her eyes and she knew that they had been riding for a couple of hours, following the river northeast. It was morning and Hawk would be returning about this time from his pig hunt, bearing fresh pork for the soldiers. How long would it be before he'd be on the trail hunting for her?

Hawk was close to tears and panic was taking over.

18

CHAPTER EIGHTEEN

HAWK RETURNED TO THE BARRACKS EARLY IN THE MORNING, tired and depressed at having failed in his hunt for the boar. He didn't find Sophie where he expected her to be, so he walked to the mess hall thinking she might be having breakfast with the troops.

Two soldiers walked out and moved toward their quarters. When he walked in, he saw no one there but the cook in the back sitting on a stool reading a book called *Hawk's Valley*.

"Has Sophie been in?"

"Nope," he said. "Ain't seen her today."

Hawk stood for a moment trying to think where she might have gone, then walked down to the river thinking she might be taking a swim, one of her favorite morning activities. She wasn't there. He walked around the fort and through the buildings and onto the prairie. He was getting worried and could feel desperation creep up on him. He ran from building to building, shouting her name. The men in the fort took up the search, but Sophie was nowhere to be found.

"Gotta get hold of myself here," he said to himself. "Think, think. Where would she go without telling me? Her horse—see if Gorgeous is there."

He ran to the stables and slid to a stop next to Sophie's mare. Now he was scared. He knew that Sophie would not be gone this long without her horse. He ran back to their quarters and shouted for her, getting no answer. The silence was frightening. He knew Sophie was in trouble and he had to find her. *How the hell do I find her in country I've never been in before?* "Who do I ask?" he said out loud. *For God's sake, use your tracking skills,* he thought to himself. *Find her tracks and follow them.* He started to circle the fort looking for her tracks, but there were so many from soldiers and horses that he couldn't pick hers out. As Hawk was studying the ground, the lieutenant came to him.

"We've searched every inch of this fort and there's not a trace of her."

"Well, she's got to be somewhere. People don't just disappear."

"Settle down, Marshal. We'll find her."

"Can you mount the troops and start a search?"

"These men are here because they can't ride. We can move around close to the fort, but we cannot ride."

"Well, you do what you can. I'm going lookin' for Sophie."

Hawk was close to tears and panic was taking over. He ran out of the fort and studied the ground there. He stopped when he saw fresh prints of a running horse in the sand and marks that looked like someone or something had been dragged across the ground. Blood rushed to his ears and his head came up as he followed the marks up the riverbank. Terror filled his soul to think that Sophie might have been dragged behind a horse. He followed the marks for four hundred yards to the ferry crossing, where he found signs of a struggle. He saw marks in the sand that were obviously made by a canoe being pushed into the water. There were also hoof prints leading into the water—and Sophie's boot prints. Sophie was at least alive. He shouted for her. It echoed up the river, but he heard no answer.

Suddenly, he remembered the recent stranger to the fort. "Where's that old Frenchman?" Hawk shouted as the men from the fort met up with him.

"He ain't in the fort, we know that. If he was, he'd be down here with us."

"He's got Sophie. He's got to be the one who's got her. Where would he take her? Anyone got a guess?"

They looked back and forth at one another and shook their heads. "North of here is Crow Wing, but I doubt he'd take her there," one man said. "Too many people. He might have taken her to Little Falls."

"He ain't going there," Hawk said. "He got in the water upstream from the fort. If he was going downstream he'da got in downstream. He crossed the river."

"How do ye figure that?"

"He took his horse. He ain't gonna swim a horse all the way to Little Falls. Where the hell would he take her, and *why* would he take her?"

"Hawk," the lieutenant said, "could this have something to do with Diggs?"

"Yeah, that could be. Diggs could'a got her," he paused. "But why?"

"Can't even guess at that, Marshal."

"Who knows this country best?"

"There's an old trapper up on the Nokay who might be able to tell you something."

"Where's he live?"

"Just follow the river east and you can't miss his place. He's got a run-down shanty right on the river just before you reach the hills."

Hawk turned and ran for the stables. He saddled his horse and Sophie's, and rode to the ferry landing. He walked his horse onto the boat.

"Did you ferry anyone across last night?" he asked the ferry operator.

"No, but I did hear someone swimming a horse across upriver a bit."

"When was that?"

"In the middle of the night. I don't know what time it was."

"Get me across this river as quick as you can."

"I can get you across, but I can't do it any faster than the river runs."

"Well, git going."

It seemed like a lifetime for the ferry to get across the river and as soon as they were close enough, Hawk ran his horses up the bank and onto dry land. An empty canoe had been pulled halfway onto land and fresh, wet sand in the bottom of the canoe told him it hadn't been there long. The small boot tracks in the sand could only be Sophie's.

He found a red bandana hanging on a branch of a nearby bush.

He knew Sophie didn't own a red bandana but remembered that the Frenchman they'd seen in the fort wore one around his neck, and that fueled his suspicion that the voyageur was involved.

There were plenty of tracks to follow, but the ones that made his heart beat faster were the fresh tracks of a running horse heading upstream. He followed them until they disappeared in the tall grass and brush along the river. The horse was easy to follow through the wet grass but when the sun rose and the wind picked up, the grass dried and he had no choice but to follow the river.

He galloped The Brute, trying to follow the winding river, but lost sight of it several times and had to go back to find it. The river twisted and turned through marshes and swamps—sometimes totally hidden by willows along its banks and other times widening into a shallow lake. The river's sinuous course made it frustrating for Hawk to follow and make good time.

Finally, he came to the trapper's cabin. He shouted across the river. "Have you seen anyone go by here?"

"Nope, no one's been by here today, leastwise not on the river. Might have gone by on land behind me, and if they did, I wouldn't have seen them."

Hawk walked his horse down the riverbank, into the water, and up the other side to the old man. "If someone was going up this crick, where would they be going?"

"Hmmm," the old man said, "that's a darn good question." He thought about it for a few seconds and said, "Well, Kelley's sawmill is up by Long Lake. That where they're headed?"

"I don't know where they're headed. It could be there or anywhere else."

"Could be they'd be going to the agency at Kathio or Mille Lac. Hell," he said, "they could be going to Superior, for that matter."

The mention of Superior put a fear in Hawk's mind that made him shake. *If it's Superior, Diggs is involved in it for sure*, he thought to himself.

"The river comes close to the road a ways up here; they might be heading there."

"Where does the road go?"

"Superior. And there's an abandoned trapper's cabin just down stream from Long Lake. Ye might check there."

"How far up is it?"

"A couple of day's ride if you know the country and ride hard. That's tough country for a horse. Plenty of hills and valleys and some big swamp country, too. If the man yer looking for knows this country, he's got a big lead on you."

"Do I just follow the river?"

"Well, if you can, you should, but it wanders through the woods and swamps, and it ain't hardly possible to stay right with it. Course you could take the trail a couple of miles north of here; that goes the same place yer going."

"No, I gotta stay on the river, that's where the tracks run."

"Suit yourself, just keep your animal's nose pointed northeast and find the river when you can. It'll take you there."

"Thanks, mister," Hawk said and turned his horses northeast.

He rode at a fast walk, keeping the river in sight as much as he could. The trees and brush were thick along the river and he was forced to dismount and lead the animals. He followed game trails where he could, but most were too small for the horses. He tried to follow logging roads that cut through the forest, but all too often they stopped abruptly, leaving him in dense new-growth with nowhere to go but backward to try another road.

Trees had been felled for lumber to build the fort and in those areas the underbrush grew thick and impenetrable. Stumps of fallen trees were everywhere, and the dried limbs that had been cut off lay on the ground where they had dropped.

A number of the brush piles had been burned, and the scorched earth beneath the horse's hooves threw up black dust that threatened to choke the life out of him. Flies and mosquitoes tormented him mercilessly. When he lost the river, he spent precious time moving in the direction he knew would take him back to it. Progress was extremely slow and frustrating, but he walked his horse till it was too dark to see the trail. He then laid out a blanket in a small opening in the brush and tried to go to sleep. Mosquitoes swarmed around him and he pulled his blanket over his head to keep them off.

When he closed his eyes, the image of Sophie's face appeared before him. He wanted to see her and touch her face. He wanted to run his fingers through her hair and touch her lips. He wanted to see her smile and kiss her lips and talk to her and hold her hand. He wanted to feel the soft skin of her neck, touch her below her ear, and see her tip her head to the side as he touched her. He wanted to see her eyes close and the soft smile come across her lips as he caressed her.

Hawk did not sleep that night. He had wanted to keep moving, but he couldn't see the trail in the darkness, and so the night dragged on eternally. He lay on the moist ground and began to shiver with cold, wondering if Sophie was cold. He wanted to go to her and wrap her in a blanket and cuddle with her to keep her warm. He could feel her warm body against his and taste her kisses and hear her breathing. He could smell her and see her and feel her— but all in his mind. He had never been so lonely.

"Even beautiful tings need to die sometime."

19

C H A P T E R   N I N E T E E N

WHERE THE HELL ARE WE GOING? Sophie desperately tried to find answers to the questions crowding her mind. She tried to think of anyone who would want her out of the way or needed money. Anyone who had the mind to do this would certainly know that Hawk would come for her. She would have to put these thoughts aside until she could think more clearly. She tried to focus on the birds that were singing. It was spring and the sound filled the woods. It was a sound that made her forget about her weary body for a few moments.

"Now we get down and rest," the Frenchman said. He climbed down first, then she swung her leg over the horse. She moaned loudly and collapsed right where her foot met the ground. "Dammit!" she said out loud. "Just give me a couple of weeks to rest here. Don't worry about me, you go on ahead."

"Huh?" He tilted his head. "Ah, *oui*. You funny lady. You make fun with Jerard; I like dat."

"Good," she said, "there is more where that came from," and under her breath, "jackass." He looked at her with an expression that made her realize he had no idea what she was saying. She decided to have a little fun and added, "It means handsome. You know the word 'handsome'?"

"*Ah, oui!* Jerard knows word. O*ui*, Jerard is handsome! Jerard is . . . jackass!"

"*Oui*," she said as she nodded her head.

She found an inviting spot in the sunlight and curled up against a huge pine tree. She felt a little more secure with something solid against her back. She curled her legs toward her body trying to conserve heat. She had no problem falling asleep. She didn't trust him, but her body took over and she couldn't argue. When she awoke, she saw some beautiful, white flowers blanketing the woods. Suddenly, those white flowers turned into hot, steaming potatoes with lots of butter. She shook her head to clear out the vision and thought, *Oh, my Gawd, I must really be hungry, or I am loosing my mind.* She settled for the first option. Nothing like a good drag behind a horse to make a woman feel really hungry.

She wished Posey were there. Posey had taught her about some of the plants that could be eaten in the wild, but she was still learning. Just then, her stomach growled. The sound caught the attention of the Frenchman who was sitting propped up against a tree with an empty brown bottle beside him. He had been drinking while she was asleep, and in a way she was glad. She thought that his fondness for liquor might make an escape easier—or perhaps, the opposite.

He looked over at her tying to focus his bloodshot eyes, then turned and started digging around in a small leather bag. He pulled out a slab of pemmican. She did her best to look the other way, not wanting him to know how hungry she was. He got up, staggered over to her, and stuck the pemmican in her face. He waved it back and forth in front of her nose and mouth. He was enjoying this game he was playing with her.

"Ah, my little one," he said, "you cannot fool Jerard—you are hungry."

"I don't need your food. I can find my own. Thanks for your concern."

He apparently did not know sarcasm, because he gave her a big, goofy grin and said, "You are getting to know what a real gentleman Jerard is. Dees deserves a drink!" He reached for a leather bag that was secured to his saddle and pulled out a buffalo horn. He took a large gulp and forced out a loud belch, then wiped his mouth with his sleeve. *Wonderful,* Sophie thought. *I love a guy with manners.* She immediately dubbed it the 'horn of plenty' because she hoped it would get him *plenty* drunk.

He continued drinking, belching, and laughing to himself. Sophie sat on the ground, watching him make a fool of himself. After a while, he came wheeling over to her, stinking of rum.

"*Pardonnez-moi, mademoiselle.* Where are my manners?" He slurred with another burp. He ran his sleeve over his bottom lip as he bent his head low to untie the tin cup attached to the sash at his waist. He went over to get a small wooden keg that was tied to his horse and poured the rum from the keg into the cup. Then he pushed the cup at her saying, "*S'il vous plaît, ma fille.* Trink. Dees ees good. Come all da way from Montreal."

When she didn't make a motion to take the cup, he bent down. "You trink viss Jerard, no?"

"You are right . . . no."

Just then, they heard the cry of a hawk circling above them. The next moment, a loud crack filled the air. Then he slurred, "See what a good shot Jerard eez?"

He walked over to Sophie, grabbed her by the arm, and yanked her off the ground. "Come," he said, as he pulled her along. "We go see what Jerard shoot."

Moving into the woods, he didn't seem to notice her stumbling, trying to keep up with him. Not too far along, he bent down to pick up a dead hawk. He held up the beautiful bird that had been alive just moments before, and without turning his head, gave her a menacing sideways glance.

"Look hard," he said. "Even beautiful tings need to die sometime."

She looked at the hawk he held and touched it, feeling the warmth that lingered. She fanned the beautiful red tail feathers outward, admiring them and the band that marked the chest running from one side to the other. Its eyes were half closed and she could still see the intelligence in them. The starkness of the blood covering the white chest seemed a perverse contrast.

With wet eyes she slowly brought her gaze up to meet his and said, "It took no talent or skill to bring this bird down. There was no reason it had to die."

She reached down and picked up some of the feathers that scattered the ground and tucked them into her shirt. When he saw her doing that, he laughed loudly and slapped his thigh saying, "What are you going to do, try to put dee damn bird back together again? I think that *you* are dee crazy one, not Jerard!"

As he looked at the bird, he said, "This will make a tasty meal, do you not agree?"

She took one step toward him, "You are not going to eat this hawk."

The Frenchman took a step backward with a look of confusion and surprise. He was not used to being told what to do by a woman. She walked to a tree and found a spot where two sturdy limbs met and placed the bird there. She closed her eyes for a moment and said a brief prayer to the Spirits who were now the keepers of its soul.

She had almost forgotten about the Frenchman her until he shouted, "You are crazy, I tell you. It ees only a worthless bird."

As he said this, from the corner of her eye Sophie caught a glimpse of a shadow darting between the trees not far from where they were standing. It gave her a strange feeling, as if she were somehow connected to whatever it was. She stood motionless with her eyes fixed on the spot.

The Frenchman stopped what he was doing, looked at Sophie's eyes, and followed her gaze to the woods where she'd seen the shadow. He glanced toward the woods then back at her.

"What? What you see up dare?" he said, looking back and forth from Sophie to the woods.

"Nothing," she said nonchalantly. "Just a jackrabbit."

"It ees time to go now." Pushing her back toward their camp, he reached into his saddlebag and threw some pemmican at her. "You eat dees now." She begrudgingly took it. He started gathering and packing his meager belongings.

Sophie could feel eyes watching them, as if they were being followed. She knew it wasn't Hawk or Jake, or the Frenchman would have been dead already. It felt more like Posey's eyes watching them. But Posey would not stay back in the woods either.

She knew Hawk was coming and wanted to leave some kind of sign. She reached into her shirt to get one of the hawk feathers she had placed there earlier. Something small and blue dropped out of her pocket. She picked it up and was quietly delighted to see it was one of the beads Hawk had given her. She took the bead and slid it up the shaft of the feather, then quickly stuck it in the bark of a tree. She walked away from the tree toward the horse and the Frenchman motioned her to get on.

They continued in a northeasterly direction, with the river still to their left most of the day. The vegetation was so thick at one point, they had to lead the horse down into the stream so they could continue. As they made their way down the embankment Sophie snapped a few of the tree branches behind her. It was not much of a clue, but doing something was better than doing nothing at all. When she got hold of a good branch, she pulled it until she was clear of it and let it go. The branch whipped back and slapped the Frenchman across the chops. She did it a half-dozen times and each time she smiled to herself.

They stopped briefly near a large rock that stood in the middle of the shallow river so the horse could drink and they could cool off. It was unusually hot for a spring day and the mosquitoes were plentiful, which added to Sophie's misery. Out of pure frustration she began yelling and swatting at the mosquitoes surrounding her. The Frenchman mimicked her, dancing around, imitating some of the words he was hearing.

She used this opportunity to place a bead on the shaft of another feather and stuck into a crack in the rock. She bent the shaft to let Hawk know they were taking the river and maintaining a northeasterly direction.

She stepped on something sharp and let out a yell, which got the Frenchman's attention. He stopped his dancing, and the imaginary music ceased.

He looked at her and asked, "Why do you stop? Jerard was having fun. Fun ees what I like. Why you stop?"

"I stepped on something sharp, that's all." She reached down to pick up a buff-colored rock with very sharp edges. She smiled to herself, thinking it could be quite useful.

"What ees it?"

She showed him the rock. "Just a pretty rock."

He started laughing and dancing around again between sips of liquor from his 'horn of plenty' singing, "Dee lady, she find pretty rock. *Une belle roche, une bella roche!*"

He stopped abruptly and said, "Now we go."

"And just where might that be? Maybe if you tell me, I might be of some assistance to you."

He stared at her as though she may have had a good idea, then got serious and said, "Ah, little one, you try to fool Jerard. That is not wise."

"Not wise? I'll tell you what's not wise—taking a woman from her bed in the middle of the night, dragging her across the ground, and taking her to some godforsaken place she does not care to go!"

He moved quickly for a man who had had too much to drink. The sting and force of his hand across her face sent her backwards into the water. As she hit the riverbed, the rock, her weapon, dropped from her hand.

"I have had enough out of your foul mout! You will learn your lesson. They cannot tell Jerard what to do or what not to do!"

He was on top of her in an instant and his hands clawed at her shirt as he pulled it upwards. She hit his face repeatedly with her fists, but it didn't seem to have any effect on him. As they tossed and turned in the water, one of her hands slapped and punched at him while the other frantically searched the bottom of the river for the rock. The strength in his arms and hands was incredible and she found trying to fight them useless as he started pulling at her pants.

For the first time she started to panic, but sheer determination took over. In the struggle, her hand landed on the rock. She picked it up and turned it so the sharp edge faced outward. She swung the rock out of the water directly at his face. The sharp edge slashed his cheek from his ear to his eye. He stopped short. Blood began pouring from the wound and for a moment she thought her retaliation had stopped him.

She took advantage of the moment and squirmed backwards far enough to follow his gaze upwards. There, on a rock above them, was an immense black wolf. She knew the wolf was the shadow she had glimpsed earlier. The hairs on his back were raised and his yellow eyes, glowing out of the black of his face, were fixed on the Frenchman. It stood perfectly still.

"Mon dieu!" cried the Frenchman, as he jumped out of the water and reached for his rifle.

"No!" Sophie sprang out of the water, trying to grab the gun, when she heard a shot ring out. The bullet flew toward its intended target, but the wolf was gone.

Suddenly, the image of Posey flashed through her mind.

"*Le lupe noir.* She ees bad omen. Dee bad spirits have sent it. But Jerard is not afraid," he said as he glanced upward to where the wolf had stood moments before. He looked at Sophie, then up to the riverbank. "You see Jerard kill wolf, *non*?" Another glance upward. "Now wolf runs to the woods to die like the coward she ees!"

She listened to his empty words and could hear the fright in his voice. She could see that he knew he hadn't killed the animal, and that he desperately wanted to believe he had.

Sophie knew there was something different about the wolf. It had appeared out of nowhere. Sophie had not had many experiences with wolves in her life, but her years told her to listen to her instincts. Her instincts told her to trust this black wolf.

"I am not done with you yet," the Frenchman said in a menacing voice. "But now we must go. You will pay for what you did." He wiped the blood from the side of his cheek then dug a handful of gray mud from the bank of the river. "I should kill you now, but you are worth more to me alive than you are if you are dead. It is not my choice." Then he slapped the mud on the wound on his cheek and rubbed it in.

She started toward the horse, then noticed a cedar tree close by. She walked over, pulled at the branches, and rubbed the needles over her face and neck, hoping to keep the mosquitoes away. This was something she had learned from Posey. The thought that she might never see Posey again brought stinging tears to her eyes.

The Frenchman slid into the saddle and pulled Sophie up in front of him.

They continued walking in the river where the horse had solid footing and they would be harder to track.

The Frenchman's hands slid around her middle and started to move upward toward her breasts. She slid her fingertips lightly over his hand as he moved upward and gently wrapped her hand around his. She pulled it up over her breast to her mouth, then bit down hard. He screamed and tried to push her off the horse, but his finger was clamped securely in her teeth. He hollered and pulled and swatted at her back, but she was too close to him for his swings to have any effect.

"Let go my finger!" he yelled. She let go and he pulled his hand away from her mouth. *"Mon Dieu! Vous êtes une femme folle!"*

Without turning around she said in a low voice, "Don't touch me again."

"I don't remember which way I was going!"

20   CHAPTER TWENTY

AFTER COUNTLESS PERIODS OF DOZING AND WAKING, the sky finally began to lighten and Hawk rolled out of his blanket, saddled the horses, and resumed his search. Riding was not practical in the dense undergrowth, so he climbed down and once again was afoot, leading the horses.

The river wound through the hills and swamps and he had to travel miles to cover even one mile as the crow flies. He twisted and turned and lost his way, but he always found his way back to the river.

He came to a place where the river ran through a tamarack swamp. The hills surrounding the swamp were high and rugged with impenetrable under-brush. He knew there must be a road following this river, but he couldn't waste precious time looking for it.

The banks of the river were too steep for the horses to cross and he was forced to double back to find a ford. He lost another mile getting across the stream. He crossed and re-crossed time and time again, eventually not knowing if the river was to his right or left. In some places he couldn't see the water from twenty feet away. The grass was five feet tall along the river, and outside of that, the willows, hazel brush, and trees concealed the water completely. At several places he fol-lowed the river around a curve, only to find it disappear; the river had changed its course, leaving oxbow lakes in the abandoned channel. It wasn't long before Hawk realized that there was no way in the world to stay with the river.

Hawk wished he had gotten more information from the trapper about the river. If he knew the river's source, he could go there in a straight line. But he knew that a man who has kidnapped a woman would not stay on the beaten path; he would keep to hidden trails. Hours passed as he came across swamps and bogs, circling them only to find more swamp or high, rugged hills. Out of sheer frustration he raised his head and yelled out to no one—only the heavy, empty silence that surrounded him.

Realizing that riding through the marshes and swamps could only lead to disaster, he decided to go northeast in as straight a line as possible and hope to find the river's source. As he turned his horses he saw another river to his left, flowing in the opposite direction.

He smiled to himself. *Nope*, he thought. *You ain't gonna fool me this time, Old River.* The river made another turn, but he stayed in a straight line, thinking he would come to it again. He rode over a tall hill and down the other side then walked his mount onto a narrow road. The road didn't lead in the direction he thought he should be going—this road went north and south. He stood in the middle of the road looking one way and then the other. He looked at his lengthening shadow, identifying north, but it didn't seem right to him. His mind and the river had him turned around. *North should be that way*, he thought, *but the shadows say it's that way.*

The day was coming to an end. It was frustrating for him to have to take the saddles off his horses again and wait out another night. "Dammit," he said to his horse, "if I hadn't gone on that hunting trip, none of this would have happened." He took the saddle off Sophie's horse and threw it to the ground. "If I'd taken Sophie with me, she'd be here with me right now. Hell, we wouldn't even be here, we'd be snuggled up in a warm tent . . . Aw, listen to me. Now I'm talking to a horse."

He rolled up in his blanket and lay awake thinking of the previous days and the boar hunt with the lieutenant. "Dammit!" he shouted. "Goddammit!" he shouted into the night air. "Goddammit!" Then he lay his head on the ground and fought to keep the tears from his eyes. "God, get this night over with so I can get moving," he pleaded.

He dozed off and saw a white light shine through his cabin window. He watched the light and just before he was about to sit up, a black horse in red harness, pulling a red sleigh appeared momentarily then disappeared. He woke up and realized it was just a dream. He rolled over and tried to get to sleep, but sleep would not come. The night dragged on and on—silent, empty, nothing moving but an occasional, cool breeze passing over him.

Hawk awoke to the raucous call of a crow. The sky was gray in the east and although he could see very little, he threw his blanket off and saddled the horses. He traveled through the dawn and watched the sun come up and the sky turn blue. His trail took him back to the road. *If Sophie's kidnapper took this road, which way would he go?* His senses told him north, so he kicked The

Brute and moved down the road at a canter. Keeping his eyes on the road for tracks Hawk realized he was seeing only *old* tracks. He turned The Brute around and galloped back to where he had come onto the road. He then realized that he had lost Sophie's trail. Once again, he turned around. He had missed the point where he came out and realized that he was retracing his own tracks.

"God!" he said out loud. "I don't remember which way I was going!" He stopped the horse and took a deep breath, turned in the saddle and saw two sets of hoof-prints in the road. "Sophie!" he hollered, and jerked the reins to turn The Brute around. Hawk was not a man to pray for help, but he knew he needed it at this time. "Oh God," he prayed out loud. "Help me find Sophie. Please dear God, let her be alright." The wind blew his tears back along the sides of his face. He galloped until the double set of tracks came to an end. Now there was just one set of tracks. Furious with himself, he realized he was following his own tracks.

Through the maze of panic he told himself that Sophie is just around the next bend, or just over this next hill, or right ahead of him. He rounded a curve in the road and ran smack into two riders, one male, and one female. In a split second, he saw that the woman was Indian and not Sophie, so he kept moving at a fast gallop. Over the thunder of The Brute's hooves he heard a faint call. He turned in the saddle and looked over his shoulder. Fifty yards behind him he saw a man riding hard toward him. He kicked The Brute to stay ahead of the man, but he could hear the hoof-beats getting closer. Suddenly, he felt his shirt being pulled backwards.

"Hawk! Stop this crazy animal a-fore ye kill 'im."

Abruptly, Hawk found himself flying backwards through the air as someone jerked him from the saddle. He landed on the ground on his back, scrambled to his feet, and ran to the man on the horse. He jumped up and knocked him to the ground then ran around the terrified animal and went to jump on the man's chest when the man rolled to the side and got to his feet. Suddenly, Hawk felt something hard and heavy hit the side of his head and saw a bright light flash in front of his eyes. He fell to the ground and in an instant the man was sitting on his chest holding his arms to his sides. "Settle down, ye crazy redhead! It's me."

As Hawk's eyes began to focus he saw a familiar, sunburned face. "Git off'a me! Sophie's just up this road. I gotta go find her!"

"Sophie ain't up this road. We jiss come from there, and there ain't no one there but a scraggly old wolf."

Hawk thrashed under Sunkist's weight and screamed, "Let me up. I gotta find Sophie!"

"Sophie ain't up this road. Yer goin' the wrong damn direction."

"Where'd she go? I gotta find her!"

Posey walked up and knelt next to the two men. She put her hand on Sunkist's shoulder and laid one hand on Hawk's forehead. Immediately, Hawk settled down and became quiet. "What's going on, Sunkist? Where's Sophie?"

"I got no idea where she is, son. The lieutenant at the fort said she was took away and you was out lookin' for her. We figured we'd come'n help. Jake will be comin', too, soon as he gets to the fort."

"I don't need no help! Let me up, Sunkist, this is my own mess!" Hawk was again thrashing under Sunkist.

"You settle down, boy, or I'm a-gonna heff'ta hitchew ag'in."

Posey touched Sunkist's arm and handed him a cup. He was about to splash it on Hawk's face when Posey stopped him and said, "He drink."

He looked at her for a moment and she nodded back. He held the cup to Hawk. "Here, son, you need to drink this, then we'll go find Sophie."

He let one of Hawk's arms loose, and Hawk took the cup. He drank the contents, threw the cup off the road, then swung a fist at Sunkist. Sunkist caught his arm before it could land the blow and trapped it beneath his knees. "Just settle down, Hawk. We'll find her."

Hawk's eyes suddenly lost their fire. Sunkist pulled him to his feet then had him lay on a blanket next to the road. He held Hawk's arms down and asked, "When's the last time you had anything to eat?"

"I don't know and I don't care. Let me up."

"You ain't ett in two days, have ye?"

"I ain't got time to eat. Let me up!"

"You ain't goin' nowhere till you git some grub in your guts."

"Sunkist, please, let me up. I gotta find Sophie."

"Boy, you jiss went crazy onna conna you ain't et. We'll go find Sophie in a few minutes."

Posey handed Sunkist a strip of venison, and he put it to Hawk's lips. Hawk bit into it and started to get up.

Sunkist pushed him down. "Jiss lay still, boy."

He stared up at Sunkist and Posey with eyes that showed no feeling. His eyelids fluttered then slowly closed and he began softly snoring. Posey and Sunkist silently moved away and laid down for a rest. "That whar some powerful medicine ye give 'im," Sunkist said.

21

CHAPTER

TWENTY-ONE

SOPHIE AND THE FRENCHMAN HAD BEEN RIDING for most of the day and Sophie was not afraid to let him know how uncomfortable and hungry she was. Her wet buckskins rubbing back and forth on the saddle added to her misery. They had been living off a few roots and offerings from the woods—and the spoiled pemmican.

She turned around in the saddle to speak to him. She was so close, she could smell the rum on his breath. "If you don't mind, I would love to get off this horse and wash up and use some of those bushes over there." He reeled back slightly and looked at her, studying her as if deciding that, yes, it did look like she needed to wash up.

"Okay, we rest. But do not forget, Jerard and his friend here will be watching you." His hand dropped to his side and touched his gun.

"Lucky me," she said softly. She slid off the horse and collapsed into the water onto her knees. She cupped her hands into the cool, clear water and drank all she could, then splashed some of it onto her face where it felt swollen. She wanted to take off all of her wet garments and soak for about a week. She decided on the next best thing and took off her boots and sloshed through the stream then limped up the bank on the other side to find a suitable bush. She squatted and peered through the branches toward the Frenchman. Sure enough, just like he said, he was watching her.

"Can't a woman have any privacy?" she yelled through the bush.

Crossing back over the river, she sat on a rock and slipped her boots on. Then she turned toward the Frenchman and caught his eyes. He was sitting cross-legged against a tree.

She jumped up and ran as hard as she could directly at him without taking her eyes off his. He saw her coming and his mouth dropped open. In a flash, he was on his feet running away from her. He ran about five steps, stopped, and quickly ran back to his rifle. He picked it up and pointed it at her, but by that time she was walking and brushing dirt from her clothing like nothing had happened.

He let the rifle down and said, "Jerard does not like any of dees. I cannot drink like I want, cannot sleep when I want, cannot have fun when I want. Being around a woman like you is too much worry. Jerard ees not use to so much worry. Jerard likes things when *he* wants, don't like someone else telling me what to do. And you do not listen to me, only wag your tongue like a little puppy dog's tail. Ha! Dat ees good. Jerard ees funny!" He laughed, amused at himself. "You talk too much. You make me tired. You are not the kind of woman I like. I never know what you tink, or what you do next. *Tu me fait stupide dans l'tête.*"

"Don't blame me for your stupidity," she said. "You can thank nature for that."

He turned to walk away from her, stopped and said, "*Tien!* It will give me great pleasure to be rid of you."

She had gathered that the "someone else" he mentioned not only referred to *her*, but to somebody who was pulling all the strings. The fact that she was worth more alive than dead meant that he needed to deliver her still breathing. Obviously, he was hired to do someone else's dirty work. She wondered who could be behind all of this. *Is it Diggs?* It had to be someone who wanted something badly, and money was a powerful motivator.

Soon they were back on the horse, heading north. As they rode along, she watched the Frenchman looking into the woods searching one side of the river, then the other. She knew he was looking for the wolf even though he denied that it had scared him.

Sophie felt a sharing of spirits with the wolf and did not feel any fear. It seemed to be *protecting* her. Once in a while, from the corner of her eye, she would catch a glimpse of something moving in the woods, but by the time she looked, she saw only the movement of the wind blowing the brush, creating shadows.

As the day passed, she had a hard time keeping awake in the saddle and welcomed the fact that night was approaching.

"We will sleep here for the night."

"You won't get any argument from me."

"Ha, some things I do not believe. That ees one. I will make small fire."

She looked around for a spot that would offer some comfort. Her body ached and she felt chilled from being wet and tired. She located a cedar tree and pulled off enough branches to make herself a bed underneath, then curled up against the night. She tried staying awake for as long as she could. The last thing she remembered was the Frenchman sitting down, leaning against a tree with his 'horn of plenty' tipped to his mouth. His face glowed as he sat staring into the fire, singing softly. She recognized some of the melodies from the time she'd spent canoeing home with the French Voyageurs. Most of the songs he sang were melancholy, but once in a while he would laugh to himself. Then he'd raise his rifle, point it her way, and snicker quietly. She knew she had to be careful; in his drunken state he was perfectly capable of shooting her, even if accidentally.

Many dreams haunted her that night. She heard Hawk's voice telling her not to worry. Then she dreamed of him kissing her. It was so real she could feel the warmth of his lips and his arms around her. Then the dream switched and Posey's face appeared, changing, and wavering into a face that was almost animal-like. In her dream she sensed that Posey was trying to tell her something, and she could feel the warmth of her breath and a soft, soothing panting.

She was then abruptly pulled out of her dream by the Frenchman's rough voice, "Come now, we must go." He threw her a small piece of pemmican.

"It ees too bad I must keep you alive. I would have such a time watching you die. Now eat."

She looked at the pemmican and imagined it was a seven-course meal, complete with dessert. She could almost taste the ice cream and the fresh, sweet tang of strawberry juice running down her chin as she bit into one.

"Come!"

The image quickly disappeared.

She thought about her dream. It had a certain quality, a depth that was different from any dream she could remember. The realness of the warm breath on her neck and the soft panting made her believe it was more than just a dream. There was a truth in it, and she was determined to find its meaning. Posey had taught her to listen to her dreams.

They rode for most of the day following the river. Jerard would dismount from the horse now and then to guide him around boulders, but most of the time he sat behind her, like he had done for most of the journey.

"We are close now," he said, interrupting Sophie's thoughts.

Her head came up and she peered into the woods as they climbed the bank of the river. The forest was thick and the breeze blew through the pines, making a soft, whispering sound. As they got closer, the form of a small shack took shape. She felt a certain foreboding. The only thing she welcomed was the fact that they had stopped riding. She was exhausted, hungry, sore, and in need of a nice, hot bath with lots of suds.

They entered a clearing with a cabin. After taking her down from the horse, the Frenchman opened the door and allowed Sophie to walk in ahead of him. As soon as she was inside he grabbed her and threw her to the floor. His powerful arms pulled her hands behind her back and tied them tightly.

"What the hell are you doing?" she yelled.

"Jerard has had enough of your tricks. You will not play your foolish games with me anymore." He pulled her to her feet and sat her on the only chair in the cabin, then pulled a scarf through her teeth and around the back of her neck. "You will stay there and do not talk. Do not come off that chair or Jerard's friend here will make sure you do not bother me again." He waved his blade in front of her face. "Do you hear me, foolish woman?" Sophie said nothing. She glued her eyes to his and didn't blink.

The Frenchman moved around the cabin as if he was not sure what he should be doing next. Sophie had not taken her eyes off him since they arrived. It made the man very uncomfortable having her stare at him so intensely. In the dim lantern light her eyes seemed to take on a glowing, yellowish hue, like those of a wild animal. They belonged to a dog or a wolf. Yes, that was it . . . they reminded him of the eyes of the black wolf—watchful, patient, and keen. There was something hidden behind that stare. He wanted to go over and blindfold her, but he did not like being that close to her. She had not made any kind of sound and her silence unnerved him. *What the hell ees wrong with her?* he thought to himself. *She ees not right.* It was as though she had completely gone into herself. He was starting to lose interest in the entire situation. He had done this for the money only, but judging by her behavior, or lack of it, he seriously doubted it was worth it.

Perhaps, he thought, *if I cut her bonds, she will run away, and I will be done with her.* She had the look of a captive animal that had been caged too long. Her hair hung straight down to her shoulders in dirty masses. She certainly had to be getting weak from lack of nourishment and was no threat to him. But what got to him most were those eyes peering up from under her bangs. Those animal eyes, studying him, patiently waiting . . . for what? An involuntary shiver made its way up his spine.

He had always done as he pleased with women and he could always read their thoughts. But not this one. This one had him scared. *What the hell ees wrong with her?*

Then, from a distance, the air was split by the sound of a single, low, long, ascending howl. Jerard shivered again; he knew it was the black wolf he had seen earlier. He quickly glanced at Sophie and he thought he saw a hint of a smile.

"Pah! Jerard ees not afraid of old wolf. I will cut her up into small pieces for my dinner." A second mournful call followed, but this time it came from right outside the window.

"But, but . . . how can dees be? Only one moment ago, she was by dee lake, no?" Silence returned and the only sound was the wind through the pines outside and the "keer, keer" call of a red tailed hawk soaring from above. Now they could hear the sound of the wolf circling the cabin. Jerard stood perfectly still as he listened.

"What does it want? Why does it do this?" He looked out the window trying to get a glimpse of the creature. There, a few feet away, sat the black wolf with yellow, piercing eyes staring back at him. Jerard jumped back from the window. "*Mon Dieu!*" he shouted. "Dee wolf, she ees right out dee window."

Sophie's eyes showed no emotion but the corner of her mouth turned up slightly.

Jerard went to the window again. Even though he was looking right at it, it was as if the wolf was not physically there. There was an unearthly presence surrounding it, which made him uneasy and he wanted to flee. But in his mind, only a scared rabbit would do such a thing. As he stood there peering out the window at the wolf, he caught his own image reflected in the window, melding into the face of the wolf. Instantly, the reflection turned back to his own frightened face—the face of a coward.

Wasting no time, he approached Sophie and paused in front of her, his mind made up to free her from her bonds. "Now, you be good girl. I take dees tings off you." He walked behind her and, working quickly, started cutting the scarf he had tied through her mouth. He abruptly stopped and backed away as he heard a low, guttural sound like a growl coming from her throat. *She ees acting more and more like a wild animal. I turn her loose. She ees bad omen like de black wolf.* He reached down and cut the rope binding her wrists.

"It ees no use keeping you here. They cannot tell Jerard what to do. I wait no more. I set you free. You understand Jerard?"

Silence followed his question; only the haunting call of a loon answered back. For a brief moment he felt sorry for her, but this feeling passed just as quickly as it had come.

She ees a creature who needs no sympathy. Without hesitation, he cut the rest of the ropes that secured her to the chair and repeated his question. He wanted to be sure she had heard his generous offer of freedom. Without a sound he watched as her head rose slowly and traced his entire form with her eyes from his feet to his face. She stopped when her eyes rested on his. Keeping their gaze, he slowly backed away from her and kept what he thought was a good distance. *What am I worrying for? What ees she going to do to me? Why then do I feel like the prey?*

He released her from her bonds and she slowly got up from the chair, keeping some distance between them. He soon realized that she was circling him, always at the same distance, never taking her eyes off him. Standing in the middle of the cabin, he followed her movements, turning slowly with her. She was crouched over as she moved, her back slightly curved. There was a slight upper curve to one side of her lips, exposing some of her teeth. In the dim light her eyes took on a yellowish glow from within. He knew she was just playing with him. *Wait*, he thought to himself as he sucked in a rush of air. *That ees it. She ees playing with me, like a predator plays with his prey . . . right before the kill.*

Caught off guard, he felt her weight on him. He heard himself gasp as he fell violently backwards, and then the sound of his dagger hitting the floor. Sophie wasted no time as she reached for it, feeling the sweet coolness of the handle.

But she wasn't quick enough. In the brief time it took her to reach for the knife, the Frenchman was gone. He did not care that he was acting like an animal on the run with its tail between its legs as he headed for the trees. The woods took on a twilight mask as the moon ascended, casting strange shadows into the night. Jerard ran through the trees, and although it was light enough to see, he found himself stumbling. He stopped when he reached a clearing, tried to catch his breath, and realized how foolish he was acting. Just as a loud laugh escaped from his lungs, a large black shadow, approaching at great speed, emerged from the woods. He felt his back slam onto the ground, then the weight of the black wolf on his chest. He could feel the hot breath in his face, and its yellow, glowing eyes burning into him. His throat fit perfectly between the wolf's jaws and Jerard knew that instant death would come with the slightest effort from the wolf.

He was mentally preparing to die when he heard a woman's voice. His eyes followed the sound and he saw Sophie step into the clearing. Her eyes were like those of the wolf and her voice was soft and distant. She spoke directly to the guardian wolf. "Let him go."

The black wolf's massive head turned up towards Sophie and as their eyes met, her eyes lost their yellow color and returned to normal. The weight of the wolf on the Frenchman's chest vanished. In the same moment, a young Indian girl stepped out from the woods, "My work here is finished, he will not bother anyone again. This man has been touched in his mind by the White Painted Lady." Then she turned and disappeared into the forest.

It took a moment before the Frenchman realized he could get up freely. Frightened, and half-crazed, he took off into the woods, and all was quiet, save for the call of a great horned owl.

Sophie looked at the knife she was holding and was grateful that she did not have to use it to defend herself. She decided to keep it and turned back in the direction of the small cabin. Exhausted, she took only a few steps, then collapsed to the ground. Sleep came instantly to her and the events of the last few days intertwined themselves in her dreams. The vision of the spirit wolf came to her once again, comforting her, protecting her, and a feeling of peace enveloped her.

When she opened her eyes the sun was in the western sky.

"Good day, young lady," a man's voice said.

It took a few seconds for her to realize that she was not alone. She sat up quickly and slid back up against the tree.

"Don't worry," a man said. "We're friendly. We're not going to hurt you."

Standing before her were four men—one an Indian and the rest dressed in clean, pressed clothes.

"Who are you?" she asked.

"We're on our way to Kelly's mill. Do you know where it is, by chance?"

"No, I have no idea where it is. I'm on my way back to Fort Ripley. Can you tell me where the road is? I got turned around back there."

"Yes," the man said. "We have been on it for several days now. You can ride with us if you'd like."

"I lost my horse and I'm on foot."

"Are you traveling alone?" the man asked.

"No. I have friends out looking for the road."

"Well, you come with us and we'll find your friends and the road."

Sophie was not sure how to handle this situation and agreed to go with them. If they meant her harm, at this point it would make no difference if she went with them or not. She decided to gamble on the chance that the men were indeed, friendly. She remembered what Sunkist had said; it's best to keep an enemy where ye kin see 'im so's he cain't sneak up on ye an' shoot holes in yer hide.

The man looked up at the sky and said, "We have a few hours before dark. I suggest we make as much time as we can before night."

"How far is the road?" Sophie asked.

"We can be there well before dark," he said and got to his feet. "Shall we?"

They mounted their horses and put Sophie on a pack mule. They traveled along the shore of the lake on an Indian trail until the sun set below the treetops, then they set up a small camp.

Sophie, still suspicious of the situation, moved to the outer edge of the camp. One of the men went behind her and stopped her. "Where are you going?" he asked.

"I have to go into the bushes," she said.

"I think you should just stay right here with us," he said.

Sophie turned and started to run, but ran directly into a man standing behind her. He grabbed her hands and held them behind her back.

She kicked at the men, trying to connect with that vulnerable organ that would cause any man to forget what he was doing. Her effort was in vain and she was dragged to the ground and tied once again.

"Who are you people and what do you want from me?"

"Oh, you'll be made aware of that in due time. Just relax. Nothing is going to happen to you if you just be quiet and wait."

Darkness fell and one of the men gathered sticks and started a fire with flint and steel. Sophie saw that across the lake, another fire began to burn. No one else seemed to notice.

"If you don't mind," Sophie said, "I need to go into the bushes."

The man untied the ropes and tied one end of a longer rope around her neck, the knot in the back. "Don't go too far," he said. "It's a short rope."

Sophie started toward the bushes walking a sinuous path to put her body between their fire and the fire across the lake several times as she walked. The fire across the lake went dark and flared each time she blocked the firelight. She then knew Hawk was on the other side of the lake and that he would come for her. She went to the bushes and stood for a few minutes, watching as the fire across the lake died out. Hawk was on his way.

She went back to the camp and sat down next to the fire. "Are you religious men?" she asked.

"No, not really. Why?"

"Maybe you should start saying a few prayers."

"Ye never know who you're going to find out here."

22

C H A P T E R

T W E N T Y - T W O

A FEW DAYS EARLIER, the heat of the morning sun woke Hawk.

"How ye feelin', son?" Sunkist asked as Hawk's eyes opened. "Posey jiss give you some of her medicine to help you get some sleep. It's somethin' the Injuns down south . . ."

Suddenly, Hawk sat up and scrambled to his feet. "I gotta git movin'!"

"Jiss take it easy. We'll go look for Sophie after we eat somethin'."

"We can eat on top of the horses."

"We can do that. Git The Brute saddled and we'll git movin'. Where do ye think she went?"

"I don't know. All I know is some old Frenchman got her. I got no idea where or why."

"We're goin' with you," Sunkist said.

"We can't all go crashing through that brush."

"Ye figger she's up this road somewhere?"

"Sunkist, I don't know where she is. Are the rest at Ripley?"

"They wasn't there when we left to find you, but they should be comin' along anytime now."

"I'm not hanging around here waiting for them. I gotta move while the trail's still fresh. You wait here for them, then follow my trail. It ain't gonna be easy but you can do it. Just stay close as you can to the river."

"Well, I ain't jiss sittin' here, neither," Sunkist said. "And there ain't no call fer all of us bein' on the same trail. We'll go up this road and see where it goes. Might be someone up there knows something."

They walked their horses up the road, side by side, looking for the place where Hawk had come onto it. Suddenly, they heard a gunshot from somewhere off to the east. It made Hawk's heart jump and he turned in the saddle to look in that direction.

"Prob'ly jist someone takin' a shot at dinner," Sunkist said.

A glint of sunlight caught Posey's attention. She turned toward the edge of the road and picked a hawk feather out of the bark of a tree and handed it to Hawk. A blue bead had been slipped over the shaft of the feather. Hawk was suddenly gripped by powerful emotion. "Oh God!" he said out loud. "She's alive! Which way? Which way?"

His heart throbbed and tears pooled in his eyes. He wiped his eyes dry with his shirtsleeve and searched for another sign but saw nothing. There were too many tracks on the road from horses and mules and wagons to find any particular one. He got down from The Brute and searched the ground. Posey touched his arm and pointed at the track of an unshod horse. They followed it until they found that the tracks went into the woods.

"They go there," Posey said.

"We can't all go through this stuff," Hawk said. "I've been in there and it's too damn thick. Three of us can cover more ground separately than we can all together. You go up the road. Maybe this trail comes out on the road somewhere up ahead. If it does, you'll be there waitin' for him when he shows up."

Hawk turned his horses into the woods. He was back on the right trail now, he was sure of it. A lump grew in his throat thinking that he might be just a few hours or even minutes from Sophie. The brush along the trail was thick and there would be no riding on top of his horse.

In his imagination he pictured what he would do when he found them. First he'd kill the Frenchman, then take Sophie home. Simple as that.

The trail led back to the river, and there, in a crack in a rock, he found another hawk feather with a blue bead on the shaft. The stalk had been broken and it leaned to the left, upstream. He knew she was telling him which way she went. Wolf and raccoon tracks led into the water then out and disappeared into the forest.

He would have run his horses up the stream but the banks were steep and slippery, and the brush was too thick. He was forced to walk slowly, keeping an eye on the ground for tracks. But there were no tracks. *Could they be riding in the middle of the river? Of course; that's why she left the feather. She knew I wouldn't be able to find her tracks in the river bottom.* He looked back. "They went into the river back there," he said to himself.

He turned The Brute and Gorgeous back to the place where he'd found the feather. He went into the creek and found solid footing in the rocky bottom. At that time of the year the river ran swiftly in the narrow channel and kept the bottom clear.

He smiled to himself at the thought of communicating with Sophie, even though he had no idea where she was. He continued upstream twisting and turning and having to go up onto dry ground at times. He saw a few horse tracks that told him he was on their trail. When he found a place where they might have climbed out of the river, he stopped and studied the ground for tracks. Under a cedar tree he found a bed make of cedar branches, the way Posey had taught them all to do. He could feel that he was close to her.

The Nokasippi ran fairly straight at that point but it was completely surrounded by marsh and swamp. He rode into the hills catching an occasional glimpse of the river.

After only two more hours of riding he saw a small log cabin and behind it, a lake. He stepped off The Brute and moved quietly to the cabin, keeping himself hidden in the brush. There was no movement around the cabin and no sounds came from inside, so he slowly slid toward the open door and glanced quickly around the inside. It was empty except for a bed on one side, and a table and chair, and a small stove.

In the dirt around the cabin he found Sophie's boot prints . . . and wolf tracks. *What would a wolf be doing so close to the cabin?*

He fought the urge to call out her name, knowing it could be disastrous for her. He moved around the cabin, looking for clues indicating where she might have gone. Then he went inside, and on the floor just inside the door, he found her belt sash.

He ran out the door, got hold of Gorgeous, got on his horse, and went down to the river. He followed it upstream to where it flowed out of Long Lake. He desperately searched the ground for tracks. By the lake he found fresh marks left by a canoe. He looked up, fearing that they might have taken the canoe and crossed the lake. If they had, it would take him days to circle the lake to find where they went. He climbed onto The Brute and started up the shore of the lake on the sand beaches, and where there was no beach, he went into the water.

The rest of the day he followed the shore and that night he made his bed on a bluff overlooking the lake. Darkness fell and the air turned cold. He built a small fire and sat close.

Across the lake he saw quick flashes of light. Light flashed several times, and then he saw a small glow, then a fire. He wondered if it could be Sophie and her captor. All at once, the fire went out, then immediately flamed again. Three times this happened, then stopped. His heart jumped into his throat as he remembered the time on the bluff overlooking the Minnesota River Valley when Sophie played a game with someone miles away. She would hold her blanket up to block the firelight, then lower it, and wait for the other person to do the same. He remembered they did that for five minutes before stopping. Tears filled his eyes and his breathing became deep and quivering.

He grabbed his blanket and held it up between his fire and the one across the lake, then lowered it. The fire on the other side disappeared and then reappeared. He repeated his signal and the person on the other side did the same. He knew then that it was Sophie and he wanted to shout to her . . . but she was probably not alone. If she were alone and saw his fire, she would shout to him, but there was no call from across the water.

Quickly, he saddled The Brute and Gorgeous and led them around the lake toward the campfire. The air was cool and damp along the lakeshore. As he came closer, he realized he could not keep the horses quiet, so he led them up the bluff and let them graze as he moved closer to the light. He jumped at the sound of a deer barking and stopped to listen. A hiss from somewhere in the darkness caused him to drop to the ground and lay flat. Again, he heard the hiss.

He hissed back.

"That you, Hawk?" he heard Sunkist whisper.

"Yeah, it's me. Where y'at?"

"Jiss keep a-comin'. Posey sees ye."

He moved quietly toward the voice. "That's Sophie out there. I don't know if she's alone or with someone."

Posey pulled at Sunkist's sleeve. She spoke to him in Cherokee and moved off into the night.

"She's goin' te see who's out there."

"Either one of us could'a done that. She didn't have to do it."

"Posey can sneak up on a jackrabbit on a frozen lake. She'll be back quicker'n a bunny's ass."

"Is Jake here?" Hawk asked.

"He's out there movin' around tuh the other side."

"You got a plan?"

"Yeah. We planned on waitin' here till *you* git here."

"How'd you know I was comin'?"

"Figgered you bein' good at trackin' an' all, you'd be showin' up sooner or later."

They sat and waited until Posey returned. "Sophie there," she said. "This many men." She held up four fingers. "They fight."

"What do you mean they fight?"

"Talk loud. Do like this." She held her fists up and shook them at Sunkist.

"They're fightin'. I like that; it'll make things easier fer us."

"Is the Frenchman there?"

She looked at Sunkist. He translated the question.

"She don't know what a Frenchman is."

"Small man," Hawk said as he indicated to her with his hand held level with his shoulders.

"No," she said and indicated taller men.

"How we gonna do this?"

"Wanna jiss walk in and take her?"

"We probably could if we knew what they was up to. But we don't. I say we git close and git the drop on 'em, *then* walk in."

"Let's go. You move straight in. Me an' Posey, we'll go around tuh the other side. Posey'll bark like a deer when we git ready."

Slowly and quietly they moved toward the camp. As he came to the edge of the woods, Hawk stopped and lay on his stomach, awaiting the signal. He could see Sophie sitting on the ground behind the men. An involuntary rush went through his body at seeing her again—alive. Her hands were tied and she looked tired, but her eyes were wide open and alert. The man sitting close to her reached out to touch her, but pulled back as her feet flashed out and kicked him hard on the thigh. He laughed at her fearlessness.

Hawk lay still and listened to the muffled sounds of angry voices coming from the camp. He searched the camp for the Frenchman. He would have been the first one to die if things came to shooting. But he was nowhere to be found.

He heard the bark of a deer. It was the signal he was waiting for. He rose to his feet and started forward. He'd taken five steps when he felt the cold steel of a gun barrel against his neck.

A hand reached around from behind and took the rifle from his hand. Then he was urged forward by his unseen captor.

The sky began to lighten as he was ushered into the camp. Hawk looked at Sophie and very slightly shook his head, indicating that she not to say anything. She looked down at the ground.

"Who are you?" a man asked.

"Just looking for a cup of coffee," Hawk responded.

"Why do you think you have to sneak into a camp for a cup of coffee?"

"Ye never know who you're going to find out here."

"Well, you found the wrong people."

"Alright, I'll just turn around and leave then."

"Like hell you will. You're staying right here."

An arrow screamed out of the woods and lodged in the chest of the man behind Hawk.

The men in camp turned toward the direction the arrow came from and started shooting. Shoots then erupted from the woods behind them. A man raised a rifle toward Hawk. Sophie jumped from her sitting position and threw her body across the back of his legs. As she flew from her seat, an arrow zipped by her and lodged in the chest of the man who'd been sitting with her. Hawk quickly grabbed his rifle from the dying man behind him while one man ran into the woods and disappeared. The shooting then stopped and Hawk had no one to shoot at. He ran to Sophie and threw his arms around her.

"God, Sophie, you're alright! I was so damn scared I'd lost you," he said as he cut the ropes that bound her wrists. "Are you alright?"

She wrapped her arms around him and said, "I'll tell you all about it later. Kiss me."

Sunkist came out of the woods with Posey behind him. Jake came in from the opposite side of the clearing, carrying his bow and a handful of arrows. "Figured this would come in handy someday," he said. As he passed, he reached down and pulled his arrow out of the first man he'd shot, then threw it into the underbrush.

"Come on," Sunkist said, "let's leave 'em alone fer a while. Let's go see if we kin find that galoot what got away."

"We ain't never gonna find . . ." Jake started, then stopped when he saw Sophie and Hawk embracing and said, "Lead the way."

They stood facing each other on the grass along the lakeshore. He pulled her tightly to his body. "I was scared to death, Sophie," he said into her hair.

The sky reflected in her eyes and made them seem even bluer as she tipped her head back. Hawk leaned forward to kiss her neck. She moaned. Their breathing came in gasps and low-pitched sounds came from deep in their hearts. He raised his lips from hers, took her face in his hands, and looked at her. "God, you are so beautiful." Tears of passion began to fill his eyes as he delicately traced the soft curves of her cheeks and chin. No words were spoken as they walked hand in hand towards the horses. Hawk helped her onto Gorgeous and they started toward the river.

They came onto the road Hawk had been on before he found Sophie. "This is the road that goes from Crow Wing to Superior," Sophie said. "It'll take us back to the fort."

"How'd you know that?"

"The Frenchman told me all about it. He's not the sharpest tool in the shed."

Sunkist, Posey, and Jake caught up with them and they rode silently back toward the fort.

When the shadows stretched across the ground and the sun was close to the horizon, Sophie and Hawk put down their blankets and lay side by side. Jake and Sunkist set their camps some distance away behind a stand of aspen. The evening became cool and still. The crescent moon came up and made its way into the sky as the stars made their appearance, one by one. The night song from the marsh lulled the reunited couple into a deep, peaceful sleep.

They were back on the road at sunrise and met Abernathy and Lorraine at Fort Ripley.

"We heard you had some trouble," Lorraine said.

"Nothing we couldn't handle."

"Do you know who it was?" she asked Sophie.

"I have no idea who it was or why they did it."

"They? There was more than one?"

"As far as I could tell there were two of them," Sophie said. "I heard them talking. One of them was a Frenchman. He's the one who took me with him. I don't know where the other man went."

"Did the other man talk like someone from out east?" Jake asked.

"No, I don't think so. They talked in whispers, so I really wouldn't know."

"What are you getting at, Jake?" Hawk asked.

"Kind of a long story."

"We gotta know it, Jake," Sunkist said. "It might have somethin' to do with what we're here fer."

Jake sat quietly for a few minutes then said, "There's someone wanting to kill Hole-in-the-Day. They tried to make me think they kidnapped Eve to get me to find him for them."

"Eve was kidnapped, too?" Sophie asked.

"No, they didn't get her. She's in Milwaukee, or some damn place like that."

As they rode, Jake told them about Robert Orley.

"When I went to meet Orley in Crow Wing he had two guards with him. They showed me a nightgown that looked like the one Eve made, and the hair they showed me before. Hell, I knew that wasn't Eve's hair, and it wasn't her nightgown, either."

"How did you know the hair wasn't hers?"

"The hair smelled like Eve's perfume, but it didn't smell like Eve. It don't matter how much you cover it up with perfume, the woman's scent is still there."

"And the nightgown?"

"It didn't have fur around the bottom like Eve's."

"Fur around the bottom?" Sophie asked.

"To keep her neck warm at night," Jake responded nonchalantly.

"So what happened to Orley?" Hawk asked.

"I threw the gown at him and that distracted his goons long enough for me to take control of the situation."

"And?"

"I killed 'em."

"All of them?"

"All three of 'em."

"And you got away with it?"

"Yeah, I told the people outside the door they'd got in a fight and shot each other." He shrugged his shoulders, saying, "I guess they believed me."

"Do you think they tried to kidnap me for the same reason?" Sophie asked.

"I doubt it. That was Orley's stupid plan to get me to take him to Hole-in-the-Day, and Orley's dead."

"What made them think you could take them to Hole-in-the-Day?"

"My brother's reputation for getting along with Indians, I guess."

"*My* reputation!" Hawk blurted out. "Yer the one who started all that Pa Hin Sa bullshit."

They entered their camp and Posey started a stew of venison and herbs. When the stew was done cooking and the animals had been taken care of, they sat in a circle around the fire. "Hawk," Sunkist said looking up from his bowl of stew, "you and Jake look a lot alike. Best you keep a hand on Sophie and don't let her out of your sight."

"What's that supposed to mean?"

"They might'a thought they was makin' off with Eve."

"That's pretty clever thinking, Sunkist," Lorraine said. "You could be right about that."

"The thing with Orley is over," Jake said. "He's dead."

"Yes, but didn't you say there are others who want Hole-in-the-Day dead?"

"Yes, but Orley's plan got him killed. Ain't nobody gonna try it again."

"Yes, I suppose you're right," Lorraine said sadly. She walked past Sunkist, patted him on the shoulder and said, "Sorry, Sunkist, that wasn't so clever after all."

"Yeah, well, I'm gonna keep an eye on 'er jiss the same."

Lorraine turned back toward the group. "I think we should take Sunkist's thought seriously. We have already seen that we are dealing with some rather ruthless men, and they seem to be quite capable of trying most anything, including kidnapping and murder."

"Well, Sophie ain't leaving my sight," Hawk said.

"May I be excused?" Sophie asked. "I need to go back in the bushes, alone." She turned to Hawk. "Some rules are just begging to be broken, aren't they."

"We're gonna have to keep a watch on from now on," Hawk said.

"I'll take the first watch," Jake said. "Someone relieve me when you wake up."

"I'm turning in," Sunkist said. "You all have a good night's sleep."

23

C H A P T E R
T W E N T Y - T H R E E

It was full morning when Sophie and Hawk came out of their tent. Jake, Lorraine, and Abernathy sat by the fire. Hawk poured himself a cup of strong coffee and one for Sophie.

"Good morning, everyone," Abernathy said. "I trust you two slept well?"

"Sleep?" Sophie asked as she shot a quick glance at Hawk.

"Is Sunkist sleeping in today?" Abernathy asked.

"No, he left early to talk with the people at the fort."

Lorraine came out of her tent, ran her fingers through her hair, and rubbed her eyes. "Good morning. What's for breakfast?"

"Well," Hawk said, "if we had some ham we could have ham and eggs, if we had some eggs."

"Well, Hawk, *if* is a big word. If a frog had wings he wouldn't bump his ass every time he jumped."

"Lorraine! Such language."

Sophie looked out over the prairie. "Someone's coming."

A lone rider came into the camp. "Sunkist said you should come to the fort right away," he said as he wheeled his horse around and headed back to the fort.

They threw their coffee into the grass and saddled their horses.

"We'll wait here," Lorraine said.

"You can't do that," Hawk said. "What if . . . ?" Then, remembering that he'd never won an argument with Lorraine, he turned his horse and rode off toward the fort.

Soon arriving at the fort, Sophie, Hawk, and Jake tied up their horses and walked into the commander's office. "What's up?"

"Got someone I think you know," the lieutenant said.

He turned and shouted to the back door. "Bring her in."

The door opened and Miss Erickson walked in.

Sophie smiled. "Well, look what the cat dragged in."

Miss Erickson stood quietly looking at the floor. Her hair was tousled and her clothing was dirty and torn.

"Where's Diggs?" Sophie asked.

Miss Erickson looked at Sophie. "He iss going nort to Grant Marais."

"What is he doing in Grand Marais?"

"I don't know notting about what he iss doing. I only know dat he vill kill anyvon who tries to stop him."

"Does this have anything to do with those two children you had in that cabin?"

"I don't know vhy he wanted to keep dose children. He didn't tell me about hiss business."

"And exactly what *is* his business, Miss Erickson?" Sophie asked dryly.

"I don't know dat either."

"You don't seem to know much of anything, Miss Erickson."

"I know dat if I tell you vhat I know, I will not live trew da day."

"If you tell us all you know, I promise no one will harm you."

"Ya sure, you vill protect me. Dat doesn't giff me much comfort. Yew can't even take care off yourself. Yew let dat ugly old Frenchman take you avay. Dat's the kind off protection I can expect from yew."

Sophie walked toward Miss Erickson. They were eye to eye. "Why did he want to kidnap me?"

"He is not da von who hed you taken. He set dat he didn't do it, but he vos glad dat it happened, it vould slow yew down."

"If Diggs didn't kidnap Sophie, who did?" Hawk asked.

"I don't know who it vos."

Sophie spoke up. "He's not really a preacher, is he?"

"Ya, he iss a gyud man who youst got mixed up vit da wrong people."

"Good men don't get mixed up with the wrong people," Sophie said.

"Reverend Diggs iss doing good tings for the Indyun children."

"Tell us where he's going," Sophie said flatly.

"I said, he iss going to Grant Marais, and den from dare I heff no idea."

"What's in Grand Marais?"

"I don't know who iss dare. Youst some off hiss business partners."

"Men of the cloth don't have business partners."

"Sophie," Miss Erickson started.

"Don't call me 'Sophie'. Only my friends call me that."

"Missus Owen," Miss Erickson said softly, "I don't know vhat he iss doing. I only know dat vhen he dropped me off hiss vagon he tolt me dat if I tell anyone where he iss he vill kill me."

"Why did he drop you off his wagon?"

"He didn't like me telling him dat he should giff himself up. I don't like all dat riding in da vagon vit him. He tolt me to get out or he vould shoot me."

"And did you believe he would have shot you?"

"Oh ya, he vould shoot me. I don't doubt dat even a little."

"How can you say he's a good man, then say he would have shot you?"

Miss Erickson looked quickly at Sophie and then at the floor without answering.

"Why didn't he just have me shot rather than kidnapped?"

"He said he didn't heff anyting to do vit it. I told yew dat."

"Does he know we are coming?"

"Ya, he knows you are coming."

"How does he know that?"

"Someone tolt him you are coming."

"And I suppose you don't know who told him."

"I do not know who told him. Somevon in Saint Cloud, I tink."

"Does he know you're here?"

"He must know dat. Vhere else vould I go?"

"Which way will he go?"

"He vill stay close to da Indyuns. He iss a man of da cloth and the Indyuns like him."

"That will take him to Crow Wing, just a few miles from here," the lieutenant said, "but as fast as he's traveling, I doubt he'll stay there long."

"That, and it's too close to the fort," Jake said.

"We'll go up there and ask some questions," Hawk said. "Maybe we can find something out about what he's doing. Lieutenant, can you hold her here for a while in case we have more questions?"

"I can keep her here till the stage comes, but then she has to be sent to Saint Paul."

"We're going back to camp, tomorrow we'll be going to . . ."

Hawk laid his hand on Sunkist's shoulder and interrupted. "We've got a sick man at the camp, so we'll be staying around there till he's better, then decide where to go."

Sunkist looked at Hawk for a second and said, "Who's sick?"

"Abernathy. He's about as sick as a man can get."

"Oh yeah, that." Then he turned to the lieutenant. "We'll be hanging around camp for a while."

They turned and walked out the door, got on their horses, and rode back to camp.

"What was all that about havin' a sick man in camp?" Sunkist asked.

"We don't need to be telling everyone where we're going and what we're doing. There's someone telling Diggs where we are and we don't know who it is or where they are. For all we know, it might be Lieutenant Holister at the fort. Ye know," he said, "Holister came and took me off on a wild boar hunt the night Sophie was taken. I've thought about this before. Do you suppose he knew Sophie was going to be swiped?"

"Could be. Did you see the pig?"

"No, but there was one out there. The sign was fresh and clear."

"He was probably being straight with you then, but we'll keep it in mind. We'll stick around here for a day or two then go to Crow Wing."

Across the prairie they saw a rider coming at full gallop. They grabbed their rifles and stood there, waiting for him to arrive.

"Don't shoot!" he hollered as he rode in. "The lieutenant wants you back at the fort right away!"

"What's going on?" Hawk asked.

"Someone got shot."

"Who was it?"

"Don't know yet. Lieutenant Holister sent me here. He wants you back there right away." The messenger galloped back to the fort.

"Well, let's go," Hawk said, moving toward The Brute.

The group saddled their horses and took off across the grass to the fort. When they got there they rode directly to the infirmary and ran inside. There on the bed lay Miss Erickson. Her face was white and her eyes were closed.

"Someone took her out from somewhere behind the stables." Lieutenant Holister said. "Hawk, you are the only people here who can ride, so I want you and your people to go out there and find the person who did this."

Sunkist and Jake ran out the door, took their mounts, and headed to the area behind the stables at full gallop.

"Did anyone see the shooter?" Hawk asked Holister.

"No, everyone was in the mess hall."

"Didn't you have a guard with her?"

"We did, but she was going to the emperor's throne and he had to leave her while she was in there."

"She was shot sitting on the . . . ?

"No, just as she was going in. Not a damn thing anyone could do to stop it."

"How about the guard you had on her, he didn't see anything?"

"He saw her go down and panicked and didn't think of going after the shooter. He just called us over and we brought her in here. She was already dead when we got her here. She was shot through the heart and died instantly."

"That tells me whoever it was, was a pretty good shot. That's about two hundred yards. Probably someone hired just for this purpose."

Hawk turned to Abernathy. "Do you think anyone could shoot good enough to hit someone in the heart at two hundred yards?"

"Most certainly; one could hit the chest area with an adequate rifle, but to strike the heart at that distance would take extraordinary shooting skill. A rifle built for long range shooting is usually used with a device on which to rest the barrel while sighting, such as sand bags, and is capable of six-inch groups as far as five hundred yards. These rifles, however, are far too cumbersome to be used in conditions such as we have here. There are, of course, rifles equipped with telescopic sights that are even more accurate than those used in the long-range competition. These arms are used . . ."

"Abernathy!" Lorraine said sharply.

"Oh, I'm very sorry. I do tend to ramble on when speaking of firearms. You see . . ."

Lorraine put her hand on his shoulder and turned him toward her. She put her index finger in front of his mouth and said, "Shhh . . ."

He nodded his head and turned back to listen to the conversation.

"Who do you know around here that can shoot that good?" Hawk asked Holister.

"The firearms we have here are old Argentine muskets the state sent us. They're more dangerous to the guy holding the gun than the guy he's pointing it at. And even if we did have good weapons, there is no one here that can shoot that good."

"Well, I guess the only thing to do is go looking for him."

They turned for the door and walked across the parade field to the stables and began searching the ground.

"What are we looking for?" Sophie asked.

"Tracks, or anything that might give us some idea where to start looking."

He bent down and picked a cartridge case from the grass.

"Abernathy, what kind of gun did this come from?"

Abernathy took the copper cartridge and examined it carefully. He looked at the base and down into the cavity, took note of the diameter, and handed it back to Hawk.

"Well?" Hawk said.

"Sir?"

"Well, what kind of gun did this come from?"

"Well, I don't know."

"I thought you were the expert on guns."

"Oh, I can shoot them quite effectively, but I know very little, indeed, absolutely nothing, about the types of the firearms that are available, or what calibers are offered with each of them. That particular cartridge is designed for bullets of forty-four one-hundredths of an inch in diameter. It is a very popular caliber for a number of weapons offered by various manufacturing firms, including a number of pistols. It has a priming compound of fulminate of mercury around the periphery of the base of the cartridge, which, when struck by the hammer, is crushed, causing it to detonate, igniting the main charge—approximately forty grains of gun power—which in turn, causes extremely high pressure behind the bullet forcing it through the barrel and sending it at a very high velocity to the target."

"Thanks a lot," Hawk said. He turned to Lorraine. "What'd he say?"

"I haven't the faintest idea."

"You don't know? I'll be dam—uh, darned."

"You are most welcome," Abernathy said. "Anytime I can be of service, please call on me. I have no trouble admitting that I am somewhat ignorant about firearms, but I must say . . ."

"I thought you said you don't know anything about guns," Hawk said.

"The more you know," Abernathy said, "the more you realize how much there is you don't know."

Lorraine laid her hand on Abernathy's shoulder and squeezed tightly. Her eyes fixed on his as she raised her index finger to him. She then lowered her finger slowly, keeping her eyes fixed on his.

"Yes, Miss Lorraine."

Lorraine kept her hand on his shoulder and squeezed the muscle slightly again. Then she glanced at Abernathy and quickly took her hand away.

They turned at the sound of horses galloping across the prairie to the west. Sunkist and Jake rode up to them. "We ain't never gonna to find him in that country. Too damn many places he could have gone and the only trail we found was covered with tracks."

"Well, let's get back to the lieutenant."

They walked into the commander's office. "Didn't figure you'd find him. He had everything on his side. He's most likely sitting in the saloon at Crow Wing right now having a beer."

"Could be that," said Sunkist, "or sittin' at the table in the mess hall rot cheer in the fort."

"No, I doubt that. I know all of the men here and there's not a one of them got the intestinal fortitude for something like this."

"Is that some kind of gun?" Hawk asked.

"Hawk," Lorraine said, "it means guts."

"You'll have to explain that one to me sometime."

"I'll let Sophie handle that."

"Lieutenant Holister," Sophie said, "where were you when this happened?"

"I was in the mess hall with the rest of the troops."

"I'm sorry, we just need to know where everyone was."

"I understand. I would have been disappointed if you hadn't asked."

Hawk turned to the gang and said, "Let's get back to camp and get ready to move." Then he turned to Lieutenant Holister. "We're gonna go down to Saint Cloud and talk with the sheriff there. We gotta get more information about Diggs."

"Hawk," Sunkist said, "we got all the information he's got. You and Sophie talked to him when you were there."

"Yeah, well, this chasing around the hills like a blind coon dog ain't gittin' us nowhere. We need to know more about Diggs."

Sunkist looked curiously at Hawk. "If ye think we need to, I recon we should."

"You gotteny better ideas? Like where to look next?"

"Well, north, that's all I know."

"Yeah, if he keeps goin' north."

"I guess that's something to think about."

Back at camp, they rolled their tents and loaded the mules.

"Hawk," Sunkist said, "what's the real reason fer going back to Saint Cloud?"

"Hell, we been to that town," Hawk said. "There ain't nothin' there we need."

"Ye mean we ain't going to Saint Cloud?"

"Nope. I just want whoever it is telling Diggs where we are to think we're going to Saint Cloud."

"You think Holister is mixed up in this?" Sophie asked.

"Someone at the fort is mixed up in it, whether it's Holister or someone else. I got a feeling that Diggs will hear we're leaving and going back."

"I wish I understood all I know about this," Sophie said.

"What I would dearly love to do is to study the natural history of this wonderful state."

24

C H A P T E R
T W E N T Y - F O U R

THEY COVERED THE FIRE PIT, cleaned up the area, and set off toward Crow Wing. They followed the line of hills for seven miles under the cover of the forest, then rode over flat, sandy ground covered with thin scrub grass and very few trees. In the distance, set back against the trees, stood an old, abandoned house and barn. The wood had turned gray with age and the windows were all broken.

Sophie halted her horse to look across the grass at the farm.

Hawk stood next to her. "It looks lonely over there," he said.

"You know what makes it look so lonely?" Sophie said quietly. "There is no smoke coming from the chimney."

They soon entered a heavy growth of tall pines. The road through the pines was good and easily traveled. To their left, the bank of the Mississippi River, forty feet below them, was covered with mixed hardwoods, short pines, and heavy undergrowth. Sophie stopped her horse next to a one-hundred-foot elm tree that stood in the middle of a stand of white and red pines.

"What do you think this old tree has witnessed?" she whispered as she touched the tree looking upwards.

"I'm sure it has plenty secrets," Hawk said. "Must be a hundred years old."

"We'll come back here someday and find it fallen and decaying, feeding the new trees," she said.

It was midday when they rode into Crow Wing. The town was alive with horses, wagons, and people moving on the street along the riverfront. The streets were lined with stores, warehouses, blacksmith shops, hotels, and boarding houses, and a church sat on the hilltop. Some buildings stood alone away from the town and some were connected by a long boardwalk. Saloons were scattered randomly throughout the town and a train of oxcarts sat on the far side. The Métis drivers roamed the streets, their haughty attitudes clearly visible to onlookers.

The women of the Métis, in their brightly patterned dresses and flowered hats, flaunted their dusky charms with arrogance and poise. Their dark eyes and wavy black hair seized the attention of men and women alike. They knew that no woman in that country could equal their natural beauty.

The town was situated on a rise overlooking the two mouths of the Crow Wing River where it joined the Mississippi. The camps of the Chippewa were seen hidden in the pines around the outskirts of town. Most were round-top wigwams made of birch bark and, for the more fortunate, canvas.

The group rode quietly into town, turning their heads and looking into each alley and window. Somewhere in this town there was probably someone with a rifle capable of hitting a mark at two hundred yards with deadly accuracy. Hawk stayed close to Sophie, moving from one side of her to the other.

A man in a gray suit stood on the boardwalk in front of a saloon and watched as they rode in. Sunkist stopped his mount in front of him and looked down into his eyes. The man cleared his throat then turned and walked into the saloon.

"What was that all about?" Jake asked.

"Didn't like the way he wuz lookin' at us," Sunkist answered.

"Think he might be trouble?"

"Jake, mu boy, any one of these people could be trouble. Might as well let them know right off we ain't gonna be messed with."

"You guys wanna get a room at the hotel?" Hawk asked.

"You can get a room if ye want," Sunkist said. "We'll be settin' up camp outside of town."

"Considering the state of affairs," Sophie said, "I think that would be the best. We'd be sitting ducks in a hotel room."

"Anyone for a beer?" Jake asked.

Sophie turned her horse, crossing in front of Hawk, and pulled up to the hitching rail in front of the saloon they were passing.

"Guess that answers that," Hawk said.

They dismounted and went into the saloon, taking a table in the corner of the room.

The bartender came to them. "What'll you have?"

"Beer all around," Jake said.

"Sasparilly fer the lady," Sunkist said, pointing his thumb to Posey.

"I would prefer a cognac, if you please," Abernathy said.

The man looked at him curiously and said, "Well, a man with a distinguishing palate."

"Yes, sir. If I'm to indulge in the spirits, I would prefer a gentleman's beverage."

"Well, Mister Gentleman, we ain't got no cognac. We got some brandy, but it ain't cognac."

"May I ask what vintage your brandy might be?"

"You can ask any damn thing you want, but you'll get what I got on the shelf behind you."

Abernathy turned in his chair and scanned the line of bottles on the shelves.

Unable to read the labels on the bottles in the dim light, he said, "I shall have beer like the rest."

The bartender looked at Abernathy, shook his head slowly, and walked away. The beer came and they talked quietly among themselves. Suddenly, a loud laugh came from two men standing at the bar. One of the men looked at Abernathy and said to his partner in a loud voice, "Looks to me like she should be in the back washing dishes or sweeping floors." Then they laughed loudly.

Sunkist turned his head and glared at the men.

"Hey, old man! That yer sister ye got sittin' there?"

"Sunkist, please ignore them," Lorraine said. "They're just having a little fun."

Sunkist looked down at his glass and said nothing.

"Maybe it would be best if we just leave," Lorraine said.

"I ain't goin' nowhere," Sunkist grumbled.

"Might be she's right," Hawk said. "We don't have anything to prove to these people."

"Hey, little girl, where'd you get those fancy duds? I thought only girls wore frilly things on their shirts."

Abernathy started to stand, but Sunkist put his hand on his shoulder and pushed him back to his chair. "Si'down. He ain't worth getting yerself all beat up over."

"He will not beat me up, Sunkist. If anything, he will learn a valuable lesson."

"You ain't no match for that galoot; he out weighs you by a hunnert pounds."

"Size has nothing to do with it, my friend. It is all in the brain," he said, tapping his head. He turned toward the man and finished the sentence loud enough for him to hear, ". . . the likes of which I suspect this man is sorely lacking."

"You talking about me, there, little girl?"

"When I address you, sir, you will be sure of it."

"You gonna undress me?" he said, and both of the men laughed hard.

"No, I will not undress you. The smell, I'm sure, would cause the swine in town to vomit and leave."

"Abernathy!" Lorraine snapped.

"Yer a damn smart mouth, and I don't like smart-mouthed little girls."

"I am not surprised that you would be afraid of people more intelligent than you. Of course, that would include most any being with intelligence greater than the lesser apes."

The man looked at Abernathy for a few seconds. He glanced at his partner, then back at Abernathy. "What the hell's that s'pose to mean," he shouted.

"Oh dear, I apologize. I realize now, considering your obvious lack of intellectual muscle, I should keep my verbalizations on a more primitive level."

"What the hell are you talking about?"

A man sitting at another table laughed and said, "Hey, Dave, he just called you stupid."

The man pushed himself from the bar and started toward Abernathy. Sunkist jumped up, put himself between them, and faced the man.

Abernathy came around from behind Sunkist, faced him, and said, "I will not have you defending me. I can handle my own affairs." He turned to Dave. "If, indeed, this ignorant primate can pose even the slightest difficulty."

Dave stood shaking and staring at Abernathy. "You little runt! I'm gonna shove my fist down your throat and grab your ass and pull you inside out!"

"Well," Abernathy said with a grin, "now that we have the easy part out of the way, may I suggest we . . ."

"What easy part?" the man growled.

"Talking about it." Abernathy said. "Talking about what one will do is always much easier than actually doing it. As I see this situation, there is no recourse but to end this with barbarism." He calmly took his glasses off his face and set them on the table. His left hand came up like a bolt of lightning and slapped Dave across the face with a loud crack.

Dave was stunned by the sound so close to his ear, the sharp, burning pain on the entire right side of his face, and the high-pitched, metallic ringing in his right ear. He started to bring his right fist up to hit Abernathy, but suddenly his left eye became blurred and he could not deliver his blow. He dropped his fist and touched his eyebrow with his left hand, feeling for blood. Suddenly, his right eye ceased to function. He did not see the cause of the discomfort, but assumed it came from the small man standing before him with his fists curled up. He let out a bellow and started toward his assailant. Abernathy's fists flashed like lightning and Dave was stopped by a sudden and painful barrage of strikes around his nose and face. Abernathy stood before him looking deeply into his swelling eyes. "Are you satisfied that you are no match for me?"

Again, Dave started toward Abernathy but caught another barrage of painful strikes that sent him to the floor. Abernathy stood over him waiting for him the get up, but Dave stayed down, knowing that to rise would only mean more punishment.

The other man stepped toward them. Sunkist grabbed him by the shirt and said, "You stay otta this."

He raised his hands and backed himself against the bar. "I was just gonna help Dave to his feet and get him otta here."

Sunkist pulled him by the shirt and said, "Good ideer. You take him otta here and you go with 'im."

The man reached down to help Dave to his feet but Dave pushed his hand away. "I can get up by myself." He stood and looked at Abernathy. "I'll get even with you for that, you little runt."

"It should be entertaining to watch you tell your friends a little runt blacked your eyes. We will be around town for a few days if you feel you can handle another trouncing."

The man stomped out the door.

Abernathy and Sunkist took their chairs. Lorraine looked at Abernathy, tipped her head slightly, and smiled.

"You ain't gonna get after him for his barbaric behavior?" Hawk said.

"That man was looking for trouble," Lorraine said, with a slight smile, "and, obviously, he found it."

"Where'd you learn to fight like that, Abby?" Sunkist asked.

Abernathy didn't respond.

"Oh, excuse me, Mister Gentleman. Abernathy, where did you learn to fight that way?"

"As I stated previously, you can never tell a horse by its color."

"Y'ain't gonna answer me, huh?"

"Someday you will know the entire story."

"You don't suppose that was one of Diggs's friends do you?" Lorraine asked.

"Naw," Sunkist said. "That was just some bully pickin' on a little guy he thought he could whip." Then he elbowed Abernathy and said, "Picked on the wrong guy, huh, Abernathy?" He grabbed his beer, clinked his glass with Abernathy's, took a sip, and said, "Diggs's men'll stay undercover till the shootin' starts."

"Do you think he'll be back?" Abernathy asked.

"Would you come back after being humiliated like that?"

"Not without a gun," Hawk said.

"Mebbe ye otta think about gettin' yerself a pistol, Abernathy."

Abernathy looked at Sunkist for a long moment, then nodded slightly and said, "Yes, I suppose I should." His eyes fixed on an empty spot on the table as he mulled his actions over. "Maybe that was not such a good thing to do."

"Well, it's done now," Sunkist said. "We'll jiss have tuh keep a closer eye on our back trail fer a while."

After an hour, they left the saloon and followed Posey to the spot she had picked for their camp. Her natural instinct for survival made her constantly aware of her surroundings, as she silently searched out cover from danger, and for safe places to camp. She'd picked an opening in the trees and underbrush about thirty yards from the road into town. They slipped through the trees and bushes to an area about twenty feet across with a floor thickly carpeted with pine needles. The camp could not be seen from the road in the daylight and only a flicker from the fire would be visible at night. When night came on, Sunkist sat away from the others, preferring to be at the edge of the camp rather than in the center close to the fire. He seldom looked directly into the fire knowing it would diminish his night vision. Abernathy sat next to Sunkist. After a minute of silence he said, "Sunkist, I know you don't think much of me, but if you don't mind, I'd like to talk with you for a while."

"Who said I don't think much of you?"

"Oh dear, no one had to say it directly. I can just feel it in the way you talk to me."

"Aw hail, Abernathy, I'm jiss havin' fun wit'cha. I don't mean nothin' by it. You ain't gotta 'splain nothin' to me. Ain't none of my bidness."

"Please, let me say this, Sunkist. I need to tell you about myself."

"Well, go ahead on, then. I'm listenin'."

"My mother had four sons. I was the youngest. She had always wanted to have a girl, so she tried to raise me as if I were a girl. She dressed me in fine clothes and taught me to talk the way she thought a girl should talk. My brothers were all raised as men and were taught by my father to live like men. They joined the Union forces and went to fight in the south with General McClellan. I was not so fortunate."

"How could a mama do that to one of her own chi'dren?" Sunkist said. "It don't make a lick'a sense."

"Oh, I don't blame my mother. She lived in a household with five men and she dearly missed the company of another female.

"My father taught my brothers to ride and shoot and work the farm. I was kept in the house helping Mother do the housework and cleaning.

I went to school and excelled in everything they taught me. One of mother's friends told her I should go to college and get to continue my education, so she enrolled me in a university in Michigan. I did very well there and was one of the top students. The other students teased me incessantly, and at times became violent with me. One night, a group of them caught me and threw a blanket over my head. They beat me so severely my eyes swelled shut and I couldn't see for days. The boys who did it were never punished for it, even though the college dean knew who they were. They were the sons of some of the administrators at the school and their friends.

"I was walking in the yard of the campus one day when the old, black groundskeeper named Roscoe Lemons stopped me and asked what had happened to me. I told him about it and he sat down next to me.

"'Massa Abernathy Wayne,' he said, 'you don't have to take that from them boys.'

"I said that I can't just leave the school.

"'No, you can't do that, that would be letting them win.'

"I asked him what I should do about it.

"'I can teach you how to fight—and win,' he said.

"I told him that I didn't think I could ever win a fight because of my size.

"'Size got nothin' to do with it, Massa Abernathy Wayne. You gots to know *how* to fight. You gots to let them boys know they can't be pickin' on you. You gots to make them respect you,' he said. Then he pointed his finger at me and said, 'Now, I said *respect*, mind you. You don't need them scared of you. If they's scared of you, they'll just come after you in bunches. They have to respect you.'

"'I understand,' I said. 'What do you propose I do?'

"'Do you want to know how to fight?' he asked me. I said, 'No, I would rather know how to avoid fighting.' He said, 'All right, there are two ways to avoid fighting. You can run and hide or you can stand tall and teach them respect. The only reason they pick on you is because you're small and they know they can beat you without getting hurt themselves. With boys like that, the only way to make them respect you is to fight them and hurt them. You will have to hurt them, but you'll only have to do it jist once.'

"I told him I could never hurt anyone deliberately, and he said, 'Then you will have to get used to running or being hurt yourself.'

"I certainly didn't want that. Then he asked me if I wanted to know how to fight. I thought that over and decided that he was right. I asked him to teach me how to fight.

"He was a slave in Alabama many years ago. His job was to fight. He fought for his very existence. His master had him fighting once a month against some of the biggest men he could find. They made bets on who would win. The man who won the fight was allowed to go back to the shed and heal up for a month before the next fight. The one who lost was beaten with whips, and he said if the man was lucky, he was killed.

"They didn't kill the man with a gun—they hung him by the neck. What made that even worse was that they put the rope around his neck and pulled him up so his toes were just touching the ground and he choked to death. That made the fighters want to win at any cost. A fighter would rather be killed by his opponent than to loose the fight and live. He said he'd had a few men ask him to kill them, and he did kill one man. He didn't do it because he wanted to. He said the man wanted to die.

"He knew all the tricks to stop a man and all the mean things to do to make him weak. He was never beaten in a street fight. The last fight he was in was the one where the man died.

"Normally, they would put fighters who grew too old to fight back in the fields to work until they died. But they didn't want him fighting anymore, so they chopped off all of his toes and sold him to the university were I was enrolled. The university gave him his freedom, but he stayed there because he had nowhere else to go.

"He offered to teach me to fight and whip any man on that campus. He said when they see that I can fight, they won't want to fight me anymore.

"So Mister Lemons began teaching me to fight. We went deep into the woods where he taught me to use my hands and feet, and teeth and knees and elbows, but mostly my brain. He taught me things I had never dreamed of doing to another man. He also taught me how to take a punch and roll with it, and how to avoid being punched, and how to fall without getting hurt. He taught me to watch my opponent's eyes to anticipate his next move. He taught me to hurt my opponent with the first blow and end the fight as soon as it started. He had me punching bags of sand to toughen my fists.

"But he also taught me to stop fighting when I knew I had defeated the other man. He said that was the most important part of gaining the respect of the other men on campus. If I were to continue to beat on a defeated man after he was down, they would begin to hate me.

"One day one of the boys came and wanted to fight. I told him I did not want to fight and to please leave me alone. He pushed me and I instinctively hit him on the end of his nose with my fist. Oh, I felt so cheap after doing that and apologized to him. But he was furious and came after me. My first instinct was to turn and run, but I suddenly remembered Roscoe's words and stood my ground. He came at me so mad, he was screaming. I knew at that point that I could defeat him because, as Roscoe said, when you loose your temper, you loose the fight.

"I struck him on the end of the nose again and bloused his left eye. My strikes were too fast for him to dodge and it was effortless to overpower him."

Sunkist clapped his hands and laughed. "That'll larn that dumb-ass."

"He walked away, tossing threats back to me, telling me that he would get me for that, and such foolishness. I never had any problem with that man again and he never did get me for anything, as he had threatened. That was the worst spring I have ever had. I had to fight several men before they finally stopped tormenting me. The dean of the school approached me one day and asked if I would like to join the college boxing team. I didn't think I could ever be a part of such a barbaric sport. But the dean convinced me that it was a very respectable sport, so I said I would do it. Then I was taught the art of fisticuffs and became the school's champion in the lightweight division. Then I learned that they were making wagers on the outcome of the contests. To me that was more barbaric than the fights and I backed out with my trophies. My trophies for that sport now lie in the bottom of a lake in eastern Michigan. It is a time in my life that I would just as soon forget."

Sunkist listened as he cleaned under his fingernails with his pocketknife.

He realized suddenly that Abernathy had stopped talking. "Is that the end of the story?" he asked.

"No. I thought you fell asleep."

"Nope. Jiss git on with it afore I do."

"By this time, I was considered one of the top students at the university and was engaged in a number of sports, non-violent sports I should stress. I was a top contender in the rifle competition and archery. It seemed I had a natural instinct for accurate placement of projectiles. I also learned the art of horsemanship. In all, Sunkist, I am very fortunate that I have been given the talents to do so many things. Unfortunately, the things I can do are not the things I wish I could do."

"And what, pray tell, are the things you would want to do?"

"Oh, my dear friend . . ."

"Stop calling me your dear friend!"

"Alright, you big lump."

"That's better."

"What I would dearly love to do is to study the natural history of this wonderful state, the geological history in particular. I have read all of the letters and books written by the great scientist Louis Aggasiz, and I have traveled with David Dale Owen when he surveyed this country in eighteen fifty-two. I also traveled with Henry Eames in eighteen fifty-six."

"So you know this area?"

"Oh no, I have never been here before. We explored the Ottertail River, and the central parts of Minnesota. Then up the north shore of Lake Superior to the Canadian border. We were assigned the task of exploring for mineral deposits."

"Did ye find inny?"

"There is a high probability that iron ore exists in the deposits north of here. Unfortunately, we were unable to prove that the deposits were present in sufficient concentration to justify the expense of further exploration."

"You speak different languages, too?"

"Oh no, my dear friend . . . Oh! Forgive me. No, you big lump. I only speak English."

"How about we jiss stick with Sunkist?"

"Very well, Sunkist."

25

CHAPTER
TWENTY-FIVE

"You say you was on a shootin' team?"

"Yes, I was."

"I can shoot better'n you," Sunkist said, without looking up from his fingernails.

Abernathy looked up to the clear blue sky. "This looks like the type of day that would be quite agreeable to a contest of skill with the trusty rifle."

"Does that mean we can shoot today?"

"Yes, we can shoot today."

"Well, git that fancy smoke pole and let's get a'goin'."

Abernathy stood and walked to his tent. He brought out his rifle and a box of ammunition. The two walked to an open meadow where a line of trees stood one hundred yards away. Sunkist pointed down range. "See that white tree yonder?"

"Yes, the smaller one?"

"Yeah, the small one. Might as well make this tough right from the start."

Abernathy loaded a round into the chamber, pulled the rifle to his shoulder, and fired. The bullet tore a hole in the center of the tree. Sunkist brought his rifle up and did the same.

"Sunkist," Abernathy said, "that tree is much too easy to hit. Let me take a target out there that will be considerably more challenging."

"Suit yerself there, team shooter."

Abernathy went to his tent and brought out paper targets with three circles and a small black spot about the size of Sunkist's thumbnail in the center. He carried them out to the trees and tacked them up, one on the birch tree and one on an elm.

"Now," he said, "we will shoot at the black spot in the center of the target, and the one who has three shots closest to the center spot wins. I will take the one on the right, you shoot at the one on the left."

"You brought your cryin' towel, I hope."

"I have one in my tent, if you care to borrow it."

"Who shoots first?" Sunkist said squinting at the distant targets.

"We will shoot three shots and count the score. We can do this as many times as you wish until, at some point during this competition, you realize you cannot shoot better than I."

"We'll jiss take the first group and stick with that."

Sunkist brought his rifle to his shoulder and fired.

Abernathy stood at an angle to the target, looking down range for a few seconds. He held his rifle in both hands, took a deep breath, then let it out. Then he smoothly lifted the rifle to his shoulder and raised his right shoulder to align the sights with his eye. The rifle came down and Abernathy adjusted his feet slightly. Then he brought the rifle to his shoulder. He stood relaxed and rested his cheek on the stock with both eyes looking down range. He took another breath, let half of it out, and focused on the target. For long seconds he stood perfectly still, peering over the sights.

Sunkist watched patiently and was about to speak when Abernathy's gun went off. The recoil took him back two inches and the muzzle of the rifle raised three inches. Abernathy held the stance and slowly brought the rifle back to rest the sights on the target. He held it in place momentarily, then raised his head. "There, if the laws of physics apply in this state, that shot went directly through the center of the bull's eye."

"Laws? What laws? The only law out here is I'm gonna show you how to shoot."

"Well, my . . . Sunkist, I see you have your piece loaded, so you may take your next shot."

Sunkist brought the rifle to his shoulder and fired. "Yer turn."

"You are quite efficient with your rifle. I can see that I will have to try my best in order to win."

"Well," said Sunkist, "it ain't yer ever'day Joe what can shoot better'n me."

"I shall do my best to avoid being an ever'day Joe."

"Want me to go gitcher cryin' towel fer ye?"

"Yes, please do that. I suspect one of us will have use for it soon."

Once again, Abernathy raised his rifle to his shoulder and, once again, went through the ritual of concentration and delivery. Sunkist made his third shot and Abernathy finished the game.

"Well," Abernathy said with a bow at the waist and a sweeping of his hat, "shall we walk together and see the results of this exciting contest?"

"Sure you don't want to bring yer cryin' towel?"

"Not unless you think *you* will need it."

"I ain't a-gonna need it, you are."

They approached the targets and Sunkist began to laugh. "Ha!" he said. "Ye only got one damn hole in yer target. It's in the bull's eye, though, I'll give ye that."

He looked at his target and found three shots grouped tightly around the bull's-eye, with one shot half inside the black spot.

"Want me to gitcher cryin' towel, Mister Gentleman?"

"Perhaps you should come over here and look at this. *You* might want that towel."

Sunkist leaned down close to Abernathy's target, then he stood and looked at his opponent. "There ain't but one hole in that target," he said with a look of amazement in his eyes. He pointed to the target. "You put all three shots in the same damn hole."

The hole was shaped like a cloverleaf and the entire black dot had been shot out.

"Will you be going after your crying towel or would you like me to get it for you?"

"How the hell'd you do that?" Sunkist asked, pulling at his beard.

"Well, I guess it boils down to one thing—I am a better shooter than you."

"Must be something wrong with this gun."

"There is only one thing wrong with that rifle, my friend. It is a muzzle-loading rifle, incapable of the accuracy achieved by a cartridge-firing weapon. You have done exceedingly well in this competition and I believe that, had you a rifle like mine, you would most likely have beaten me."

"Abernathy?"

"Yes, Sunkist?"

"Kin I shoot yer rifle?"

"Well, I don't know if you can or not. You certainly didn't impress me with that club you call a rifle."

"Look you little . . . Ye know, ye really hadn't aught'a insult a man's rifle. It's kinda like his lover. Ye know?"

"That is a wonderful analogy, Sunkist. I'll remember it."

"Well? Kin I shoot that piece-a-shit gun o' your'n?"

"Yes, Sunkist, you may shoot my rifle. But," he said with his finger pointed toward the sky, "you will be so kind as to allow me to give you pointers on the proper use of this fine weapon."

"*Yer* gonna teach *me* how to shoot?"

Abernathy pointed at his target as he looked Sunkist in the eye.

Sunkist rolled his eyes to the targets and said, "Well, I guess I can't argue about you knowin' how it's done."

"If you want to hit the center of the target, you will allow me to show you how to accomplish that goal."

"Oh, please, teach me," Sunkist said sarcastically.

"Good. Now I want you to shoot the rifle at that birch tree and try to strike the knot halfway up the trunk. I will watch and see what you are doing wrong and attempt to correct it."

Sunkist looked at Abernathy, obviously troubled by the thought of him teaching him anything. "Where do I aim?"

"This rifle is sighted to hit a mark at one hundred yards. Aim directly at the spot you wish to hit."

Sunkist raised the rifle to his shoulder and fired. The bullet hit an inch to the right of the knot.

"All right, I see what you're doing wrong," Abernathy said.

"What?"

"Everything."

"I didn't do nothin' wrong."

"You missed that rather simple target out there. That means you did something wrong."

"I s'pose yer gonna tell me you can hit that knot."

"Sunkist, that knot is not even a slight challenge. If you were to put it out another hundred yards there would be a chance—be it ever so slight—that I would miss."

"Boy, you jist don't quit, do ye."

"First of all, my friend, you have to stand perfectly relaxed. Let your body settle on your hips and put your weight equally on both feet." Sunkist stood straight and shook himself down onto his hips.

"What if there's an Injun shootin' at you with a gun?"

"There are no Indians shooting at you at this moment."

"Yeah, well, if there was, I wouldn't be standin' up like this."

"No, I do not suppose you would be. You would most likely be shooting holes in the trees behind them."

Sunkist looked at Abernathy and envisioned picking him up, holding him at arm's length and shaking him like he'd shake the fleas out of a fox hide. He drove the thought from his mind and said, "Wha' do I do now?"

"Stand so your feet are directly under your shoulders at a forty-five degree angle to the target."

Sunkist turned.

"Now let the rifle hang comfortably in your hands while you concentrate on relaxation. Your shoulders should droop naturally with the weight of the rifle. Take a deep breath and let it out. Now, concentrate on the target. In your mind, visualize the bullet going where you want it to go. Keep that vision in your mind as you sight down the barrel. Now raise the stock to your shoulder."

Sunkist raised the rifle quickly and bent his head so his cheek lay on the stock.

"No-no-no!" Abernathy shouted as he took hold of the rifle and pulled it from Sunkist's shoulder. "You raise the rifle *smoothly*. You do not jerk it up. And do not lower your head to the sights. Raise your right elbow. The rear sight will come up with your shoulder until it is lined up with your eye. Keep both eyes open . . . take a deep breath . . . let half of it out as you align the sights on the target. Stop breathing . . . Now," Abernathy hissed, "squeeze that trigger slo-o-o-owly. Do not jerk it. You do not want to know when the rifle is going off. Your mind is not on the rifle. You are concentrating on holding your sight picture. Your mind should be on just these three things: sight picture, breathing, and," he spoke in a hoarse whisper, "sque-e-e-eze that trigger."

Sunkist did what Abernathy told him and suddenly, the rifle went off. He lowered the rifle and said, "How wuz that?"

"You did it wrong," Abernathy said softly, looking at the ground, scratching behind his ear, and slowly shaking his head.

"I did not. Where'd it hit?"

"You hit the mark, but you should never bring the rifle down after you shoot. You should always roll with the recoil and bring the rifle back to battery before lowering the piece."

"What the hell fer? After the bullet's on its way there ain't nothin' you kin do to change it."

"It is all part of the concentration, my friend. You need to stay focused on your sight picture and not worry about where the bullet hits until the competition is over. If you do everything correctly, you will not have to be concerned about where the bullet hit. You will know it hit its intended mark. And, as you said, once the bullet is on its way there is nothing you can do to change its course. The reason most people bring the rifle down after they fire is to look and see where the bullet hit. Oftentimes, one starts lowering the rifle before the bullet is on its way."

"Guess that makes sense. I'll admit to doing that muself a time or two."

"Make a mental picture of where the sights were when the rifle went off and you will know where the bullet hit. If you have the sights on the bull's-eye then you know the bullet went there. If your sights were to the left or right of the bull's-eye, you will know the bullet went there. If you can tell exactly where that shot went each time you shoot, you are doing it correctly, even if the bullet did not hit the bull's-eye. There will be times when your sight picture wanders off the mark just before the shot goes off. That has even happened to me on occasion."

Sunkist looked closely at Abernathy's rifle. "Mebbe it's time for me to retire that old Springfield and git me one of these here cat'ridge shootin' repeaters."

"They are a great improvement over the older weapons."

"I got me a Sharps in mu plunder. She's all took apart so's I kin carry 'er, but she'll shoot if I put 'er back together."

"You have a Sharps rifle?" Abernathy asked with surprise.

"Yeah. Took it off'n a pack of Injuns what made a big mistake last fall."

"Why in the world are you carrying this relic if you have a Sharps?"

"This old Springfield ain't never let me down, an it's kinda hard to let 'er go. Kinda like tellin' yer best friend ye found a new best friend. Know what uh mean?"

"I know what you mean. I have never allowed anyone to handle my rifle, until now. It's kind of like allowing someone to handle your lover."

Sunkist scratched at his whiskers as he looked deeply at Abernathy.

"You ready to go back to camp?" Abernathy asked.

"Yup," Sunkist said. He threw his Springfield over his shoulder, holding it by the barrel, and slapped Abernathy on the back, causing him to hop one step forward. "Hey, Abby, yer alright. I'll admit I was a little worried about you at first but, hey, yer alright."

"Thanks, Jim."

Sunkist looked sternly at Abernathy then began to laugh. "Alright, 'Abernathy' it is from now on."

They walked on toward the camp. "Hey, Abernathy, wanna go to town and kick some ass?"

"Oh dear, no, I've had my excitement for a while." Abernathy stopped and turned to Sunkist. "You know?" he said with his fingertip touching his lips. "I should have kicked his ass on his way out the door." Then he clapped his hands, twirled around on one toe, and laughed. They walked back to camp and Abernathy picked up the ax and started to split firewood. "This is a wonderful exercise to relieve frustration."

"Tomorrow we go to Crow Wing and talk to someone about Diggs," Hawk said. "They must have a sheriff there."

"We don't need no saw-bones taggin' along."

26

CHAPTER
TWENTY-SIX

IN THE MORNING THEY WALKED the quarter mile into town. They stopped a man and asked where they could get a meal. He pointed at a two-story building and said, "Brown House Inn."

"Thanks."

They walked into the hotel and took a table against the back wall and ordered their meal. As they sat talking, Sunkist suddenly got up from his chair and walked to the door. He went outside then came back to the table.

"What was that all about?" Hawk asked.

"Some guy just came in the door and saw us sitting here, turnt around, and left. I think we aught'a git outta here. Now!"

They each pulled money out of their bags, laid it on the table, and walked to the door. Sunkist walked ahead and opened the door slowly, poked his head out, and looked up and down the street.

"Come on," he said as he motioned with his hand, "and keep yer eyeballs skinned."

They cautiously walked through the street avoiding the buildings as much as they could. They went toward the nearest exit out of town and headed into the pine forest and back to their camp.

"Are we being a little overly cautious, Sunkist?" Lorraine asked.

"Ain't no sech'a thing as over cautious. We don't know who's out there gunnin' fer us. We don't even know if anyone's gunnin' fer us. The only way fer us to know fer sure is to get someone shot, then we'd know. I ain't willin' to take that chance."

"He's right, Lorraine," Hawk said. "They already tried to take Sophie and it didn't work. Next time they'll use other ways to stop us."

"I see your point."

"That guy what came in the saloon knew who we are," Sunkist said. "He ducked out as soon as he saw us, and I figger he went to tell someone we was there."

"Do you suppose Diggs is in town right now?" Jake asked.

"Ain't no way to know that, but you can be sure he's got people here keeping an eye on us."

Hawk looked at Lorraine. "Are you sure you want to come with us on this? You and Abernathy can turn around and go back to Yellow Medicine if you want."

"Now, why in the world would I do that? I came along for a reason. I did not expect this to be a picnic. This is about two Indian children who were brought into the agency."

"What Indian children?"

"One day a group of Indians from Chief Wabasha's band came in with two Indian children. You remember Wabasha; he was against the war and fought to keep the Sioux from attacking the agencies."

"I remember him, but you had lots of Indian kids at the agency. What's so special about these two?"

"They were Chippewa Indians."

"Boys? Girls?"

"A young girl and a boy. They said they had been attacked by a band of Sioux and their grandmother and one of the girls got away. The children were captured and taken to a camp where there were white men. Wabasha's men threatened the band and rescued the children."

"What were white men doing in the camp of warring Indians?" Sophie asked.

"I don't know, but these children were from the Chippewa tribe. They had no business being in Sioux country. Ordinarily, the Sioux would have killed any Chippewa they found. My question is, why would these two be taken prisoner?"

"Indians will take captured children to replace the ones they lost in wars."

"I know that, but now answer this. Why were there white men there?"

"Missionaries?" Sophie suggested.

"We could wish they were missionaries," Lorraine said, "but I know all of the missionaries in the valley, and no new ones would have come in during the war."

"Want to go to the Indian camp tomorrow and ask some questions?" Sophie asked.

"Yes, I'd like that."

Jake moved next to Hawk. "Remember those Chippewa we met on the road going back to your place last fall?"

"You suppose that's them?"

"I'll bet if we looked hard enough in the camps around this town," Jake said, "we could find that girl that got away."

"You thinkin' somethin'?" Sunkist asked.

"If we can find her, she might know if one of the missionaries at that Sioux camp was Diggs."

"What would that tell us?" Hawk asked.

"Probably nothing, but it could tell us what we're up against here. I don't think Diggs is really doing this to help the Indians, do you?"

"No, not after Miss Erickson was shot. There's something goin' on that's worth killing over."

"Tomorrow we'll go talk to the Indians."

There was no moon that night and they slept without a fire. The men took turns on watch and each of the women sat with them.

In the morning they were up with the sun.

"I could sure use a cup of coffee right now," Sophie said.

The sky was cloudy and a light drizzle wetted the ground. The damp air had them shivering in their blankets, even though it was early July.

"Ain't no use tryin' to start a fire in this," Hawk said. "Let's go to town and get breakfast."

"I'm with you," Jake said.

In the Brown House Inn they had their breakfast and warmed up near the kitchen fires. No one seemed to pay any attention to them and they ate in peace. Suddenly, something out the window caught Hawk's eye.

Sunkist jumped out of his chair and ran to the window. "Wha'd ye see out there?" he said as he pulled the edge of the curtain aside and looked out.

"That man in the buggy. I've seen him before."

"Where at?"

"Don't remember. Sophie, come here."

Sophie came and looked out the window. "Well, I'll be jiggered. That's Doc Bernier."

"You know 'im?" Sunkist asked.

"He's the doctor who fixed Hawk's hip. I should go thank him for that—right now."

"You just stay put till we know why he's here."

"Why don't we just go ask why he's here?"

Sunkist looked at her for a moment, winked at her, and said, "I recon that would be the quickest way to find out."

They stepped out the door and walked quickly down the road to catch up with the buggy.

The buggy stopped, and the man turned toward them. "Good morning." Then, with a look of surprise, he said, "Well, I'll be darned. Hello, Sophie. Hello, Hawk."

"Hello, Doctor, what brings you up here?"

"Might as well git right to the point," Sunkist grumbled.

"I heard you folks were heading to Superior. If it's all the same to you, I'll tag along."

"We'd be delighted to have you," Sophie said.

Sunkist turned his back to the doctor and said in a low voice, "We don't need no saw-bones taggin' along."

"Sunkist," Jake said, "judging by what we've been through so far, it might not be a bad idea to have a surgeon with us."

Sunkist turned his head to look at the doctor in the buggy, then turned back to Jake. "He don't look like much of a fightin' man."

"I knew a few fightin' men who'd still be alive if they had a doctor around," Hawk said.

Sunkist turned to the doctor. "Kin ye shoot?"

"I do a fair job with a rifle but I'd rather not make holes I'd have to patch up."

"Ye got a gun?"

"I've got more guns than I can ever use."

"You got so many guns, how come you don't shoot?"

"I just told you why."

"Yer gonna have to take care of yerself. Ain't no one here gonna do it fer ye."

Sophie nudged Sunkist aside, "You're more than welcome to ride with us, Doctor."

"Thank you. I won't be any bother to anyone." Then he reached in the back of the buggy and pulled out a pistol. "Anyone want to buy a pistol? I'm running a little short on cash."

"Lemme see that thing," Hawk said.

The doctor tossed the pistol down. "Eighteen fifty-one Colt, sheriff's model. Forty-four caliber revolver."

Hawk looked it over and handed it to Sunkist.

"Nice lookin' piece. Where'd ye git it?"

"Someone paid his bill with it. That's where I get all the guns I mentioned."

Sunkist handed the pistol to Abernathy. "What do ye know about this thing?"

"I know very little about pistols. This one was probably built in Samuel Colt's factory in Hartford, Connecticut. Mister Colt built hundreds of thousands of these revolvers to be used by the Union Army in the Civil War. As to be expected, some were purchased and used by the confederate soldiers, as well. It is a very reliable weapon and well worth having in your arsenal. Judging by its excellent condition, I would say it was built fairly recently and has seen very little use. This lever under the barrel is to facilitate loading. However, it is a bit cumbersome to load while under fire. Also, I see that . . ."

"How much ye want for it?" Hawk interrupted, looking at Abernathy.

"Twenty dollars sound fair to you?"

Hawk turned to Abernathy. "How much do they cost new?"

"It would be speculation," Abernathy said, "but I believe the cost would be comparable to the monthly wages of a working man. Perhaps twenty-five dollars."

"I'll take it." Hawk said. "Do you have ammunition for it?"

"Yes. I have everything that came with the pistol."

Hawk handed the pistol to Sophie. "Here, this is yours."

"I've got the dragoon," she said. "I don't need another gun."

"This one is smaller and lighter. It shoots the same ammunition the dragoon does and it'll be easier to handle when you need it."

"How will I carry it?"

"We'll make a holster for it. You can carry it on your belt."

"And the dragoon?"

"Stick it in your saddlebag."

"Stick it in yer own saddlebag."

"So, Hawk," Jake said, "what do we do now? We can't just sit here and do nothin'."

"What do you propose?"

Lorraine spoke up, "Let's go out and talk to the Indians."

"Good idea. Let's go. Come on, Doc."

"I will catch up with you later. I want to see what they have for medical services in this town."

"Have it your way. See ye later."

As they walked into the Indian camp at the edge of town, they were greeted by several women asking for food. Some of them held small children in their arms. A man sat on the ground in front of his wigwam obviously inebriated. Others sat around in groups doing nothing but watching the strangers walk in.

"Does anyone here speak English?" Hawk asked the Indians.

A voice from behind them said, "Very few people in this camp speak English."

They turned to see an older man walking up to them. "Good afternoon. May I be of service? I'm Reverend Ottomer Cloeter, the Lutheran minister. If you'd like to talk to a Catholic priest, Father Pierz has a chapel over in Belle Prairie—although I have no idea why anyone would want to talk to him, unless you wish to acquire a few trinkets and beads."

Hawk extended his hand. "I'm Hawk Owen." He then introduced each of his friends.

Reverend Cloeter was a heavyset man pushing seventy. He wore a thick, white beard, wire-rimmed glasses set high on his nose, and a black frock coat that reached to his mud-caked boots. His face presented a stern demeanor and the lines around his eyes showed the years of struggle trying to convert Chippewa Indians to Christianity. In his hand he carried a small black book.

"Do you know a man named Diggs?"

"Reverend Diggs? Oh, of course—well, I don't know the man personally, but I know of him. He's well known amongst the Indians. Why do you ask?"

"Do you have any idea where he might be?"

"I understand he was through here a few days back, but I have no idea where he's gone. He may still be here, in fact. I don't spend much time around town, so I wouldn't know."

"Do the Indians talk about him?" Lorraine asked.

"I hear his name mentioned occasionally. May I ask why you are so curious?"

Lorraine stepped in front of the rest of the group. "We are seeking his help in finding homes for Indian children in our orphanage."

"Where is your orphanage, if I may ask?"

"West of here a few miles."

Reverend Cloeter searched his memory. "That's strange. I know of no orphanage around here. Where exactly is it?"

"It's down in Sioux country. The Yellow Medicine Agency."

"I see." Cloeter looked puzzled. "Why are you looking in Chippewa country for homes for Sioux?"

"We have some Chippewa children who were captured by a Sioux war party and later rescued and brought to us."

Cloeter looked into Lorraine's eyes for a long moment. "I'm afraid I'm a bit confused. Why were these children not killed by the Sioux? That would be the expected behavior in this time of struggle."

"That's what bothers me," Lorraine said, "and that's exactly why we are looking for Reverend Diggs, to see if he can shed some light on this."

"Reverend Diggs may know something. He is one of the men who has taken it upon himself to take Indian children and put them through school. He is doing a great service for the natives of this land," Reverend Cloeter said, sounding as if he were preaching from his pulpit.

"We hope that is the truth in the matter, but we must find him and ask for ourselves."

Reverend Cloeter reached into his waist pocket and pulled out a timepiece. "I'm going to Rabbit Lake tomorrow to talk to the Indians. If I hear anything about Reverend Diggs, I'll send a messenger to you, but now I must go and rest. It is a long walk to Rabbit Lake."

"Is there someone in this camp who speaks English?"

"As I said, very few can, and even fewer who will talk at all."

"Thank you, Reverend. Have a good journey."

"A good journey would be any journey that would result in the conversion of even one soul to the gospel of the Lord," he said as he walked away.

Lorraine looked at Sophie. "Prostitution?"

"You think so?"

"What made you think that?" Hawk asked.

"There are schools right here at the agency for Indian children," Lorraine said. "Why take them to Saint Paul?"

"It hardly seems prostitution would be lucrative enough to kill over."

Suddenly, Posey turned and walked away.

"Where's she going?" Hawk asked.

"Don't know," Sunkist said, "but I know that look. She's feelin' somethin'. C'mon, follow her, but stay back."

Posey walked slowly into the Indian camp looking straight ahead. She walked to a bark shelter and stood at the doorway. Hawk and Jake started to walk to her but Sunkist put out his hand.

"Let her be."

"What's going on?"

"Ye jiss have to wait and see like the rest of us."

Slowly, Posey pushed aside the blanket that covered the entry to the shelter and went inside. Five minutes passed before the blanket opened and Posey stepped out. "She is Dream Talker. She has words for us."

"Does she speak English?"

"She speak Anishinabe, the first language of the Chippewa. I talk with her with sign. She will come to our camp tonight and talk."

"It's time to get back there ennaway," Sunkist said. "Let's go."

Doc Bernier joined them as they came into their camp. They built the fire and sat on blankets on the ground. "Well, here we sit, waiting again," Jake said.

"A little impatient, Jake?"

"I hate waiting for people. We've been here for two days and ain't found nothing."

"Who's this Diggs you keep talking about?" Doc asked.

"You probably know him," Sophie said. "He ran the Good Samaritan Church in Hutchinson."

"Oh yes. I knew the man."

"So, what do you know about him?"

"Nothing. I only know he took in orphaned children and found homes for them."

"Did he ever bring them to you when they were sick?"

"No, none that I knew of."

"You would have known if he did bring them in though, right?"

"I suppose so."

"Then he never did bring any in."

Doc just shook his head.

Silence prevailed for a long minute. Then Sophie said, "Okay, let's go over what we *do* know about him."

Lorraine was the first to speak. "We learned that he's taking Indian kids to schools to educate them, or at least that's what people believe."

"We learned that Diggs is well liked by the Indians," Hawk said, "but we know he's rotten to the core."

"And has anyone got a doubt that he's the one who had ol' lady Erickson killed?" Sunkist asked.

"We don't believe he's taking them to school," Sophie said. "Lorraine and I think he may be taking them somewhere for prostitution."

"What makes you so sure about that?" Hawk asked.

"When we were in the camp, did you see any young girls?"

"I guess I didn't notice."

"Most of the children there were under twelve and there were very few between twelve and twenty to be seen. If they were going to school, they would have started much younger than that."

"That sounds reasonable," Abernathy said, "but we must not jump to conclusions. We must keep an open mind and look at all of the facts. Otherwise, we are like the scientist who dreams up a theory and goes looking for whatever will support that theory. All too often, he overlooks important information that would prove his theory wrong."

"Abernathy," Sophie said, "are you suggesting Diggs might be legitimate?"

"I have no doubt that the subject of our search is running for a reason. Whether that reason is legitimate or not is yet to be seen."

"If Diggs is legitimate, why'd he take off after Sophie and Hawk rescued those two girls?" Sunkist asked.

"It's obvious that he's running for some reason, but I don't believe he's taking girls for prostitution," Jake said.

"I would have to agree with Jake," Abernathy said. "There would not be enough profit in prostitution to cause one to kill."

"He's right," Jake said. "Lord knows there's enough whorehouses the way it is."

Sophie looked at Jake with raised eyebrows. "Really? And how would you know that?"

"Hawk told me."

Sophie let out a laugh. "You're quick, Jake.

"You are the one the Old Ones tell me about"

27

C H A P T E R
T W E N T Y - S E V E N

POSEY STOOD AND WALKED TO THE EDGE OF THE CAMP. Through the thickest part of the surrounding forest came Dream Talker. Posey led her to the group. Sophie brought out a blanket and laid it on the ground and motioned Dream Talker to sit.

"Thank you," she said.

"You speak English?"

"Yes, I was educated by Father Pierz."

"Do you know who we are?" Sophie asked the girl.

"Yes. When we were in the south you gave us food."

"What is your name?"

"I am Dream Talker."

"Posey said you wanted to talk with us."

"Yes. Grandmother and my brother and sister and I came to see our cousin who lived at Wabasha's camp. We were told that it is not safe for us to stay there and we should go back to Red Lake where our people are. We were sad to leave but what he told us was true, so we started to go home. We talked to you and you gave us food. You were friends. After we left you, we went on our way and when we had walked for half the day, a band of Sioux attacked us. I knew they were there but did not know where they hid. When I knew they would attack us, I took Grandmother and hid in the sumac. They searched the woods and found my brother and sister and took them away."

"Have you seen them since?"

"I did not see them again after that day, but they are alive."

"How do you know they are alive?"

"I know they were not killed. I will see them again."

"Do you know anything about where your brother and sister were taken when they were captured?"

"No, I do not. Indian children are taken for many reasons. Sometimes they are taken and given to the traders to work for them to pay the money the father owes them."

"How long do they work for them?"

"Sometimes until a year and sometimes more. Sometimes they are never seen again."

"Where are all the girls who should be in the camp?"

"I do not know. They are gone."

"How is it that you are left and not taken?" Jake asked.

"I know when they come and I hide from them."

"How do you know when they are coming?"

"The Old Ones tell me in my dreams. That is why I am called Dream Talker. The Indians will not listen to me when I tell them the traders are coming. They want to stay and get the whiskey the traders have. The Indians like to get drunk from the whiskey, and the traders know this. They give the man whiskey and get him drunk, then take the children. They say the child will work for them to pay for the whiskey and the fathers say it is good."

"Does that explain the missing kids?" Jake asked.

"That explains nothing," Lorraine said. "I saw no Indian children working in any of the shops in Crow Wing. That means they're being taken away from here."

"I see no connection here to Reverend Diggs," Abernathy said.

"Diggs's name has come up too many times. He is connected with the missing children, Abernathy," Lorraine said. "Whether his involvement is legitimate or not, he is connected."

"He is connected to the missing children," Abernathy said, "but we have also heard that he is taking them to schools."

"Dream Talker," Lorraine said. "What else can you tell us?"

"There are things about the white man that I do not understand. I do not understand the things the Old Ones tell me."

"What do the Old Ones tell you?"

Dream Talker's eyes closed and she lowered her head with her hands on her lap. "I see white man's money and gold. I see strange people who do not dress like Indians or white men. I see the great water and canoes as big as Mister Beaulieu's house that fly on the wind. I do not understand these things."

"The great water you see—is that Mille Lacs Lake?"

"No, it is not that lake. I have never seen the place the Old Ones show me. I do not know where it is."

"Do you know a man named Reverend Diggs?" Lorraine asked.

"I have seen him in the Indian camp but I have never talked with him. The white men here do not know I can speak English."

She became silent and a frown crossed her face. Then her face became calm. She looked up at Sunkist and said in a soft voice, "You are the one the Old Ones tell me about. They told of a giant man with fire for hair, riding fast on a giant horse, and swinging a flaming tomahawk. He comes out of a storm in the sky," Dream Talker said.

"That is the same dream I had when Sunkist came to me," Posey said. "The Old Ones have brought us here."

"Do you know who killed Miss Erickson?" Sophie asked.

"I do not know that person," she said slowly in a soft voice.

"She's the one who rode with Diggs."

"I do not know of her."

"Do you know where Reverend Diggs is now?" Lorraine asked.

"I do not know. There are many white men here but I must stay. The Old Ones said you would come."

"Why did the Old Ones send us to you?"

Seconds passed before she spoke. Her eyebrows lowered as if she was in pain. "You will help my people."

"Yes, we want to help your people. Please tell us how we can do that," Sophie said.

"Stop the whiskey trade and help us get our land back from the white man. Help us get our deer and our elk back so we can feed our children. Stop the men who cut our trees and leave the ground bare so the deer have nowhere to live."

With her eyes closed, she raised her hands into the air as she talked. "Stop the traders who take our children and make them work for them. Indians do not know how to work like the white man. Mother Earth has given us all that we need to live, and the white men are taking it away from us.

"Before the white men came our men were proud warriors and hunters and did not need help from anyone. Now they are beggars and drunks because the white men have taken all of the deer and buffalo and our men have forgotten how to hunt and take care of their women. Our women go to the white man's house whenever he wants, even though they know he does not love them."

She folded her hands in her lap and talked softly with her head bowed and eyes closed. "They move us from our homes and give us the land that they cannot use for their farms. The land they give us is not good for their farms and it is not good for us, but they make us live there and buy our food from them with the money they give us."

Doc sat quietly studying the girl. The others looked back and forth at each other as they listened.

She paused and took a deep breath. "They give us the money then the traders come and say that the Indian owes him this much and that much and they take the money and leave us with nothing.

"The men who cut the trees come to our camp and give the mother glass beads and the mother gives the white man a girl for his pleasure."

Her voice became angry and she pounded her fist on the ground. "Sometimes the girl is not yet a woman, but the white man does not care and he takes her anyway! Sometimes he beats the girl and even kills her." She made a motion like she was swinging a club. "He says he did not do that and he is not punished for it."

Sophie's eyes teared and she reached out to touch the girl. "Dream Talker, we will do all we can to help . . . but sadly, we cannot stop the white man from coming. I am sorry. I wish things were different."

"I know that," Dream Talker said sadly, "but you will help."

Dream Talker raised her head and opened her eyes. "I must go now," she said, and she got up and disappeared into the woods.

Silence fell on the camp. The pines above them moaned and drops of rain began to fall. They all sat quietly contemplating what they had just witnessed.

"*Que penses-tu, Docteur Bernier?*" Lorraine asked.

Doc was taken by surprise by the French. "It's been a long time since anyone pronounced my name correctly. Thank you."

"*Docteur*, my name is also Bernier. I am quite familiar with the pronunciation."

"There are a lot of Berniers in Canada," Doc said. "They apparently reproduced quite successfully."

"Bones," Sunkist interrupted. "What about the gurl?"

"Well, it appears that she was in a state of self-hypnosis."

"Meaning?" Sophie asked.

"It's a sort of sleep condition during which she was able to block out all outside influences and concentrate completely on one thought. In her mind she was actually experiencing what she was saying."

"What about the Old Ones talking to her?"

"There is nothing unusual about that. Many people have prophetic dreams, especially the Indian people."

"Why mostly Indian people?" Hawk said.

"Because unlike those of white people, the Indian's mind is not encumbered by thoughts of self elevation. They don't consider it a special power of their own. They believe it's the spirits of the Old Ones—the deceased—talking to them, and they don't try to interpret their dreams. They simply tell what they see."

"Well," Hawk finally said, "I guess Dream Talker shot down the idea about prostitution."

"We're back to where we started," Sophie said, letting out a sigh. "Let's get some sleep. Maybe tomorrow things will be more clear."

28

C H A P T E R

T W E N T Y - E I G H T

MORNING FOUND THEM HUDDLED under their shelters in a pouring rain. Lightning flashed and thunder rolled. The wind picked up and the trees swayed and cracked. The horses stood with their tails to the wind and their heads low.

"Anyone wanna go to town for something to eat?" Jake asked.

Everyone stood and started to town on foot. They walked in the wind and rain with their canvas ponchos around them to the Brown House Inn. They walked in and took a table in the back corner where Sunkist could see out the window.

"Someone tole me the drumsticks off'n a hawk ain't got no meat on 'em," a voice said from across the room.

Hawk looked into his coffee cup and said loudly. "Anyone in this room cares to find out if this hawk's got meat on his drumsticks, just stand up."

The sound of a chair sliding on the board floor caught their ears. Hawk turned and looked at a scruffy man walking his way and stood.

"Hawk," Jake said, "sit down."

Hawk stepped by him and patted him on the shoulder. The two men met in the middle of the room and the room went silent. The ticking of the clock was interrupted by the footsteps of the waiter as he rushed to put himself between the two men. Distant thunder rumbled as Hawk's hand came up. The waiter ducked back expecting to catch a fist.

"Hey, Hayes," Hawk said as he shook the man's hand.

"What brings you up to this country, Hawk?"

"The Old Ones, I'm told. Come sit with us."

They walked to the table and Hawk pulled a chair from another table.

"Hello, Hayes," Sophie said with a smile.

"Hi, Soph. Glad to see yer still kickin'." His voice was small and seemed to come from the back of his throat.

"I have to stick around and keep an eye on these outlaws."

Sunkist glared suspiciously at the man.

"You remember Hayes, Sunkist. He was with us going out to talk with Little Crow."

Sunkist's head went up in recognition. "Oh yeah, ye look a little fatter'n ye did back then."

"Better eatin' up here."

"They let chuh outta the army?"

"More like they kicked me out. Couldn't handle that military bullshit."

"What are you doing up here, Hayes?" Sophie asked.

"On my way back home."

Hawk looked at Sophie then at Hayes. "Grand Marais?"

"Yep, doing a little prospectin' up there."

"Prospecting for what?" Sophie asked.

"Gold, silver, copper—whatever I can find to make me rich."

"There ain't no gold in them hills," Sunkist said.

"Maybe not, but there is copper and silver. Iron, too, I hear."

Sophie looked at Hawk. "Diggs?"

"Yeah," Hayes said, "got me some digs goin' up there. It ain't much, but . . ."

"No, I mean Reverend Diggs."

"Who's Reverend Diggs?"

"Never mind."

"Hayes Mayhew," Sophie said, "this is Abernathy Wayne, Lorraine's secretary."

"Good to meet you," Hayes said and put his hand out to Abernathy.

"Please. Tell us more about the prospecting up by Grand Marais."

"Not much to tell. A few guys up there found copper and silver, and now they're thinking they can get rich from it. Not many people know about it and the men up there ain't talkin'. Too far away and too damn cold in the winter anyway, for most of 'em. It takes a special kind of man to winter up there."

"And what kind of man is that?" Sophie asked.

"If you ain't too smart, but you can lift heavy things, you'll do alright."

"And that's you?" Jake said.

"Yep, I guess so." Hayes held a slight grin on his face as he talked.

"Has anyone made any good strikes?"

"Not that I know of. They're digging up copper on the Canadian side but nothing worth mentioning on this side. Yet."

"How much do you think a man could take out of that ground?" Hawk asked. "Enough to make it worth killing over?"

"Up there men get killed over a frozen p'tatee."

"But if someone found a rich strike he'd kill to protect it, right?"

"I suppose he would—I would."

Abernathy looked at Hayes. "You'd kill a man for gold or silver?"

"No, but I'd kill someone who's trying to kill me and take it away from me."

"Do you have a mine, Hayes?" Sophie asked.

"Not yet, but I got some good places to look. Why are you guys so interested in what's going on up there?"

Hawk started, "We're . . ." Sophie nudged him with her knee. He looked at her, then at Hayes. "Just curious, that's all."

"Say, what brings you up here anyway?" Hayes asked. "Don't you have a place down by Hawk Creek?"

"Yeah, we do. We're just out exploring the countryside."

Abernathy turned to Hayes. "We're continuing the research David Owen started back in the fifties. We want to see all of the places he wrote about in his diaries. It's very interesting. You would enjoy it immensely."

"Naw. I don't know much about geology, and I care even less. I got all the geology I can stand for one lifetime when I ran with Henry Eames back in fifty-six."

"It might offer you clues as to the location of the silver and copper deposits." Abernathy added. "If you know the types of rocks that bear copper ore, you would find your wealth much more quickly."

"Do you know what kind of rocks to look for?" Hayes asked arching and eyebrow.

"Oh dear, no. I know nothing about prospecting for minerals. I'm afraid mineralogy is far to complex for my rather limited capacity, so I shall limit my interests to surface geology."

"There ye go ag'in'," Sunkist barked. "Talkin' so's no one kin figger out what the hail yer talkin' about."

"It is the study of the surface of the earth and the means by which it was formed."

"Go talk to Father Pierz," Hayes said with a chuckle. "He'll tell you all about how the earth was formed."

"The fact of the matter is, Mister Mayhew, the ground on which this hotel is built is alive and changing as we speak. The wind and rain falling outside are at this moment, washing the soil from the land and into the Mississippi River to be carried further . . ."

"I think this would be a good time to think about a place to stay, don't you, Abernathy?" Sunkist interrupted.

"It is exceedingly rude to interrupt a conversation, Sunkist."

"You weren't having a conversation, ye little rat. A conversation takes two 'er more people. You was the only one talkin'."

The weather outside was turning worse. The wind blew hard and the rain poured down in sheets. Though they were reluctant to leave the shelter of the restaurant, they knew that sooner or later they'd have to, regardless of the weather conditions.

"Where do we find a dry place to stay?" Hawk asked.

"Stay here, in the hotel," Hayes answered. "I'm sure they got plenty of rooms."

"I ain't stayin' in this place," Sunkist said. "Too damn many people comin' and goin'."

"Put your animals in the stable and stay in the warehouse down by the river," Hayes said. "It ain't the Brown House, but it's dry."

"Sounds better'n this," Sunkist said. "Who do we talk to about it?"

"It belongs to Clement Beaulieu. He lives in that big, white house on the hill," Mayhew said. "But he's out of town now, so just go make yourselves at home. You can ask forgiveness when he comes back in the morning."

"I'll go git the animals an' put 'em up in the stable," Sunkist said. "You guys go find us a room."

"I'll stay here in the hotel," Doc said.

"You got a horse, Sawbones?" Sunkist asked.

Doc chuckled, "Yes, I can ride the one hitched to my buggy."

Lorraine looked hard at Sunkist. "I don't think the doctor wants to be called 'Sawbones'."

Doc chuckled again and said, "No, it's alright. That's what everyone called me at the fort."

"And you don't mind?"

"Not at all," he said softly. "I got used to it and now I answer to it pretty much automatically."

"So you prefer it?"

"Well, let's just say I will answer to 'Sawbones'."

"I'll git the horses," Sunkist said. Without hesitation, he stepped out into the storm and walked leisurely through the driving rain to the camp and the horses. The rest of the group ran to the warehouse with their coats pulled over their heads and crashed through the door. Inside it was dry, but the wind blew through the cracks in the walls. They found their comfort under blankets they found bundled on stacks of miscellaneous goods. What little light there was came through a few dirty windows and the same cracks as the wind.

The thunderstorm lasted through the rest of the day and into the night. In the morning they were up early, and the air in the warehouse was heavy. Sophie threw the blankets off and fanned herself with her hand. "Whew! Sticky." She pulled her shirt away from her damp body. "I could use a jump in the river."

Sunkist was looking out the window toward the house on the hill a hundred yards away. He turned and said, "Stay away from these wenders; there's someone with rifles in that house up there."

"Do you think they're after us?"

"I don't know if they're gunnin' fer us, but I ain't gonna step out there to find out."

They heard laughing from outside. Hawk looked out the window and saw two young Métis women washing themselves under the pump.

He turned to the others and said, "Now's our chance. Sunkist, you come with me. Jake, you and Abernathy stay with the women." Quickly, he stepped out the backdoor with Sunkist behind him.

"Where we a-goin'?" Sunkist asked.

"We're gonna go down to the riverbank and make our way to that house while those women out there are distracting those rifles. Come on, let's go."

They crept through the tall grass to the river, keeping the warehouse between them and Beaulieu's house. They made a wide circle around another large building and two smaller ones, then around the house at the top of a hill. They stopped and crouched down in the wet grass as they came up behind Beaulieu's house and peeked in the window.

"No one there," Hawk said and put his ear to the door. He took hold of the knob and turned it slowly. The door came open and he carefully looked inside. He reached back, caught Sunkist's shirtsleeve, and stepped inside. To the left they saw the stairs going to the second floor. Hawk pointed at Sunkist's feet then to the edge of the stairs. Slowly they climbed the steps. They heard soft mumbling voices from above, then someone laughed. "Gimme them," a voice said from above.

"Jest wait a second," another voice said.

They heard shuffling, "Gimme them glasses, dammit!"

Then a moment of silence. "That you, Boots? Come on up here and look at this."

Hawk mumbled a fake response, then whispered to Sunkist almost silently, "Don't kill 'em."

One of the men upstairs laughed. At that moment Hawk made the top of the stairs and stepped out to the men at the window five feet away.

Without turning, one of the men said, "Come and look at this."

"Turn around and look at this," Sunkist said.

They turned quickly and saw Hawk with his rifle pointed at them. They dropped a pair of binoculars to the floor as Sunkist stepped next to Hawk. At once the two men pulled their rifles from the windows and started to swing them around, but they weren't fast enough. Sunkist's rifle cracked simultaneously with Hawk's Henry. The two men spun around, their rifles clattering to the floor. They fell and one of them turned white and went limp.

"I told you not to kill 'em," Hawk said.

"He ain't dead."

Hawk stepped to the man and kicked the rifle out of his reach. "Who are you and why you wanna shoot at us?"

"We didn't shoot at you!" the man hollered.

"Yeah, well, that's just 'cause we shot you first."

"I need a doctor!" the man shouted.

"The doc's over at the hotel," Sunkist said. "Yer gonna need an undertaker if you don't tell us why you wanna shoot us."

The man who lay next to him groaned and stopped breathing.

Sunkist touched the other man's wounded shoulder with his toe. "You gonna tell me who yer workin' fer?"

The man screamed in pain. "We weren't workin' for nobody, and we weren't gonna shoot nobody."

"Why the hell are you up here with rifles pointed at us then?"

"We was just supposed to keep an eye on you. We wasn't gonna shoot anyone."

"Then why the rifles?"

The man looked at Sunkist then at Hawk. "I'm gonna die, ain't I?"

"Looks that-a-way," Sunkist said.

"We was hired by some men to take care of you guys."

"Who were the men who hired you? And who's Boots?"

"Boots said we should stay here and keep an eye on you. He said if we didn't do it, he'd shoot us."

"Do you know a man named Diggs?"

"Yeah, he's the preacher who . . ." The man's body suddenly stiffened, his eyes turned up and he got a frightened look on his face. Slowly his face started to turn blue.

Sunkist kicked him on the leg. "Don't you go dyin' on me now! Diggs is the man who what?"

He gasped for air then went limp. His head dropped to the floor and he let out his last breath.

"Damn tenderfoots," Sunkist said. "A wound like that shouldn't kill a man that quick."

"Any idea what we do next?" Hawk asked.

"We'll tell the law about these men and they can bury 'em."

They walked down the stairs and Hawk opened the door. He looked to the right, then to the left, and cautiously stepped out. "Looks like we're alone." They followed their path around the buildings back to the warehouse.

They sat in the dim light of the warehouse listening to the increasing activity on main street.

"Well," Hawk said, "now we know we're bein' hunted. I say we git the hell outta this town before someone gets killed."

"I agree," Jake said. "But where to? We can't just go chasing around hoping to bump into Diggs. We gotta have some idea where to look."

"How about Boots?" Hawk asked. "You ain't wonderin' who he is?"

"If there's a Boots, he's long gone by now. We can go to the saloon and see if anyone there knows anything about him, and who he was runnin' with, but I doubt we'll learn anything."

"We could go and talk to Dream Talker. Maybe she can help us," Sophie said.

"You don't believe that stuff about seeing things in her dreams do you?" Hawk said.

"Don't ever doubt the powers of the Indian visionaries and medicine men," Lorraine said. "Some of them have exceptionally clear connections with the spirit world and are capable of seeing things hidden from the rest of us."

"Lorraine . . ."

"They have been known to cure illnesses with ceremonies and prayers so powerful that we will never hope to understand."

"Lorraine . . ."

"You may scoff at what I'm telling you, Hawk, but I assure you, it is not a practice to be dismissed as paganism. The medicine men have been known to cause persons to conduct themselves in manners uncharacteristic of their normal behavioral patterns."

"Lorraine . . ."

"Dream Talker could very well be one of those people."

"Lorraine . . ."

"Perhaps I should talk to Dream Talker about *your* behavioral patterns."

"Lorraine!"

"Oh, what is it, Hawk?"

He pointed at the front of Lorraine's shirt.

She pulled her lower shirt out away from her body so she could see below her breasts and looked down to see a large spider climbing up her body. She screamed and swatted the spider off.

"See? I'm capable of seeing things hidden from you, too."

Lorraine clenched her jaw and started to turn to walk away from him.

"Lorraine, come here," Hawk said. "I'm not real sure what you just said, but if you think it'll work, let's go see Dream Talker."

"I didn't say she will be able to help us, I simply said she may have the power to do so."

"You didn't say anything simply."

"That would depend on the listener's ability to comprehend the exchange of ideas."

"Give it up, Hawk," Sunkist said, "yer an unarmed man fightin' an army. You guys go over to the Indian camp. I'll catch up with you there. I'm going to find someone and tell 'em what happened. Abernathy, you come with me."

"Sir?" Abernathy said quizzically.

"Two sets of ears is better than one." They walked out of the warehouse and up the slope onto the street. Very few people were out, and they had the street to themselves. A wagon came into town on the south road and stopped at the saloon.

"Folks are scared they'll melt in this rain," Sunkist said as the rain fell from his hat in front of his eyes.

Abernathy stopped and looked back. "You're not bringing Posey with you?"

"Nope. She's gotta find the Injun gurl."

"But we know where her home is."

"We know where she was yesterday, but I doubt she'll be in the same place after talking with us."

"Sometimes you do amaze me with your perception, my dear friend."

"I tole you to stop calling me your dear friend!"

"I'm sorry, it's just that . . ."

"Never mind. Jiss call me Sunkist."

"Yes, sir." Abernathy paused and asked, "Why did you ask me to come with you?"

"I didn't ask you, I tole you."

"I took it as an invitation."

"Yer comin' with me onna conna you kin write and I cain't."

"You cannot write?"

"I used to. My pa learnt me some but I ain't writ nothin' fer so long I fergit how."

"I could teach you?"

"What fer? I got you to do it fer me."

"I may not be with you forever."

"Can you make that a promise?"

"All things come to pass, my friend. Do you know where the local law enforcement officer is?"

"That's prob'ly him going to the house right now. He musta heard the shootin'." Sunkist pointed to several people sloshing through the mud on their way to the house where the dead men lay.

As the men entered the house, Sunkist and Abernathy came up to them. One man turned and asked, "Do you know what the shooting was about?"

"Who the hail are you?" Sunkist asked.

"I'm Clement Beaulieu and this is my house. Do you know what happened here?"

"Yeah, we killed two men afore they could kill us."

"Where are they?"

"Top of the stairs."

They climbed up the stairs to the room, looked around, and saw nothing.

"What the hail's this? There outta be two dead men layin' there."

"Well, they're obviously not here now." Beaulieu knelt down and examined the blood on the floor. "But the blood tells me they were." He turned to Sunkist. "Are you sure there were two dead men there?"

"Well, I didn't do no physical inventory but I'm perty sure there was only two."

"And you say you shot them?"

"I did."

"Would you like to explain that?"

"No."

"Well, I'm asking you to explain why you shot two men here."

"We was stayin' in the warehouse down by the river . . ."

"That's my warehouse. Why were you in there?"

"Cause it ain't rainin' in there."

"Go on with your story."

"They was up here in these here wenders with rifles. We snuck up on 'em and when they started to pull their rifles on us, we shot 'em."

"We? Who else was in on this?"

"Jiss me and some other guy."

"This man?" Beaulieu asked turning to Abernathy.

"No. Someone else."

"Who was the other man?"

"An Injun. He went back to his people."

"And, of course, you don't know his name."

"Course not. He told me, but it was a Chipaway name and I cain't remember it."

"Who are the men in your party?"

"Ain't givin' ye their names onna conna they don't know what happened up here."

"They know nothing about this?"

"No, they don't know nothin' about it."

"You're claiming it was self-defense then?"

"It was us or them."

"Since there are no other witnesses and no bodies, we'll assume, for the present, that you are telling the truth."

"Well, hail yes I'm tellin' the truth! What the hail would I lie fer?"

"May I ask your names? For the record."

"Name's Whistler, James Whistler."

Beaulieu turned to Abernathy. "Your name please?"

Surprised at the abrupt attention, Abernathy raised his hand to cover his mouth. "Oh dear me," he said, "I was not party to this. I was in the warehouse, but I was not involved in the disturbance here."

"I still need your name, as a witness to this interview. You understand."

"Oh yes, I understand."

"Your name?"

Abernathy turned to Sunkist then to Beaulieu. "Abernathy Wayne."

"Your last name?"

Again Abernathy turned to Sunkist then back to Beaulieu. "Sir—that is my full name. Abernathy Wayne."

"Did you know these men?" Beaulieu asked Sunkist.

"Nope, I don't hang around with people who wanna shoot me."

"Is that all you can tell us about this?"

"Yup. We shot 'em afore they could shoot us. By the looks of things they ain't even dead. Dead men don't get up and walk away."

"Well, there is nothing we can do about it now. Where will you be if we learn more?"

"We ain't stayin' in this town. People here ain't friendly."

"I'll need to know where you're going."

"North."

"Your destination?"

"North."

Beaulieu looked at Sunkist. "I would suggest you leave at the earliest convenience."

Sunkist and Abernathy started down the stairs. Sunkist stopped, turned, and said, "Hey, Beaulieu! You know a guy named Boots?"

Beaulieu thought for a second. "No, I don't believe I do. Did he have something to do with this?"

"One of the men we shot said his name b'fore he died. Figgered if you knew who Boots was, we might find out who's trying to shoot us."

Beaulieu scratched at is chin, "Hmm, nope."

"He said the name before we shot 'im. I figger he was mixed up in whatever's goin' on 'round cheer."

"As far as I know, there is no one in this town by that name. Mister Whistler, just what is it you think is going on here?"

"Prob'ly nothin'. Just people shootin' at each other. Nothin' outta the ordinary. You know a preacher name'a Diggs?"

"Why, yes. He was through here just a few days ago. He stopped and talked to the Indians for a bit. I believe he took two of the girls down to Saint Paul for schooling."

"What'a guy," Sunkist said in a low tone.

"Why do you ask?"

"We know a lady school teacher who's lookin' fer 'im."

"Is she a nun?"

"No, she ain't no nun, but she might as well be. She's a schoolteacher. Guess we'll be on our way."

They stepped off the boardwalk and started toward the Indian camp on the north edge of town.

Sophie, Hawk, and the rest were waiting for them when they arrived.

"Ye find that gurl?" Sunkist asked.

"No. She left camp right after we talked to her yesterday," Hawk said. "No one seems to know where she went."

"What say we go get the animals and move on?" Jake said.

"I say let's do it now while we can," Hawk added.

Walking back to town, Sunkist turned to Hawk. "Ye know those two men we shot?"

"Yeah?"

"They wasn't there when we went to see 'em."

"You thinking they weren't dead when we left 'em?"

"No, they was dead. Someone came and carried 'em away. Prob'ly Boots, whoever the hell he is."

"Did you ask Beaulieu about Boots?"

"Yep. Ain't no one in this town by that name."

"Let's get the sawbones and git out of here."

"I'll go get him," Jake said and walked to the hotel.

Mayhew, who had been waiting for them, walked up to them and said, "If there are no objections, I'd like to ride with you."

"Why you wanna ride with us?" Sunkist asked.

"You're going to Grand Marais and so am I. You got troubles and so do I.

One more rifle in the group can't hurt."

Sunkist looked at the man from under thick eyebrows. "You know the trail to Grand Marais?"

"Yup, been up there and back three times."

"You know a galoot named Diggs?"

"Nope, don't know the man. I think I told you that once."

"You ridin' alone?"

"Yes, I'm alone," he said, showing some impatience.

"Okay, you ride in front of us."

"Whatever you say," he said with a slight grin. "I'm not a dangerous man, my friend." Then his eyes narrowed and locked onto Sunkist's. He nodded slightly and added, "Unless you are."

"That I am."

Mayhew chuckled and stepped up onto his mule. "Follow me," he said.

"Where we goin'?"

"If you want to know about people, you go ask people who know."

"You know someone like that?"

"Yes. A lady who runs a saloon on the edge of town. It's on the road to Grand Marais."

Sunkist nodded at Mayhew. "You jiss lead the way."

*"This aye no regular hang-around joint, ye knew.
This is a farst-rate Irish pub."*

29

THEY RODE UP THE HILL and onto the road leading out of town. Mayhew led them to a small frame building with a sign over the door that read, 'Kathleen's Irish Pub.'

Hawk reached for the outside door handle of the tavern just as a gust of wind caught the door, banging it hard against the wall.

From somewhere inside they heard a female voice. "Well, whud ye look whah the wind blew in now! Aye and a thirsty lot they are from whah aye ken see. Coom in out of thet wind 'fore ye git yourselves blown away." The woman stood from cleaning a table top. "I ken say that ye've ne'r been 'ere before, so welcome to me 'umble establishment." This was followed by a loud, hearty laugh. "Ello, me name is Kathleen Marie. O'Rourke, that is. This is me tavern, thanks to me late 'usband. God rest his soul." She abruptly turned her head, spat into the sawdust on the floor, and walked behind the bar. Jake laughed out loud at this sudden, unexpected act.

"Ye knew," she said, wiping the back of her hand across her lower lip, "I was just tellin' Andy there, the only reason I married the bloke was so's I could coom over 'ere from Dublin, me 'ometown. And I'm right glad at that, tew!" This was again followed by a gusty laugh that shook her ample bosom. Sophie caught Hawk's downward glance and gave him a curt jab in the ribs with her elbow, smirking while she did it. She instantly liked this woman.

Kathleen was studying Jake and Hawk. She leaned over the bar, reached up she tousled both heads of hair simultaneously, remarking, "Aye, tew redheads, and good-lookin' at that. Hmmm . . . Bookends—I like that. I may have tew find room on the bookshelves in me bedroom far the tew of ye."

"Well, now, that deserves a drink, Kathleen Marie O'Rourke," Sophie said. "A round for the lot, and make that six beers and a sasparilly." She looked around to make sure this was correct.

"Aye, ye've got it!" She spun around on her five-foot-five frame and walked behind the bar and grabbed the glasses and started pouring a round. Hawk watched her as she busied herself behind the bar. Her long, thick red hair fell in curls past her shoulders. She wore a man's white cotton shirt knotted in the front, and a long, brown, pleated skirt that was pulled tightly around her narrow waist, accenting the roundness of her hips. Sophie smiled as she watched Hawk and Jake focus their eyes on the flare of the Irish woman's bottom. Kathleen turned with the beer glasses on a tray and set them on the bar. She had emerald-green eyes that sparked with mischief and looked as if they were ready to ignite at the slightest provocation.

"Well, now, I see ye've got me friend Ennery wi' ye."

"Ennery?"

"Aye. Ennery, here," she pointed to Hayes.

"Henry? Why do you call him Henry?"

"Ow, he goes by Ennery, or Hayes, and soomtimes he even uses his real name, Hazael."

Sophie looked back and forth from Kathleen to Hayes. "You two know each other?"

"Aye," she said with a wave of her hand. "Ennery an' me, we go wa-a-ay back. We've been friends for couple o' years now."

"You have? How do you know Hayes?"

"Ow, he cooms through 'ere once er twice a year, just to see Kathleen." She reached across the bar and shook Hayes's hand. "Ow's the world treatin' ye, Ennery?"

"Not that often," he said quietly. Hayes's eyes were wide and fixed on the woman behind the bar.

"It certainly is a small world, huh, Hayes?" Sunkist said.

"Um, yeah," Hayes said softly while staring at Kathleen's white shirt. "Um, no, not all that small." He suddenly realized he was being spoken to— and he was answering. Then, as if he were abruptly awakened from a dream, he cleared is throat and took a long drink from his mug.

Sunkist turned to Kathleen. "Do you know Abernathy, too?"

She thought about it a moment and shook her head. "No, aye don't believe I knew anyone by thet name." She laughed and said, "It does sound like a good Irish name, though. May haps I should get te know the lad."

"Naw, maybe you should just keep things like they are," Sunkist said. "Ye got ennything stronger'n beer in this place?"

"Jesus, Mary, and Joseph, mon! This aye no regular hang-around joint, ye knew. This is a farst-rate Irish pub. I've got the finest Irish whiskey mooney ken buy! Farst-class it is."

"Well, stop dawdlin' around bring me some of that farst-rate Irish whiskey."

Without taking her eyes off Sunkist she reached under the counter, brought out a clear glass bottle, and slammed it on the bar. She put her face in her hands, dropped her elbows on the bar, and said with mischief in her eyes, "There ye be, me good mon. Have at it."

Sunkist looked at the bottle from under his bushy eyebrows.

"Well, go on mon, have a sip! It's called Tullamore Dew, the best damn Irish whiskey ye've ever 'ad." She stepped back from the bar, threw out her chest and hooked her thumbs in her belt. "I have te boast about it a bit now, ye knew," she said with a wide smile. "It's made in the town of Tullamore— County Offaly—just a wee bit west o' me 'ometown. I knew one of the gentlemen who worked there. He brought me my supply every time he came tew me 'ouse." She glanced around the bar and leaned toward Sunkist. "I suppose I ken tell ye his name since he ain't livin' around 'ere. His name is Daniel Edwin Williams. The D E W in the name on the bottle are 'is initials."

Sunkist pulled the cork from the bottle with a squeak and a thump.

"Aye, I love thet sound," Kathleen said with a slight tilt to her head.

Sunkist tipped the bottle up for a taste, smacked his lips once, then turned the bottle up, filling his mouth and swallowing hard. His head went back and his eyes closed and a smile crossed his lips. He raised one eyebrow and looked at Kathleen through the corner of his left eye. "Arrrr," he growled, "now *that's* good Irish whiskey."

Kathleen came over and slapped him hard on the back. "Now 'ere's a mon after me own 'eart. Would ye be needin' a glass far yer whiskey, sar?"

"Nope, this bottle's got a hole in the neck and that's all I'll be needin'. It ain't quite Fraley's heaven in a jore, but it slides down jiss fine."

"Fraley's what, ye say?"

"Walt Fraley's heaven in a jore. Feller down by Courtland makes the stuff. Best damn squeezin's in the world."

"Me good mon," Kathleen said. "Have I go' a surprise fare yew. Ye see, I just happen to know that scalawag. I was down there me self a couple'a months back and I just 'appen to have a jar of his venom right . . ." she paused and reached under the counter, brought out a pint jar and slammed it on the bar, "'ear!"

Sunkist looked at the jar with his mouth hanging open. "That's Fraley's stuff?"

"Aye, that it tis. Packed it all the way up 'ere in me poke."

"How much?"

"Five dollars for the jar," Kathleen said, staring into Sunkist's eyes.

"Make it ten," Sunkist replied without taking his eyes off the jar.

"Four," Kathleen said.

"Fifteen," he grumbled.

"Three dollars and the jar is yours."

"Twenty it is then." He reached into his pocket, pulled out a handful of money, dropped it on the bar, and wrapped his hands around the jar.

Kathleen took a bill out from the stack, tucked it inside her shirt between her breasts, then slid the remainder back to Sunkist. "And 'ere's yer change."

Sunkist reached up, pulled the bill from her cleavage with his thumb and index finger, then pushed a twenty-dollar gold piece deep down into the cleft. "We agreed on twenty."

Kathleen turned to Sophie. "I like this mon." She moved away from Sunkist and stood before Sophie. "So, what brings the lot of ye up to Kathleen's country?"

"The Old Ones," Hawk grumbled.

"Ye mean Sunkist and Ennery?" she asked with a bosom-shaking laugh.

"Now, that wasn't nice, Kathleen."

She reached over the bar and grabbed his whiskers. "I wos just ruffling yer feathers, Sunny."

"You call me Sunny agin and yer gonna get yer feathers ruffled," he said without looking up.

"Aye, a mon who knows a good woman."

Kathleen stopped abruptly. Her head turned slowly and she looked directly at Hawk. Her eyes narrowed slightly and her face became serious. She started to move to her left around the bar, sliding her right hand behind her along the polished wood. Her eyes held Hawk's as she moved very slowly. He had a strong urge to break and run but resisted. With a cat-like movement, she placed herself between him and Jake. She slowly looked them up and down and said, in a low, sultry tone, "We 'aven't been properly introduced."

"Um, I'm Hawk and he's Jake." Hawk was visibly shaken by this unexpected attention.

"Now, don't ye be tellin' me yer Hawk and Jake Owen."

"How'd? . . ." He stopped to clear his throat. "How'd you know that?"

"Mister Fraley told me all about the tew of ye." She hooked her arms with Jake and Hawk. "Coom with me. We'll take a table."

Her bosom pressed against their arms as they walked across the room to a table. "Sit yerselves down." Hawk felt her pat his backside and jumped. Then Jake jumped. Sophie grinned as Hawk's face turned red. Kathleen stopped and turned slowly toward Jake. "Aye," she said as she turned with a faint smile on her lips. "Thank yew. Ye've got a nice touch."

Kathleen turned to Posey. "And who have we 'ere?"

A voice from the bottom of a pint jar said, "That's mu wife, Posey."

"Well," she said as she looked at Posey and then at Sunkist. One eyebrow came up and, with a sly smile on her lips, she looked back at Posey. "Aye ken see that she's not Sioux, and she's certainly not Chippewa. What I dew see is a very beautiful woman."

"Cherokee."

Quickly she turned to Sophie. "So, tell Kathleen what brings ye up to this country." Then she turned to Hayes. "Well, sit yerself down, Ennery, aye won't be goin' anywhere for a while."

"We're on a geological research trip," Sophie said.

"Aye, there's been a lot of that goin on 'ere abouts. I love it. What is it?"

"She's okay," Hayes said. He then turned to Kathleen and said, "They're looking for a man called Diggs. You heard of him?"

She thought for a moment and said, "I've heard the name, but no, aye don't believe I know the mon. Whot's 'e look like? May haps 'e's been through 'ere."

"Tall and thin," Jake said, "wears a black hat and coat. Oh, and his eyebrows meet in the middle, above his nose."

Kathleen sat down close to Jake and looked directly at him. "Aye, I've seen a mon like thet around 'ere, but I'm thinkin' he was a preacher." She cocked her head to the side. "Do ye go te church, Jake Owen?"

"That's him. Where'd you see him?"

Kathleen didn't respond, she just looked into Jake's eyes.

"No, I don't go to church. Where did you see him?"

"Too bad. I wondered if ye ever called upon the Lord at the end of the sarvices. Aye don't make a habit of goin' te church. They put too many restrictions on a lady's activities."

"When did you see this preacher?"

"He stopped in about a week past and asked for wine. Well, I'll be tellin' ye new, this is a farst-class establishment, don't ye knew, boot we don't have wine in here. He took a bottle of spirits and left."

"Did he say where he's going?"

"New, and I didn't ask 'im. He was a bit shy, I believe."

"Did you see which way he went when he left?"

"Back to town I would guess. Where he went frum there, I wouldn't knew. People talk aboot one another all the time, but they don't talk aboot the men of the cloth in 'ere. I was raised to be a good Irish Catholic girl, boot, I have me own religion. I love hearing a mon shouting, 'Oh, Lord—oh, God!' at the end of sarvices."

She leaned her elbows on the table and put her face in her hands. "Would ye be Irish, Hawk Owen? I knew some Owens back in Ireland."

Hawk backed away and sat straight up in his chair. He looked at Kathleen silently for a moment, then glanced at Sophie, then back to Kathleen. "No. Um, no. My grandpa came from Wales."

"Close enough," she said.

Kathleen slowly turned her attention to Jake sitting to her right.

"The ladies in town will be askin' about yew, ye knew."

"Yeah, well, you can tell 'em you don't know nothin' about me."

"Anything yew say," she said with a wink. "Boot I'd like te know absolutely everything aboot yew."

Jake took a sip from his glass. "Did he have anyone with him?"

"Who?"

"The preacher."

"Ow, 'im again. We've got lumbermen and businessmen comin' and goin' through 'ere all the time. I don't pay attention to who is with who."

The door flew open and a small man with thin chin whiskers walked in. He wore a red and green plaid cap and a brown wool overcoat. He stopped at the door and looked around the small room.

Kathleen jumped up from her chair nearly turning it over. "Well, Chauncey O'Riley! It's aboot time ye got 'ere. Ye've guests to entertain!"

Chauncey took one step back, pulled the door shut, then walked into the room. Kathleen went quickly to him, wrapped her arms tightly around him, and kissed him on the lips. "Ye best be gittin' out of thet coat now and start playin'."

Hayes got up and quickly walked out the door.

"What's wrong with him?" Jake asked.

Sophie looked toward the closing door. "I think our friend Hayes is in love with our Irish spitfire."

"Now what makes you think that?" Hawk said. "Maybe he just hadda go water the trees."

"Haven't you seen how he looks at her? He's hardly taken his eyes off her since we came in here."

"Well, she's a damn good-lookin' woman," Sunkist said. "Havin' a little trouble keepin' my eyes off'n them . . ." he glanced quickly at Posey, "um, green eyes."

"Right, her green eyes—I think it's a little further south than that."

The room suddenly filled with fiddle music. Chauncey stood in the corner playing a lively Irish jig, stomping his foot, and showing his tobacco-stained teeth. Kathleen carried a cuspidor over and set it on the floor next to him. She grabbed Jake's arm and dragged him to the middle of the floor and started to dance around him, her skirt flaring out and showing her stockings with white and green horizontal stripes. Her feet danced quickly to the music while Jake stood with his hands at his side not knowing what he should be doing.

"Well, come on, lad, dance with me!"

"But, I ain't never danced before."

"Well, now's the parfect time te learn!"

He tried a few quick steps but decided he would never be able do dance, especially a fast dance like Kathleen was doing. He walked back to the table, embarrassed by his inexperience.

Sophie jumped up and joined Kathleen on the floor. Together they danced and twirled and laughed. Sophie had once again surrendered to the call of music. Aside from being free to move about as she wished, dance was her first love, and a lively Irish jig was the perfect outlet for her energetic nature.

Sophie came back to the table, breathing hard, beads of perspiration on her forehead. She took a drink of beer and said, "Come on, Hawk." She took hold of his arm and dragged him out onto the floor. He stood looking down at Sophie's feet, trying to pick up the rhythm. People watched and clapped their hands in time with the music. Soon the floor was filled with people dancing and laughing and spilling their beers.

Jake sat alone at the table. Kathleen walked over to him. "Would ye like te try it again, Jake?" She took his arm. "Coom on lad, no boody's going te laugh at ye."

He stood and quickstepped his way onto the floor. Kathleen hooked her arm with his and danced around him while Jake bounced on his feet and watched.

The party went on until well past midnight. Eventually everyone left the dance floor and gathered around the scattered tables.

"What say we git back to camp and git some shut-eye." Sunkist said.

"Getting tired, Sunkist?" Sophie asked.

"When I blink mu eyes it's an effort tu git 'em back open."

They stood and started out the door, but Jake kept his chair.

"Coming, Jake?"

"I'm gonna hang around here a bit. I'll catch up with you later."

Kathleen came to Jake's table. "Would ye be havin' another mug a beer, Jake?"

"What time do you close this place?"

"Ow, aye ken close any time. I own the place ye know."

"Well, how about you close it right now and let's go for a walk."

"Aye, I'd luv that."

She chased the few remaining customers from the bar and turned down the oil lamps, then she wrapped a shawl around her shoulders and motioned to Jake. "Let's go."

The wind had died down, the sky had cleared, and the stars shone brightly. They walked around the building and stopped to look up at the stars. "The night is so romontic," she said.

They walked toward the woods, down to the creek and sat on the bank. They sat close and Jake took her hand. Her arms went around him and they kissed. His hand started to move down her back and she moaned softly. "Ye've got nice hands," she said and pressed her body to his. They slowly lay back on the grass and Jake leaned over her and kissed her again. His hands explored her body and she responded with soft moans and held him tight to her. They kissed hard and Kathleen's body began moving rhythmically against Jake.

She stood up unexpectedly and smoothed out her skirt and said, "Coom on, Jake. I need to go to me bed far the night."

Jake's heart was hammering in his chest as they approached the door.

She opened the door and stepped inside, then turned around and gave him a light kiss on the lips. "Good night, Jake. Thank yew, it was a lovely evening. I'll see you in the marnin'," she said and closed the door.

Jake stood facing the door and heard the lock inside slip into place.

Loneliness.

He took a deep breath then turned and walked back toward town.

He started toward the camp but stopped thirty yards from it. He stood for some minutes before joining the group. Sitting on the ground with all of his friends around him, he still felt alone.

Abernathy sat on a fallen log with his face cradled in his hands.

"Are you alright?"

"Oh, Miss Lorraine, I feel absolutely dreadful."

"Why? What's wrong?"

"I suspect I have a serious illness."

Lorraine felt his forehead. "You're burning up! You have a fever."

"I do hope it is not something serious that will slow our progress," he said with a groan. "I must go in and lie down."

"I'll get you some water."

"Oh, would you please? That would be so nice. Thank you."

Abernathy wrapped himself tightly in a blanket and walked slowly to his lean-to. He lay down on the blanket and pulled another over himself, letting out a soft whimper.

Sunkist came to his tent. "What's eatin' you? You don't look so good."

"Oh, my dear friend, I am so ill."

"What the hell you been eatin'? Y'ain't been eatin' mushrooms, have ye?"

"Oh no, I know better than that. I have had nothing the rest of you have not. I think the cold rain has got me down."

"Ye got yerself a damn cold, that's all. You'll git over it someday."

Lorraine came over with a cup of water. "Here, drink all you can. It will help you fight this cold."

Abernathy took a sip from the tin cup. His face showed the pain as he swallowed. "Oh dear! My throat is so inflamed I can't swallow."

"Best thing ye kin do is ignore it and let it work its way otta ye," Sunkist said.

"Abernathy needs to lie still and stay warm. This is nothing to take lightly.

If it should turn into pneumonia, it could . . ." She glanced towards Abernathy, then back to Sunkist, "Well, it could be very serious."

"Thank you, Miss Lorraine," Abernathy whined.

"He ain't that bad. He prob'ly jiss drank too much beer. We ride in the morning."

"Mister Wayne did not drink beer."

"Well, thar ye go. That's the problem."

Lorraine stayed near Abernathy, feeding him oatmeal sweetened with maple sugar.

The morning found her sitting next to him, rubbing his temples gently while he slept. Posey made a tea from yarrow to reduce the fever and another to help rid his system of bad spirits.

"Come on, git up!" Sunkist shouted. "We gotta git goin'!"

"Sunkist!" Lorraine shouted back, "Mister Wayne cannot ride."

"We can make a travois and he can lay on that," Hawk said. "Tie it to his horse."

"Yes, I suppose we could do that," Lorraine responded softly, as if reluctant to admit Hawk had made a rational suggestion.

"Ye cain't tie it to that critter he's ridin'," Sunkist said. "It'll break his spirit."

"Thank you, Sunkist. My horse is not trained as a draft horse. May we attach the travois to your horse?"

Sunkist thought about it a moment then, with a grin, he said, "Yeah, sure, we kin do that."

Posey helped Sunkist build the travois, and with a display of intense agony, Abernathy crawled aboard and wrapped himself in blankets.

Sunkist turned in the saddle grinning at the suffering Abernathy. "How ye doin' back there, Abby?"

"Please use the name Abernathy on my tombstone, Jim, not Abby."

As they passed the saloon, Kathleen came out and stopped them.

"Top o' the marnin' tew ya," she said. "I've got a bit of news ye might find interestin'."

Sunkist answered. "Mornin'. What's on that naughty little mind of yers t'day?"

"Ye'd like te know that, now wouldn't ye, Soonkest," she said.

"Naw, I don't think muh heart could handle that right now. What's the news ye got fer us?"

"This marnin' I overheard a couple o' gentlemen talking about a preacher they passed last night. He was camped on the Superior road. I thought ye might be interested in such news."

"Was it Diggs?" Hawk asked.

"They didn't say who he was. They just said he woos a preacher."

"Last night, huh? Did they say how far out he was?"

"The lads were still laughing when they came in, so he can't be that far out."

Hawk turned to Sunkist. "Figger we can ketch up with 'im?"

"Not with Abernathy on that travois."

"We'll leave him here with Lorraine."

"Aye," Kathleen said. "I've got a cabin out back that'll suit him."

"Sunkist, you and me and Jake'll go out an' see if we can catch him in camp," Hawk said.

"Sophie and Posey come, too," Posey added.

"Of course. That goes without saying." Hawk said. "If Diggs is there, we'll bring him back here. If he ain't, we'll just move on."

Riding around to the back of the tavern, Lorraine helped Abernathy out of the travois and into the cabin. The door was small and they had to bend down to get through. Inside the cabin were two chairs and a small table and four beds. A small, rusted-out stove stood to one side of the room, and the floor was rough boards that were simply laid on the ground. Abernathy sat on a chair wrapped in blankets, shivering, coughing, sneezing, and sniffing while Lorraine lit a coal-oil lantern.

"Oh, I dread the thought of another night," Abernathy whined. "All I do is cough and sniffle, and I can't seem to get warm."

Hawk stood in the doorway watching the activity. "Lorraine, remember those nights with Rolette when it got so cold? We slept under the same blankets and stayed warm. You could do that for Abernathy tonight."

"Oh, don't be ridiculous."

"What would it hurt?" Sophie asked.

"If I did that, you'd have two sick people to take care of."

"Okay," Hawk said with a shrug of her shoulders. "It was just a thought."

"Timid men don't start barroom brawls."

30

CHAPTER   THIRTY

THEY LEFT KATHLEEN AND CAUGHT UP WITH JAKE, who waited thirty yards away. They rode east out of Crow Wing on the Superior road.

The forest along the side of the road had been cut for lumber several years before, and new-growth aspens and willows enclosed them as they rode on. The air was damp and still and mosquitoes and flies buzzed around them, making travel miserable.

They each had a loaded rifle laid across their laps and pistols in holsters attached to their saddles. At one point, Posey turned off the road and into a cornfield and came back with a small bundle of leaves from the stalks. She pushed them down into her side bag. Sophie looked at Sunkist, then at the bundle of leaves.

"Jiss some of her Injun medicine, I recon."

An hour went by and Hawk raised his hand to signal a halt. He looked at Posey. "Did you hear a horse?"

She nodded her head.

"Come on, let's go," Hawk said, "but ride slow, like you're just another traveler."

"My," Sunkist said in a loud voice, "ain't this a awful road to be travlin' on setch a hot day?"

They looked at him wondering what had gotten into him.

"Well, come on, talk it up." Sunkist said. "Make like yer some dumb tourist from Saint Paul out here enjoyin' the great outdoors."

Hawk shrugged his shoulders and said louder than he needed to, "It ain't that hot out today, Sunkist."

Sunkist turned quickly in the saddle toward Hawk, "Don't use muh name, ye damn fool. Diggs prob'ly knows who we are. It'll tip 'im off."

"How about I just keep my mouth shut?"

"Good idea."

Ahead they heard men talking and saw smoke from a campfire. They came to an opening in the brush and found five men seated around a fire.

"God bless you this fine morning, my friends," one of the men said. "Come in and have some coffee."

"No thanks," Hawk said. "You a preacher?"

"My friend, we should all be ministers of the Lord and bring the message of the gospel to all people."

One of the men put his hand out to the preacher. "Uncle Ernie, hush up."

"You a preacher?"

"I am not ordained by any church," Uncle Ernie said. "But I am ordained by . . ."

"You seen a preacher on this road today?"

"No. We've been here all night and haven't seen a soul this morning," another man said. "You're the first to come by. Why are you looking for a preacher? You get your squaw in trouble and want to get married?"

Sunkist rode his horse close to the man seated on the ground and pointed his rifle at his face.

"What the hell are you doing?" the man cried as he scrambled backwards to get distance between himself and the rifle.

Uncle Ernie stood and lifted his hands to the sky. "Lord have mercy on this man's soul, for he is about to die!"

"Say yer sorry to the lady."

"What lady? What the hell are you talking about?"

"You jiss called my wife a squaw. She ain't no squaw. Now you say yer sorry."

The man looked back and forth between Sunkist and Posey. "Sir, I am Jonathan Whipplemeister. I am a well-respected attorney from Saint Paul, and I will not be treated in this manner."

Sunkist tapped the muzzle of his rifle on the man's forehead. "Say yer sorry, Mister Whipplesnapper, er you won't be gittin' no treats a'tall."

"Alright," he said. "In the interest of peace, I'm sorry I called your wife a squaw."

"Don't tell me— tell her," he said pointing with his thumb.

The man looked up at Posey. "I'm sorry . . ."

"Git on yer gaddamn feet when you talk to her!" Sunkist barked.

The man stood quickly and looked at Posey. "I'm sorry, I . . ."

Posey looked down at the man. "Ignoramus," she said as she turned her horse around and walked away from him before he could finish. Everyone stopped and looked at Posey.

"Where'd you learn that?" Sophie asked.

"L'raine say to Hawk sometimes."

Everyone's eyes turned to Hawk.

"Let's git back to town," he said.

They rode into Crow Wing and passed a line of people going into the church.

They got to Kathleen's tavern and went inside. The place was wrecked. Tables and chairs were thrown around and beer had been spilled on the floor. "What the hell happened in here?" Jake asked.

"Ow, we 'ad a bit of a brawl in 'er this marnin'."

"Looks like more than a bit of a brawl."

"It was that rascal Boudreaux Jardin again. He's the warst scalawag in this county."

"What was it all about?"

"Boudreaux doesn't need an excuse tuh coom in 'ere and start a brawl. He walks in the door and starts pickin' fights."

"Cain't ye jiss boot his ass out when he comes in here?" Sunkist asked.

"Ow, no, Boudreaux brings buckets o' money when he cooms in and it all ends oop in me cash drawer."

"Where's he get all that money?" Jake asked.

"I don't knew where he gets it, and I don't care where he gets it. I only care where he leaves it."

"What's going on at the church?" Sophie asked.

"There's a mon over there that ye might want to talk with. His name is Reverend Cloeter."

"We met Cloeter in Crow Wing."

"May haps he knows soomthin' about the man yer lookin' far."

"Good idea. Let's have another beer and go over there," Sophie said.

"I'm gonna hang around here a minute," Jake said.

"We'll see you there later."

He leaned his elbows on the bar and Kathleen leaned on the bar in front of him. "Jake, aboot last night."

"Never mind that. Tell me more about this Boudreaux," he said.

"I don't knew anything aboot him. He cooms in here and gets himself a belly full of whiskey and leaves."

"And picks fights."

"Ow, everyone knows about Boots. He's always gettin' into fights with someone. He'd be lookin' te fight yew if he was in 'ere right now."

"They call him Boots?"

"Aye, no one calls 'im by his name. He's just Boots."

"That's what I figured. Where can I find him?" Jake asked.

"He stays at the hotel when he's in town. They've got a flophouse in back for scalawags like 'im."

"I'm goin' over there," Jake said.

"I don't think that's sootch a good idea. Boots is not a genial mon."

"I'm just gonna talk to him. I'll be back."

Jake walked out the door and headed to the hotel.

When Jake stepped up to the desk, the man said, "Need a room, mister?"

"Nope. Looking for a man calls himself Boots."

"Bunkhouse in back. Fifteen beds and all the fleas you can eat fer free. He'll be in there sleeping it off. I wouldn't wake him if I were you."

"Thanks," Jake said. He walked out the door and around the hotel to the bunkhouse. He opened the door and shouted, "Is there a man in here calls himself Boots?"

"Quiet down over there. Can't ye see there's people tryin' to sleep?"

One of the men rolled over and looked at Jake with half-opened eyes. "Who's looking for Boots?"

"You Boots?"

The man swung his legs over the edge of the bed and stood. He started to walk towards Jake, tucking his shirt into his belt. "Yeah, I'm Boots. What of it?"

"Did you know the two men who were killed in Beaulieu's house a couple of days ago?"

"I don't know nothin' about that," he said and started to walk away.

"One of 'em called your name just before he died."

Boots stopped and turned to Jake. "You the one who killed 'em?"

"Nope, but I talked to the one who did."

"Who's that?"

"Friend of mine."

"You a lawman?"

"No, I'm not a lawman. I just want to know who those men were."

"Well, I don't know nothin' about it, and I don't know the men who was killed." Again, Boots started toward his bunk.

"You got any idea where I can find Hole-in-the-Day?"

Boots stopped and paused for a split second then turned and looked at Jake. "What you want with Hole-in-the-Day?"

"Got a message for him from Beaulieu."

"Beaulieu ain't got no time for that Injun. He'd rather see him dead than anything."

"You know Beaulieu?"

"Yeah, I know him. Ever'body in town knows him. He practically runs this town."

"You working for him?"

"I ain't workin' for nobody. Why don't you just get the hell out of here and let me get some sleep."

"I think I've learned all I can here," Jake said.

"Where ye stayin'? If I hear anything I'll let ye know."

"Got me a camp just outside of town on the south road."

"Can't say I'll learn anything, but if ye hear me coming, don't start shootin'."

"Don't worry, Boots, I'll let ye in."

Jake walked out the door and back toward Kathleen's tavern. The crowd at the church had grown to nearly twenty people, Sophie and Hawk among them.

Jake walked up to Hawk. "What's goin' on?"

"Going to church. Get your business taken care of in town?"

"Found out who Boots is."

They talked quietly as they walked.

"So who's Boots?"

"Just some tough guy hangs around town. Claims he didn't know anything about the guys in Beaulieu's house."

"You think it's him?"

"I know it is."

"What makes you so sure?"

"I don't know. Maybe the way he was so timid when I talked to him."

Reverend Cloeter greeted them at the door with his book in his hand. "So glad you could make it. Did you know the deceased?"

"No," Hawk said, "we come to see if you've heard anything about Diggs."

"I'm sorry, no, I have not. I've been too busy to pay much attention to what's going on around the community. Mister Diggs is not one of our citizens and if he's been through here, I would have paid no attention to him. Please come in and have a seat, there will be a luncheon served afterward. Father Pierz should be here soon. You might want to talk to him about your Mister Diggs."

"I ain't been inside a church in many a year," Sunkist said. "Figger we'll just wait out here."

"Sunkist," Sophie said, "if Diggs is really a man of the cloth, he might show up for church."

Sunkist looked into the church and back at Sophie, then into the church again and back at Sophie. "You sure that buildin' ain't gonna git struck by lightnin' er nothin' if I go in?"

"I think the only thing in here that might strike you is some fire and brimstone."

"I'd feel like a hippycrit."

"I think the Lord will tolerate one more hypocrite," Reverend Cloeter said. "Come on in."

As they entered the church, Reverend Cloeter stopped them. "Um, gentlemen, your hats."

"What about 'em?" Sunkist said.

"It is customary to remove your hat in the house of the Lord."

"What fer?"

Sophie reached up and pulled Sunkist's hat from his head and handed it to him. He took his hat in his hand, reached up, and pulled Hawk's hat from his head.

Sunkist hesitated at the door and looked up and around the small building. "I don't know about this," he said softly.

Sophie took him by the sleeve and led him in. They found a bench in the back of the church and sat down. Sunkist sat closest to the isle.

In a few minutes, two dozen people crowded the small church, filling the back pews first.

Hawk leaned toward Jake and whispered, "You said Boots was timid. Why shouldn't Boots be timid?"

"Timid men don't start barroom brawls."

"Did he know you?"

"Who?" Jake asked.

"Boots."

"No, but I know him. He was with Orley in Courtland."

"He should know you, then."

"I didn't have a beard then."

"Does he know Orley's dead?"

"I didn't say anything about Orley. I didn't want to tip him off about who I am. I don't think this has anything to do with killing Hole-in-the-Day. I think it has to do with Diggs."

Sunkist suddenly looked up and around the church. "Did ye hear that?" he asked Sophie in a hoarse whisper.

"What?"

"I thought I heard thunder. You sure we ain't gonna get hit by lightnin'?"

"Probably just a squirrel on the roof."

Reverend Cloeter stopped his sermon and focused on Hawk and Jake. Hawk caught the look and sat quietly for a moment, then turned to Jake. "Why do you say that?"

"He don't care about Hole-in-the-Day. I figure Orley was paying Boots for protection."

"Think he's a hired killer?"

"Could be."

Sunkist watched the preacher as he handed each of the people in line a small wafer. "What're they a-doin'?" he asked Sophie.

"They're receiving communion," she said quietly.

"Ol' Gabe used to do that on Sundays. I never did understand it."

"It's a symbolic eating of the body and blood of Christ. Apparently this is a Catholic funeral being conducted by a Lutheran minister."

"Mebbe you can 'splain it to me sometime." He paused briefly, put his hat on his head, and turned to Sophie, "Never mind. I don't think I wanna know."

"Who's this Ol' Gabe?" Sophie whispered.

"Jim Bridger," Sunkist said out loud. Then he stopped, corrected himself, and whispered, "Best damn tracker and trapper and beaver skinner in the west. He's still out there, so they say—him an' the Liver Eater. Liver Eater, he used tuh eat the livers outta the Injuns he . . ." He stopped himself and looked up to see the preacher glaring at him. He held the preachers gaze as he leaned over to Sophie. "Ain't no Injun alive can take either one of 'em down. Them ol' boys ain't never gonna die."

Sunkist then noticed the church had gone completely silent and all eyes were on him. He looked up at Reverend Cloeter behind the alter. Cloeter tapped his finger against his forehead indicating the removal of Sunkist's hat. Sunkist quickly grabbed his hat off his head and said aloud, "'Scuse me,

Reverend . . . Uh, I mean, beg pardon. Guiss I fergot."

Sophie turned to Hawk and whispered, "I prefer my own church."

"Your church?" Hawk asked.

"Yeah, the Church of the Great Outdoors. It's open every day of the year, and there's no doors or rules."

A woman sitting in front of them turned around and shushed him.

Sunkist looked quickly at Sophie. "There. Did'ja hear it?"

"Hear what?"

"Thunder. I jiss heard thunder agin."

"I didn't hear anything."

The sacrament continued.

Jake leaned toward Hawk and whispered, "Don't say nothin' to the rest of 'em till I get some answers."

Suddenly, someone dropped a thick hymnal on the floor with a loud bang, and Sunkist bolted out into the isle and out the door.

Six men stood and walked to the front of the church and lined up on both sides of the casket. They lifted it up onto their shoulders, carried it out the front door, and loaded it onto a wagon. The wagon drove away, followed by some of the mourners on horses, mules, and in buggies. Hawk and the gang stood in the street and watched the procession leave.

"Well? Wanna go back to Kathleen's?" Sophie asked. "Sunkist is probably over there sucking down Tullamore Dew."

"We could go sit with Abby and Lorraine in that cabin," Hawk said with a smile.

"If you think hunting Diggs is dangerous," Sophie said, "you just try to get in that cabin and you'll see what dangerous really is."

"Back to the saloon, then."

Sunkist turned on his heel as they walked in. "Don't you never ax me tuh go in a place like that agin," he growled. "I got my pride, ye know."

"Don't worry, you weren't the only one uncomfortable in there."

"We gotta get some shuteye before we do ennathin' more," Sunkist said.

"Getting sleepy there, Sunkist?" Hayes asked.

"I sleep with one eye open, little man," he said with a stern look at Hayes.

Outside they heard wagons coming down the road at a gallop. The riders stopped in front of the church and went inside.

Reverend Cloeter peeked in the door of the saloon. "Would you care to join us in feast?"

"I ain't goin' back in there. It ain't safe."

"It's not a church anymore, Sunkist, it's a dining hall now," Sophie said.

"Well, in that case," Sunkist said with a grin, "a belly full'a hot grub always helps me sleep."

They walked into the church to find the benches had been moved to the outer walls and tables covered with white cloths set in their place. Sunkist stopped abruptly and raised his nose to the ceiling. The room was filled with the aroma of roasted turkey and ham, fried chicken, baked beans, and potato hotdish. And coffee. Ladies walked from one end of the tables to the other, taking the lids off pots and pans.

Reverend Cloeter clapped his hands to get the attention of the congregation. "Let us give thanks," he said as he lowered his head. "Come, Lord Jesus, be our guest. Let these gifts to us be blessed."

The assemblage responded with a low, "Amen."

"Amen," Sunkist said louder than the rest. "Let's eat."

"Come," Reverend Cloeter said, "fill your plates and rejoice in the bounty of the Lord."

Hoping to be first to get at the turkey, Hawk grabbed a plate and went to the end of the first table. A line formed at the opposite end and people stood with their plates in their hands, looking intently at the feast laid out before them. Hawk left his preferred place and walked around to take a place at the end of the line. When he finally made it to the food, he found only the mangled remains of the coveted roasted turkey. A lady standing across the table in a white apron asked, "White meat or dark?"

"Um, don't matter to me."

Sunkist stepped up to an outsized pan containing a large fish surrounded by boiled potatoes, green peas, and onion slices, all swimming in a sea of melted butter. "What's this?" he asked the lady standing across the table.

"Dat, sir, iss lutefisk. It's a delicacy from Norvay. It vos my modder's faverit recipe."

Sunkist started to reach his plate over to receive his portion but Posey took his arm and pulled it back. She looked at him and shook her head ever so slightly, then urged him to the next dish. He took her arm and turned her to him. "Why can't I have some of that fish?" he asked in Cherokee.

"Smell bad."

Then they came to something none of them had ever seen before. It was red, and looked like liquid—but it didn't pour like liquid. It *jiggled*.

"What the hail's this?" Sunkist asked.

The lady behind the table gave him a sour look and said, "It is a gelatin dessert. I have mixed fresh strawberries into it to give it a wonderful flavor. Try some." She scooped a serving from the bowl and held it out to him. Sunkist stared at the strange creation as the lady dropped it onto his plate then added a big dollop of whipped cream on top. He shook the plate slightly, watching it jiggle, then looked up at the lady. "Looks like clotted blood."

She looked at him with a frown, annoyed by his crude manners. "It's good. Try it."

"Looks like I need to git my gun and put it out of its misery."

Hawk's plate was filled to overflowing. Sophie's had small amounts of each of her favorite dishes, including potato hotdish. Each of them had a portion of the jelly-like substance on their plate. Sunkist went right for the gelatin. With the edge of his fork he cut a piece off and scooped it up. It dropped off. He tried again with the same results. Then he stabbed it and quickly brought it his mouth. He swallowed and gave Sophie a sour look.

"Damn stuff slips down like raw hawk eggs." He glanced at Hawk. "No offense."

"None taken."

A lady, tall and thin as a whip, came to the table carrying a coffee pot. "Would you like coffee?" she asked.

Sophie took the cup from the saucer and turned it over. "Yes, please."

"Ye gotten thing stronger?" Sunkist asked.

"Sir, this is a funeral, not a party."

"A funeral? I'll be damned. Who died?"

"Eunice Gibbons, poor thing. She passed away unexpectedly, two days ago."

"Eunice?! Oh my Gawd, not Eunice!" Sunkist gasped with his hand over his chest.

"Yes, God rest her soul, did you know her?"

"How'd she die? I though she was in the best of health."

"The poor thing. She choked to death on her own hotdish . . . must have been the potatoes." She smiled into Sunkist's eyes. "You know," she said softly, "Eunice attended all of these community functions, and she always brought her hotdish. She was so proud of it. It was her own recipe, you know."

"Musta been perty good, huh?"

"Yes, Eunice's hotdish was—well—it was very nice. But as you know, everyone has their own preferences." The lady looked quickly around the room, then leaned close and whispered into Sunkist's ear, "Personally, I think she over did it a little with the raisins."

She straightened herself and turned toward a specimen of questionable masculinity sitting on a bench next to the far wall. "Elmer," she said sharply, "come over here and join the rest of us." She looked down at Sunkist. "Excuse me," she said and stepped over to Elmer.

Sophie grinned at Sunkist and said, "I think she likes you."

"Too damn skinny fer me," he said as he watched her walk away. "Be like crawlin' inta bed with a bag'a antlers."

Elmer wore canvas overalls covered by a dirty plaid shirt, and he had a tie around his neck knotted in a simple square knot. He looked down over a five-day growth of beard at the red blob on the plate he held in his grimy hands.

"Elmer," the lady said as she pulled his greasy, shapeless hat from his head and dropped it on the bench next to him. She wiped her hand on her apron. "That gelatin isn't going anywhere. Come and sit with the rest of us."

Without taking his eyes off the gelatin, Elmer wrapped his fist around the crown of his hat and pushed it back down onto his head. He then went back to jiggling his plate and ignored the people around him.

The thin lady walked to the door, peeked out, and came back to Sunkist. "That old man is out there again with his books."

"What old man?"

She glanced towards the door. "An old geezer they call Smoky. He sells books." She looked around the room then leaned toward Sunkist. "Now, I ask you, how many people around here have the time to read books?"

"What's yer name, lady?" Sunkist asked.

"Oh," the lady said with a giggle, "my name is Elsa Bjorgstrom." She smoothed her hair back and said with a wide smile, "May I ask your name, sir?"

Her question fell on deaf ears; Sunkist had resumed eating and was paying no attention to her.

Elsa had a narrow face, long slender nose, and a sharp, protruding chin. Her front teeth extended over her lower lip, making it necessary for her to lick her lower lip frequently to manage the overflow of saliva.

Sophie looked up from her plate to Elsa. "Do you know Ester Erickson?"

"Oh, the poor woman who was killed at the fort? No, I didn't know her."

"That old geezer out there," Sunkist said around a slip of ham hanging from the corner of his mouth. "Has he been 'round here long?"

"He usually shows up wherever there's a gathering of people."

"No, I mean has he lived here long?"

"He's been around as long as I've been here."

Sunkist turned to Sophie. "Let's go talk to the old geezer."

"What do you think we can learn from him?"

"Dunno. Maybe he knows Diggs."

"Anything's worth a try."

3I

CHAPTER

THIRTY-ONE

THE GANG WALKED OUT THE DOOR with Hawk behind them, gnawing on a drumstick. They found Smoky sitting on a wooden box watching them approach. He wore wool trousers and a calico shirt covered with a faded, knit sweater. His well-worn hat sat back on his head exposing a bald crown, and a white beard covered his chin and neck.

"Hi there, lad," he said looking at Hawk over the top of his small, wire-rimmed glasses. "Who's the pretty girl?"

"Sophie."

"You'd be Hawk Owen, then."

"That's me. How'd you know."

"Heard about ye." His gaze went to Sunkist. "Howdy there, Sunkist. Been a while."

"You know me?"

"Yeah, with Ol' Gabe back in Kansas."

"You was there?"

"Yep. 'Member Ozzy Russell?"

"Yeah, all the time writin' in that damn book. Didn't figger he was patched real tight."

"Why's that? He seemed tuh be all there tuh me."

"Well, I figger there's gotta be somethin' wrong with a man who sits an' writes in a gaddamn book when there's better things he could be a-doin'."

Smoky paused for a brief moment before nodding his head in agreement.

Sunkist got a grin on his face. "Remember that time he found that Ree war party in that patch of willers?"

"Hail, yeah! Put them diggers on the run, din we?"

Sunkist turned to Sophie and offered for justification. "I'da jist as soon left 'em be. But they was the ones kilt that trappin' party and that preacher down by Saint Mary's Crik." He turned back to Smoky. "What was that preacher's name? D'ye remember?"

"Nope. Don't recollect," Smoky said. "Them Injuns wasn't up to no good, and we knew that. Rees got no bidness in that part of the country enna ways."

Sophie was paging through a book she'd picked out of Smokey's stock. Smoky lost the smile from his face and frowned up at her. "This ain't no gaddamn lib'ary," he growled.

She looked down at him and laughed. "Well, I'm not going to buy a book without knowing what's in it first."

"If ye read the gaddamn thing, ye won't need tuh buy it."

"How much for the book, Smoky?"

"Ten cents."

"That's the cost of a new book."

"It's got all the pages jiss like a new book, ain't it? And jiss cuz somebody read it, don't mean the words ain't there no more."

"Makes sense. Ten cents it is."

"Y'ain't gonna argue about it?"

"Nope."

"Aw hail, jiss gimme a nickel then," he grumbled. "A body could starve tuh death around here an' nobody'd give a damn."

"Smoky," Hawk said, "do you know a man named Diggs? He's a preacher."

"I know the man," Smoky grumbled. "Worthless as tits on a stovepipe."

"Ye seen him lately?"

"Heard he was through here a couple'a days back. Don't know where he is now and don't much care."

"Any idea where he's going?" Hawk asked.

"Nope. Don't care 'bout that neither."

"You don't like him, I take it."

"Bible thumper."

A mother came out of the church yelling and pulling a squalling boy by the ear. Smoky glanced over and mumbled, "Brat." Then he turned away and said in a low tone, "Ye know what she aught'a do with 'im, don't cha? She aught'a jiss grab 'im and slap the gaddamn li'l bastard."

"Looks like that's what she's about to do."

"Hey, Smoky," Sunkist said, "hang around a while. Let's jaw about the old days."

"Cain't. Big weddin' goin on down by Saint Cloud. Gotta git down there and sell some books."

"We'll catch up with ye down the road, then."

"Mebbe so, mebbe not."

"Yeah, I recon."

Smoky didn't look up as they walked off. "Hey, Sunkist!" he shouted. "What ever happened to Curly Jack?"

"Last I heard of Curly Jack he had a farm down by Lime Springs, Ioway."

"Well, I'll be dipped in shit an' called a petunia. Never figured Curly Jack tuh be no farmer." He paused, then looked up at Sunkist. "But then, I never figgered you tuh be no depuddy marshal neither."

"I ain't no depuddy marshal."

Smoky turned quickly toward Sunkist. "The hell ye ain't!" he snapped. "Yer chasin' that no good Diggs all over hell's half acre. Yer a lawman, like it er not."

"Ornery old cuss," Sunkist mumbled. "Let's git outta here."

"Hey, Sunkist," Smoky said.

"Whut?"

"Ain't nothin' wrong with bein' a lawman, 'specially one who's goin' after the likes of Diggs. Git that son of a bitch, lawman, and stretch his rotten hide over the roof of some Injun's shithouse."

"Smoky, do you know something about Diggs we should know about?" Sophie asked.

"I know there's a lot of young folks disappearing from around these parts. The law tried to find something out, but up here no one talks about missing Indian kids. People jiss don't care 'bout 'em. Agent Walker damn sure wasn't worried about it."

"Injuns pretend they love Diggs, but the truth is, they're scared to death of him."

"Who's this Agent Walker? Someone we should talk to?"

"Walker's dead. Killed hisself down by Monticello a couple'a years back. He figgered the Injuns was out to kill him, so the dumb-ass went and done it hisself. Took a pistol an' blowed his own brains out." Smoky shook his head slightly and said, "Don't make no sense ta me."

"We're gonna do what we kin to find out what's going on with the Injun chi'drin," Sunkist said.

"You do that, Depuddy. I'll be around."

"Well? Now what?" Hawk said.

"It looks like there's no secret to our working for the law," Sophie said.

"That could make things worrisome," Sunkist said. "We're gonna hefta watch our backs even tighter."

"Mister Owen!" they heard from behind. They turned to see Reverend Cloeter coming toward them. "That's Father Pierz coming down the road. You might ask him about your Mister Diggs."

A man came down the road on foot and approached Cloeter. They shook hands and Cloeter brought him to Hawk. "Mister Owen, I'd like you to meet Father Francis Pierz. Father Pierz, Mister Hawk Owen, his wife Sophie, Sunkist and his wife . . . I didn't get your wife's name, sir."

"Posey."

"And your full name?"

"James Whistler. They call me Sunkist."

"So glad to meet all of you," Father Pierz said. "What can I do for you?"

"Now, don't be digging in your sack for beads," Cloeter said, "they're not here to be baptized."

"I had no intention of baptizing them. I expect they are good Christians already."

"This man has baptized more Indians than all the preachers from here to Boston," Cloeter said.

"That, my friend, is because I do the Lord's work daily. I don't sit in a cabin and try to learn a language that will be obsolete in a few years. That book you have in your hands was written by a Catholic bishop by the name of Frederic Baraga. He wrote that Chippewa-English dictionary while he was traveling the country teaching and converting Indians to the Catholic faith. He did not hide in his house studying books to learn the language. He went out and talked to the Indians. And, by the way, he has baptized and confirmed more Indians than you or I have ever seen."

"You baptized more Indians because you trade them beads for their pledge," Cloeter said.

"The beads, as you are fully aware, are rosaries. It is part of the Roman Catholic heritage."

"Yeah, you give them beads and they take them apart and decorate their war shirts with them."

"The Chippewa do not wear war shirts."

"They didn't until you came around."

"You buried Mrs. Gibbons?"

"Yes, once again, I've done your work for you."

"I'll have you know, Mister Cloeter, I was out winning souls for Jesus."

"You were out decorating war shirts."

"Umm, Father Pierz," Hawk said. "Do you know a preacher named Diggs?"

"Yes, I know Reverend Diggs," Pierz said.

Cloeter turned to Hawk. "I guess you were right. Diggs is a scoundrel."

"Why do you say that?"

"Consider the company he keeps."

"Don't you have work to do in the church, Mister Cloeter?" Pierz asked.

"Yes, I do. I really should finish your work before I leave. Someone has to do it."

"About Mister Diggs. Is he a friend of yours?"

"Well, let's say we're acquainted. What is your reason for asking about him?"

"We're looking for him for some people in Saint Cloud."

"Is there trouble?"

"Not yet," Hawk said.

Sophie elbowed him. "We'd just like to catch up with him and talk to him about the orphans he had at his church in Hutchinson," she said.

"Mister Diggs is on his way to Saint Paul right now with two orphaned Chippewa children. He'll be taking them to a school down there to learn the ways of the white man."

"Did he get the children from here?" Sophie asked.

"Oh, I don't know where the children came from. I saw him in Crow Wing two days ago and he had them with him then."

"Where did you see him?"

"At mister Beaulieu's residence. Reverend Diggs and a Mister Jardin."

Jake elbowed Hawk hard on the arm. "There ye go," he said.

"What?"

"Boots is working for Diggs"

"Who's working for Diggs?" Sophie asked.

"Boots."

"Who's Boots?

"Jardin."

"Jardin down in Courtland?"

"Yeah."

"What's he got to do with Boots?"

"Boots *is* Jardin."

"Who's Jardin?"

"Boudreaux Jardin."

"I'm confused."

"Tell ye all about it later," Jake said.

"What was Diggs doing there?"

"I don't know. Where he goes is none of my business."

"When did he leave there?"

"I was there for just a few minutes. I don't know when Reverend Diggs left, and I don't know where he went either."

"Are you sure he's going to Saint Paul?"

"Yes, that's what he told me. He said that he would hate to have anything bad happen to the girls, so he's taking them there. I don't know what he meant by that, but he made a point to tell me and make sure I heard it. It was almost like a warning of impending trouble." Pierz shook his head slightly as he said it. "Now that I think about it, it was a very curious statement coming from him. He was not referring to you, was he?"

"Tell me about the girls. What did they look like?"

"Very pretty young ladies, probably around ten or twelve years old. They appeared to be well cared for, clean and tidy. Dressed in white men's clothing, you see."

"You didn't know them?"

"No, I have never seen them before."

"Can you tell us anything more about Mister Diggs?"

"Only that he has been a friend to me and to the Indians in this part of the country."

"Was he traveling alone?"

"He was alone when I talked to him here, but I doubt very seriously that he would travel alone in this country. That would be foolish, considering the state of affairs with the Indians."

"Did he have guns with him?"

"I didn't see them, but of course he did. It would be doubly foolish to travel without protection."

"You don't carry protection."

Father Pierz raised one finger and pointed to the sky.

HAWK'S QUEST

"About the best protection money can buy," Hawk said.

"I'm afraid the Lord's protection cannot be bought, Mister Owen. We must earn it."

"Sorry."

"Did you know he had a church in Hutchinson?" Sophie asked.

"Yes, I know that."

"Do you know that church no longer exists?"

"Oh no! What happened?"

"Money problems."

"I see. The curse of the Devil. We can't run a church without money."

"Thank you, Father. We'll leave you now."

"Have a safe journey, and God go with you," Father Pierz said.

They started to walk away from Father Pierz, but Hawk stopped and turned back. "How long have you been in this area, Father?" he asked.

"I came here in eighteen fifty-one. Why do you ask?"

"Just curious."

"Off to Grand Marais?" Sophie asked.

"Yup," Hawk said, walking straight ahead.

"What fer we goin' to Grand Marais?" Sunkist asked. "He said Diggs is goin' to Saint Paul."

"That's what he told Father Pierz, expecting we'd be talking to him. And the thing about not wanting anything to happen to the girls was a warning for us to hear."

"I knew that. Jiss wondered if you did."

"Let's go back and talk to Kathleen."

Back in the tavern, Sophie asked Kathleen, "Is there another trail to Grand Marais from here?"

"New, not thet I knew of. There be a few trails thet the Indians use, boot they're not fit for white men or horses."

"That's what I thought."

"Does this road go all the way to Grand Marais?"

"Aye. It'll take ye through the city of Oneota and from there tis just a trail thet follows the shore of Lake Superior clear oop inta Canada."

They took chairs at a table. "Well," Sophie said, "all we can do now is follow what we know about Diggs and go to Grand Marais."

"Fer all we know we've walked past 'im a hunnert times since we got up here." Sunkist grumbled.

They looked back and forth at each other. "Now why didn't we think of that before?" Sophie said. "He could be right here under our noses."

"That could be, but . . ."

"Hawk, what's a deer's favorite way of escaping danger?"

"Gittin' down in the brush and layin' still."

"I'm guessing Diggs is hunkered down right here."

"What makes you think he hasn't left?"

"Those men we talked to this morning said no one has gone by there, and they certainly would have noticed a preacher."

"So how do we find him if he *is* here?"

"This is the only road to Grand Marais, right? Tomorrow we pack up and head out. We can pack Abernathy on travois and make a big issue of leaving. We travel a day or two and then hunker down and wait for him."

"It works for deer, it might just work on Diggs, too," Hawk said. "Lots of times a deer will watch you go by, then git up and follow you just to see what yer up to."

"Diggs won't be curious, but he's probably hoping that we're on our way to Saint Paul."

"You know, don't ye," Sunkist said, "that if he's got two brats with him, he ain't taking 'em to school. He's got 'em fer pertection."

"You know, don't cha," Hawk said, "that those kids Diggs had are not from around here."

"Where do you think they're from?" Sophie asked.

"Dunno. He's probably had them since he left Hutchinson."

"Explain, please," Lorraine said.

"Pierz has been here since eighteen fifty-one. That's more'n ten years."

"That's thirteen years, Hawk," Lorraine said.

"He said the kids were ten or twelve years old, but he didn't baptize them. They would've been baptized by a missionary close to their birthplace, right?"

"Right."

"They had to come from someplace where Diggs has been, and we haven't passed any Indian villages on our way here."

"The children Father Pierz told us about were Chippewa," Lorraine said, "so they can't be Dakota. Father Pierz would know a Chippewa from a Dakota."

"That's right."

"There are no Chippewa in Dakota country, Hawk," Lorraine said.

"Not anymore."

"What is that supposed to mean?"

"Dream Talker said her brother and sister were captured by the Sioux and taken to a camp where there were white men."

"Are you saying Diggs has Dream Talker's brother and sister?" Sophie asked.

"As much as I hate to admit it," Lorraine said, "Hawk has a very good point."

"This could also explain why Dream Talker singled us out," Jake said. "We're the only white people she's met who were willing to help her and her family. She trusts us."

"So, why isn't she here with us?"

"Can't answer that one," Hawk said.

"Diggs's got the kids for protection," Sophie said. "That means we're going to have to be extra careful when we get close to him."

"Right now," Sunkist said, "finding 'im and knowing we're on the right trail helps a lot." He turned toward the bar. "Kathleen! Where's Mayhew?"

Kathleen got a wide grin on her face. "'E's over visiting the widow Bjorgstrom."

"Elsa?"

"Aye, 'e slips over to her house after dark and don't coom oot till joost befar the soon cooms oop. Everyone in town knows about it, boot he doesn't know thet."

"Didn't know the little tramp had it in 'im," Sunkist grumbled.

"Jealous?" Sophie said with a grin.

"I don't like fickle wimmin."

"Let's go get some rest," Hawk said.

They walked out of the saloon and into the street.

"I've got business in town," Jake said. "I'll be staying at the other camp."

"What business you got in town?" Sunkist asked. "Goin' in and see Kathleen?"

"Yeah, goin' to see Kathleen," he said not wanting them to know he was planning on seeing Boots.

"Best you be careful with that wildcat. She's liable to claw the hide clean off'n yer back."

"I'll take that chance."

They set up their shelters in the woods behind Kathleen's tavern, had something to eat, and turned in.

32

C H A P T E R

T H I R T Y - T W O

Jake mounted his animal and rode to the other side of town to the camp in the woods. He built a small fire and had coffee and venison jerky.

The night got dark, cool, and silent. Jake moved back into the underbrush and sat against a tree with one blanket under him and another over his legs. He listened to the night sounds and the sounds of people coming out of the taverns, laughing with one another. A wagon rumbled past him on the road thirty yards away.

From the river below he heard the sounds of canoe paddles in the water and low mumbling sounds from men in the canoe. A few minutes later he heard them unloading the canoe and heading for the saloons.

Jake was having trouble keeping his eyes open and dozed briefly when the snap of a twig woke him. He checked the chamber of his rifle and adjusted his position so he could use it if he needed.

On the other side of the camp he saw a figure move slowly. He stopped, looked around, and quickly ducked back in the brush.

"Come on in, Boots," Jake said softly.

"Where y'at?"

"Put the rifle down and come on in."

"I ain't putting this gun down till I know where yer at."

Jake got up and stepped out of the woods with his rifle at his shoulder pointed straight at Boots. "I'm right here. Put the rifle down."

Boots stayed in the shadows, not realizing he was silhouetted against the sky. He started to raise his rifle, and Jake shot a round into the ground at his feet. He jacked another shell in the chamber and said, "I can see every move you make. Throw the rifle away."

Boots started to lay the rifle on the ground. Jake fired another round at his feet. "I said throw the rifle away, not put it down."

"Alright, alright," he said and tossed the rifle in the brush.

"Come on in and sit down."

Boots walked slowly into camp and stood close to the fire.

"So you must have learned something or you wouldn't be here, right?"

"No, I didn't learn nothin'. I want to know why yer so interested in the men who got shot."

"I figure they were after me."

He looked hard at Jake. "Who are you? Don't I know you from somewhere?"

"Courtland."

Boots studied Jake's face. "What's yer name?"

"Jacob Owen."

Boots started to step back.

"Where you going?" Jake said. "We've got some unfinished business to take care of."

"You goin' after that Injun?"

"Nope. I'm here to find out what you know about those two men who were shot in Beaulieu's house."

"I don't know nothin' about that. I told you that."

"Bullshit!" Jake barked. "One of the men called your name before he died. Who was it, and why did they have rifles on us?"

"I told you!" Boots started, but suddenly made a dive for Jake. Jake dodged the move and hit Boots on the back of his head. Boots went to the ground and quickly got to his feet. Jake hit him in the mouth and knocked him back. Boots took a swing and connected with Jake's cheekbone. Jake was stunned by the blow but quickly recovered and struck out, connecting with Boots's nose. Boots backed away and held his hand over his nose.

"Come on, tough guy," Jake said with a grin. "They tell me you're the meanest man in town. Let's see what you got."

Boots made a dive toward Jake and caught a hammering blow to the top of his head. He went down to one knee, shook his head, then stood.

Jake backed away. "Had enough?"

Boots suddenly kicked at Jake and caught him in the upper thigh.

"Oh, you wanna play that game. Well, that's fine with me," Jake said.

Boots made another swing. Jake caught his arm, spun him around, and wrapped his arms around Boots's chest. He pulled back and at the same time thrust his hips forward. Boots's feet came of the ground and Jake slammed him down on his back. Boots started to get up, but Jake kicked him in the face with the instep of his foot, snapping Boots's neck backward. Boots dropped to the ground and lay still.

"Git up. We ain't done."

Boots didn't move. Jake touched him with his toe and Boots moaned.

"Well, you ain't dead. We'll take care of that another time."

As Jake started out of camp he kicked something with his toe. He bent down to pick a pair of binoculars off the ground. He looked back at Boots who was starting to move. "Thanks," he said. "If you want these back just come find me."

He walked out of camp, found Boots's rifle, and tossed it into the river below, then headed back to Crow Wing.

In the morning Jake joined the rest in Kathleen's tavern for breakfast and coffee. "Looks like ye lost that one, Jake," Sunkist said.

"Just a little scrap. Nothin' to worry about."

"Anyone we know?"

"Nope."

"Let's go get some supplies," Hawk said.

In the traders store they found Henry Mayhew buying supplies.

"Looks like yer plannin' on coming with us," Sunkist said.

"I told you I would. You might need a guide, and I know the road."

They bought the supplies they'd need for a week's ride, including cheesecloth for protection from mosquitoes and biting flies. They packed the new supplies onto the mules, tucking some packages around Abernathy who was bundled in the travois.

"If we go east on this road, Diggs is gonna know we ain't goin' to Saint Paul."

"So we go south and circle around," Mayhew said. "I know a trail, but it's a lot of hill, and that travois is going to be a problem."

"We'll work it out. Let's go."

Mounting their horses, they moved out of Crow Wing to the south toward the fort. About a mile out Sunkist reigned up to Hawk. "I got a feelin' we're being follered."

"What makes you think that?" Hawk asked.

"Lone rider back there. He's been keeping pace with us since we left Crow Wing."

"Try to ignore him. He'll have to turn back and report to whoever he's working for sooner or later."

The rider stayed with them for another five miles when they turned east on a seldom-used trail. The trail took them over an open prairie toward a line of hills a half-mile away. Sunkist glanced back in time to see the man pull off the road and get down from his horse. He pulled the saddle off and started setting up a camp.

"It don't figger," Sunkist said. "Mebbe he wasn't follerin' us."

"He was following us, alright," Jake said. "I know that man."

"Who is it?"

"That's Boudreaux Jardin."

"How do you know that?" Sophie asked.

"Just from his size and the brains it takes to follow someone this close. Boudreaux ain't real smart."

"What're we gonna do about him?"

"Let me take care of that little problem," Jake said with a half grin.

They stayed on the road until it climbed a steep hill. At the top of the hill they found a trail that followed a ridge back toward the fort. Mayhew led them along the crest of the hills.

Lorraine stopped the column. "Abernathy!" she said excitedly. "Do you know what this is?"

Abernathy was sitting up on the travois. "Yes, Miss Lorraine. This is the esker David Dale Owen wrote about in his journals."

"What's an esker?" Hawk asked.

Lorraine pulled maps from her saddlebags and spread them on the ground next to Abernathy. They talked softly, tracing their fingers over the maps, then turned to look up and down the ridge.

"What's so interesting on them maps?" Hawk asked.

"These are maps of the geological structure of Minnesota," Lorraine said. "They were drawn by surveyors and geologists in eighteen fifty-two."

"What's a geologist?"

"A person who studies the structure of the land and how it came to be the way it is," Abernathy interjected. "He has knowledge that will tell him of mineral deposits in a particular area."

"You mean like gold?"

"There ain't no gold in Minnesota," Hawk said.

"There is gold in Minnesota," Hayes said, "but not much of it has been found."

"The fact is, Mister Mayhew," Lorraine said, "there is gold almost everywhere on the face of the earth. However, I am not aware of any significant amounts being found anywhere in Minnesota."

"I'll give you that," Hayes conceded.

"Lorraine seems to know everything there is to know about Minnesota," Hawk said.

Lorraine stood, rolled the maps into tubes, and said, "Though you have lived in Minnesota all your life, Hawk, I suspect I know more about it than you do."

"That's nothing to brag about."

"I do not brag. I simply state facts, and the fact is, I know more about Minnesota than you do."

"Okay, why are these hills here?"

"These hills were built by glaciers that came through this country a hundred thousand years ago."

"I knew that."

"Hawk, do you know what a glacier is?"

"No, but I think I'm about to find out."

"Glaciers are made up of snow that is compressed into ice by its own weight, and they stay throughout the seasons. The glaciers that came through here were formed in the northern latitudes when the mean temperature of the earth, for some unknown reason, dropped several degrees. Hundreds of years of snow accumulated until the weight of overlying layers squeezed the lower layers out and pushed them south to cover the northern parts of this country. At least, that is what Louis Aggasiz theorizes."

"You don't really believe that, Lorraine."

"These hills around us are evidence of those glaciers."

"So, what made this ridge?"

"As the temperature of the earth finally began to rise, a river of meltwater formed a valley in the ice. Gravel that was suspended in the ice settled to the bottom of that valley. The moving water carried the lighter dust and silt away and left the heavier material—gravel, rocks, and boulders—in the bottom of the channel."

Hawk reached for the coffeepot and poured himself a cup.

"Are you listening to me?"

"Who me? Yes, I'm listening. You said there's a river up here."

"Oh, my dear God," Lorraine said softly. "Why do I even try?"

"How can there be a river up *here*?"

"She is referring to a river that formed inside the ice," Abernathy interrupted.

"Wait a minute," Hawk said. "How thick was this ice?"

"It may have been as much as a several thousand feet thick."

"Must have been a long winter."

"It was. Probably a hundred thousand years long."

"When the ice surrounding that river melted," Abernathy continued, "the sediments were left where they were deposited. Then, as the ice melted, the deposits along the flanks of the river dropped away, inverting the formation and leaving it as you see it today. It has a high center and lower outer edges. Doctor Aggasiz called the ridges eskers. It is a Swiss word that means, as one would expect, ridges."

Hawk touched Lorraine's arm then pointed down the hill. "There's a puddle down there. Maybe that's the river you're looking for."

"Hawk, get the hell away from me!"

"There is no reason to use that kind of language with me, Lorraine."

"It seems to be the only language you understand. Please, Hawk, this is serious business here. Will you please stop tormenting me?"

"I'm sorry, Lorraine, I won't do it no more."

"You won't do it *anymore*."

"Ain't that what I just said?"

Sophie took Hawk's arm. "She likes you, but I wouldn't push it too far. That could change."

Hawk stepped up to Lorraine. "I have to admit, this is pretty interesting. Is this really the bottom of a river?"

"Yes," she said almost in a whisper. "This is the remnant of a river that flowed beneath ice perhaps a thousand feet thick, ten or even fifty thousand years ago."

Hawk looked at her face, her eyes wide and her lips slightly parted in a soft smile. He started walking along the crest and stopped to pick an oak leaf from a tree whose roots were thirty feet below.

Sophie reached up and grabbed a limb and swung up into the tree. "I've always loved climbing trees, 'specially oaks. They were designed by Mother Nature for just that purpose."

They followed the ridge for six miles until they could see Fort Ripley, then they set up camp.

"I'm going to see about Boots," Jake said.

"Want me to come along?" Hawk asked.

"Na, me and Boots have a special relationship. He won't be any problem."

Jake walked his horse out of camp and down the low hill to the road. Ahead he could see Boots' campfire. He walked the horse into camp.

"Ain't nothin' for you here," Boots said without looking up. "Keep movin'."

"Can't do that, Boots. I come to see why you're following us."

Boots jumped up and reached for his rifle. Jake kicked his horse and bowled Boots off his feet, then jumped down and took the rifle. With a grunt and a hard swing, he tossed it far into the grass. His own rifle stayed with the horse. "I ain't armed. Wanna try that ass-kickin' game again?"

Boots got to his feet and brushed himself off. "I ain't following no one. I was just headin' back to town."

"You followed us till we turned off the road. I say you were sent to follow us."

"I wasn't following you!" Boots shouted.

Jake took a step toward him and Boots stepped back.

"Who sent you?"

"Wasn't nobody sent me."

Jake punched him in the middle of his chest and Boots stumbled and fell backwards.

Jake stepped up to him and put one foot next to Boots's head.

"Alright, alright," Boots said. "Beaulieu said I should keep an eye on you till I knew you was on yer way to Saint Paul. That's where yer goin', ain't it?"

"That's where we're going. Give me your boots."

"What?! I ain't giving you my boots!"

"Yeah, you are. You're giving me your boots and I'm taking your horse."

"That's horse-stealing. You can git shot fer that!"

"I ain't gonna steal him. I'm just gonna let him go. You can go find him later."

"Come on, Jake, you can't leave me out here without my boots. These damn sticker burrs will eat my feet off."

"Keep yer boots then. They probably wouldn't fit me anyway."

"When you get back to Crow Wing, tell Beaulieu that you saw us heading for Saint Paul. And tell him you quit. You ain't chasing Jacob Owen no more, 'cause if you catch Jacob Owen, Jacob Owen is gonna cut yer gizzard out and feed it to the crows."

"You takin' my horse?"

Jake walked to Boots's horse, cut the hobbles from its legs, and turned it south. Firing his rifle in the air and slapping the horse on the rump, he sent it down the road.

"Good night, Boots," Jake said. He mounted his horse and rode south.

"This town is full of strange people,
and by the looks of it, it ain't getting any better."

33

C H A P T E R
T H I R T Y - T H R E E

IN THE MORNING THEY WERE UP AT SUNRISE. Hawk came out of the tent and walked to the fire. Lorraine sat on a folding chair reading the Bible. "Morning, Lorraine."

She didn't answer.

"Lorraine?"

She kept on reading. Hawk squatted by the fire and poured himself a cup of coffee and looked at Lorraine.

Sophie came out and said, "Good morning, Lorraine."

Still no response.

Then Jake came out of his tent. "Church this morning?" he said without looking up.

"Is she alright?" Sophie asked.

"Dunno. She's been sitting like that since I came out."

Suddenly, Lorraine slammed the book shut with a resounding pop, and stood up. "Hawk, there is nothing in this damned book that tells me how to deal with you." Then she walked away.

"Lorraine! Such language!" He grinned at Sophie. "Damn, I love that woman."

"I know," Sophie said and kissed him on the cheek.

They rode four hours through the prairie and around Crow Wing until they found the road to Grand Marais. Then Posey got off her horse and studied the tracks, talking to Sunkist in Cherokee.

"She says no one has been on the road this morning. That's a good sign."

"Let's turn off the road and set a spell," Sunkist said. "Don't matter to me where we git Diggs. Here's as good a place as any."

They sat in a grove of white pines while Posey set the corn leaves to boil.

HAWK'S QUEST

When they had cooked a few minutes she brought a cup of the tea to Abernathy. "You drink. You be better rot quick."

"Rot quick?" Lorraine said. "What kind of language is that?"

"She's learning English from Sunkist," Sophie said.

"How unfortunate," Lorraine said with a sigh.

"Is that tea something we should know about, Sunkist?"

"Yeah. Boiled corn leaves. Comanches use it to break up a cold in the chest."

Abernathy drank the tea and they got on their horses and moved on. Mayhew, on his brown mule, took the lead. Sunkist and Posey rode directly behind him, with Jake in the middle of the column. Lorraine watched over Abernathy who had resumed his position on the travois. Sophie and Hawk brought up the rear.

The road was littered with rocks of all sizes and shapes. Along the edge of the road were stones that had been cleared from the roadbed. "Hey, Abernathy!" Sunkist shouted. "How'd all these rocks get here? Was that one of them there glayshers?"

Abernathy held tightly to the sides to keep from being thrown off as the travois bounced and jumped over the rocks. "Must we go over every rock on this road?"

"Hail, we ain't hittin' hardly any of 'em. Look over there," Sunkist said as he pointed to his right. "And look over there!" he said pointing to the left. "Hunnerts of rocks. Big ones, small ones, green ones, speckled ones, an' black ones—the country is covered with 'em. What makes dat?"

"These rocks were brought here by the glaciers. This appears to be one of the places where the glacier stopped its forward movement and melted away leaving its load where it stood. This field of rocks lies on a very gentle slope, and the work of thousands of years of wind, rain, and snow have eroded the overlying layers of lighter material down-slope. I suspect we will find a swiftly moving stream ahead or perhaps a low wetland."

Abernathy had lost awareness of his discomfort in favor of his favorite subject, geology. Suddenly, he was dragged up and over a large block of granite and dropped on the opposite side.

Sunkist heard a groan from the travois behind him.

"Are you uncomfortable back there, Mister Gentleman?"

"Sunkist, may we stop for a moment?" Abernathy whined. "I have to go into the woods."

"What fer ye wanna go in the woods? Ye gotta pee?"

"Yes, I have to pee! Now please stop!"

"That's the tea Posey made fer 'im," he said to Lorraine as Abernathy got up. "Yer givin' 'im plenty of water, I hope."

"Yes, she told me about it. It seems to be working quite well."

"How's the fever doin'?"

"She has that under control, too, no thanks to you."

Abernathy resumed his position on the travois and they rode on.

At sundown they stopped in a grove of pines and set up a small camp for the night.

Sunkist walked to Abernathy. "How ye feelin'?"

"I think I'm over the worst of it. I'll be on my horse tomorrow."

"Enny thing ye need, you jiss holler."

"Well, thank you, my dear friend. That is very . . ."

"How many times I gotta tell ye? Stop callin' me your dear friend!"

"You have just demonstrated what a dear friend you really are."

"Yeah, well, I meant, I jiss don't wanna be diggin' no holes in this rocky ground. How good are you with that fancy rifle of yourn?"

"Who is the best shooter in this group?" Abernathy asked.

"Figger me or Hawk."

"I'm better than either of you."

"How come I ain't surprised at that? Think you could hit Diggs at, say, two hundred yards?"

"I have no doubt any one of you could do that."

"Anyone of us could, Abby, but we ain't got good enough guns for the kind of shootin' I'm talking about."

"And may I inquire as to the nature of the shooting to which you refer, Jim?"

"Well, Abby, Diggs is going to have those girls right close to him. I wanna know if you could put a bullet between the girls and into Diggs."

"Yes, I could, Jim, that would be no problem."

"They're gonna be moving. That make a difference, Abby?"

"I see what you're getting at, Jim, but I do not think that is what we're here for. We were hired to bring him back alive."

"Yer right about that, Abby, I'm just thinkin' we might hefta."

"If and when the time comes, it can be done."

"You got no problem with killing a man?"

"If a man is endangering the lives of two young people, it would be necessary to stop him."

"Better git back to Lorraine, Abernathy, I think she misses you."

"I doubt that, Sunkist."

They traveled another day until they came to the top of a rise. Before them, a flat, open area stretched out for five miles. The area was covered with tall grass and small patches of tamarack and willow. "That's perty open country out there," Hawk said, "and there ain't no going around it."

"Well, this is as good a place as any to stop and wait for Diggs," Sunkist said.

They found a place fifty yards from the road and set up a camp in plain view of the road. Posey built a fire and they had a warm meal. "We'll keep one man on watch all the time while the rest of us get some shuteye," Hawk said.

In the morning of the second day, Posey spotted a rider coming up the road. When he saw their camp, he turned around and went back the way he came.

"Probably just someone lost his way," Hawk said.

"Could'a been a point rider fer Diggs, too."

"We'll just keep a closer watch on the road."

For two days they stayed in their camp. They kept a fire smoldering with the coffeepot next to it. Around the middle of the third day, Posey shook Sunkist's sleeve and pointed down the road.

"Someone comin'," Sunkist said.

"Abernathy, you and Mayhew go back in the woods out of sight and cover this spot," Hawk said. "Don't do any shootin' unless I give you the okay. Everone just act like we're just a bunch of city folks havin' a hot meal. Soph, you'd better cover your hair or Diggs will surely recognize you."

Ten minutes passed as they waited. A group of riders and a buggy came around the curve of the road. Diggs sat in the middle of the seat with an Indian girl on each side of him. He held the reins in one hand and in the other, a pistol pointed at the stomach of one of the girls. Four men on horseback with rifles across their laps rode close around the buggy.

"Don't do anything to endanger those girls," Lorraine whispered.

Sophie had a scarf over her hair and Hawk had his hat pulled low over his face. Sunkist waved at the riders. They waved back and kept moving.

"Is that Diggs?" he asked still smiling at the riders.

Hawk looked from under the brim of his hat. "Yup, that's Diggs."

They watched as Diggs and his men rode by them, down the slope, and onto the grass. When they were a safe distance away, Hawk motioned Abernathy and Mayhew in.

Jake took out the binoculars and watched as the men rode away.

"Where'd you get them?" Hawk asked.

"Got 'em from Boots."

"He gave them to you?"

"No, I had to kick his ass to get 'em."

"When did that happen?"

"That night you thought I was gettin' my ass kicked by Kathleen."

"You fought Boots?"

"Yup."

"Why didn't you tell us?"

"Don't figure he's gonna be a problem no more."

"You didn't kill him, I hope."

"Nope. Just showed him why he shouldn't be chasing us around."

"Those men we shot at Beaulieu's had binoculars," Hawk said.

"That makes Boots the one who dragged the bodies out," Jake said.

"I guess so."

"There's no question now about Boots working for Diggs."

"Sunkist," Abernathy said as he came into camp, "One of those men could be the one who shot Miss Erickson at Fort Ripley."

"What makes you think that?"

"In the boot of his saddle I saw a rifle with a telescopic aiming devise, the type that would enable a shooter to strike a mark quite effectively as far away as he can see."

"How come he didn't have it out?"

"At this short range it would not be necessary. He will not shoot that rifle unless he has sufficient cause."

"Well, we'll let him get across this grass, then we'll go after 'im. We ain't gonna just turn around and go home."

"He has the girls. He could not have better protection than that," Sophie said. "If we get too close he'll probably kill one of them. We can't let that happen."

One of the men dropped behind Diggs' group and stopped about three hundred yards out. He got down from his horse and pulled a rifle from the boot under his saddle, rested the rifle on a forked stick, and took aim.

"Get down!" Abernathy yelled.

They all hit the ground just as a bullet hit the canteen on Sunkist's horse. The canteen split open and showered them with water. They watched as the man calmly put the rifle in the scabbard, climbed onto his horse, and cantered ahead to rejoin Diggs.

"Well, whoever he was shootin' at, he missed," Sunkist said as he stood up.

"He did not miss, Sunkist. He hit exactly what he was aiming at."

"Ye mean he was aiming at my canteen?"

"Sir, that shot with a telescopic sight is child's play at that range."

"Why didn't he just shoot one of us?"

"According to our plan, he thinks we are ahead of him and probably doesn't know who we are. That shot was a warning to anyone who gets close—not just us. He could kill any one of us whenever he wished."

"Think you could hit him from here?"

"Yes, I could."

"Wanna try?"

"No."

"Why not?"

"Those two girls."

Sunkist stood and watched them ride away then disappear into the forest on the far side of the bog. "We're gonna heff-ta git rid of the man with the rifle."

"It seems there is no alternative."

"You can shoot 'im cold?"

"As I said, there is no alternative."

"Well, let's give 'em some time to get out a ways, then we'll go after him. We ain't gonna let 'im know we're following 'im. We'll git 'im somehow."

"Diggs ain't stupid enough to think we ain't following him," Jake said.

"He just told us not to get close or one of us is gonna get hurt," Hawk said. Silence prevailed as they looked across the bog.

"Getting across this grass is gonna be dangerous till we get to the woods."

"Well, might as well pack up and get movin'," Hawk said. "We'll keep a fair distance between us and get across as fast as we can."

"Mayhew, you take point," Sunkist said.

"Whatever you say, boss."

They packed their camps onto the backs of their horses and mules moved down the grade and onto the grass. They'd left the rocky ground behind them and the road was now soft and muddy with water standing in the tracks left by Diggs's wagon. Mayhew moved at a fast walk toward the tree line on the far side. Half an hour out Hawk yelled for Mayhew to hold up and wait for them.

Mayhew stopped and turned his mule to face the group. "What's going on?"

"Nothin', just ain't no use putting one man out there to take whatever's comin' alone."

"What do you think is coming?"

"That line of trees up there could hide an army of shooters. A sharp-shooter would have all the time he needs to pick us off one at a time, and we wouldn't even know where the shot came from."

"We're a lot like targets on a shooting range," Abernathy said.

"Can you hit a moving target, Abernathy?" Hawk asked.

"Yes."

"It's harder to hit when it's running though, right? Like trying to hit fast food."

"Fast food, sir?"

"Yeah, that's what chuh call a white tailed deer after he's been shot at an' missed."

"Are you suggesting we make a run to the woods?" Jake asked.

"Yup. Let's go."

All at once, they kicked their horses and made a mad dash toward the woods. When they entered the trees, they slowed to a walk. The trail was nar-row, but under the trees the ground was open and free of underbrush, giving them a comfortable range of view. With Mayhew in the lead, they moved as quietly as possible through the forest. The moist ground softened the plod of the horses' hooves, and all that could be heard was the creak of saddle leather, the drone of deer flies circling their heads, and birds singing in the trees.

The air was heavy and carried the sweet smell of damp, rotting vegetation from the forest floor. The wind moaned softly in the treetops, but the air was motionless on the road. A soft rumble sounded from the distance. "Feels like we're gonna have some weather to deal with," Sunkist said. "Ye see how the wind keeps a-shiftin'?"

Posey stopped and pointed toward an opening in the forest. "Looks like she's found us a place to ride out this storm," Sunkist said.

"What storm?" Mayhew asked.

"Well, cain't cha feel it? The wind in the trees, it keeps switchin'. It stops then blows from another direction, and the air feels like ye gotta drink yer way through it."

"It ain't that way up on Superior," Mayhew said. "Storms don't give you any warning. They just come in and raise all kinda hell and soak you down good, then leave."

They moved into the opening and began setting up camp. The sky above them was blue, but in the northeast a sharp line of clouds moved quickly towards them. The front of the dark-green cloud rolled bottom-up and flickered with lightning. The silence was as eerie as the yellow light, and a warm breeze stirred the tops of the trees.

"Hang onto yer hats when this one gits here, chi'dren." Sunkist said as they watched the evil-looking cloud roll in. The tops of the trees started swaying wildly, and leaves drifted down around them. But the air on the ground was still. Gradually, the wind picked up and shifted to blow directly towards the storm. The clouds blocked the sun so it was nearly as dark as night and the wind picked up until it was a roaring, whistling gale. Trees creaked and cracked and pulled at their roots. The sky filled with flying debris and the rain started as the black cloud rolled directly over them. The wind shifted again and a sudden downpour of cold rain drenched them before they could scurry into their tents.

Lightning flashed and thunder cracked while rain pounded their tents, forcing a fine spray through the canvas. Then hail threatened to blast the canvas apart. A quick sizzle followed by an ear-splitting explosion made them cover their ears and throw themselves flat to the ground.

Sophie shouted, "Usually this tent is so nice and cozy in the rain, but this storm might prove a little too much for it."

Hawk just looked at her, shook his head, and shrugged his shoulders. There was no use attempting conversation over the noise from the wind, rain, and hail and the constant explosions and reverberating rumble of thunder. Outside the tents, the wind increased and they heard trees cracking and falling in the forest. Then a loud, screaming roar shook the smile from Sophie's lips. The tent shook and flapped in the wind so violently they thought it would be torn to shreds. A sudden blast of wind blew in through the front of the tent, inflating the walls, ripping the tent stakes from the ground, and sending their canvas through the air to wrap around a tree. They quickly ran in the pouring rain to the canvas and scrambled to get it wrapped around them. They sat huddled together against a large white pine. The ground beneath them rose and fell as the wind pulled at the tree trying to tear its roots from the ground. Hawk wrapped Sophie in his arms as much for his own security as for hers. They clung to one another under the soaked canvas, listening to the wind blow the forest apart. Then, as quickly as it started, the wind died down and the rain stopped.

Drops of water pattered down from the tree above them as the world became quiet, as quiet as it had been before the storm. They crawled from under the canvas and saw broken branches all around and trees lying against one another with their roots torn from the ground. The grass that had been standing tall and luxuriant was laid out flat and soaked with rain. Slowly the rest of the group moved together to watch the storm clouds roll away. The air was crystal clear and the world had taken on a golden hue as the clouds allowed the sun to shine on them. The birds began to sing.

"What the hell they singing about?" Hawk asked sarcastically.

"Y'ever seen a cyclone b'fore, Hawk?"

"That was a tornado, not a cyclone," Lorraine said as she wrung the rainwater from her shirt.

"Looked like one of them there cyclones they have down in Kansas tuh me. The ol' Liver Eater claims he was in one of 'em once and got blowed clear inta the next week. I figger a tree fell on 'is head."

"Sunkist," Lorraine said, "what we saw today was a tornado."

Sunkist looked at Hawk and shrugged his shoulders. "Let's git this mess cleaned up and git goin'."

"Sunkist, are you listening to me?" Lorraine shouted.

"No!" he barked then turned to Hawk. "Is there anythin' she don't know?" Sunkist asked.

"She don't know much about keeping her yap shut."

They found the animals grazing peacefully in an open field and brought them back to camp.

"Wonder how Diggs liked that little squall," Abernathy said.

"Be alright with me if he drowned," Mayhew said quietly.

"We've got a few hours of daylight left. What say we get movin'?"

A steady rain began to fall. They traveled for another two hours, then set up camp on a piece of high ground. Everything they owned was wet, which made sleep hard to come by. One man stayed on watch while the rest tried to sleep. Morning brought bright blue skies and a warm, dry wind. They built a small fire and made coffee and biscuits for their breakfast then mounted and rode east.

Halfway through the day, they came upon a dead horse twenty feet off the road. Sunkist rode over to it, looked it over, and came back. "Been shot. Broke his laig. Prob'ly one of Diggs's men's horse. They'll be traveling a little slower for a while till they can git another horse."

The road they traveled was mostly mud from the previous day's rain. Rocks and stumps that hadn't been removed when the road was built slowed their travel.

Later in the day they came to a small settlement called Twin Lakes. As they rode in they passed a general store, a post office, a livery stable, and several small shops. Few people were out and those they passed paid no attention to them. They reined up in front of the Lac Le Belle Hotel, a two-story, unpainted, clapboard building, with one large chimney up the south side.

"What say we take a room and get dried out?" Sunkist said.

"Sunkist wants to take a room?" Sophie asked.

"I've had a belly full of sleeping in the rain, and Abernathy, he don't look like he's enjoying it a'tall."

They went into the hotel and took three rooms on the second floor. Mayhew took a bed amongst the dozens in the dormitory on the first floor.

Soon they gathered in Sophie and Hawk's room. "Anyone thought of going to the saloon and getting a beer?" Sophie asked.

"I'm goin' down to the stables and see if anyone's bought a horse lately," Sunkist said. "We can get beer later."

"I'll walk with you," Hawk said. "Four eyes is better'n two."

"Let's go."

As they walked into the stable, the man turned and glanced at them then went back pitching manure into a wagon.

"Anyone been in to buy a horse lately?" Sunkist asked.

"Ain't no use buying a horse when you can steal one for free," the man said without looking up.

"You loose a horse?"

"Probably Indians."

"Where'd they take it from?"

"Right outta my pasture. Took the best horse I had."

Sunkist turned to Hawk. "Diggs?"

"That'd be my guess."

"You had Injun troubles around here?" Hawk asked the hostler.

"Not for a while. Just a few renegades running around, but this is the first horse-stealing we've seen in a long time. Don't know how the hell they expect me to furnish horses for the stage if people keep steeling 'em."

"Stagecoach?"

"Yeah, this is the last relay station for the stage lines from Saint Paul before you get to Oneota."

"Did anyone see the thief?"

"Nope. No tracks to follow neither. That's why we think it was Injuns."

"Have you seen any strangers come through town?" Hawk asked.

"This town is full of strange people, and by the looks of it, it ain't getting any better. Hell, I don't even know my next-door neighbor. The damn hotel is full of strange people complaining about the rain. Farmers ain't complaining though."

"We're looking for a man riding in a buggy with four riders with him."

"A preacher?"

"That's him. When did he go through?"

"Couple of days ago. Seemed to be in a hurry. He didn't even stop; just went right on through."

"How many riders?"

"Three riders and two men in the buggy."

"Did he have a couple of Indian kids with him?"

"Nope, didn't see no Injuns." _

"Did you see what was in the buggy?"

"I don't pay no attention to what people got in their wagons. I see horses, that's all."

"Well," Hawk said, "guess we learned all we can here. Let's get back to the hotel."

"Missin' someone?" Sunkist asked.

"Yeah, a warm body in a dry bed."

"Race ye back."

Sunkist turned to the hostler. "We're bringin' our animals over fer some feed. We'll be right back."

They ran back to the hotel. Hawk was far ahead of Sunkist but waited for him catch up before going in.

In their room, Sophie was kneeling on the bed in one of Hawk's shirts when he walked in. "What's going on?" she asked.

"Just had a race with Sunkist. That old man can still run."

"What's the big hurry?" she asked as she settled back onto the pillows.

It was dark when they heard a knock on their door. "You comin' with us?"

"Where are you going?" Sophie asked.

"Down to the saloon."

"You go ahead, we'll catch up."

They quickly dressed and went to the saloon. Inside, three men leaned over beer mugs. Two tables had poker games going, and one table had a man sitting with an oversized woman. The woman laughed often as the man talked. They took the fourth table and ordered beer. Abernathy asked for cognac and was again disappointed. He settled for beer.

"So, what'd you learn at the stables?" Jake asked.

"We learned that someone swiped a horse from there a couple of days ago."

"Diggs?"

"We can think that, but we don't know fer sure," Sunkist said.

Hawk said, "Diggs has been through here and the man without a horse was riding in the buggy. If they got the horse, they did it after they were here."

"We'll just figure Diggs's men got the horse and they're on their way east. Ain't no one gonna go fer long without a horse."

Sunkist turned his head around and looked around the room. "I'm gettin' tired of this shit."

"We're all a little weary of it," Lorraine said. "We'll catch up with Diggs in due time."

"I ain't talkin' about that. I'm talkin' about—where the hell is Mayhew? He knew we was comin' over here. How come he didn't come, too?"

"You're going to have to ask *him* about that when you see him."

"Yeah, well, I don't like the way he disappears without tellin' us where he's a-goin'."

"Well, you don't always tell us where you're going," Lorraine said.

"That's diff'ernt. Ain't nobody's bidness where I'm a-goin'."

"Maybe that's the way he sees it. Maybe it is none of your bidness where *he's* a-goin'."

A very large woman walked into the room and shouted, "Howdy, boys! Oh, and ladies." She wore a long, full, dark blue dress and an ostrich plume in her bonnet. Her lips were painted a bright red with exaggerated points accenting her upper lip, and the redness of her cheeks matched her lips. Her eyelashes were coated with black paint so it was hard to tell where she was looking. Her hair was piled high on top of her head and around the edges it looked like she'd been in a strong wind. She walked in with a wide smile on her face and stood at the bar. The bartender brought her a glass of brandy and she took a long drink. She slammed the empty glass onto the bar, "Aah . . . that's better."

Hawk studied her for a moment. "She sure ain't no Kathleen, is she?" he said.

Sophie turned back to her beer. "Let's just say that if they were standing side by side, I'd have no problem telling them apart."

"Why is it so quiet in here?" the woman hollered. "Ain't nobody having no fun?"

The room became quiet. "Anyone here wanna have some fun with Lily?"

"Gittin' stuffy in here," Sunkist said, "Let's go."

The lady sauntered over to their table and leaned down over Sunkist. "How about you there, handsome?"

"I ain't handsome and you ain't no lady."

"Well, that's no way to talk to Lily."

"Lil," the bartender shouted, "leave the customers alone."

"I was just trying to liven things up a little!" Lily yelled as she backed away from the table. Mayhew walked in the back door.

"Hayes," Lily said, "come with me, you sweet thing, and we'll have another party . . . somewhere else."

Hayes's face turned red and he pushed Lily aside and sat down, straddling a chair.

"Guess there ain't no wonderin' where you been," Sunkist grumbled.

"I had business."

"I'll say. Ye got enny money left?"

"I'm down two bits."

Sunkist looked at Lily then at Hayes. "Ye spent way too much."

Jake started to get out of his chair. "I'm going back to the hotel. You people can stay if you want."

"We're right behind you," Hawk said.

Hours later, a knock on the door woke Sophie and Hawk. "You guys gonna sleep all day?"

"Damn, it's daylight," Hawk said. He got out of bed and opened the door.

"I got the horses out front and ready to move," Sunkist said.

"The rest of them ready?"

"Nope, I figgered I'd wake you up first so's you can take yer time gittin' outta bed. Hostler lost another horse last night. He's convinced it was Injuns. Best we keep an eye peeled today. Could be we're gonna have more problems than Diggs and his sharpshooter."

"He's too damn good with that rifle
to be jiss another gentleman shootin' pigeons."

34

CHAPTER

THIRTY-FOUR

THEY RODE OUT OF TWIN LAKE ON THE GOVERNMENT ROAD.

About two miles out of town they saw a wagon coming their way. Jake rode ahead to talk to the people in the wagon. "You folks seen a buggy and outriders on this road?"

"Yeah, some guy turned his buggy right in front of us. Damn near run us off the road."

"What'd he look like?"

"Looked tall and skinny. Course he was sitting down, so I can't say for sure. Had a hat on like he was a preacher."

"How many riders?"

"Two."

"You don't know who it was, do you?"

"Nope. Never seen him before. I'd know him if I ever saw him again, though. He only had one eyebrow. It stretched clear across his head."

"Thanks a lot," Jake said and turned back to the rest.

"Learn anything?" Hawk asked. "Yeah. They said a buggy damn near run 'em off the road. A preacher and two riders. They turned north toward the river."

Hawk turned to Mayhew. "What's north of here?"

"The only thing I know of up there is a few settlers and one of the wildest parts of the Saint Louis River."

"Figure he's goin' to see that settler?"

"Can't say. He can't cross the river up there; it's too wide and too fast. His horses would never get across, and that buggy sure as hell wouldn't make it."

"Maybe it wasn't even Diggs. Might'a been that settler."

"Might'a been, but how many buggies have you seen on this road. Hell,

HAWK'S QUEST

the heavy freight wagons are havin' trouble gettin' through."

"Diggs could be trying to throw us off his trail," Mayhew said. "There's a road up there that follows the river to Fond du Lac. It's a tough road and not very many people travel it."

"Can we get through on horseback?"

"Yeah, I've done it, but it's damn hard on horses and riders."

"The road does go to Fond du Lac, though, right?"

"It does, but it's a great place to set up an ambush. Lots of rock, and forest, and underbrush you can't see through for fifty feet."

"If he was going to ambush us, he's had a dozen chances already," Hawk said. "I say we follow him."

"All agreed?" Jake said.

"Let's move," Sunkist said.

Two miles out of Twin Lakes they came to the road that led northeast then, after a quarter mile, turned straight north.

The road was a narrow mud track through two miles of tall pines. They crossed two small streams and arrived on the banks overlooking the Saint Louis River.

Mayhew stopped them and said, "It's going to be dark soon and we don't want to be on that road at night. Neither will Diggs. I say we set up camp."

Abernathy and Lorraine walked to the edge and gazed down into the gorge the river had cut into the slate. Slabs of black rock rose from the bottom of the gorge like countless books on a shelf. The water rushed over and around rock islands and outcrops of slate, shale, and gray whack. They moved slowly upstream, examining each spire of slate as they passed. Some had been polished as smooth as glass from thousands of years of water coursing over their surfaces. There were potholes that had been cut by sand and pebbles trapped in the holes and swirled round and round, cutting deeper and deeper into the solid rock. They found channels where small rivulets had worn and dissolved the rock over millennium of continuous water flow. They climbed over the outcrops of slate and through thick undergrowth and majestic white pines.

Sunkist and Posey watched from above. "Whatcha seein' down there?"

"This black rock you see is slate," Abernathy said. "It was formed by sediments on the bottom of seas that covered this continent several million years ago."

By this time, Hawk and the rest had joined them. "How did rocks that big get out in the ocean?" Hawk asked.

"They were not carried to the ocean as rocks. It is fine sediment that accumulated at the bottom of a very calm sea. It was compressed into shale by overlying layers of sediment and further altered by heat and compression into the finer grained rock we see here."

"How come it's all tipped up like that if it was dropped on the ocean floor?"

"As time went on, more sediment was deposited on top of the older sediments and pressed down hard enough to break the horizontal layers of rock and tilt them upward, almost on edge."

Two hundred yards from camp, Lorraine stopped and pointed down the bank at a mass of white rock amidst the black slate. "Sunkist," Lorraine said. "Do you see that white rock formation over there?"

"Looks like the birds been using it fer a shithouse."

"That is a perfect example of a quartz intrusion breaking through the slate as magma."

Hawk turned to Sunkist. "Any idea what magma is?"

"Sure. It's melted rock that comes outta volcanoes."

"How do you know that?"

"I been out to Oregon and Californee. I seen volcanoes and lava, and lava flows and all this stuff. She ain't teachin' me nothin'." He tapped Hawk on the shoulder and nodded toward Lorraine. "She don't hefta know that."

Lorraine took Abernathy by the sleeve and tugged at him. "I want to go down there and look at those rocks," she said.

"You ain't goin' down there. You'll gitcher self kilt on them rocks," Sunkist said.

"I have to go down there and see it."

"Alright, you go ahead on down there, but if you go an' gitcher self kilt, don't come cryin' tuh me about it."

Lorraine was already on her way along the rim of the gorge toward the white formation. Sunkist shrugged his shoulders and followed along. "You comin', Hawk? Ain't no point in arguin' with her, she's goin' down there whether we like it or not. Ye might even learn something."

"I got no doubt about that."

They followed Lorraine and Abernathy along the rocky rim, through brush and trees to the place where she'd seen the white rocks. She stopped with Abernathy by her side and bent down and picked up a stone about the size of her hand. "This is almost pure quartz," she said as she turned to Sunkist.

"I seen lots of that stuff out in the Sierras. Ain't nothin' special about it."

"No, as far as it being quartz, there is nothing remarkable about it. However, the size of this formation is quite remarkable."

She started to crawl down the white rocks, stepping carefully from one broken bulge to another. She moved on hands and feet as she went down into the gorge. Abernathy handed Sunkist his rifle and followed Lorraine down the rocks. He stood silently observing Lorraine's studies from ten feet above her. He scratched at a piece of slate with his pocketknife. "This material appears to be soft, but is very hard. My knife won't scratch it."

"Told-ja we'd be learning stuff," Hawk said.

"I'll be a-goin' to muh grave with a head full'a useless information."

Posey pulled at Sunkist's sleeve and pointed to the rim on the other side of the valley.

"Lorraine! Get up here!" Sunkist shouted down to her. She looked up at him. He pointed to a rider that had appeared on the opposite side of the gorge.

"What is the problem?" she asked. "He's probably just a sightseer enjoying this spectacular river just as we are."

"Get up here. NOW!" he shouted back at her.

The rider turned and moved away from the river. Lorraine and Abernathy scrambled toward the top. Suddenly, a shot rang out and a bullet shattered the rocks close to Abernathy. There was no place to hide—they were open targets.

"Keep moving!" Sunkist shouted as he fired his Springfield across the gap. Hawk and Jake had taken positions alongside Sunkist and Posey.

"Shoot as fast as them guns'll load," he said. "Keep their heads down till Lorraine gets back up here."

Another shot bit the slate next to Abernathy, showering him with fragments of rock. Sunkist grabbed Abernathy's rifle and started shooting. Lorraine and Abernathy scrambled faster as the rifles above them kept a steady fire. After a long, hard climb, they made it to the top. The shooting from across the river had stopped.

"Keep down," Sunkist said. "Jiss cause we cain't see 'em don't mean they ain't there."

They watched and waited until Sunkist decided it was safe to move.

"Come on," he said, "but keep low."

They started slowly along the rim toward their horses. Suddenly, a bullet ricocheted off the rocks next to Abernathy. They dove for the ground and scrambled behind the rocks.

Jake took out his binoculars and scanned the rim on the other side of the gorge.

"Figure they're waitin' fer someone to show hisself," Sunkist said. "We're gonna heffta wait, too."

"The shot came from above," Abernathy said. "He is hitting very close to his intended target from a considerable distance, which brings me to the conclusion that he is at the very least two hundred yards away. The man who is doing the shooting is not the man who shot at us on the road earlier."

"How do ye figger that?" Sunkist asked.

"If that man had done this shooting, one of us, either Lorraine or I, would be dead. Most likely, both of us." He turned quickly and pointed up the gorge to a high prominence of slate. "I just saw a movement up there among those rocks."

"Looks like there's just one of 'em up there," Jake said as he looked through the field glasses.

A cloud of smoke erupted from the right of the rock. An instant later a bullet smacked against a tree behind them. "Did ye see where the shot came from?" Hawk said.

"I saw the smoke but not the man," Abernathy said.

"We're stuck. He can see us but we cain't see him."

Jake jumped up and ran to another rock and ducked behind to watch through his binoculars.

Minutes went by with no sign of the shooter.

"Mebbe he took off," Sunkist said.

"Would you like to stand up and find out?"

"Yeah, I'll do just that." Sunkist got his feet under him but stayed in a crouched position. "Ready?"

"You're not really going to stand up, are you?" Lorraine asked.

"Yup," he said and rose to his feet and just as quickly dropped down. The expected shot didn't come about.

"You must have gotten down before he could get a bead on you."

"Well, I ain't gonna do it ag'in. He's got a bead on my position now."

"Get ready," Jake said.

Abernathy, Sunkist, and Hawk raised their rifles and aimed toward the opposite side of the gorge. Jake quickly stood and dropped, but his effort was wasted. No shooting came from the sniper.

"This is positively stupid," Lorraine said. "One of you is going to be killed if this keeps up."

"You got a better idee how tuh smoke 'im out?"

"We could wait until dark and steal away unseen."

"Miss Lorraine," Abernathy said as he started to rise. "In the morning..." His comment was interrupted by an explosion and a shower of splinters as a bullet shattered the rocks next to him.

"There he is," Jake said. "Just a small dark spot between two layers of slate." He looked through the glasses again then raised his head, looked at Abernathy and said. "He's wearing a Confederate uniform."

Abernathy squinted to the spot where Jake pointed. "Yes, I thought he might be. His eyes must be going bad on him."

"Who?"

"The man up in those rocks."

"You know him?"

Abernathy looked at Sunkist for a brief moment and said, "No, I have no idea who he is."

"How far ye figger he is?"

"Two hundred and twenty-five yards."

"Kin ye hit 'im from here?"

"Of course I can," Abernathy said as he cradled his rifle between two rocks. He laid his cheek on the stock of the rifle, took a deep breath, and let it out. He held the sights tightly and began to squeeze the trigger.

"We ain't got all day," Sunkist said.

The rifle went off and the sound echoed up the gorge and back.

Seconds went by until from behind the rocks, a body tumbled down a small wash, bounced off another rock, slid down a small rivulet, and plunged into the river. They watched as it was carried by the current, tumbling over the rocks and rapids toward them. It hung up on an outcrop of slate for a few seconds before being shot through a narrow gap between two rocks. Abernathy watched the body tumble among the rocks as the current carried it by directly below them.

Sunkist gazed at Abernathy with a confused look in his eye. "That was one hell of a shot," he said softly.

"Yes, I suppose it was," Abernathy said.

"That the first man you ever kilt?"

"I do not make a habit of shooting men from hiding."

"That the first man you ever kilt?" Sunkist repeated.

"No," Abernathy answered without looking up.

"Ye kilt 'im dead."

"As I recall, that was the objective."

Sunkist watched as Abernathy started toward his horse while wiping his rifle with an oiled cloth.

"Something bothering you?" Hawk asked.

"Yeah. He said he's kilt men b'fore."

"Well, ask him about it."

"A man's past ain't no one's bidness but 'is own."

Jake came close. "They could still be around here, so we gotta keep our eyeballs skinned."

"It wasn't Diggs," Mayhew said.

"Why wasn't it Diggs?"

"Because there is no way he could have gotten across that river."

"You don't think it was Diggs's men?"

"It might have been someone working for Diggs. Probably someone planted there to slow us down."

"So that means he'll be running."

"Unless Diggs knows something about this road that I don't," Mayhew said, "he's not going to travel it in the dark."

"So if he *is* on this road, he'll be camping for the night, too."

"Right, and we'd ride right by him if we traveled tonight."

"We'll stay put till daylight, then get moving as early as we can," Mayhew said. "We should be in Fond by mid-morning. I'm going to suggest you do not stay in Fond du Lac. Just ride through. Diggs is not there."

Sunkist and Hawk looked quizzically at each other.

"What the hell's going on here?" Sunkist said. "Who put this guy in charge?"

"There are people in Fond du Lac who know me," Mayhew continued.

"Yeah, mostly in the whorehouses," Sunkist grumbled.

"That's the most likely place to find these men, don't you think? I need to stop in Fond du Lac," Mayhew said. "You people don't."

Hawk looked at him deeply. "You know something you ain't tellin' us, Hayes. What is it?"

"I jiss figgered it out, Mayhew," Sunkist said.

"What did you just *figger* out?"

Sunkist waved his index finger between Hayes and Abernathy. "You an' Abernathy here, you ain't strangers. You two was both with that geologisser back in fifty-six."

Hayes looked at Abernathy, shrugged his shoulders, turned back to Sunkist and said, "Alright, here it is."

Hawk looked around the area, and said, "This looks like as good a camping spot as any. Si'down. We ain't goin' nowhere till we know what this is all about." He looked at Mayhew. "Tell us what we don't know."

Hayes looked at Abernathy. "Guess it's time to let them in on it."

"Go ahead."

"My name is Hazael Mayhew. Abernathy is my cousin."

"Yer damn cousin!" Sunkist said. "What the hail's goin' on here?"

Hawk put his hand on Sunkist's arm and said, "Let him talk."

"I have a brother named Thomas Mayhew. He worked as an intelligence agent against the Confederate Army in the Civil War. He took orders directly from President Lincoln. He's in Washington right now. Or at least that's the last I've heard of him."

"So what are you doing here?"

"Thomas wrote me a letter a couple of years ago advising me not to join the Union Army. Well, I didn't need to be told that, so in September of sixty-two, I joined the Army at Fort Snelling to fight the Indians. That would keep me from going to the south. I was sent to Devil's Lake with you by Captain Vander Horck at Fort Abercrombie. That wouldn't have been my choice of duty either, but it was either that or be sent to the South. When we got back to Fort Abercrombie there was a letter waiting for me from Thomas. He asked me to investigate some illegal trade that has been going on with foreign countries."

"What illegal trade?" Hawk asked.

"We're not sure, but it has to do with smuggling illegal goods out of the country."

"What goods?"

"That has yet to be determined, but we are quite sure it's akin to slave trade."

"Slave trade?" Sophie said.

"We think Indian children are being sent overseas." Lorraine said.

"My God! What for? Where are they being taken?"

"We don't know that," Lorraine said, "and we're not even sure that's what it's all about. But all indications point to it."

"You're in on this, too, Lorraine?" Hawk said.

"Mister Lincoln has asked that we find the very best people to work on this," Mayhew said. "Lorraine is the best. She speaks several foreign languages and a number of Siouan and Algonquin dialects. After I fought with you in Dakota, I knew you would be the very best available for tracking and finding whoever is controlling this business."

Sunkist turned to Abernathy. "What's yer part in all this?"

"Have you heard the name Hiram Berdan?"

"I figgered something like this. Yer one of Berdan's sharpshooters, ain't chuh?"

"That is correct, sir."

"How'd you figure that out?" Jake asked.

"He's too damn good with that rifle to be jiss another gentleman shootin' pigeons."

"There are lots of good shooters out there, Sunkist."

"Yeah, well, he was too damn cold-blooded after he picked that guy off'n that rock. An' back in Crow Wing he slapped the whiskers off'n that hooligan in the bar an' he didn't have no worry about gettin' his ass whipped. Ain't yer ever'day Joe does that. Specially a scrawny little rat like that. An' all that stuff you tole me about bein' in college and learnin' all that stuff was bullshit, right?"

"Oh no. All that is true—as it happened."

"How the hail did you get mixed up in this?"

"Abernathy's fighting abilities are legendary in the Mayhew family," Hayes said. "We needed someone good with a rifle, and Abernathy is the best there is. He even whipped Berdan in shooting competitions."

"Berdan's the best in the country," Sunkist said. "I been hearin' about him fer years."

"Mister Berdan is the best of those who compete in the organized shooting sports," Abernathy said. "Competitive shooting is done over measured distances, and the shooting is practiced at those ranges. To be effective in combat, a man must be able to judge distances by sight and hit his target at any range. That is what Mister Berdan trained us to do."

"So back to the children," Sophie said. "Why would they want to sell Indian children as slaves? Indian people are hunters, not workers."

"They're just taking girls," Mayhew said. "Figure it out."

"Why the hail wasn't we told all this before we took on this chase?" Sunkist asked.

"Because this is supposed to be top-secret, but now it has become time for you to know everything we know."

"What do you know that we don't?" Sophie asked.

"We know that Reverend Diggs is not in this alone, but he is one of the ringleaders. His church was the perfect cover-up for their activities. He *is* an ordained minister, which made it possible for him to collect all the Indian children he needed without having to answer questions."

"What church?" Sunkist asked.

"That has nothing to do with it," Lorraine said. "There are good people and bad people everywhere you look. Thank goodness the good people out number the bad. Unfortunately, not by a large margin."

"Diggs had white children at his church," Sophie said.

"Color has nothing to do with it. What counts is children who have no one to come looking for them, such as white orphans assumed dead from the wars, or Indian children whose parents are used up by alcohol."

"Ol' lady Erickson," Sunkist said. "What was she doin' in this?"

"Miss Erickson was Diggs's housekeeper, nothing more."

"Then why was she killed?"

"Because she talked to you."

"Diggs already knew we were after him when we got to Ripley?" Hawk asked.

"Yes. He's known since Saint Cloud."

"Why do you say that?"

"We caught one of his men in Saint Cloud. He was in the same hotel you were in."

"We didn't talk to anyone there but the man at the desk."

"And the southern woman at the table next to you at breakfast."

"She was part of this?"

"Yes. We have her and the man she was with in jail in Saint Paul."

"On what charge?" Hawk asked.

"Conspiracy to commit murder."

"Murder who?"

"You."

"*Me!* Why would they wanna murder me?"

"Because you're chasing Diggs."

"I've got another question, and I want an answer," Hawk said. "Why was Sophie kidnapped?"

"I don't really know," Mayhew said, "but here's a reasonable guess. When the fur companies moved to Canada, they left a lot of men out of work. Some of them had accumulated vast amounts of money and did alright afterwards. Some of them were left with nothing. One of those men was a man named Beaumont Greenwood. Greenwood was one of the few honest men in the fur trade and stayed on as the fur traders made the transition to fishing and then to lumber. Along with the lumber and fishing, some men set up a smuggling ring and were shipping goods to Europe through Canada without paying duties.

"When Mister Greenwood learned of the illegal activities, he confiscated a very large amount of money and headed south. He bought a small claim along the Mississippi River in Saint Paul but sold it soon afterward and moved south. He was found murdered in a cornfield in Iowa."

Sophie took hold of Hawk's arm and squeezed tightly. He put his arm around her shoulder and pulled her close. "What?" he asked.

"Wait a minute," she said, then asked Mayhew. "How much do you know about this Mister Greenwood?"

"I know he died a broken man. He had absolutely nothing when he died. No money, no home, and a mistress who left him just after he left Saint Paul. She was killed in Mankato two years ago, probably by the same men who killed Beaumont Greenwood."

"Why do you say that?"

"Because she was executed in the same manner as Greenwood. Shot in the back of the head at close range."

"Why was she in Mankato?" Sophie asked.

"Because you were there."

"She was looking for *me*?" Sophie asked.

"No, she was looking for the money she thought you had."

"I don't have any money."

"I know that, and you know that. But, apparently, she had reason to believe you did."

"What did Mister Greenwood do for the fur companies?"

"He was a clerk."

"What happened to the money he took?"

"I don't know. I'm not convinced there ever *was* any money. But what we're dealing with here is not about the money, it's about those children."

"Why was Sophie kidnapped?" Hawk asked again.

"We're not sure, but we believe it's because the money that Greenwood supposedly took was never found."

"Why would they think Sophie has it?"

Sophie turned and looked at Hawk. "I'll tell you why they think I have the money. They think my name is Greenwood."

"Why would they think that?"

"My last name—Boisvert. Translated to English, *bois* means wood, and *vert* means green. In French, the adjective follows the noun. Therefore, *bois*, being the French word for wood, and the descriptive word, *vert*, meaning green, would be said in English as wood-green. In English, the adjective precedes the noun. So we turn them around and they mean green wood."

"What the hell was that all about?"

"It means my name is Greenwood."

"You're quite right, Sophie," Mayhew said. "I can't be absolutely sure, but I think you are the daughter of Beaumont Greenwood, formerly known as Beaumont Boisvert."

"So where's all the money?" she asked.

"That money hasn't been heard of for twenty years and you don't have to be a steamship engineer to know that after that long a time there is no money left. The money, if it ever existed, is gone."

"You still haven't said why Sophie was kidnapped."

"Someone apparently believes Sophie has the money. We know that money is gone, so anything else we come up with will be speculation."

"What's speculation?"

"Bullshit," Sunkist grumbled.

"Why are you telling us this now?" Hawk asked.

"Because from here on, things are going to get *very* interesting. We're close to the Great Lakes, and this is where we will run into international criminals who have no qualms about killing someone—anyone—male or female, even children. I would suggest you leave your women . . ."

Sunkist interrupted, "What can we expect to find in Fond du Lac?"

"Fond du Lac is a relatively large town," Lorraine said.

"You got relatives there?" Sunkist interrupted.

"No, Sunkist, I do not have relatives there." She leaned close to his face and looked directly into his eyes. "What I meant to say is, thar's a passel uh folks thar what moght take a notion tuh take a shot at chuh from one uh them thar wenders." She looked into his eyes for a moment then shook her head slightly and turned away. "Good Lord, I can't believe I just did that."

"Have you been to Fond du Lac, Lorraine?" Hawk asked.

"Yes, but it was a number of years ago."

"I have to go into Fond," Mayhew interrupted. "Jake, I'd like you to come in with me."

"Will do," Jake said.

"Anyone else?"

"We won't be stopping," Hawk said.

"Ain't nothin' in there I want," Sunkist said. "If yer sure ye don't need us, we stick with Hawk."

"Abernathy and Lorraine?"

"We're going around," Abernathy said. "We'll take the road around the north edge of town and meet you on the other side. There's a beautiful over-look there. You will just love it."

Lorraine looked at Abernathy, surprised that she wasn't consulted about the decision. "You know this road, Abernathy?" she asked.

"Oh yes. I've been on this road several times."

"When were you ever on this road?"

"With Henry Eames in eighteen fifty-six."

"Let's get some sleep," Mayhew said. "We've got a lot to do tomorrow."

35

C H A P T E R

T H I R T Y - F I V E

ON THE ROAD INTO FOND DU LAC THE NEXT DAY, Jake asked Mayhew, "Is Boudreau Jardin mixed up in this?"

"Boudreau Jardin is a thug with the brains of a goose."

"Is he working for Diggs?"

"No, I don't think so."

"Why was he seen with him at Beaulieu's house?"

"I have no idea."

As they came in view of the town of Fond du Lac, they passed a trading post and descended a long hill toward the Saint Louis River. At the bottom they walked their horses into the river to the small island, crossed it, and waded to the bank on the other side. The horses struggled to the top and they continued on into town.

They rode quietly as they came into Fond du Lac. Jake stopped and looked into the cluster of small houses and shops.

"You know where you're going?" he asked.

"Yup. Going to see a friend. You can go do what you like. I'll meet you at the saloon in an hour.

Jake walked down the street until he came to the sign that led him into the saloon. He stepped up to the bar and ordered a glass of beer.

The bartender set the glass in front of him. "That'll be a nickel," he said.

Jake paid the man and turned to look over the crowd. At one table, four men sat quietly playing a game of euchre. Cards landed on the table and were picked up without an exchange of words.

He remembered his mother playing whist with some of the ladies back in Ottertail County. He never could figure out how they read the cards so fast. His mother would toss a card on the table, and before it could land, the next lady would toss her card out. Then, before Jake could see what the cards were, a hand would swipe across the table, scoop up the cards, tap them once on each edge, and put them in a pile as neat as if they had just come out of the box. And the play would resume. "Rather be fishing," he mumbled to himself.

Two men stood at the bar nursing glasses of beer and staring at the back of the bar. Jake downed his beer and started toward the door. He stopped on the boardwalk and looked up and down the street. Fifty yards away he saw a big man on horseback coming his way.

"Aw, jeez," Jake grumbled. "Not him again."

He leaned against a post that held the roof up over the boardwalk, pulled his hat down to cover his eyes, and waited for Boots to get to him. As Boots walked his horse past him, Jake stepped onto the street and walked quickly to get close behind Boots. He didn't see Jake come up behind him and kept moving. Jake pulled his pistol from his belt and fired a shot into the air and simultaneously slapped Boots's horse on the rump. The horse jumped forward and took off down the street at full, terrified gallop. The sudden acceleration laid Boots on his back over the horse's rump until he let go of the reins and fell onto his back on the dusty street. He lay there, staring at the sky for a moment, trying to figure out how he got there so suddenly. As he heard footsteps coming from behind, he slowly rolled his eyes up to look over his forehead and focused on Jake's smiling face.

"Howdy, Boots," Jake said, looking down at him. "Come to finish that ass-kickin'?"

"Howdy, Jake," Boots said as he looked between his knees and down the street in time to his horse rounding bend in the road and disappearing into the countryside. "You gonna go git my horse?"

"Nope," Jake said watching the dust left by the horse drift away on the warm, westerly breeze. "That's the second time I've had to run yer horse off. If I hafta do it again, I'll shoot the son of a bitch."

"What do you want from me?" Boots asked as he got to his feet.

"I don't want nothin' from you. You was following me, remember?"

"Yeah, I was. I gotta talk to you."

"Want to go get a beer and talk?"

"Where's the rest of your gang?"

"They're watching every move you make," Jake said as he pointed toward the bank with a flick of his thumb.

"Ain't no need for that," Boots said. "Let's go get that beer."

"You buying?"

"Yeah, I guess so."

"You know which bar we're goin' to?"

Boots turned to Jake. "This ain't no trap. You tell me what bar."

Jake motioned to the bar he'd just left.

"Keep that pistol out like you was in control," Boots said as he moved toward the bar.

"I *am* in control," Jake said. "Why should you want it to look like I'm in control?"

"Let's go in, I'll tell you all about it."

Jake held the door and sent Boots in first. Boots took a step inside and stopped to look around.

"What are you scared of?" Jake asked.

"Just making sure no one sees me talking to you."

"Okay, let's take that table in the corner. You sit with your back to the door in case someone comes in."

Boots took a chair and Jake went to the bar and ordered two glasses of beer.

He set a mug in front of Boots. "What's this all about?"

"Guess there ain't no trying to hide the fact that I was working for Diggs."

"Nope. What did you do for him?"

"My job was to keep the buck and the squaw away while his men hauled the kids off."

"We won't be using those words anymore, Boots. How about we use mother and father?"

Boots looked at Jake inquisitively. "What the hell's wrong with buck and squaw?"

"We won't be using those words, because using those words can get you killed."

"How's that?"

"Never mind. Just don't use them. It's for your own good. How did you keep the parents away?"

"Get 'em drunk, mostly. Sometimes the buck hadda be slapped around to get him to stay away." Boots heard the hammer of Jake's pistol click back to half cock. "What?" He turned quickly and glanced around the room, then back at Jake. "What's the gun for?"

"You just used that word."

"What word? What the hell's wrong with you?"

"You just heard me raise the hammer on this pistol. If you use buck or squaw again, you'll hear it fall." Jake had Boots scared, and he was going to keep it that way. Jake knew that scared men were only dangerous when they panicked, and then they're more dangerous to themselves than anyone else.

"Damn, Jake, you can't just shoot me, just like that!"

"Yer a hired killer and I'm the law. Ain't nobody gonna ask questions if you fall off that chair dead."

"Yer a lawman?"

"Genuine deputy marshal. Sworn in down in Hutchinson."

"Where's yer badge?"

Jake laid his forty-four caliber dragoon horse pistol on the table with a loud thump. "Right here."

Boots glanced down at it then back to Jake's eyes. "Hell, I never knew you was a lawman. I swear."

"Don't swear neither, goddammit."

Boots looked at Jake like he'd lost his mind. "Yer nuts, ain't chuh?"

"Maybe a little. If I am, I wouldn't know it, now would I? Now, tell me, sometimes you had to kill the father, right?"

"No. I never killed anyone doing this job."

"You have killed men, though, right?"

"Just like you, Jake—only when I had to."

"What's Diggs doing with the Indian kids?"

"I never did talk to Diggs himself. I got my orders from one of his men."

"Any names?"

"Naw. Hell, I could never talk to those men. They all got school learning and dress in fine clothes and talk that funny talk like a school teacher or something. The only time they talked straight to me was when they was giving me orders. They told me the parents don't want their kids going to white man's schools, but he's taking them for the government because the government made deals with the Indians and now the kids have to go."

"You believed that?"

"He paid me a lot of money for doing it. I ain't real smart about money and school and all that. So I just did what I was told and he gave me money."

"How much did he pay you?"

"Sometimes twenty bucks a kid. That's a lot of money for a guy like me."

"What makes you come to me with this now?"

"Well, a couple of days ago I found out he was gonna take a white kid.

Taking Indian kids is one thing, Jake, but taking white kids is something else."

"What's the difference? Ain't Indian kids just as important as white kids?"

"Well . . ." Boots stopped and looked down into his glass. "Well, it's just that—well, Indians loose their kids all the time. It ain't nothing to them like it is for white folks. They just go and steal someone else's kid to take the place of the one they lost. And on top of that, it's for their own good.

"That's just plain stupid, Boots. Where the hell did you get such an idea?"

"I know it's stupid. It ain't my idea. That's why I'm here. Diggs's men made it all sound so . . . so . . . well, honest."

"Where's Diggs gonna get this white kid?"

"If he ain't already got her, he'll get her here in Fond, or maybe up in Oneota or Superior."

"Her? He's taking a girl?"

"Yeah, a girl."

"Why a girl?"

"I don't know. Hell, I just know what I was supposed to do. They don't tell me why they do things."

"Does he know who's kid he's gonna take?"

"I don't know. I never heard anything about that."

"What else can you tell me about this?"

"Nothing. You know everything I know."

"Who told you about this?"

"Nobody told me. I heard 'em arguing about it when I was pissin' in the bushes."

"Can you remember anything they said?"

"Yeah. One of 'em said just what I said. He said taking her ain't like taking an Indian girl. He said people all around the country will be looking for her."

"But no one said who she is?"

"Nope. I got the hell out of there as soon as I heard it."

"Any idea when this is going to happen?"

"Nope. You guys just have to be damn careful so you don't get anyone else killed over this."

"Where were you when you heard this?"

"On the road a while back. Maybe ten miles out."

"Before you got to Fond?"

"Yup."

"Tell me what you know about Sophie being kidnapped."

"I don't know any Sophie. Who's she?"

"Never mind. You're better off not knowing."

Boots slid his chair back and started to rise. "I gotta go, Jake. Hope you guys get all this cleared up."

"One more question, Boots. Who killed Miss Erickson?"

"Diggs. Diggs did that one himself. See ye, Jake."

"Where is Diggs now? Is he in Fond du Lac?"

"Hell, Diggs is twenty mile ahead of you guys. I got no idea where he is, but you ain't nowhere near him."

With that, Boots started for the door. He stopped when he heard the bartender holler, "Hey, you! You gonna pay for that beer?"

Boots glanced at Jake then walked to the bar, paid for the beer, and left.

Jake sat for a few minutes contemplating Boots' story. He ordered another beer and watched the door for Mayhew.

Ten minutes later Mayhew walked in. "Jake, we gotta go."

"Can I finish this beer?"

"No, let's go."

"What's the big hurry?"

"Hawk and them are walking into an ambush. Let's move."

"How do you know about this ambush?" Jake asked as they mounted their horses.

"An informer told my contact about it."

"Boots?"

"Might'a been. How did you know he was in town?"

"I just got done talking with him. Where is this ambush gonna happen?"

"Down this road, I hope."

"What d'ya mean, you hope?"

"If it don't happen down this road, we're going the wrong way."

They turned their mounts down the street and up the hill, out of Fond du Lac. They rode side by side at a canter.

"What did Boots have to say?" Mayhew asked.

"Said Diggs is gonna kidnap a white girl."

"Protection, I'd guess. There were some of Diggs's men in town. Did you know that?"

"I'm not surprised."

"If you'd known, would you have gone in?"

"That's why I went in. I figured there'd be some. Did you know they were there?"

"Yup. That's why I asked you to come with me."

Mayhew lightly slapped Jake's coat with the back of his fingers to get his attention. "Boots just wrote his own death warrant. You know that, don't you?"

"I know that, and you know that. But does he know that?"

"I don't think Boots would risk his life for anyone, not even a little girl."

"He knows talking to me could get him killed, but he was being real careful about being seen with me."

"Hell, they saw him, you can count on that."

"He made it look like I captured him. He even told me to keep my pistol out while we went into the bar . . . and I chose the bar we went into."

"Maybe ol' Boots isn't as stupid as we thought."

"Yes, he is.

"Could he be setting a trap?"

"No. I doubt that. He didn't know when or where the kid was going to be taken."

They stopped at a junction with another road and followed it east. After ten more minutes of travel they heard Hawk's voice from a thicket of new-growth aspen. "Hey! Over here."

Soft thunder rolled in from the west and a cool wind blew over them.

"Figgered we best find a place to hole up fer a while. Looks like one of them rain showers what don't go away jiss cuz ye cuss 'em."

"We can't sit here," Jake said. "Diggs is getting' a big lead on us. Boots told me he's twenty miles ahead of us. That's a whole day's ride."

"Boots! Were did you see him?" Hawk asked.

"He dropped in to talk to me in Fond du Lac."

"Hawk," Mayhew said. "I also learned that we are riding into an ambush."

"I'd say an ambush is highly unlikely on this road," Lorraine said. "There's far too much traffic. My goodness, there's been four wagons and a dozen horses that have gone by in the three hours or so that we've been here."

"That's just what I was told," Mayhew said.

"Boots told me that Diggs is going to kidnap a white girl."

"Why a white girl?" Sophie asked.

"Don't know that. Don't know when or where, either."

"We will be learning the reason for that when Mister Diggs is ready to tell us," Abernathy said. "He will probably threaten to kill the girl if we continue to chase him."

"Sounds like a good guess to me," Hawk said. "Do you think he'd kill her?"

"He is perfectly capable of killing anyone who stands in his way. However, he will kill her only as a last resort. He knows killing her will only increase our determination. Mister Diggs is not a stupid person. He realizes that causing a lot of commotion will just draw attention to him. The people he works for don't like attention, and that is probably one reason we have not been ambushed before now. That and the fact we outnumber him in manpower and firepower."

"Jake," Hawk said. "I don't s'pose Boots said anything about how old the girl might be?"

"No, nothing. Why?"

"Might be that's why they took Sophie. For protection."

"Could be."

"He ain't gonna get close enough to take any of these women," Sunkist said, "and he knows that."

Posey shook Sunkist's shirt and pointed down the road. A quarter mile away, a wagon pulled by two horses was moving toward them from the west.

"What?" Hawk said.

"Wagon comin'," Sunkist said.

"There's been wagons runnin' up and down this road all day."

"Yeah, but this one went by here b'fore, goin' the other way. It's got a canvas over the bed."

"Nothing unusual about that with those rain clouds moving in."

"This one ain't tied down. And what's under it is movin'."

They all started to move toward the brush.

"Stand still and check your rifles," Hawk said softly. "We'll just wait here and wave at them as they pass. Don't shoot unless they shoot first." He turned to Posey. "Get the horses ready. We're riding out."

"Hawk," Jake said. "If that's Diggs's men in there, we can't just ride off and leave them."

"We're gonna keep them close," Hawk said.

The driver of the wagon didn't appear to notice the group of people alongside the road watching the wagon pass. As he drew abreast of them, he started to whistle. The canvas covering the wagon began to rise along the edges. Hawk, Sophie, Jake, Sunkist, Mayhew, and Abernathy raised their rifles and aimed at the wagon box. The edge of the canvas lowered quickly and driver snapped the reins to get the horses to move a little faster.

"Git on your horses," Hawk said.

They mounted and took up positions behind the wagon with their rifles across their laps.

The driver turned and shouted, "Something I can do for you folks?"

"Yeah," Hawk answered. "Just keep that wagon moving. You're in our way."

"What ye gonna do with 'em?" Sunkist asked.

"Ain't thought that far ahead," Hawk said. "Maybe we should find out who's under that canvas."

Sunkist moved his horse up behind the wagon and took hold of the canvas. He stopped the horse and let the wagon slide out from under the canvas. Four men slowly turned their heads and looked at the troop surrounding them.

As the wagon stopped, Jake asked, "Any of you know a man named Diggs?"

One man toward the front of the wagon rose up and said, "We don't know anyone named Diggs. We were just going hunting."

Jake moved his horse close and bumped the muzzle of his rifle off the man's forehead. "Do we look that damn stupid to you? Who sent you after us?"

"Nobody sent us after you. We were just going hunting."

Jake turned to Hawk. "What are we gonna do with 'em?"

"Dunno. We can't just shoot 'em."

"Get out of the wagon!" Jake shouted at the men. "And leave the guns there."

They looked back and forth at one another.

"Git out of the wagon!" he repeated more quietly but with more insistence.

Slowly, the men worked their way onto the ground.

"Take off your boots."

"What?"

"You heard what the man said—git them boots off!" Sunkist demanded.

"You can't leave us out here without our boots."

"Well, we can't have you following us around, either, so it's that or . . . well, I guess there's something to be said for dyin' with your boots on."

Again, they looked at each other. One of the men sat on the ground and began pulling his boots off. Another did the same. Another stood firm. "I ain't taking off my boots for no man."

Jake's rifle barrel flashed out and caught the man on the side of the head knocking him to the ground. "Take those boots off. Now!"

When all four men were barefoot, Jake said, "Throw the boots in the wagon."

When that was done, Jake walked to the front of the wagon turned the horses around and started them back toward Fond du Lac. "When ye get to where these horses take this wagon, you can pick up your guns and boots."

"You'll pay for this!" One of the men shouted as they walked away.

"Why did you let them go?" Abernathy asked.

"What were we going to do with them?" Jake said. "I don't think they were Diggs's men, anyhow."

"Why weren't they Diggs's men?"

"According to Boots, Diggs's men are all educated men and dress in clean clothes. Those guys weren't in clean clothes, and they sure as hell weren't educated."

"He took my Jessica!" she screamed.

36

THE COUNTRYSIDE THEY MOVED THROUGH WAS GETTING ROUGHER. There were steep hills to climb and descend, and outcrops of rock that could easily conceal the expected bushwhackers. They saw few wagons on the road and even fewer horses. Abernathy stopped next to a rock outcrop about ten feet high and picked at it with a pointed hammer.

"Whatcha find there, Abernathy?" Sunkist shouted.

"I am attempting to break a sample from this rather fragile-looking rock, but it is much harder than it appears. It has the large crystals like granite but lacks the coloring. It is obviously of plutonic origin and was probably deposited here by a shield volcano, since there are no tall mountains nearby."

"I seen some of them high volcanoes out west. Some of 'em put ye in mind of a woman's . . ."

Suddenly, Abernathy's body jerked violently and they heard the sound of a shot from the rocks above. Abernathy looked down at his chest then fell to the ground. Sunkist dropped off his horse and ran to him. Abernathy groaned and coughed up blood as Sunkist dragged him behind the rocks. Posey ripped open his shirt.

Lorraine ran over and knelt down beside him. "How bad is it?"

"He's got a hole in his chest the size of a hen's egg," Sunkist said.

"Bullet go through." Posey said. "He not good. Maybe bullet break bones in Ab'nathy."

"Can you do anything?" Lorraine asked.

"Plenty much bad. Maybe he die."

Tears began to flow as Lorraine looked into Posey's eyes. "Is there nothing you can do?"

"Bullet hit bad place. Make hole in Ab'nathy wind place."

"Men have survived lung wounds," Lorraine said. "We have to get him to a doctor."

Abernathy looked up at Lorraine with a pleading look. He tried to speak but the pain in his chest would not allow it. He held her eyes until his lost their focus. His face turned white, consciousness left him, and merciful nothingness relieved him from the pain.

"Where the hell is that sawbones when you need him?" Sunkist grumbled.

Hawk came and stood next to Sophie. "There ain't no one up in those rocks. This was another sniper shot. Shoot and run. We should'a hung on to that wagon."

"It can't be that far down the road."

Before the last words were out Jake had jumped onto his horse and whipped him to full gallop back toward Fond du Lac.

He passed the men they'd taken the boots from and, in another mile, he found the horses grazing along the road. He tied his horse to the back of the wagon, jumped up into the seat, and whipped the horses back toward Abernathy. As he came to the men without boots, he slowed and shouted, "Get in the wagon!" The men ran up to the wagon and hopped in. They hung on as they were jolted up and down and sideways as the wheels bounced over rocks and dropped into potholes.

Jake turned his head slightly and yelled, "Where's there a doctor?"

"Doc Thompson, but he's probably over in Superior."

"There's a new one in Oneota," another of the men said. "He just showed up. What's this all about?"

"One of our men's been shot. We need to get him to a doctor."

"Oneota is the best place. If Doc Thompson is there, he'll fix him up."

The wagon made a sharp turn to the right and nearly threw the men out.

"What the hell's the big hurry? You trying to get us killed?" One of the men yelled.

Jake whipped the horses with the reins.

"What do you need us for, anyway?"

"You're working for me, now. You'll do as I say," Jake shouted back.

As the wagon came to Abernathy, Jake slowed and stopped the horses. He told one of the men to hold the horses. "And stay away from those guns," he said. "Gitcher boots on, yer coming with us. Which one of you knows where to find the doctor?"

"We all do," one of the men said. "Ever'body knows Doc Thompson."

"Hey, one of my boots is gone!"

"Well, get up in the seat. Yer driving us to Oneota."

"What about us?" another man said.

"Make your own way and find us at the doctor's place."

Hawk and Sunkist had Abernathy wrapped in a blanket and brought him to the wagon.

"How's he doing?" Jake asked.

"It don't look good, Jake. They got one of his lungs."

"Any sign of the sniper?"

"Not hide nor hair. Close as I can figure the shot came from up in those rocks." Hawk pointed up to a cluster of black rock three hundred feet up the slope. "There ain't no use going up there looking for him. He's long gone."

"That might be," Sunkist said, "but me and Posey's going up there and track that cowardly son of a bitch snake down."

"Won't do no good, Sunkist, he's gone and . . ."

"Don't make no difference if he's gone. Twixt me an' Posey we'll track him down and bring his flea-bitten skelp back fer Abernathy. He kin hang it in the shithouse when he gets home. You go ahead on and git Abernathy to the doctor. We'll ketch up with ye down the road."

The driver snapped the reins and started down the road at a gallop with Lorraine in the wagon beside Abernathy. She reached forward and slapped the driver hard on the back of his head. "Slow these damn horses down," she yelled. "You're going to kill him driving like this!"

Sunkist looked at the blood spattered on the rock and the gray smear where the bullet splattered when it hit. Then he stood on the spot where Abernathy stood when he was hit.

He pointed up toward the rocks. "It come from right up there. There's two rocks side by side. That's where the shot come from." Mounting their horses, he and Posey rode at a canter along the road to find a place to climb the hill. He stopped when he found a wash about four feet wide that came down between the rocks. He stepped down from his horse and studied the steep incline. "We're gonna hefta walk the horses up this hill."

They moved slowly, leading the horses over the black rock and through the brush and weeds to the top. Slowly they moved along the crest. Posey stopped, "There," she said, and pointed. She left her horse and walked to a cleft between the rocks. She bent down and picked a rifle cartridge from the ground and held it up for Sunkist to see.

"That's it," he said. "Which way'd he go?"

She pointed toward the brush behind them. There they found horse tracks and dog tracks.

Sunkist studied the tracks and said, "Foundered. This horse ain't goin' far."

"What is foundered?" Posey asked.

"Ain't been took care of. His feet's all outta shape. Looky here." He traced his finger around the oval shape of the tracks—longer than they were wide. "His front feet grew too fast fer to wear 'em down proper. Prob'ly kept in the barn or in a corral too long." He looked up and said, "The damn fool—he stole a dead horse."

They mounted and followed the trail along the crest of the hill and back into the heavy timber, into a ravine and up onto a patch of rock covered with gray-green lichen. The tracks were short, which told him the horse was in pain and would not last much longer in this steep, rocky terrain. The trail turned east toward the road the wagon traveled. In the muddy places, they saw dog tracks. The tracks took them down a wash between the lava flows and onto the road. The tracks turned east and showed that the horse was struggling down the slight grade.

"Ain't no need tuh run these horses. That horse ain't gonna make another mile."

They walked the horses along the road keeping an eye on the tracks. The road was rutted from side to side from the wheels of the many wagons that had passed.

Thunder rumbled in the west. "We're gonna have to ketch up with that horse afore that rain gits here and washes out the tracks."

The Saint Louis River was to their right as they entered Oneota. Tall, rugged hills to their left reached up six hundred feet, obscuring rain clouds in the west.

Oneota was a settlement with about thirty small, simple shacks, a one-room schoolhouse, a sawmill, and a church.

Several people walked on the streets and horses pulling buggies and wagons moved about. Sunkist stopped a man and asked, "You seen a foundered horse go through here?"

"I ain't sure what a foundered horse looks like. Seen a wagon come in with a man layin' in the bed. Been shot, I hear. They got him at Doc Thompson's."

"That horse would be walkin' real slow. Feet all outta whack. Ye seen 'im?"

"Just saw the preacher going toward the doctor's house. Hope ever'things…"

Sunkist put his hand up to the man's face to quiet him. "You seen a sick horse go through here?"

"Yeah, sure, come to think of it, someone rode through just a little bit ago on a sick horse. Right after them people brought the man in, in the wagon. Horse's head was hanging down, like this." The man hung his head low and drooped his shoulders so his arms hung limp in front of him, then glanced up at Sunkist. "Ye see? I noticed him because he didn't look like a lumberjack or a fisherman. He had on some fancy duds like you might see in church. You know this man?"

"Yeah. Me an' him gonna have some words."

"Well, he went down toward the end of town. Probably on his way to church."

"Is there a livery down there?"

"Yeah, the livery's down on the right just past the saloon. He might'a went there. Ye s'pose?"

"That's where I'd go if I had a sick horse."

They left the man standing and walked toward the edge of town. Sunkist and Posey stopped and studied the road, hoping to find the tracks, but none were there.

"He either took another road or he's still in town. Let's find the livery. Might be he's there gittin' another horse."

They rode further and found the livery stables. Inside was a man looking over the horse they'd been following.

"That horse jiss come in?" Sunkist asked.

"Yup, a guy brought the horse in and ran right out the door. You know him?"

"Not yet. Which way'd he go?"

"Don't know. He wanted to trade this wreck for a good horse. Well, I ain't stupid. I wouldn't do it. He ran out the back door and I ain't seen him since."

Posey studied the boot tracks around the horse. She pointed to the round toe and wide heels. "He not wear boots. He wear slippers."

"Slippers? What the hell are slippers?"

"Yeah, he had shoes on, not boots," the hostler said.

Sunkist studied on that for a few seconds then looked down at the tracks. "Guess I don't know the differ'nce."

Posey took him by the shirtsleeve and urged him to follow her to the backdoor.

"This horse ain't gonna make it!" the hostler hollered after them. "I'm gonna have to put him down!" He watched as Sunkist and Posey left the barn. "Don't know who this critter belongs to," he grumbled, "but I ain't feedin' no dead horse."

Sunkist and Posey walked out onto the street and looked for the tracks of the slippers. Posey pointed to the east and they climbed onto their mounts and walked in that direction.

Suddenly, a horse burst out from an alley and ran passed them. A screaming girl was in the saddle with a man in fine clothes. A crowd came running out with a screaming woman right behind them.

"He took my Jessica!" she yelled.

Sunkist and Posey took off after the horse. A man ran out in front of them with a rifle pointed at them. "Stop, or I'll shoot!"

They pulled their horses to a stop just before they came to the man.

"Put the goddamn gun down!" Sunkist yelled. "We're going after that gurl!"

"You ain't going nowhere," the man yelled. "Get down off them horses."

A crowd had moved around in front of them blocking their path.

"If you don't git outta my way you ain't never gonna see that gurl ag'in," Sunkist said and started to move forward. One of the men took his horse by the reins and pulled him to a stop. Sunkist lowered his rifle at the man's chest and said, "Git outta my way."

The man dropped the reins and backed away.

They kicked their horses to full gallop. Someone from behind fired a shot and they heard shouting, but they kept on going.

They rode out of the town on the main road. Ahead they could see the dust from the horse but he'd gotten ahead of them and turned out of sight. They rode fast for a mile when Sunkist reined to a stop. "He ain't on this road,"

Horses came from behind. Sunkist turned his horse around and raised his hands. The men came up with guns pointed at him.

"Muh name's James Whistler. I'm a depuddy marshal fer the United States Gov'ment. We're lookin' fer that man who stole the gurl."

"We don't know about any deputy marshals around here," one of the men said. "You'll come with us."

Sunkist turned and looked down the road. "That gurl's gonna be long gone if you don't get movin' right now," he said.

"You're coming with us. We'll find the girl."

"You ain't takin' me nowhere. I'm turning this animal around and if you wanna shoot me in the back, then go ahead. I'm gonna find that gurl," he said and turned his horse around.

"Stop, or I'll shoot!" One of the men shouted.

Sunkist didn't turn around. He walked his horse away from them. "Come on along if you want that gurl back!" he shouted without turning his head. He rode for twenty yards and heard the sound of hooves coming behind. He kicked Dan in the ribs and headed back toward town.

"Where the hell you going?" someone yelled.

"He ain't down this road. He turned off back here somewhere."

He led the group up the road till he found a narrow trail that led north off the main road and up a steep hill. He stopped while Posey studied the tracks, then turned to the men behind him. "He went up this road."

The road was rough and steep and they had to walk the horses. Posey rode in front of Sunkist, watching the tracks. They followed the road for half an hour, then Posey stopped and pointed to a cabin set back in the woods. "White men," she said.

Sunkist turned back to the riders. Most of them had left and only two were there. "Stay back," he said in a soft tone.

Posey slipped from her horse and into the woods. Sunkist rode at a walk toward the cabin. Suddenly, they heard a scream. He stopped and stared ahead. Then he raised his hand and motioned for the riders to follow. He heard no sound from behind and turned around. No one was there. "Damn cowards," he grumbled.

He walked Dan forward into an opening in the forest. A lathered horse stood free in the field fifty yards from a small cabin. He was walking slowly toward the cabin when a shot rang out and a bullet spat by his head. He dove from his horse and rolled into the woods.

"Turn the gurl loose!" he shouted toward the house.

"Get away from here or I'll kill the girl!"

Sunkist started moving to the side to get behind the house. He heard the hammer of a rifle clicking back and ducked behind a tall white pine.

Meanwhile, Posey crept through the woods around the house with her pistol in her hand. She looked though the window and saw a man with his arm around the neck of a young girl, holding her against his body. In the corner of the cabin a woman sat with her hands over her mouth, staring at the man and crying. Posey picked a stone from the ground and tossed it up onto the roof of the cabin. She saw him look up toward the roof and instantly broke the window with her pistol. The man turned loose of the girl and swung his rifle at Posey. His bullet blasted through the window frame just as Posey fired her pistol. He doubled over from the pain of the bullet ripping into his guts, then he turned and ran out the door.

Sunkist heard the shots from inside the house. For an instant his mind pictured the man shooting the girl. A second later the man ran out of the house while trying to load his rifle. Sunkist followed the man over his sights and fired. The man stumbled and fell to his knees, then toppled to the ground. Sunkist waited a few more minutes then stepped out and walked over to him. Posey came out of the house.

A woman came out crying and holding a girl about ten years old.

A small brown dog walked over and licked the dead man's face.

Sunkist scratched the dog's ears and ruffled his back. "Was this your man?" he said to the dog.

The dog looked up at him with sorrowful eyes.

Sunkist took the dog's face in his hands and said, "One day he was some momma's little boy." He glanced at the body. "But today he had to die."

The woman came close. "Who are you?" she asked.

"James Whistler, United States Marshal."

He looked at Posey. "Yeah, I kinda like the sound of that. James V. Whistler, United States Marshal."

Posey looked curiously at him. "What is 'nited state . . . ?"

"It means I'm a lawman, jiss like Smoky said. And yer Posey, um, Flower in the Rocks, Whistler—United States Marshal."

"Can we get rid of this body?" the woman asked.

"Oh yeah. We'll bury 'im back in the woods. Coyotes need tuh eat, too, ye know."

"Take him far away and bury him. I don't want to know where."

"Do you know this gurl?"

"Yes, her name is Jessica. Her parents live in Oneota."

"I'll bury this scum and we can take Jessica home."

Sunkist threw a rope around the dead man, tied the other end to the pommel of his saddle, and dragged the body far back into the woods to the bank of a fast-flowing stream. He went through the man's pockets and pulled out a wallet full of money. "I'll jiss hang onto this fer safe keepin'," he said to himself. He slipped the wallet into his bag then rolled the body into the stream and watched it move slowly with the current. When it slipped around a bend, he went back to the cabin for Posey and the girl. He took the stolen horse's reins and led him back to town with him. Tied to the saddle of the horse was a fresh coyote skin, which Sunkist decided was fair payment for rescuing the girl, so he tied it to his own saddle.

As they rode into Oneota a woman ran up to them. "Oh, thank God! You found my Jessica!" She reached up and pulled Jessica from Posey's arms. "Thank you, thank you, thank you!" she sobbed as she cradled her daughter.

"Where is the man who took her?" Someone asked.

"He went fer a swim."

"Excuse me?"

"He fell in the crick."

"He's dead?"

"Figger he had too many holes in 'im tuh float, so, yeah, he's dead. If ye wanna hang 'im, I could take ye there. Ye kin pull 'im out an' do whatever tickles yer fancy."

The woman holding Jessica said, "The man is dead, and Jessica is home. Let's leave it at that."

"Where's the doctor's house?" Sunkist asked.

A man pointed down the road. "Right down there. You can't miss it. He's got his shingle hanging over the front gate." He reached his hand up toward Sunkist and said, "We want to thank you for . . ."

Sunkist and Posey didn't stay for the thanks. They turned their horses around and headed toward the doctor's house.

As they walked their horses down the main street, a man walked up to them and pointed at the coyote skin hanging from Sunkist's saddle.

"You want that skin tanned?"

Sunkist looked at Posey. "Ye know someone who kin do 'er fer me?

"Sure do. Me."

"How much?"

"Five bucks. Have 'er done in three days."

"Good enough." He pulled the skin from his saddle and started to hand it to the man but pulled it back. "How do I know yer gonna bring me that skin when yer done with it?"

"I'm honest," he said. "Hell, I gotta be honest, I'm too easy to find."

"Where kin we find ye?"

"They call me Skinner. Got a place north of here back in the woods, not far from Fond du Lac. I ain't hard to find. Everybody in the county knows me, they all got dead animals they want stuffed."

Skinner had light blue eyes, his face was tanned, and he wore wire-rimmed spectacles and a white goatee on his chin. He was dressed in a buckskin vest with no shirt underneath, a bear claw necklace, and brown canvas trousers.

"Kin ye bring it to the doctor's house?" Sunkist asked.

"I don't think the doctor can do anything for this critter. Looks like he's about done in."

Sunkist put out his hand. "Sunkist Whistler."

"Skinner Parks, critter-stuffer. Glad to meet you."

"Ye know where the doc lives?"

"Yup."

"See y'in two days."

"I said three days."

"I know you said three days. I said two."

Skinner chuckled. "Alright, two days. It ain't gonna be dry, but if that's what you want . . ."

"See y'in two days."

They rode to the building with the sign over the gate and dismounted. Walking in, they found Hawk, Sophie, Jake, and Lorraine sitting on chairs in the front room.

"How's Abernathy doin'?"

Sophie stood and hugged Sunkist. "The doctor says he's in real bad shape." She looked up into his eyes. "I'm afraid there's not much hope."

"As long as he's suckin' wind there's still hope." Sunkist started for the door to the backroom.

"You probably shouldn't go in there, Sunkist. The doctor's working on him."

"I'll jiss step in an' see if there's enna thin' I kin do tuh hep."

Sophie shrugged one shoulder and shook her head. "Might as well try to stop a thunderstorm."

Sunkist stepped into the room. The doctor stood by the bed and a woman stood on the other side. Doc turned to him. "Sir, please step out of the . . . Oh, it's you. Hello, Sunkist."

"Hey, Bones. What the hell brings you up here?"

"Doctor Thompson hasn't had any experience with gunshot wounds and asked me to come and do what I can for your friend."

The doctor indicated the woman. "This is my nurse, Kathy. She was a nurse in the war with the South. She is very familiar with wounds of this sort."

"How's he doin'?"

The doctor took Sunkist's arm. "Let's step out for a moment." They moved into an adjacent room. "Mister Wayne is in serious trouble. It will take a lot of fortitude on his part to pull through this. Frankly, I don't see any hope for his survival. The bullet smashed a rib very close to his spine and tore up his right lung, and there may be damage that I can't find. He's bleeding into his lungs, and as I said, I'm afraid there is no hope."

They walked back into the room. Sunkist looked down at Abernathy's pale face. He turned to the doctor, slapped him on the shoulder and said, "Keep 'im goin', Doc. He's worth havin' around."

He walked out the door and stood before the rest and took a deep breath. "Don't look good. I seen guys shot up like that, and ain't none of 'em made it. But Abernathy, he's gonna make it. You watch. Rot quick he'll be aggervatin' me jiss like b'fore."

"We'll keep hoping and praying," Lorraine said, drying a tear from her cheek.

Sunkist sat on the edge of a chair and rested his elbows on his knees. He ran his hands up, over his face, and rubbed his eyes, "Ye know?" he said, "I didn't like the guy at first, but he kinda grows on ye, kinda like a wart. It grows on ye, and ye don't like it, but when it gets ripped off, it hurts like hell."

He got off his chair and hurried out the door. Hawk started to get up but Sophie put her hand on his arm and urged him to sit down. "Leave him. He's hurting like the rest of us but he can't let us see it."

Mayhew walked in the door. "I hate to break this up but Diggs is gaining on us with every minute we sit here."

"We can't just leave him here to . . ." Lorraine started, then stopped and glanced to the door leading to the room where Abernathy lay. "Well," she said, "we can't leave him alone in there."

Hawk stood and spoke. "Mayhew's right. Abernathy knew what he was getting into just like the rest of us did. We all knew that some of us might not be coming back, and having that reality staring at us from a doctor's bed can't change that. We have to finish this job or Abernathy's death will be for nothing."

"I know," Lorraine said softly. "It just seems so cold."

"He ain't dead, and he ain't gonna be," Sunkist said from the doorway. "Hawk's right. If it was any one of us in there we'd say 'leave me here and git the job done'. Let's git on the trail and take care of that snake afore he gits any further away."

"Did you find the man who did this?" Mayhew asked.

"We found 'im, and his shootin' days is over."

"Were you able to identify him?"

Sunkist reached into his shirt and pulled out the wallet. "Took this off'n 'im."

Mayhew took the wallet, pulled the money from it, and handed it to Sunkist, then shuffled threw the papers to find some identification.

"His name was Hogan Suggs."

"Does that name mean anything to you?" Lorraine asked.

"He was a Confederate soldier who surrendered and came north to join the Union Army. Most of these men deserted and came north just to get out of the war. Apparently he has now deserted the Union Army. But this is not the time to get into it. We have to get moving." He turned to Sunkist. "You didn't happen to pick up his rifle, did you?"

"Nope, never give it a thought."

"Doc," Hawk said. "If there's anything we can do, just say so. If not, we're leaving." He turned to Lorraine. "Are you staying with Abernathy?"

"Absolutely not! Abernathy is lying in that bed, probably dying. I want to get Diggs and hold him accountable for what has happened."

"Lorraine," Jake said. "You can't make this a personal revenge thing. When you do that, you make mistakes, and we can't afford mistakes."

The gang moved outside. "Whether this becomes personal or not is not a choice we can make for ourselves. A dear friend has been wounded, probably mortally, and our feelings for that man will make it personal. We have no control over that."

Jake stopped and looked into her eyes not knowing how to respond. He pulled himself into the saddle and said, "Getting yourself killed for revenge is not getting you revenge. It's getting yourself killed for nothing. You know, don't you, that you could end up like Abernathy if you come with us?"

"I am aware of it just as I was when we started."

She turned and took hold of Abernathy's rifle and handed it to Sunkist. "He told me if anything happens to him, he wants you to have his rifle."

Sunkist took the rifle, looked at it for a few seconds, then looked at Lorraine. "I . . . he . . ." His chin trembled and he grumbled, "Goddammit," then hurried out the door.

Outside they gathered on the street. A light drizzle had begun to fall and the roads were forming puddles.

"Which way, Haze?" Hawk asked.

"From here there aren't too many places he can go but back the way he came or north to Grand Marais or the Canadian border. If he's going to Grand Marais, as we know he is, he will go by water."

"By water?"

"Yes. He'll take a boat."

"If Diggs gets on a boat, where could he go besides Grand Marais?"

"He can go anywhere in the world from here," Lorraine said. "Some of the ships you see out in the lake came here from the Atlantic Ocean, through the Saint Laurence Seaway and the Sault Saint Marie canal."

"What's that?" Hawk asked.

"In eighteen fifty-six the State of Michigan completed a canal between Lake Superior and Lake Huron wide enough for ocean-going vessels to make the journey from the Atlantic Ocean to Duluth. Before that, goods had to be portaged around the rapids of the Saint Mary's River. Now ships from England and France and some from as far away as the Orient can come in to the center of the continent to trade."

"That doesn't mean much to me," Hawk said. "I got no idea where any of those places are."

"The Orient is halfway around the world."

"Is that a big town?"

"What?"

"Orient."

"It's a region of the world, Hawk," Lorraine said as she turned and started toward the main part of town. "We're wasting valuable time. Let's get going."

Sunkist turned to Posey who was looking out over the mouth of the Saint Louis River. "You coming?" he said.

She turned her head toward him and pointed out over the water. "Husband," she said. "Canoe big, like Beaulieu house."

Hawk turned and looked. "What did she say?"

"She's bamboozled by the big canoes," Sunkist said.

"No. Did you hear what she said?"

"Yeah, she said big canoe like . . ."

"Yeah, a big canoe like Beaulieu's house . . . and the sails . . . they fly on the wind, just like Dream Talker said."

"Why in hail din' we see that?"

"Because," Lorraine said, "we are not Indian. We saw sailing ships because we have seen them before in pictures or in real life. Indians have never seen such a sight, and they can only relate to them as things with which they are familiar—canoes and teepees."

"What else did Dream talker tell about?"

"Men who are not white and not Indian," Sophie said.

"Perhaps she is referring to people from other countries," Lorraine said. "Africa, for instance, or Asia."

"Where's Asia?" Hawk asked.

"That's what we've been calling the Orient."

"Why would you . . ."

Lorraine interrupted abruptly, "I think we should find someone who can tell us about foreign people in this town, people with whom Mister Diggs might be dealing. It is entirely possible that the people we are looking for are right in this town."

"There's gonna be comin' a feller in a couple of days who might know somethin'." Sunkist said. "He says he knows ever'one around here. Calls hisself Skinner Parks."

"We can't wait a couple of days," Mayhew said. "Where can we find this man?"

"Holt on a bit," Sunkist said as he reached out and grabbed a man buy his coat. "I think I know how we kin find out where Skinner lives." The man pulled back and turned toward Sunkist with a show of surprise mixed with fear.

"You know a guy calls hisseff Skinner?"

"No," the man said. "I don't know anyone by that name. You the law?"

"James Whistler, United States Marshal."

"He ain't in trouble is he?"

"No, he ain't in trouble. You ain't neither. Not yet, enna ways. You know him?"

"Yeah, I know him. He lives down close to Fond. Down some road called Yndestad.

"Called what?"

"In-di-stad, or something like that."

"What the hell kind'a name is that?"

"Hell, I don't know. I didn't name the goddamn road."

"Ye know how tuh git there?"

"Sure. Me an' him drink whiskey, sometimes."

"Well, if'n y'ain't got nothin' better tuh do, maybe you'd like to take us there."

"Well, I hadn't planned on going out there for a while, but what's it worth to you?"

"Tell ye what," Sunkist said as he took the man by the coat and urged him away from the group. He leaned close to the man and said, "Now here's the deal. I know yer broke. I seen ye panhandlin' yer way up this street."

"Okay, so I'm broke. There's no law against that."

"An' I seen ye take the money outta that man's coat pocket. I think there's a law ag'in that."

"I didn't take no . . ."

"Yeah, ye did—I seen ye. Now let's make a deal." He leaned close to the man. "Yer part of the deal is, you take us to see Skinner."

"Okay, and what's your part of the deal?"

"My part is, you take us to see him an' I won't kick your ass and throw you in jail."

The man stood silently contemplating the deal while staring into Sunkist's green eyes.

"Well?" Sunkist said with an overly friendly smile on his face. "Whad'ya say?"

"Kind of a hard deal to turn down."

"You'll take us then?"

"Sure. I'll take you to see Skinner."

"Good. Oh yeah, the other part of the deal is you take us to see 'im and I'll give ye a ten-dollar gold piece."

"Now *that's* what I call a deal."

"What's yer name? We'll try tuh giddit right on yer tombstone if this Skinner takes a shot at ye."

"Danger, Bob Danger. Why would skinner take a shot at me?"

"Hail, I don't know. People been shooting at us all damn summer."

Sunkist led Danger back to the group. "This here's Bob Danger. He's gonna take us to see Skinner."

"You got a mount, Danger?" Hawk asked.

"I guess you could call her a mount." He walked across the street and climbed aboard a broken down jenny mule.

They followed Danger up the road they came in on. After ten minutes, he stopped next to a saloon and stepped off his mule.

"We ain't got time fer no drinkin'," Sunkist scolded.

Danger turned to face Sunkist. "You wanted to see Skinner, didn't you? Well he's in there," he said pointing to the front door of the saloon.

"Why the hail din you tell me that in the first gaddamn place?"

"You didn't ask where he was. You told me to take you to him. He's in there." He held out his hand, palm up. Sunkist gazed at him with a look of defeat, reached into his bag, pulled out a ten-dollar gold piece, and put it in Danger's hand. Danger flipped the coin into the air and caught it, then turned to walk into the bar.

Sunkist yelled loud enough to be heard in the bar. "Skinner! You in there?"

"Yeah, I'm in here. Who's asking?"

"Sunkist Whistler! Gitcher ass out here!"

The door came open slowly and Skinner appeared with a mug of beer in his hand. He saluted with his glass and nodded at Sophie.

"That's all the invite I need," Sophie said. "Let's go in and have a beer."

The words no sooner left her mouth when they all dropped to the ground and headed into the saloon. They sat at the table with Skinner and Danger.

"What's on your mind?" Skinner asked.

"I hear you know everybody in this country," Hawk said.

"More like they all know me."

"Who would we ask to find out about people from other countries?"

"Your best bet would be the lady who lives on the side of the hill north of here. Lady named Neena Lassard."

"Why would she know about foreigners?"

"Her father was the town surgeon for a while but now he travels around the world being a doctor."

"Kin ye take us up to see her?" Sunkist asked.

"I can show you where she lives, but I ain't taking you up there—too steep."

Hawk looked around the group then back to Skinner. "What else can you tell us about her father?"

"Nothing. I know he spends most of his time in the Orient practicing medicine."

"Where is he now?"

"I don't know. He could be next door or on the other side of the world. He don't tell me where he goes."

"Did he leave recently?"

"Don't know." Skinner drank down his beer. "Look, I don't know anything about the doctor. I stuff animals and that's it. All I know about her is where she lives, and most anyone in this town could tell you that."

"Can you take us up there and introduce us?"

"I know her and talk with her once in a while, but she's not going to just open her door and invite you in. I wouldn't either, and I doubt if you would."

"How about just one person?" Sophie asked. "Me, for instance."

"I'm not saying she won't let you all in, but it would be easier for just one person, especially a woman. I can take you up there and introduce you, but from there you're on your own."

"I'll go in with you," Lorraine said.

"Something we should consider before we all go lining up at her door," Hawk said. "Diggs is on his way north and we're spending time on something we're not sure is going to get us anywhere."

"Are you saying we should let this go and head out?" Jake asked.

"No. I'm suggesting that some of us take off up the shore and see if we can get a look at Diggs."

"You can't get to Grand Marais or anywhere else up the shore from here unless you take a boat," Mayhew said.

"Why not?" Hawk asked.

"Because there's no road that goes up there. The only thing that resembles a road is an Ojibwa footpath trappers and mail carriers use in the wintertime. It's called the Lake Shore Trail. It follows the shore all the way from Oneota to Fort William."

"So why can't we take that trail?" Hawk asked.

"It would take you two weeks longer to get to Grand Marais on foot than it would take Diggs to get there on a boat. Horses can't handle that trail. It's filled with deep, forested ravines, and hundreds of small streams and gorges cut by rivers that come down out of the hills like a bat outta hell. You slip into one of those and yer dead . . . no two ways about it. When it rains, you got slippery mud, windfalls, and thick underbrush blocking the trail. Winter blizzards build drifts you could disappear in, and they wouldn't find yer carcass till spring—if the wolves and bear don't find you first. Summertime, you got mosquitoes, flies, ticks, bears, moose, and wolves all around you. I'm telling you,

Diggs will be taking a boat."

"Where do we get a boat?" Hawk asked.

"The commercial boats you want don't come in that often, but there's always fishing boats here. You might hitch a ride on one of them."

"Diggs will likely take one," Sophie suggested.

"That would make sense to me," Jake said. "But which one?"

"One with sails," she answered.

"Why do you say that?"

"Dream Talker said so."

"You take what she says pretty seriously, don't you?"

"Yes, I do."

"If we're on a boat and Diggs is still here on dry ground we're going to lose him," Lorraine said. "We will have to know without a doubt that he's on a boat before *we* get on one."

"So how do we find that out?"

"We'll scout around the area while Sophie's up the hill with the lady," Jake said, "and see if we can get any information about him. Mayhew knows the area . . . Lorraine, I think you should stay with us."

"And why do you think I should stay with you?"

"Because you're such a sweetheart, and because you know Diggs better than the rest of us."

"Well spoken, Jacob. I will go with you."

"Let's get on the road," Jake said and headed for the door.

"Well," Hawk said to Skinner. "Take us to see the lady on the hill."

Once outside the saloon, they climbed onto their horses and headed north out of Oneota. The road took them up to the top of a high cliff over looking Lake Superior. Sophie stopped, got down from her horse, and walked to the edge.

About three miles out of Oneota, they looked down the hill to their right at Minnesota Point—a seven-mile long sandbar, five hundred feet wide, that stretched out in a slow, crescent shape ending in a shroud of fog. On the bar of sand lay a gathering of a dozen buildings, a sawmill, a trading post, and Indian tepees.

"What's that town down there?" Jake asked.

"They call it Duluth. That town ain't never gonna amount to nothing. I know the guy who owns the store and sawmill down there," Mayhew said. "George Nettleton. He'll have a place we can stay for the night if we need to."

Skinner stood with Sophie looking up at the rocky slope.

"What chuh seein' up there?" Sunkist asked.

Skinner pointed up the cliff. "See about halfway up there? There's a small house. You can barely see it through the brush."

"Yeah," Hawk said. "I see it. What is it?"

"That's where Neena lives."

Hawk squinted his eyes up the hill. "How do we get up there?"

Skinner pointed to a narrow trail that wound through the brush. "Follow that trail."

"Cain't take no horses up *there*," Sunkist said.

"Guess we climb."

"I thought I was going alone," Sophie said.

"You are, but we'll be close, waiting till you come out."

"We'll go find someplace to spend the night," Jake said. "By the time you get back, it's gonna be too late to travel."

They climbed until they were a hundred feet from the house. Hawk stopped and kissed Sophie lightly on the lips. "There ye go," he said. "Good luck."

Jake, Mayhew, and Lorraine took the trail along the shore toward Duluth. They rode over ancient lava flows that sloped downward toward the lake and disappeared beneath the waves. Lake Superior stretched to the horizon and mingled with the sky so that the water and the sky appeared as one. Behind them the black rocks rose nearly vertically to incredible heights. Jake turned his head this way and that, trying to take in all of the fascinating geology surrounding him. They went down close to the lake and over the smooth lava flows.

Lorraine jumped from her horse and knelt down on the rocks. "Abernathy!" she hollered, "come . . ." She stopped and looked up at Jake and Mayhew. "I'm sorry," she said. "I meant to say, Jake, come here."

Jake got down and walked over to her. "What'd you find?"

She ran her index finger over a groove cut into the rock. "These are the actual scratches left by rocks embedded in the base of the glacier that went through here thousands of years ago. Who knows how long ago these lava flows were laid down." She stopped and stared silently across the lake. "These rocks we're crossing were laid down by volcanic activity probably millions of years ago." She said it so softly that Jake and Mayhew didn't hear it. She turned to them and pointed to the edge of the water. "Look down there. You can actually see how the lava flowed . . ." her voice trailed off as she spoke, "into the water. Oh, how I wish Abernathy could . . ." She stopped talking abruptly and went back to her horse and started down the trail without finishing the sentence.

Jake looked at Mayhew. "I was afraid of this."

"What's that?"

"I think she's hurting for Abernathy a little too much. We're gonna have to keep an eye on her."

"Is that why you suggested she come with us rather than going with Sophie to see Neena?"

"No. That's because she's not smooth like Sophie is. She'd say something to aggravate the lady and mess it up."

"You kinda sweet on her, Jake?" Mayhew asked and touched his horse.

"She's nice to look at, but I'd get damn tired of being told I'm wrong all the time."

"Let's go find Nettleton."

George Nettleton sat behind the counter working on his papers when they walked in. He looked up and said, "Well, Henry, I didn't expect to see you till fall." He stood and walked around the counter and took Mayhew's hand. "Welcome," he said. "Introduce me to your friends."

After introductions, and a short lie about what brought him to Duluth too early in the year for trapping, Mayhew asked if Nettleton could put them up for the night.

"Of course, Henry. Your friends are always welcome here, you know that. I have four empty rooms and a parlor where you can entertain yourselves as you wish."

"We won't be doin' no innertainin', Mister Middleton." Sunkist said. "We jiss need a place to lay our heads fer the night."

"You have come to the right place, Mister Wrestler. You can take any room you like."

"Muh name ain't Wrestler, it's Whistler."

"And my name is not Middleton, it's Nettleton."

"I'll try tuh remember that if I ever decide tuh call you ag'in."

Their lodging for the night was in the back of George Nettleton's store at the land end of Minnesota Point. In the back of the store was a small parlor with a stove and four chairs surrounding a table covered with a white cloth. There were four very small bedrooms that had been added after the main building had been erected. The parlor had a door that led to the lake and another door led out the back of the building through a narrow hallway. The doors to rooms were situated along the hallway. A third door, which led into the store, was kept closed and locked.

37

CHAPTER

THIRTY-SEVEN

SOPHIE WALKED TOWARD THE SMALL SHACK on the top of the hill. It stood out against the fading light of the evening sky. She could see the silhouettes of the tall, statuesque pines surrounding the house and smell the smoke rising from the chimney.

The same breeze that touched her face made the needles on the trees sing their hollow, whispering notes. What stood out most was the sound of waves endlessly crashing against ancient rocks of Lake Superior. As she climbed the steps, she could hear a woman softly humming. The whole effect was very inviting and somehow Sophie already knew she would like the woman inside. When she reached the door she paused, listening to the song, and it made her think of faraway places she had not yet traveled. Before she could knock on the door, Sophie heard a voice from within.

"*Swaagat*. My door is always open to friends." Sophie entered and saw a tall, dark-haired woman in the kitchen. Without turning around she said, "Please sit. There are pillows on the floor. Make yourself comfortable. Would you like some tea?"

"Yes, thank you." Sophie walked over to a large, silk, midnight-blue pillow patterned with whimsical stars and moons, and sat down.

"How did you know I was at your door before I knocked?"

"Some things one must not question, they are not meant for us to understand . . . they are given as gifts, and we must accept them graciously. One must be open, both in heart and in mind. You will be amazed at what starts happening in your life. It is like a beautiful flower unfolding."

Neena handed Sophie a cup and joined her on the floor.

"I agree," Sophie said while watching her image dance inside the teacup. They sat quietly, sharing without speaking. Sophie studied her surroundings. "You have a very interesting home." There were various types of candles burning and an intoxicating fragrance filled the room. "What *is* that scent?"

"It is jasmine oil. It is exquisite, is it not? It is one of my favorite fragrances." She looked up from her tea at Sophie and added, "It is the oil of romance."

"Is that a guarantee?"

Neena laughed. "You will need no guarantee, and *that's* a guarantee." She rose easily from the pillow and walked to the corner of the room. She picked something up then turned around and walked back, placing the strange object in Sophie's hand. "I brought it back from Egypt, where it was made. It is blown glass and is quite unique. I have never seen another like it in all my travels. It's an Egyptian oil burner. The heat from the candle below releases the vapors from the oil above." Sophie studied the small treasure. It was slightly smaller than her hand from fingertips to the base of her palm and was shaped like a backwards C. The base rose to meet the area in which the candle rested. Above that, and resembling a round head wearing a top hat, was where the oil was placed. A clear glass handle with gold rings connected the base and the top. "The dragonflies painted around the base are made of pure gold. My father bought it for me as a gift. It is one of my most treasured possessions."

Sophie gently put the gift down, "It's like nothing I've seen before . . . it's beautiful. The only thing I have that has anything to do with my father is a set of pewter dishes he left behind. I'm an orphan and never knew my father, and I've held on to them purely for sentimental reasons."

"I would love to hear about your childhood. It seems as though we have much in common."

"I'll tell you whatever you want to hear, but I would love to hear all about you, first. Obviously you have traveled a great deal. What language did you use when you asked me in?"

"The word I used is East Indian in origin. It means 'welcome'."

"It sounds so far away, like from another world. Is it somewhere you travel to often?"

"It *is* another world. I go there whenever I can. If I am away too long, I miss the smells, the land, and the people. I don't even mind the voyage; it's all part of the adventure."

"How long is the voyage?"

"It usually takes around eight weeks or more, depending upon Mother Nature—she can be very unpredictable. But I put much faith in our dear friend, Anatole. He is the captain and a very competent sailor. The ocean has become part of my life. It has a way of capturing your soul. In many ways, Lake Superior shares the same qualities. One thing that is noticeably different, however, is that it lacks that warm, salty, organic smell." She closed her eyes, lost in the moment, and took in a long, slow breath. "But, as you know, the lake has its own unique beauty that is never the same from day to day, like that of the ocean. Have you ever seen the ocean?"

"No, I haven't. I know I would love it, though, because I'm totally enraptured by Lake Superior."

Sophie was already feeling a deep kinship with the intriguing woman. She was different from anyone she knew and had a quiet wisdom about her. Her eyes were the most commanding of all her features. They were the lightest of blue and exceptionally clear. Her raven hair was thick and wavy and hung down to the middle of her back. It shone like smooth, dark obsidian and contrasted with the paleness of her skin. She was slender, with graceful arms and hands, and was perhaps five inches taller than Sophie. There was a determined strength about her. Sophie sensed she was no stranger to work, and she possessed a distinct self-assurance, the kind that comes from having had an abundance of life experiences.

"Would you like more tea?"

"Yes, it's delicious. What is it?"

"It is masala tea. It pleases me that you like it. This particular mixture is black tea with ginger, cardamom, and cinnamon." She got up to get more tea.

"May I ask your last name?"

Neena stopped and turned around, and as she did, the bottom of her red, silk dress twisted slightly from the movement. "It's Lessard—Neena Lessard." She disappeared into the kitchen through a curtain of long, blue, glass beads that hung from the doorframe. They made a soft clicking sound as they gently swayed. Neena returned with a pot of fresh tea and sat down. "And you are Sophie, the woman of Hawk Owen, of the respected Pa Hin Sa . . . notorious to others."

"How did you . . . ?" Sophie stopped, remembering what Neena had said earlier. "Neena . . . what a pretty name, I've never known anyone by that name."

Neena laughed, "That is not surprising. My father named me. He heard the name somewhere in his travels and liked it. I have the feeling you would like traveling. Perhaps we will travel together sometime."

Sophie laughed, "Believe me, I would need no convincing. But . . . I know someone who *would*. He's rather attached to Minnesota, especially his beloved Minnesota Valley. I love it, too, but I am always ready for new adventures. Tell me, do you ever travel alone?"

"I often travel alone. However, I am never truly alone because the ship I travel on belongs to my father's dearest friend, Anatole. In return for passage, I offer to cook for the crew and any travelers aboard. It is a nice arrangement for everyone."

"Is someone there to meet you when you land?"

"My father or one of his friends is there to greet me at the port. My father spends most of his time traveling and healing the sick in the Orient. There are so many people who need his help and seek him out for his expertise. I have been helping him since I was about seven years of age. My mother died while giving me birth at home in England. I was an early baby. My father was not expecting that and was away in Persia. He has never forgiven himself for being gone. He took on the sole responsibility of caring for me. Over time he realized I needed more care and schooling than he could provide. He also realized my need for female companionship, so on one of his return trips he brought back Alisha, my nanny. She was also my father's mistress. She is from East India and strikingly beautiful, as so many of the Indian women are. For years we traveled together caring for the sick. Alisha and I became fast friends. She became the mother I never knew. We admired each other and I learned much from her. I have adopted much of her culture into my life, including Eastern medicine."

"Did Alisha come here with you?"

"No, she went home to be with her parents. When I travel to the East, I visit them whenever I can. She was married for only a short while and did not have children. Her husband died after an extended illness. I think that was a powerful factor for wanting to work alongside my father, healing others."

"You must miss her very much."

"I do. Even though she loved us, I know she missed her parents and friends, but she never complained. Eventually, as I grew and matured and became more worldly, she could see that I had developed my own self-confidence. One day she announced that she would be leaving and going home. I know that took great courage."

"You mentioned you're from England."

"Yes, I was born in Laxfield, just north and east of London. My mother's family came from that area."

Sophie laughed, "How did you end up in Duluth?"

"My father had heard from Anatole that this area would soon become a developed port and would be in need of a town surgeon. So we settled in Oneota where he opened a modest medical practice. However, he was not accustomed to being in one place and soon grew restless and tired of treating the same illnesses. He wanted to make a real difference and felt that his skills were not being used to their full capacity."

"It sounds like he has tremendous drive. I wonder what compels a man like that?"

"I know exactly what compels him . . . my mother."

"Your mother?"

"Yes, he feels he could have saved her life if he had been with her. It haunts him to this day, but because of this, I feel we have an exceptional bond."

"You live a fascinating life."

"I am only living the life I know, doing and being the best I can . . . and having fun in the meantime.

"Speaking of fun, I have some food to share. Care to sample some Eastern fare?" She gave Sophie a quick embrace. "Come! You can help me, and you are in luck. Paul, who works as a dockhand in Oneota, just delivered some fresh whitefish today. I hope you like fish."

Sophie laughed, "As a true Minnesotan, I think it's a requirement."

"Do true Minnesotans also like potatoes?"

"I believe that is the second requirement."

"Good, then you will like the batata vada we are about to prepare."

"The batata vada?" Sophie asked, "Sounds more like a dance step."

Neena laughed, "I do have *something* that I am sure you have never had that might make you want to dance." She took out two small, porcelain liqueur glasses and a matching decanter and poured them each a glass. She handed one to Sophie and took one for herself, then raised it and said, "To my new friend, Sophie. *Swaggat.*"

"Thank you, Neena, for welcoming me into your home." They clinked their glasses together and drank.

"Mmm, what is it? You're right, I've not had the pleasure . . . beer's always had that honor."

"I thought you might like it. It is toddy. It comes from the tadh tree—a palm tree. It was traditionally drunk at midmornings to increase the strength of farm workers and keep them from getting tired. Anatole brings it from India

374   HAWK'S QUEST

from time to time. He must be concerned about my energy level!"

"Well," Sophie said, "here's to Anatole. I'd say he has some doctor qualities himself."

"Yes, to Anatole!" They laughed and touched glasses once more.

"I will get the food prepared then join you by the fire."

"Looks like the fire needs more wood. Do you have an ax?" Sophie asked.

"There is one outside by the outhouse."

From a distance Hawk watched as Sophie walked out of the house toward
the outhouse. She leaned over and picked up an ax and scanned the area for
wood. Sunkist and Posey stretched their necks up over the brush to watch.
They continued watching Sophie from the brush until she had chopped
enough wood and headed back to the house. Hawk signaled to Sunkist and
Posey that things were fine, then sat down as the day turned to evening.

Sophie walked in, laid the bundle near the fireplace, and fed the fire one
piece at a time. She sat down, reached over, and finished what was left of the
sweet, soothing liquid in her glass. She savored the smoothness as it slid down
her throat, warming her from inside, and she felt her body relax.

Neena returned with a tray full of various food items. There were two
whitefish, some potatoes, a small bowl of spice, as well as flour and oil. "I
thought we would start by peeling the potatoes." She glanced down at her new
friend's empty glass. "That glass looks pretty empty without anything in it, do
you not agree?" Neena's eyes sparkled with mischief. "Here, let's remedy that.
After all, I *am* a doctor." They both laughed,

"Well," Sophie added, "I can't let the doctor drink alone . . . cheers."

"Cheers."

"I'm good at peeling potatoes. I did a lot of that in the orphanage."
Sophie said.

"And I will prepare the besan batter to dip the potatoes in."

"Besan?"

"Yes, it is the Indian word for gram flour. The batter is made of flour,
water, red chili powder, salt, and just a touch of bicarbonate."

"I'm learning all kinds of things."

Neena laughed, "I think traveling is the best kind of education one can
receive. Books are wonderful, but there is nothing like experiencing the world
with all of one's senses, drinking in the very essence of life—it seems I am never
full. It has become a way of life, and I thank both my mother and father for
that."

"Did your mother like traveling, too?"

"Yes, very much. She loved the arts and they would travel far just to see a play or hear a performance. Sometimes they would be gone for weeks."

"That reminds me . . . we're on our way to Grand Marais now, but it's *not* a pleasure trip."

Sophie realized this would be a good time to share what she knew about the events leading them to Grand Marais. She knew Neena could be trusted, and any kind of information she could get would be helpful. She took another sip of toddy. Her cheeks started to flush. Neena poured the water into the pot hanging over the fire and Sophie added the potatoes. She smiled at Neena. "Team work."

Neena reached over and lightly touched Sophie's hand. "I'm a good listener." So while the potatoes boiled, Sophie told Neena about the missing children, Diggs, Abernathy being shot, and about her being kidnapped. Neena continued to listen while she mashed the potatoes and added the turmeric and coriander leaves.

Sophie stopped her story, "I'm doing all the talking. What can I do to help you?"

"The paste I prepared needs to be added to hot oil."

"Paste?"

"Yes, it is a combination of ginger, garlic, and green chilies."

"That should heat things up."

"Sophie, if your party is in need of a boat to get to Grand Marais, I can talk to Anatole."

"That would be greatly appreciated."

"How many people will be making the trip?"

"Let's see . . ." Sophie held up her fingers and began counting.

"There's Jake, Mayhew, Sunkist, Posey, Hawk, and me. That's six of us."

"I will talk to Anatole about using his boat, the Athens Queen. You will find it more than adequate."

"Do you know how long it will take to reach Grand Marais?"

"It is just a day's journey. We can work out the details after I talk with Anatole at first light tomorrow."

"Thank you, Neena."

"I am only happy to help out."

"I added the potatoes to the paste and mixed it together, and set aside to cool slightly. Now the fun part. We roll the potatoes into balls, and dip them into the batter, then fry them with the fish. Would you like to try some currant wine?"

"I assume that's a rhetorical question. I couldn't say no to my hostess."

"No, that would not make for good relations! I also have some fruit chutney with mangoes, figs, and dates to accompany the dinner."

"We're having company for dinner? Whew, is it hot in here?"

Neena smiled, "I think we should have some food. I do hope you find it satisfying."

They sat down with full plates. Sophie made a quick pass with her nose over the food. "Should I be feeling guilty when I have no idea what Hawk is having to eat?" They looked at each other for a brief moment and together said just one word. "Nah!" They clinked glasses and laughed.

Outside, Hawk rose to his knees to peer over the brush that concealed him from the house. *What the hell are they doing in there?* he thought. *What could be that funny? Sounds like they're drinkin'. Sure hope she ain't plannin' on keepin' me up all night. Well, that might not be a bad thing . . .* His thoughts raced as he envisioned the possibilities. He ripped off a chunk of jerky with his teeth with more effort than was needed.

"Neena, that meal was hea-ven-ly." This was followed by a hiccup. "Oh, was that me? Sorry." Sophie put her hand over her mouth. Neena burst out laughing.

Something caught Sophie's eye, and she got up and walked over to a small table in the corner of the room. She spun around, "What *is* this!?" She held out a triangular piece of lavender-colored silk decorated around the edges with small gold coins. They sparkled and danced and made lots of noise as she held the fabric with both hands above her head and twirled around in circles. "I've never seen anything so beautiful." She stopped suddenly. "Where'd'ya get it?"

"I bought it in Turkey, at a bazaar. It was a huge tent filled with costumes of every color and all kinds of accessories. I knew I wouldn't leave there empty-handed. It was a hard decision, but I finally decided on the lavender scarf . . . with the matching skirt and the gold belt and the gold wrist and ankle bracelets and, of course, a matching headpiece for my forehead. Traditional dancers wear these."

"These are great!" Sophie started to slip the bracelets on. "May I?"

"Please."

Sophie raised an eyebrow. "Were you expecting company or somethin'?"

"No, I practice on my own. It is quite good exercise, you know. Somehow, it helps me feel connected to the East. I leave it on the table for when the mood strikes."

"What are the chances of it striking right now? I'd love to see this on you, and I bet you know exactly how to use it," she said, winking at Neena, ". . . if you know what I mean."

Once again, the sounds of laughter floated in the air surrounding Hawk's green fortress. "Oh, fer da cripe sake," he said. He found himself laughing at the mutual exuberance.

"I would feel honored, and it would be most appropriate. The dance that I am about to show you was historically performed *for* women *by* women and dates back to the Middle Ages. It was considered a sacred dance. It was never intended for men to see. It actually began as a ritual to prepare for childbirth."

"Well, I can assure you, that isn't the case now . . . you can just leave that part out, or just change a few of the steps." She stifled a hiccup. "Please, put these on and show me how it's done." Sophie turned around and yelled into the air. "All you men get out of here!"

Outside, two bodies popped up simultaneously. Hawk could barely make out Sunkist in the dim moonlight. They both shrugged their shoulders and sat down again.

Sophie walked over and put a few more pieces of wood into the fireplace, then sat down on her pillow. She was instantly captured by the fire's allure and watched its shifting shapes, fascinated. This gave Neena a moment to sneak from her room to the kitchen, where she could make a more dramatic entrance. The next thing Sophie heard was the sound of finger cymbals keeping rhythm as Neena moved through the doorframe, parting the glass beads hanging from above. She slowly walked forward while moving her hips from side to side. The motion was accentuated as she extended each leg, pushing out with her hip and quickly touching the floor with her toes. The movement made the coins dance and jingle. Her hips moved in a figure eight pattern and she alternated between a fast and slow cadence. Her arms went gracefully over her head, the backs of her hands lightly touching while keeping tempo with the finger cymbals. Then her arms came down to her sides, and she pulled in her stomach, rolling it in and out like it was divided in half. It reminded Sophie of a snake. She then raised one shoulder and arm up in one fluid motion, while her other shoulder and arm made a downward motion. Each shoulder and arm took turns moving upward and downward. This, too, resembled a snake. Sophie sat totally mesmerized and caught herself with her mouth open. Neena saw this, and laughed. "Here, take the zills, you can keep time for me."

"The what?"

"The finger cymbals."

Sophie put the straps over her thumbs and middle fingers. She tapped them together. Neena smiled, "Yes, yes, that is good!" Sophie's grin grew wider.

Neena grabbed the veil and began twirling around and around while holding it over her head. Sophie responded accordingly and increased the tempo. The spinning motion sent the long, gold fringe attached to her top whirling outward, and allowed a glimpse of her leg now and then through the slit in her skirt. Neena continued playing with the veil, twisting it in front of her as she bent forward, then bringing it behind her, doing a slight backward bend and making large circles around her body. She slowed the tempo while moving her hips side to side, raised the veil behind her head with both hands extended, then folded it in half, meeting the other hand. It made a tunnel that hid her entire face. She continued moving her hips, then slowly lowered the fabric to reveal her eyes and then her face. She then opened the veil and made a large figure eight motion.

"Oh, that's beautiful . . . it looks like a butterfly's wing." Sophie said reverently while taking another sip of wine.

Neena circled a few more times with the veil over her head, then dropped to her knees and did a back bend while shimmying her shoulders. She finished in this position looking up with one hand touching the floor behind her and the other arm extended above her.

The next thing Neena heard was the sound of Sophie clapping, making the cymbals resound in exuberant celebration.

"Bravo! Bravo! Where did you ever learn that?"

Neena glistened with perspiration and was slightly out of breath. "Oh, I had many opportunities to watch other dancers when I was in Turkey."

"Do you think you could teach me some of that?"

"It would be my pleasure."

They spent the rest of the evening dancing, laughing, and drinking together.

Outside the house, Sunkist stood up and shouted, "What in tarnation are they doin' in there?"

Hawk motioned Sunkist down, "Wanna wake up the whole damn shore?"

A moment later Hawk felt a hand on his shoulder and jumped, "How the hell do you do that?"

"Do whut?"

"Move like that."

"Move like whut?"

"Like you did."

"Did whut?"

"Oh, for . . . never mind. I'm glad you're on *our* side. They have to be coming out sometime soon."

They sat staring at the house. "Don't count on it."

Then they heard the sound of a door opening. Hawk knew that if anything were going to happen, it would be now. He was ready, but he thought to himself, *no amount of preparation can ever prepare a man for the affairs of a woman—no matter how well he thinks he knows her.* This became obvious as he scanned the scene in front of them. Sophie was walking down the steps a few feet in front of Neena, talking all the way. Once in a while Sophie would stop and turn around and say something to Neena and they would both laugh. Sometimes, Sophie would mumble something that Neena obviously could not hear and laugh even louder.

"Wimmin," Sunkist grumbled into the night.

The women were invisibly escorted down the hill toward Nettleton's store. Once there, Neena touched Sophie on the shoulder, "Are you going to be alright, my friend?"

"Me? Oh, never felt bedder in all my life."

"Good." This was followed by a hug. Neena pointed at the bag Sophie was carrying that contained the dancing costume. "Enjoy yourself. He will love you all the more."

"He bedder."

Neena closed her hands, palms together, gave a slight bow, then turned back into the night. She could not see Sunkist keeping some distance from her as he followed her back to her house.

Hawk ran ahead of Sophie, which was not too difficult to do, given her condition. He went inside their room, took off his clothing, and jumped into bed. He had been thinking about her all night. He could almost taste and feel her soft, warm lips when the door slammed open.

"Oh! You're here . . ." She hiccupped into her hand and laughed. "Sorry, been doing that the whole damn night. Mus' be this mountain air." She teetered and waved her hand around the room.

"Come here. I'll make them go away for you." He pulled her to him and kissed her. Feelings swelled inside him as he undressed her while they continued to kiss. She stood in front of him, naked. His eyes closed, he started to kiss her neck, and he felt himself sinking into another world.

"Be right back!" Her abrupt statement made his eyes fly open. She grabbed her bag, disappeared into the hallway, then came back and leaned into the room, holding the doorframe. "Juss wanna let you know . . . you are *really* gonna like this. "Don't go away. You juss wait over there." He sat there, unsure of what had just happened. Time passed and he nearly fell asleep when he was aroused in a most unexpected manner. When he opened his eyes, she was standing over him on the bed, swaying back and forth wearing the most revealing outfit he had ever seen. She was keeping rhythm with small cymbals between her fingers. Words escaped him and his hands instinctively reached for her legs. The only feature of her face that was showing was her eyes. She was holding a veil over the rest as she moved, undulating her hips, making the coins jingle and shake.

"Oh, my Gawd, Sophie . . ."

"Shhh." She bent down, minimizing Hawk's view and maximizing that of two lovely breasts stuffed neatly into a lavender top.

She was humming a melody that was slightly off key. Hawk didn't know if it was her unique situation, or if the song was suppose to sound that way. It made no difference; he was a slave to her womanhood. His hands were enjoying her backside as his breathing became deeper. She leaned over him shaking the assets nature gave her. He could feel and taste the fringes that hung from her top as they brushed vigorously over his lips. The next thing he felt was her entire weight on his chest. He shook her gently. "Soph? Soph?" *Is she snoring? So much for taking hiccups away.* Hawk gently covered her then went out and jumped into the icy waters of Lake Superior.

38

C H A P T E R

T H I R T Y - E I G H T

IN THE MORNING, HAWK PULLED THE BLANKETS ASIDE and slipped out of bed quietly so he wouldn't wake Sophie. His wool trousers felt cold, damp, and sticky as he pulled them up his legs. He put on a coat, walked through the parlor, and went out the door into the cold, damp air. Pebbles clattered and crunched under his feet as he walked slowly down to the beach. The air was still and a heavy blanket of fog lay on the water of Lake Superior. The waves made no noise as they lapped ever so lightly at the shore. He bent down and picked up a flat stone and studied it, wondering why all of the stones on this beach were flat and so very smooth. He was tempted to throw it and make it skip over the water but was reluctant to disturb the silence. He held the stone in his hand and unconsciously rubbed his thumb on its satin finish. The silence was stressed by the shrill cry of a gull overhead and the soft clang of a ship's bell hidden somewhere in the dense fog. He squinted into the cloud to find the source of the sounds and saw nothing but rippling water and slowly swirling fog.

The cold air and dampness were slowly creeping through his coat, and he felt himself shiver slightly.

"Cold ott cheer, ain't it?"

The voice came like a cannon shot in the cold air. Hawk jumped and nearly cried out. He wheeled around quickly, ready to defend himself. With his heart just below his tonsils he said, "Goddammit, Sunkist; one of these times you're gonna get your face busted sneaking up on me like that!"

"I didn't sneak up on ye. Ye jiss wasn't payin' no attention on account you bein' all b'fuddled by thet ocean ott thar."

"Is this going to be a regular thing?"

"Whut?"

"You sneakin' up on me like that."

Sunkist nodded toward the lake. "She is a sight tuh put a kink in yer thinker, ain't she."

Hawk turned again toward the lake. "I'm not sure what you mean by that, but it is hard to not just stare out there and think about nothing . . . Oh, I get it."

He pointed out into the fog at the silhouette of a boat slipping silently around the far end of Minnesota Point and out of the harbor. "It's almost scary the way it moves with no noise at all."

"That'd be one of them there small steam ingines," Sunkist said. "They use 'em on the Missoura sometimes. They don't make hardly no noise, jiss a hiss when the steam comes out."

They heard bells as boats rocked lazily back and forth inside the harbor, and the sharp cry of seagulls overhead. Under their feet came the crunch of the flat stones as they moved back to the cabin.

Jake came out of the backroom looking for coffee. Sophie heard the activity and came from her room, bright-eyed and smiling. "Good morning, everyone. Just a bit chilly out there this morning."

"Just a bit chilly out there every morning up here," Mayhew said as he came in the side door.

Lorraine appeared from another room. Her eyes were bloodshot and her hair mussed and tangled.

"Are you alright?" Jake asked.

"Yes," she said. "It's just this humidity."

"Is it always so foggy out on the lake?" Jake asked.

"It is a lot, but not always. If you hear the bells on the lake before you get up in the morning, you might as well stay in bed."

"Are those bells just used in the fog?"

"For the most part, yes. Sometimes they sound them if there's a lot of activity in the harbor. But if they're going to try sailing in the fog, they always have the bells going."

"Do you have a boat for us to take to Grand Marais?" Hawk asked.

"I do," Sophie said. "Neena is arranging one for us."

"We need it right now," Hawk said.

"What's the hurry?" Mayhew asked.

"You said the boats always sound their bells when they sail in the fog."

"Yeah?"

"And if they didn't?"

"They could run aground or into another ship. They always ring the bells in the fog."

"One went out of the harbor this morning without sounding a bell."

"How do you know that?"

"Me and Sunkist saw it not fifteen minutes ago."

"Sunkist and I," Lorraine mumbled softly into her coffee cup.

"You saw it, too, Lorraine?" Hawk asked.

"No, I was just . . ." She glanced up at him then returned to her coffee. "Never mind," she said with a slight shake of her head.

"No level-headed captain is going to sail in this fog without a bell or a horn," Mayhew said. "Unless you're in a big hurry or don't want to be seen . . . or both. I think Hawk is right. We should find a boat as soon as we can."

"Did Neena say when she could get us a boat?" Hawk asked.

"She's talking with a man named Anatole this morning," Sophie said. "He owns a ship called the Athens Queen."

"Any idea where we can find him?"

"Nope. She said he'll find us."

"He's probably going to wait till this fog burns off," Mayhew said.

"So do we sit here and wait?" Jake asked impatiently.

Someone knocked on the door that led to the shore. Hawk and Jake each went to different sides of the door. "Who's out there?" Hawk shouted.

"George Nettleton," came the response as the door opened and Nettleton walked in.

"Mister Nettleton." Hawk said. "Do you know of any boats going to Grand Marais that we might hitch a ride on?"

"What do you want in Grand Marais?"

"Vacation."

"None of my business, right? Well, a boat left this morning heading up the shore. I don't know . . ."

"Where was it going?"

"Up the shore, that's all I know. That's none of my business either, I guess."

"Well, that boat is gone. Any more going you know about?"

"I saw the Greek loading this morning. Ye might check with him."

"His name ain't Anatole, is it?"

"Yes, Anatole," Nettleton said. "He was a fisherman by trade, but now he makes his living carrying people and cargo up and down the shore and overseas. You might be able to ride with him."

Another heavy knock made Jake and Hawk move toward the door, but Nettleton stepped in front of them and opened it. He turned to Hawk, "You're a jumpy bunch. What are you worried about?" He opened the door and in walked a big man in a heavy coat and boots. His hat sat on his head like a small, gray flour sack, its bill decorated with braided cord. He had a beard that followed the line of his jaw and covered his chin. He wore no mustache. "You the folks wanting a ride up the shore?"

"Yes," Hawk said and stepped up to the man. "Are you Anatole?"

"Get your belongings together if you're coming with me. I don't have all day to wait."

"Can you sail in this fog?"

"The fog will be gone by the time we leave, and if it's not, we're leaving anyway. Be at the dock in fifteen minutes."

"What about our horses?"

"My boat is not equipped for horses and I'm loaded down with supplies bound for Port Arthur. You're going to have to leave them here. George can take care of them."

Hawk looked to George.

"You have no choice, Mister Owen. I'll take care of your animals."

"Well," Hawk said turning to the others, "Let's go."

"Last time I was on a boat was on the Missoura," Sunkist said. "Hey, Anatole! Y'ever bin on the . . ."

Anatole was walking quickly toward his boat and out of earshot. He stopped and turned around to check the progress of his passengers. He shook his head in disgust and turned to walk on.

When they arrived at the dock, they found Anatole and two men on the ship waiting for them. One man was skinny and exceedingly soiled. A big, floppy hat was pulled low on his head so the tips of his ears lay forward. He stared at the newcomers with wide, fear-filled eyes.

The other man was a tall black man who stood a head taller than both Anatole and the other man.

"Welcome aboard the Athens Queen," Anatole said loudly.

He put his hand out toward the tall black man. "Allow me to introduce Hector, my first mate. Hector is in charge of everything aboard this vessel except stoking the boiler." Then he pointed to the small man. "And this is Samuel, my boiler tender. *He* is in charge of stoking the boiler."

As they stepped aboard the boat, Anatole shook hands with each of the men and steadied the hand of the ladies.

"How long is this trip gonna take?" Hawk asked.

"You will be in Grand Marais by evening, weather permitting."

"A ship left here this morning with no bells sounding," Mayhew said. "Do you know who that might have been?"

"Any ship's captain who left port in this morning's fog without bells or a horn is a damn fool."

"Do you know who it was?"

"No. I assume it was that bucket that's been anchored in the harbor for the past few days. Considering the condition of her rigging, she's not very well cared for."

"Sailing ship or steamer?" Mayhew asked.

"She carried one mast, but even though I didn't see any of her crew on board, her boilers were kept hot and ready for departure." Anatole turned and searched the water. "Apparently, she's sailed. We'll probably be picking some of her crew from the water on our way."

"Did you notice a name?"

"I didn't pay that much attention."

Anatole's boat was ninety-five feet long and about twenty-five feet across her deck. Her hull was painted white with red trim. Large bundles of rope hung from her sides between the ship and the pier. A pilothouse with glass windows all around stood amidships, ten feet above the deck. It, too, was painted white, with red trim around the windows. Gray smoke rose straight up from the smokestack just behind the pilothouse and disappeared in the fog. She had three masts rigged with folded sails, and on the bow, a boom reached out over the water with ropes attached from it to the deck. Ropes and nets lay in neat piles around the deck and a winch sat directly in front of the pilot-house. Barrels, bundles, and boxes were stacked fore and aft, giving the appearance that there was no room to move about.

"Where do we ride?" Hawk asked.

"You will stay topside the entire trip. The only cabin we have besides the captain's quarters is occupied by a crew sent by the U.S. General Land Office to survey the northern coast of Lake Superior. They asked not to be disturbed. You will meet them when Hector serves lunch. Samuel has a full head of steam, and if you are ready, we will be underway as soon as the lines are cast."

Hector went to the bow, expertly walking the narrow space between the cargo and the toe-rail on the edge of the ship. He tossed the mooring ropes onto the pier then went to the stern and did the same. The ship started to drift slowly away from the dock. Anatole climbed the ladder to the pilothouse, and the engine started puffing gray smoke from the stack.

"You're gonna go out in that fog?" Hawk asked.

"You have just volunteered for official bell ringer duty," Anatole said. "The rope for the bell is hanging right in front of the pilothouse. Go start pulling on it."

Hawk went and grabbed the rope and began ringing the bell.

"Not so fast!" Anatole yelled. "You'll drive us all insane."

Hawk slowed the pace of the bell to match what he'd heard earlier. The chug of the steam engine became faster and the Athens Queen pushed a wake in front of her bow as she picked up speed. Sophie, Lorraine, and Posey stood on the deck, their hands gripping the railings that surrounded the ship. Posey's eyes were wide, and despite her seemingly emotionless expression, Sophie could see her great excitement. Hawk and Sunkist stood at the stern with Jake and Mayhew, watching the great blades of the propeller churn the water behind them. Suddenly, and without warning, the sound of the steam whistle atop the pilothouse shattered the silence. They all jumped and covered their ears. The shrill whistle echoed around the lake for ten seconds then sounded again. Posey was on her knees and elbows on the deck, her hands tight against her ears.

Sunkist took three steps up the ladder toward the pilothouse and yelled, "You blow that gaddamn whistle ag'in an' I'll come up there and shove it up yer ass!"

Anatole looked down at him with a surprised look on his face. "Sir, we have to blow the whistle in this fog or we could collide with another ship. You understand."

Sunkist took another step up the ladder. "Understand this, you gaddamn mop-jockey. You blow that whistle one more time and yer gonna be sittin' on it all the way to Grand Marais. You understand?"

The ship moved slowly forward then made a wide turn around Minnesota Point into open water. Hawk kept the bell ringing, and the whistle stayed silent. Sunkist sat next to Posey and Sophie. Posey was shaken by the experience and Sunkist tried his best to calm her.

"Mop-jockey?" Sophie said to Sunkist with a mischievous grin.

"Yeah, that's what they call them boys on the riverboats down on the Missoura. They keep 'em moppin' the decks tuh keep 'em outta trouble."

Gradually the fog lifted and they were able to see the shore. Hawk stopped ringing the bell and the engine settled into a monotonous *chunk-hiss, chunk-hiss, chunk-hiss.*

After a while, the hatch to the lower compartment opened and Hector came topside. He stood without looking at them and said in a voice that came from deep in his throat, "Lunch is ready."

"Thank you, Hector," Anatole said. "You may bring it up. And please have the rest of our guests come topside and have lunch with us."

Five men stepped onto the deck.

"I'm terribly sorry for the inconvenience," Anatole said, "but, as you can see, we don't have room on deck for tables and chairs. Please understand."

Hector brought kettles of food and placed them on the boxes and crates about the deck. Each person introduced himself as they came close to the food line. Lorraine brightened up when she heard that the group they had with them were surveyors and geologists. She sat next to a man and started a conversation. They talked through the meal while the rest sat quietly and enjoyed the feast of smoked salmon with lemon and boiled potatoes in butter sauce.

Late in the afternoon, Anatole yelled down from the pilothouse and pointed toward shore "See over there," he said. "That is Grand Marais Harbor."

"Well, why in hail ain't we goin' in there then?" Sunkist yelled back.

"We're taking the survey crew up a few miles, then we will come back and anchor in the harbor."

Hawk and Jake pulled the levers of their rifles down, checked to be sure there was a round in the chamber, then looked up toward Anatole.

Anatole climbed down the ladder. "I assure you, gentlemen," he said, "you will land safely in Grand Marais before nightfall. There is no need for weapons aboard this ship. These surveyors have to be ashore before dark or we would be anchoring in Grand Marais right now."

As they continued on, the wind changed and picked up. Waves began rocking the boat, and they were forced to stay seated or risk being thrown overboard.

"Are we there yet?" Hawk yelled against the wind.

"This reminds me of the last squall the Queen went through," Anatole shouted down from the pilothouse. "She rolled so far that the stack scooped fish from the water and smoked them for our dinner."

"So, *that's* how Hector prepared the salmon." Sophie said with a spirited laugh.

The ship turned sharply toward the shore where a small river flowed into the lake.

"We'll be letting some passengers off here, then we'll be underway back to Grand Marais Harbor."

Hector came topside and lowered a small skiff off the back of the ship.

The man Lorraine sat with during lunch came over to her. "It was very nice to meet you, Lorraine." He took her hand and said, "I wish you all the luck in the world on your journey." Then he said good-bye and lowered himself into the skiff.

"He was a nice man," Sophie said to Lorraine.

"His name is Charles Kimball. He is very well informed about the geology of this area." She watched as Hector rowed Charles Kimball and his companions to shore. She lowered her eyebrows, and said, "He is quite curious, however. He seemed to have emotional problems and I don't think his mind was entirely on our conversation." She threw her arms out to the side and said, "Oh well, you certainly meet some interesting people out here."

Anatole, overhearing Lorraine's remarks, came to her and said, "We'll be picking them up on our way back from Port Arthur. Perhaps you will meet him again."

"That would be nice," Lorraine said, "but I don't think we'll be seeing him again."

Kimball jumped from the boat and ran into the forest, leaving the other men to unload his gear. When all of the surveyors were on shore, Hector turned the skiff into the surf and rowed back to the Athens Queen.

Once the skiff was secured to the Queen, Anatole told Hector, "Take us to Grand Marais, my good man."

The engine chugged and water boiled from the propeller, and the boat began moving forward. In an hour they were turning in to Grand Marais Harbor.

39

C H A P T E R

T H I R T Y - N I N E

SILENCE FELL OVER THE GROUP as the ship made its way around the north end of the harbor. "Well, this is it," Hawk said. "This is where it all ends."

"What do you mean by that?" Sophie asked.

"I'm not sure, but I think we're going to find out what Diggs is up to. By the looks of Grand Marais, there's not much here and not much reason for anyone to be here. Jake, get your binoculars and see what's on shore."

"Not a soul around," Jake said as he scanned the beach, "just a couple of old cabins, a rotting boat on the beach, and two smaller boats pulled up on shore."

"Anyone on that boat?" Hawk said indicating a small, steam-driven boat on the opposite side of the harbor.

"I don't see anyone. In fact, it looks like the boat is drifting toward the rocks on the other side."

"That is that bucket that was in the harbor in Duluth," Anatole said. "It appears that it has been deserted."

"Whoever is on shore must be waiting for another boat or they wouldn't let that boat drift."

"Hawk," Jake said softly. "On that hill, there's a line of people moving, going up."

"There's nothing up there anyone would want," Mayhew said. "Just a lot of trees and rocks, and a lake the Indians call, *Manito Bimi-tagico-wini*. It means the place where Spirits walk on ice. It's six miles of climbing up steep hills and rocks. Come to think of it, if I was looking for a place to hide, that's where I'd go."

"To the lake?"

"No, but that trail takes you to some pretty desolate country."

The Athens Queen made its way into the harbor. Jake kept watch over the shore with his binoculars. Lorraine observed ancient lava flows that had broken into angular blocks and columns as the lava cooled. Next to the water the rocks were worn smooth from thousands of years of the relentless pounding of waves. The top surfaces were scarred by rocks that had been dragged against them by ancient continental glaciers.

The ship slowed and came to a stop one hundred yards from shore. The sound of the anchor being lowered and plunging into the water told them they had reached their destination. They sat silently scanning the shore for any movement.

"Well, here we are," Hawk said. "Guess there's nothing to do now but go ashore and see what's there."

"Gentlemen," Anatole said. "I would advise you to wait until morning to go ashore. There will be a moon tonight and a boat on the water will be seen as clearly as in daylight."

They agreed, and Hector brought them blankets. They spent the night huddled together on the deck.

Morning brought heavy fog to Grand Marais Harbor and shivers to the sleepy people on the deck of the Athens Queen. The sun hadn't completely cleared the horizon when Hector came out with hot coffee and corn biscuits with blackberry jam.

Anatole sat with them while they ate. "Are you folks expecting trouble in Grand Marais?"

"We're hoping we don't have trouble," Lorraine said. "We would just as soon take care of this problem without trouble, but it does not appear that peace will prevail."

"Lorraine, what is peace?" Hawk asked.

Lorraine thought about it for a few seconds and answered, "Peace is that period of time when we can find nothing to quarrel about. It is generally of very limited duration and is considered by some to be nonproductive time."

"Sunkist, what is peace to you?" Hawk asked.

"That's that aggervatin' time b'tween fights when ye got nothin' tuh do an' ye yawn a lot."

"It looks as if peace is something that's easier to talk about than to find." Lorraine said.

"I feel it my duty," Anatole said, "to inform you that the legend of a big silver strike is just that . . . a legend."

"What legend?" Hawk asked.

"Aren't you folks out to find the silver?"

"We don't know about any silver, and this is not about money."

"I will stay in the harbor for one night on our way back. If you're not here at that time, you will have to make your way back to Duluth on your own."

"Good enough," Hawk said.

Hector was at the stern of the ship untying the ropes that held the skiff. They gathered their belongings, leaving all but the bare essentials on the ship, then made their way through the boxes and bundles to the stern. The skiff was lowered into the water and one by one they got into the boat. The air was cold and wet, and they could barely see the shore through the fog.

Five minutes of rowing brought them to the rocky shore. Hector stepped into the water and pulled the boat onto land. Jake sat in the middle with his binoculars, searching the shore for any movement.

Grand Marais was nothing but a sparse collection of abandoned trappers' cabins and a few broken-down wigwams. Two boats, barely hanging onto shore, rocked with the waves.

"Let's pull these boats up," Jake said. "They might come in handy when this is over."

Posey pulled on Sunkist's shirt and pointed at tracks that led toward the hills.

"Appears like they went up them mountains, yonder," Sunkist said.

"Husband," Posey said while pointing to more tracks. "Injuns."

The tracks led them west and gradually the trail became steeper and the climb more difficult.

After an hour of climbing, the trail turned north and they stopped for a rest.

"Where's this trail taking us, Hayes?" Hawk asked.

"Well, if we'd stayed on the main trail it would take us to Devil Track Lake. But these tracks are going toward the river."

"Why the river?"

"It's a connection back to Superior . . . and maybe to that ship you said they'd be waiting for."

Posey suddenly shook Sunkist's sleeve again and pointed into the forest.

"Whut?" he said.

"Injun," Posey said.

They all peered into the brush but saw nothing. "Check your weapons," Hawk said.

"No," Posey said. "Friends."

"How do you know that?"

"If they wasn't friends," Sunkist said, "we'd be fightin' fer our scalps right now."

"Well, let's keep these guns handy, anyway."

"Let's move," Jake said.

They followed the tracks along the trail, keeping a close eye on their surroundings. Now and then they caught a glimpse of movement in the brush.

Jake stopped and turned to the forest. "Wait here," he said and stepped into the brush.

"What are you seeing?" Lorraine asked.

"Just wait here."

He moved farther into the brush. Lorraine, Sophie, and Hawk stepped up behind him. "What is it?" Lorraine asked as she pulled a branch aside. There before her, the naked body of a man hung upside-down from a tree by one leg. His throat had been cut and fresh blood puddled beneath it. Between his legs was nothing but a bloody gash, and blood covered his body from head to foot. Lorraine let out a cry and started to fall.

Jake caught her and said, "You should'a stayed back like I told you."

Sophie turned away quickly and started back toward the trail with Lorraine. Hawk pulled his knife and cut the rope that held the body. A rush of wind came from the lungs as the body dropped in a heap to the ground.

Jake turned the dead man's head to see the face. "Aw Gawd," he said as he turned away, "it's Boots."

"This ain't the work of Indians," Hawk said. "Diggs did this."

"Yeah," Jake said. "Like Mayhew said, Boots signed his own death warrant when he talked to me."

"Gonna bury him?" Hawk asked.

"We don't have time now. We'll do it later." He went to his pack and pulled out a blanket and covered Boots' body. "Let's go. We got people who need killin'."

Lorraine sat on a large rock with her face in her hands. Sophie sat next to her, rubbing her back and talking softly to her.

"You alright, Lorraine?" Jake asked.

She looked up at him. Her face was white and tears ran freely from her bloodshot eyes. "Next time you tell me to wait here, I'm going to wait right here."

"Hawk . . ." Sunkist said softly.

Hawk turned and saw an Indian standing on the trail fifty feet ahead of them. He was tall and wore buckskin clothing. Half of his face was painted black and the other half was painted white. Long black braids hung down the front of his shoulders. He stood motionless and soundless. Jake got up and turned toward the Indian. He walked deliberately toward him, and when he reached him, he put out his hand. The Indian took it and said, "It is good to see you, Jacob Owen."

"Come and sit with us, Crow. We must talk."

They came back to the group. Crow nodded to each of them as he lowered himself to sit cross-legged on the ground.

"This is Dead Crow," Jake said. "We know him from Dakota Territory."

Crow looked at Hawk and said, "Cetan. It is good to see you are not killed yet." Then he nodded to Sophie. "Situpsa, it is always good to see you."

"And you, too, my friend."

"How many men do you have, Crow?" Hawk asked.

"We are ten. More will come."

"All Dakota?"

"We are not Dakota and we are not Ojibwa."

"Do you know where Diggs is?"

"Yes. He has many men, men from places we do not know."

"This is where we'll find the people Dream Talker mentioned," Sophie said, "the one's who are not white and not Indian."

"Show us where they are," Jake said.

"Stay on this trail and you will find them. The men do not know the way of the forest. It will be easy to overpower them."

Crow stood and started to walk away. He stopped and turned. "Hawk," he said as he pointed towards the dead man, "these are bad men, you must be careful." Then he disappeared into the woods.

They took up their rifles and packs and moved a quarter of a mile up the trail where Mayhew stopped them and pointed into the woods. "Jake," he said, "come with me."

"I think we should stay together from here on," Hawk said.

"Aright, but this ain't gonna be pretty."

"What'd ye find?" Sunkist said.

"Nothing yet, but I can smell it." They stepped off the trail and into the woods. In a clearing, they saw an area fifty feet in diameter with poplar saplings snapped off or uprooted. The ground was scraped bare in places and there was blood and hair everywhere. Blood was smeared six feet up the trees that were left standing. A dead moose lay on the ground in the middle of the area, its insides completely gone.

"Moose kill," Jake said surveying the scene in front of them.

"Yeah," Mayhew added, "but I've never seen anything like this one before."

They walked into the clearing and studied the area.

"Here's how it happened," Mayhew said with excitement in his voice. He proceeded to take on the posture of the different animals and choreographed the fight. He pawed the ground with his boots, pantomiming the moose, and reenacted the actions of the badly wounded timber wolf that had been repeatedly flung against the trees. He pointed to a blood trail that most likely led to the dead wolf. As they approached the moose carcass, he explained that wolves preferred entrails over good leg meat.

"Must'a been one sick or injured moose fer wolves to take a beatin' like this fer a meal," Sunkist said.

Mayhew bent over the carcass. "Look here." He reached in and pulled out a broken arrow shaft that was lodged between the ribs. "This is what made him sick, and the wolves could smell it."

"That'll ruin yer day," Sunkist said.

"The other critters will take care of the rest," Mayhew said.

Hawk looked at them, "You kids done playing now? Let's get moving."

They walked back along the narrow trail until they came to a deep ravine with a small river at the bottom. Posey and Sunkist went to the edge of the ravine and studied it for tracks. "They go there," Posey said pointing at tracks that followed the river to the east.

"I think I know where they're going," Mayhew said. "This river connects up with the Devil Track River a couple of miles down. The Devil Track dumps into Superior a mile and a half farther down."

"Why would they come clear up here just to go back to Superior?"

"I can only guess about that, but Grand Marais is a fairly well-known port, and illegal trade would be risky there. There's a sand bar at the mouth of this river. It breaks up the waves and gives enough shelter for ships to anchor."

"Alright," Hawk said. "Why are these people taking the long way around to get there?"

"You're asking me to speculate. Alright, I will. I'm thinking they're doing their business inland and transporting the goods down the Devil Track to meet ships."

"Sound's reasonable to me. We'll follow the river. One more thing," Hawk said. "What's this legend about silver?"

"There's a story about a big silver strike somewhere around here. They say someone found pure silver nuggets but didn't tell anyone about it."

"Is it true?"

"I think there's some truth to it, but the part about silver nuggets makes it hard to believe. You don't find silver in nuggets. The story says a man found a big silver vein on an island and would go out at night and dig in his mine, then take it back before daylight."

"What happened to the man?"

"That's the fun part of it. No one knows where he went. He just disappeared."

"Does anyone know who it was?"

"Hawk, it's just one of those ghost stories they tell around campfires. There was no silver or gold or anything else. Well, copper, maybe, but no one's found a big vein of that either. They say his ghost can be seen moving around at night looking for his silver. It's a great story to scare kids with, but that's all."

After two miles of climbing and descending hills, they heard the rush of water. At the edge of a ridge, they spotted a camp one hundred feet below. They crouched down and peered through the brush. Three tents were set up on the river's floodplain. One was circular with high walls and was decorated with vertical stripes of various colors. The rest were cabin type, plain, white wall-tents. A group of men stood in the middle of the compound. They wore long robes and hats that appeared to be cloths wrapped around their heads. They all had long, full beards and their skin was dark like that of the Indians. But their eyes were like those of white men.

"Jake, what's going on down there," Hawk whispered.

"Doesn't look like much of anything. Just a bunch of people standing . . . Wait a minute." He handed the binoculars to Hawk. "Someone just came out of that tent. I've never seen this Diggs before, but that man fits your description."

Hawk took the glasses. "I'll be damned, that *is* Diggs." He looked through the glasses for a few moments and handed them back. Jake scanned the group, counting the people he saw. "Wish they'd hold still so I can count 'em," he said. "Hawk, there's a bunch of girls coming out of one of the tents."

"Let me see those," Hawk said and reached for the glasses. "What the hell's going on down there?"

One of the girls was led away from the rest and stood in the middle of the clearing. Diggs stepped up to her, grabbed the front of her dress, and jerked it down, exposing her breasts. He spoke to her and the girl started to cry. He stood next to her and spoke out to the men gathered around the girl. Hawk handed the glasses to Jake. "Ye know what this is?"

"What?"

"It's a goddamn auction. They're auctioning off the girls."

"Hawk," Jake said. "Look down there at the girls. Third from the right. Tell me what you see."

Hawk took the glasses. "Damn," he said softly and handed the glasses to Sophie. "Take a look down there at the girls."

Sophie took the glasses and looked through then. "Oh, my God," she whispered. "That's Dream Talker."

She handed the glasses back to Hawk. Dream Talker stood below, expressionless, looking up the hill and directly into Hawk's eyes. Shivers ran up his spine and the hair on his arms raised. His heart skipped a beat when he saw Dream Talker nod her head at him.

Dream Talker started to sing. The girl who was being auctioned stopped crying and looked straight into Diggs's eyes. He stopped for a brief moment, studied her, then turned back to the men standing around him.

"How many men are down there, Jake?"

"Looks to be about thirty, give or take."

"That's too damn many."

"I don't see anyone guarding the perimeter," Jake said, "and I don't see any guns."

"No guns?"

"This here's one time we cain't jiss jump in an' kill 'em," Sunkist said.

"Crow said they don't know the way of the forest. I think we can use that to get close," Jake said.

"We can't let anything happen to those girls," Sophie said.

"Nothing's going to happen to any of those girls as long as they don't suspect trouble."

"No guns?" Mayhew said.

"No guns." Jake replied.

"No guns means they're not expecting trouble," Mayhew said.

"Just because we don't see 'em don't mean they're not there, Haze." Jake said while watching below through the glasses.

"We're going to have to get down there," Hawk said. "We can't do much from up here." He turned to Mayhew. "How far is the lake from here?"

"Around two miles. You thinking about going to the lake and waiting for them?"

"That's a thought, but do you know what they plan on doing with the girls after they're sold?"

"No. What?"

"I don't know, I'm asking *you.*"

"I don't know."

"And what happens to the ones who *do not* get sold?" Lorraine asked.

"We have to get them out of there—now."

"Yer right. We can move down stream where they can't see us and climb down to the river and come back to them," Hawk suggested.

"Hawk," Jake said and handed him the glasses. Below, the girl was being led away by one of the men in long robes. Hawk watched as another girl was taken into the middle of the circle. Again, Diggs grabbed the front of her dress and started to pull it down, but the girl pushed his hand away and slapped at him. Diggs slapped her hard and knocked her to the ground. Two men came, took the girl's arms, stood her on her feet, and held her while Diggs ripped and tore at her clothing, completely disrobing her. Dream Talker was still looking up at Hawk, still showing no emotion.

"Come on," he said as he handed the glasses back to Jake. Let's get down there and get this taken care of."

"Wait," Jake said, "Something's going on down there."

Diggs went to the girls and dragged another one out and stood her next to the one that was already there.

Dream Talker stepped out of the gathering and raised her arms into the air. She looked up the hill into the binoculars.

Diggs grabbed the girl's dress but before he could pull it off, both of the young girls jumped at him, knocking him to the ground. All at once, the girls in the group ran at the men, screaming and clawing at them with tooth and nail. A sudden cloud of smoke erupted from the forest on the opposite side of the valley and three of the men below dropped to the ground. The girls kept up their attack as gunfire echoed up and down the valley.

"Hold your fire!" Hawk said. "We can't risk hitting any of those girls."

"That there's Crow and his army on the other side," Sunkist said. "I say we git on down there and git Diggs afore he disappears."

As a unit, they slipped over the bank and started toward the river. From one of the tents below came five men holding rifles. They ran into the clearing, aiming their rifles up the bank and into the woods. A cloud of white smoke blasted from the woods, and one of the men fell. The girls turned their attack to the riflemen. Several of them were knocked to the ground, but the attack made the men's defense useless.

Dream Talker's voice could be heard now. She shouted a loud song that called the girls to her, and as a group they ran and vanished into the forest. Diggs had disappeared, along with the men with rifles. The men in robes stood in a tight circle with their hands high in the air. Hawk, Jake, and Sunkist tried to move along the bank of the river to catch Diggs, but the bank was too steep and made movement difficult and dangerous. They climbed to the top where travel was easier but the going was still slow through the heavy brush. Lorraine and Sophie followed, each carrying a repeating rifle.

Seventy-five feet below, they saw Diggs and his men moving along the edge of the river, scrambling over rocks and wading into the rushing water. Hawk followed their progress moving along the rim of the valley.

"How about we jiss shoot 'em," Sunkist suggested.

"We're supposed to bring Diggs back alive," Hawk said, "and I intend to do just that. I want him behind bars where I can go in and slap the son of a bitch once or twice a day."

One of the men with Diggs stopped and looked up the bluff. Hawk stopped and stood motionless for a few seconds until he saw the man's rifle come to his shoulder, then Hawk dropped to the ground. No shot came. Hawk peered over the bank and saw Diggs moving again.

"Ye could pick 'im off so easy from up here." Sunkist said.

"Well, pick one of those riflemen off. We want Diggs alive."

Sunkist laid his Sharps over a rock and took aim. The men below moved behind a pile of rocks. Sunkist lowered his rifle.

"Kind of a standoff here," he said. "We cain't see him and he cain't see us. But neither of us can move."

"You stay here and keep a bead on the rock," Hawk said. "I'm going downstream and set up a little surprise for them. We got him trapped with nowhere to go. Jake, you come with me. Lorraine, you stay here with Sunkist and Haze."

"I'm coming with you," Sophie said.

"That kinda goes unsaid," Hawk replied.

They moved back into the forest and down along the rim of the valley until they found a place where the slope was more gradual, then moved toward the river and found a cluster of large boulders to hide behind. They sat quietly, watching the river tumble over rocks as it rushed toward Lake Superior. They were still thirty feet above the water and could hear the rapids. The water rushed over the cascade for a quarter of a mile before the channel turned out of sight.

Then they heard a rapid series of shots from the direction they had just come. After a quick exchange of shots, the shooting slowed. Then silence. They waited. There were no sounds, no movement, just the steady rush of water over the rapids. Jake tapped Hawk's shoulder and pointed up the river. There they saw a dark object tumbling over the rapids and coming their way. It tumbled closer. Sophie's hand came to her mouth. "Oh, my dear God!" she shouted, "Oh, God, no! That's Lorraine." She jumped up and started climbing down the rocks toward the river, but before she could get close, the water had carried the body out of sight.

"Hawk!" she shouted. "We have to find her. We can't just leave her."

"Sophie! Get back up here!" Hawk shouted. "There's nothing we can do for her now. We'll find her when this is over."

Sophie scrambled up to Hawk, threw her arms around him, laid her head on his shoulder, and cried loudly. They held their position for fifteen minutes watching the river. Hawk stood and said. "Let's go see what happened up there."

From above they saw Mayhew coming down the slope toward them. Sunkist was leaning against him with Posey holding him on the other side. Jake jumped to his feet and ran to meet them. "What the hell happened up there?" he asked.

Sunkist looked at him with a laugh in his eyes. "Damn, that guy can shoot."

"What guy? How many were there?"

"Don't know how many there was to start, but there ain't but one shooter left . . . and Diggs." They sat Sunkist on a rock and Posey opened his shirt to show the bandaging she'd already done.

"How bad is it?" Sophie asked.

"Figger he got muh liver," Sunkist said. "Recon I'll be back in the Rockies b'fore sundown."

"You ain't goin' nowhere," Hawk said. "You just sit right here till this is over and we'll get you back to Doc Bernier. Yer gonna git better rot quick."

Sunkist looked at Hawk and smiled. "Appears like I finally learnt ye how tuh talk 'merican."

"Hawk," Jake said and pointed up the river. Diggs and two men were moving slowly their way.

Posey turned to look, then grabbed Sunkist's rifle. She laid the barrel over a rock and took aim. Sophie started to reach for the rifle but Jake stopped her. "She's gotta get revenge," he said. "It's the Indian way."

The rifle went off. The man fell backward and disappeared. Diggs ducked quickly behind the boulders.

"Come on out, Diggs!" Hawk shouted. "You got nowhere to go!"

"I'm not finished yet, Owen," the reply came back. "You show your face just once and you're a dead man!"

"Where the hell did those Indians go?" Jake asked softly. "We could use them right now."

"The Indians came to get their women back," Mayhew said. "They've gone back home, now."

Jake backed away from Hawk and Sophie and slipped into the brush. Sunkist lay on the sand between two rocks with Posey by his side. On the ground next to Posey was a leather bag of herbs and Cherokee medicines. No emotion showed as she looked down at Sunkist's face. His eyes were closed and his breathing was slow and shallow. "He's still alive." Hawk said. "We'll get him down to Oneota."

Hawk watched across the river, waiting for the chance to take a shot at Diggs. Clouds began to cover the sky and darkness started to close in.

Across the river they saw Diggs stand up behind a rock with Jake right behind him, a pistol at his head. They moved down to the edge of the river. Jake hooked his foot with Diggs's, causing him to fall face first onto the river's stony edge. Jake was on top of him in an instant and quickly had his hands tied behind his back.

He looked across the river toward Hawk. "He's finished now!" He pulled Diggs to his feet by the back of shirt and prodded him forward with the muzzle of his pistol. Then he motioned for Hawk to move downstream. He walked Diggs for a few feet then gave him a shove, causing Diggs to fall onto the rocks. Jake pulled him to his feet and they started moving again. Once more Jake shoved Diggs, and again Diggs fell.

Hawk turned to Mayhew. "What happened back there?"

ARVID LLOYD WILLIAMS
BONNIE SHALLBETTER

401

"We had Diggs in a trap. He couldn't move and we couldn't move. His rifles were behind some rocks and we couldn't see any of them. Somehow one of them got away from the rest of them and got a bead on us from the side. That's when Sunkist got it. First shot caught him in the guts. He didn't go down, though. He ups and kills the man who shot him. Then he started pumping bullets down at Diggs. One of Diggs's men took off and got behind a boulder. Sunkist got a bead on him, but fired a little too late. That's when Lorraine got hit." Mayhew choked on a sob. "I tried to catch her when she went over . . ." Mayhew tried to continue the story, but his sobbing wouldn't allow it.

Hawk patted him on the back, "We'll talk about it later."

"What happened to the other men who were there?" Sophie asked through her own tears.

"Mayhew wiped his eyes and said, "I'm not sure what happened to them. They just stood there with their hands in the air through the entire battle. When it was over, they were gone."

"What about the Indians?"

"I'm just guessing, but that's probably what happened to the other men. I'd rather be dead than have to go through what those Indians have planned for them."

They saw Jake coming along the face of the slope with Diggs in front of him. Suddenly, Diggs fell face-first to the ground. Jake grabbed his shirt and pulled him to his feet. "The man's got trouble staying on his feet," Jake said with a grin, then kicked Diggs's left foot to the side so it hooked his right foot, and Diggs hit the ground again.

"Git up!" Jake commanded as he kicked Diggs in the ribs. Diggs rolled to his side and sat halfway up. His face was bleeding from several cuts and blood dripped from the side of his mouth.

"He don't look so good," Hawk said.

"I'll bet he looks better than those foreigners right now."

"What d'ye mean?"

"Crow and the boys got 'em. I saw smoke back in the woods and heard 'em screaming. I don't think those ol' boys are real comfortable by that fire." Jake poked Diggs in the ribs with his pistol. "What d'ya think, Reverend? Ye wanna go get warm by the Indian's fire?"

"We gotta get Sunkist down to the lake and we gotta find Lorraine, too."

"We're not going anywhere tonight. It's going to be dark in two hours, and we can't be carrying Sunkist over these rocks in the dark."

"You stay here with Sunkist and Posey, then," Jake said. "I'm going to leave this trash with you and go downstream and see if I can locate Lorraine."

"I'm going with you," Mayhew said.

"Alright," Jake said. "Four eyes are better than two. Let's go."

Jake and Mayhew started down the bluff to the river and disappeared around the bend. Hawk took Diggs and tied him to a tree in a sitting position.

"You can't leave me tied to this tree all night," Diggs complained.

"Oh," Hawk said, "I can't? Well, alright then, I'll . . ." He stepped up to Diggs, paused for a moment, and said, "Yes, I can." Then he walked back to the rest.

Sunkist slept with Posey by his side. Sophie and Hawk curled up together and wrapped themselves in a blanket. Sophie was awake most of the night thinking about Lorraine and talking about the memories she had of her. Darkness fell and they dropped off to sleep.

Morning came and Hawk rolled out from his blanket. Sunkist was not where he had been the night before. From a thicket he heard Sophie call, "Hawk, over here." He went into the brush and found Sophie sitting next to Sunkist and Posey. Sunkist's face was as white as the clouds above them, and Posey lay motionless by his side. The bag of Cherokee medicine lay open and herbs had spilled out onto the ground. Posey's arm lay over Sunkist's chest and her head was on his shoulder. Sophie sat staring at the ground. She looked up at Hawk. "She poisoned herself." Hawk sat down next to Sophie and they cried together.

40

C H A P T E R   F O R T Y

LATER IN THE MORNING, JAKE CAME BACK with Mayhew and saw a single grave. "We buried them together," Hawk said.

"As it should be," Jake said. His shoulders began to shake and he turned away. When he turned back around, his eyes showed the tears he tried to hide, and his face showed the pain that gripped his heart.

"I didn't find any sign of Lorraine," he said. "But there's a ship out on the lake."

"It comes from the Mediterranean Sea," Mayhew said.

"How do you know that?"

"The flag. It's the Persian flag. That's where those men came from that were trying to buy the girls."

"We have to do something about that ship," Hawk said. "We can't just let them go so they can go find someone else to buy their slaves from."

"Those girls were not going to be slaves," Diggs said from his sitting position by the tree.

Hawk walked over to him and sat down. "Just what were they going to do with those girls, Diggs?"

"They were going to a land where women are treated like ladies. They would have fine homes and men who would take care of their every need."

"You don't believe that any more than I do, Diggs. Those girls were going to be slaves and you know it."

"Hawk," Jake said softly. Hawk looked up. Standing fifty feet away was Crow and nine warriors dressed in breachclouts and moccasins. Crow walked in and stood in front of Diggs. "We want this man," he said.

"No." Hawk said. "He's coming back to Oneota with us.

"He is the one who took our women. He must pay."

Diggs looked up at Hawk with true fear in his eyes. "You can't let them have me," he said. "They'll kill me."

"If that's all they were gonna do, I might not let them have you, but I think they have more in mind than just putting you out of your misery."

Diggs looked into Crow's black eyes then back at Hawk. "Please," he said.

"Tell me something, Diggs," Hawk said. "How much did you get for the girls?"

"Gold. They paid in gold."

"How much is a human life worth in gold?"

Diggs didn't answer. He simply stared.

"Well? How much did you get for one of the girls?"

He still didn't answer. Hawk looked up at Crow. Crow took hold of the handle of his knife and started to pull it out.

"They got fifty dollars gold for the one they sold yesterday."

"Who's 'they'?"

"The people who . . ." Hawk backhanded him across the mouth.

"Don't hand me that shit! You were the one who took the goddamn money, not *they*."

Diggs stared.

"Well, if you got fifty dollars for a pretty young girl, an ugly old son of a bitch like you should bring, what, about five bucks?"

He turned to Crow. "You got five bucks, Crow?"

"I have five bucks," Crow said.

Hawk stood up and shouted to the rest of the Indians standing fifty feet away. "Crow here has offered five bucks for the child stealer. Does anyone offer six?"

The Indians looked back and forth amongst themselves and finally one raised his hand, "Six!" he shouted.

"Does any one want to offer seven dollars?" All hands went in the air.

"What are you doing?" Diggs cried. "You can't do this."

"We're holding an auction. Isn't that the way we sell human beings?"

Diggs' head turned to the ground and began sobbing. "You can't do this. Please don't do this."

"Tell me something, Diggs. What do you know about Sophie being kidnapped?"

"That was not me. I had nothing to do with that."

Sophie stood and came to stand in front of Diggs. She touched him with her toe and looked directly into his eyes. "Who had me taken?"

"I don't know anything about it."

Sophie turned toward the Indians. "What is the highest bid?"

"Ten dollars," one man said.

"Ten dollars. Going once . . ."

"Alright!" Diggs said. "I had nothing to do with it. I mentioned to some people that you were with Hawk Owen. I didn't mean to do it. It just slipped out."

"I don't understand. What do they care if I'm with Hawk? Who knows me well enough to want to know where I am?"

Diggs looked as confused as Sophie was at that time. "You don't know, do you?"

"Know what?"

"About the silver."

"What silver?"

"You are the daughter of Beaumont Boisvert, are you not?"

"So the story goes."

"Let me interrupt here," Mayhew said. "I think this has something to do with the legend we discussed earlier." He turned to Diggs. "Is this Boisvert supposed to be the one who got away with a ton of silver?"

"That is what the stories say."

"So someone actually thinks Sophie Boisvert has that silver."

"Yes. They had people out looking for her for years."

"Do *you* think she has it?"

"I don't believe that silver ever existed," Diggs said.

"Did you know the Frenchman who took Sophie?"

"That Frenchman. What an absolute fool."

"You knew him, then."

"He was one of the men they sent out on Sophie Boisvert's trail twenty years ago. He heard that she was spotted in Saint Cloud and was headed to Fort Ripley. How such a damn fool even remembered her name is beyond me."

"What about the men who took me after the Frenchman ran away?"

Diggs looked into her eyes without responding. Sophie's eyes narrowed and she scowled at him. "Those were your men." She kicked him on the shin. "You were with them, weren't you?"

Diggs didn't answer. She turned towards the Indians. "Anyone with two bucks can do what he pleases with this man, I don't care." She started to turn away then stopped and turned toward him. "Oh . . . *Reverend*, I believe there is a passage from the Bible that states you reap what you sow."

The Indians started moving toward Diggs. "No, please," Diggs pleaded. "I'll tell you anything you want to know." His voice trailed off. "Just don't let them have me."

"What did you want from me?"

"I thought if I had you I could get Owen off my trail."

"That Frenchman wasn't the damn fool—*you* were. Did you really think that Hawk would just give up if you had me?"

Diggs sat quietly.

"Who are the people buying Indian girls?" Hawk asked.

"Some people from across the ocean."

Hawk kicked his leg.

"Alright! Most of them are bought by Persian kings and princes to become their wives."

"And you think this is alright to do?"

"I'm giving these girls a place to live where they will be well fed and treated as ladies. That's a far cry from what they had living in the woods with savages."

"No, it's not," Hawk said. "Get on your feet."

"What are you going to do?"

"I haven't decided that yet. These Indians want you but they're just going to burn you alive. That's too good for you."

Jake made a motion to the Indians and they turned and walked away. Then he stepped up to Diggs, took him by the shirt, and raised him to his feet. He turned to Mayhew. "Which way, Haze?"

"I say we go down the river to the lake."

"I agree," Sophie said. "Maybe we can find Lorraine."

"That's damn rough country down there," Jake said. "Tougher than the way we came."

"What are the chances of finding Lorraine?"

"Slim to none."

"If there's one chance in a million we have to take it," Sophie said. "We're not going to just let her . . ." She broke down and cried.

"We have to go look for her," Hawk said, wiping tears from his eyes. "If she's alive . . ."

"She's dead, Hawk." Jake said. "No one could have lived through that ride down the river."

Hawk pushed Jake aside. "I know she is."

Sophie walked up to Diggs and slapped him hard across the face and walked off. Jake went behind him and gave him a push. Diggs stumbled and started down the path toward Lake Superior.

The terrain was rocky and wet. They stumbled and slipped along, keeping their eyes on the river. Two hours later they could see the lake and a ship anchored off shore.

"That's the ship from Persia," Mayhew said.

"They're waiting for Diggs to bring the goods."

"I say we head back to Grand Marais," Mayhew said.

"Is there a road?"

"There's a trail, and it's not near as rough as the trail we just came on."

"How far?"

"Three, maybe four miles."

"Let's go. Lead the way, Haze."

They moved down to the shore of Lake Superior and walked single file southwest toward Grand Marais. Diggs's hands were kept tied in front of him and a long rope was tied around his neck. Jake held the end of the rope and gave it a jerk now and then.

By nightfall they were on the beach of Grand Marais Harbor. "Anatole couldn't have been here and gone already, could he?"

"No, I doubt it. He'll be along any time now," Mayhew said.

"Let's go make one of those cabins home for tonight," Hawk said.

"I'll stay out here with Diggs for a while incase the ship comes in," Jake said. "Hey, Hawk! Did you notice one of the boats is gone?"

"Prob'ly just drifted away. You should'a pulled it farther up."

The next morning Sophie and Hawk walked around the shore and out onto a lava flow that stretched into the water. They climbed up the jagged rocks.

She stood at the precipice, looking down on the lake the French called Le Lac Superior, the uppermost, the final headwaters. She stood for a long while, saying nothing, just looking, captured by what has captured trappers, voyageurs, clergyman, and adventurers for hundreds of years. The rocks she was standing on were ancient rocks more than two billion years old.

She realized she had been holding her breath and let it out slowly. As she stood there with Hawk behind her, his arms around her waist, her voice came out in a low whisper, so soft that he had a hard time hearing her.

"Hawk, I've never seen anything so beautiful in my life."

He felt a tear drop on his hand. He quietly moved away from her, knowing she needed to be alone.

Looking at the lake was like being with a lover for the first time. It was hard for Sophie to take her eyes off or look away, fearing a moment missed, a moment she could not reclaim.

As the sun shone on the lake it reflected a sea of crystal jewels dancing on the surface in a menagerie of sparkling light—a gift for all those who choose to take the time to look. The lake was a deep blue, offset by the pale blue of the sky and the whiteness of the clouds above. Sophie watched as the waves moved, carrying molecules of life dating back to the glaciers. She needed to be closer, to climb down the rocks to the water's edge so she could feel more a part of it.

When she reached the rocky beach, she picked up a handful of pebbles and tried to imagine how long they had been there. Each was like a storybook with its own unique history. She watched a wave as it rolled towards the shore into a small enclosure of rocks where it caressed and lapped, creating a sculpted, smooth surface. It playfully teased the rock, moving sensuously up, over, and around, leaving no part untouched. She watched this for a long while and was suddenly aware that her breath was in unison with the ebb and flow of the water. She took off her moccasins and waded into the water, wanting to feel the coolness. A sudden feeling of emotion swept over her body as recent tragedies became realities. She stumbled back to the shore and collapsed. Uncontrollable sobbing came from deep within her soul.

Soon afterward Hawk and Sophie found Jake talking with Hector on the beach. Diggs sat on a rock, shivering. They all climbed into the skiff and Hector rowed them out to the ship.

"Well, how was your trip?" Anatole asked cheerfully.

"We have a prisoner. Do you have a place where he won't be very happy?"

"Well, of course—the brig down below. But we haven't used it for prisoners for years."

"Put him down there."

"Perfect," Jake said. "Where is it?"

Anatole motioned to Hector. "Hector, please show him where the brig is."

Jake and Diggs followed Hector to the bottom of the ship, and Jake ushered Diggs into a small space enclosed with iron bars. Then he untied the ropes from Diggs's hands and closed the iron door. Once Jake was satisfied the door was secure, he joined the others on deck.

"Did you pick up the survey crew?"

"Yes, all but one, the one your friend . . ." He looked around and said, "Oh, where is the young lady who was with you?"

"She stayed behind," Hawk said fighting a lump that was growing in his throat.

"Her friend, Mister Kimball, didn't come back with us either."

"Decided to stay, huh?"

"No. In fact, they don't know what happened to him. They say he jumped out of the boat when they landed and ran into the forest and disappeared. They found his clothing on the shore of the lake and his tracks leading into the water. But they couldn't find any tracks coming out. It is a very curious situation. They named the creek where he disappeared after him. It is now officially called Kimball Creek. Surveyors can do that, you know."

"Devil Track River is properly named, too," Hawk said and went to watch the water go by.

They sat on chairs as Hector brought them lunch. Mayhew took one of Sophie's pewter plates and scratched at it with his pocketknife. "Sophie, where did you get these plates?"

"My father left them for me."

"Your father was Beaumont Boisvert, right?" He stood and moved closer to Sophie. He leaned down and scratched at the edge of the plate. "It's mighty shiny under this pewter."

"So what does that mean?"

"It means these plates are not pewter—they're silver."

Sophie took the plate and looked at it closely. She looked into his eyes. "Are you sure about that?"

Mayhew looked at her. "Yes, Sophie, these are silver. This is the money people have been looking for for twenty years."

"Mister Mayhew, for the time being, let's just say they're pewter."

"Sounds like a wise decision," he replied, and went back to his chair.

A man in a boat close to shore waved as the ship went by and they waved back. "People in boats are always so friendly," Sophie said. The man waved again with both arms.

Hawk watched as the ship passed the boat until it could no longer be seen around the bends of the lakeshore.

Slowly the ship rounded the end of Minnesota Point, slipped into Duluth

Harbor, and pulled up to the dock where they had boarded the Athens Queen three days before.

Hector came to Anatole and whispered in his ear.

"Oh dear," Anatole said. "What happened?" Then he turned to Hawk. "I'm afraid there has been a tragedy in the brig."

"What tragedy?" Hawk said.

"Hector went to bring your prisoner up and found him hanging by the neck. I'm afraid he is dead."

Hawk turned and went below. As he came close to the cell where Diggs had been housed, he was assaulted by a horrible smell. He walked to the cell and saw Diggs hanging from a rafter by the rope his hands had been tied with. He rushed to the top deck and vomited over the side, spit a few times, and wiped his mouth with the back of his sleeve. "Diggs hung himself."

Sophie looked into Hawk's eyes for a few seconds then said, "After everything that has gone on, I'm afraid I don't feel anything. He has no one to blame but himself."

They all picked up their horses and rode to Oneota, then directly to the doctor's house to see Abernathy.

"Hello," the doctor said as they walked in. "Your friend seems to have recovered from his wounds. He is taking nutrition and can sit up for short periods."

"Can we go in and see him?"

"Yes, of course." Doctor Bernier led them to the backroom where Abernathy lay. Abernathy was asleep when they walked in, so they took chairs and sat next to his bed. The doctor came in and brought them coffee and offered sweet bread, which they graciously turned down.

Abernathy moaned softly and opened his eyes. Sophie stood and looked down at him.

"Oh, my dear God!" Abernathy said. "Where have you been? I have missed you so."

"It's good to see you recovering, Abernathy" Sophie said and gave him a hug.

"We found Diggs," Hawk said. "He's dead."

"He is? How did you find him so quickly?"

"We didn't find him that quickly," Hawk said. "We've been gone for about a week."

"Oh dear. I have missed five days of my life. One can never reclaim those days once they are gone." He raised his head and looked about the room. "Where is Lorraine? Didn't she come with you?"

"Abernathy," Sophie said and started crying. "Lorraine didn't make it."

Tears began to fill his eyes. "What do you mean 'she didn't make it'?"

Sophie tried to tell him but couldn't speak.

Hawk leaned in from the other side of the bed and said, "Abernathy, Lorraine is dead." Then he broke down and cried.

"And my dear friend Sunkist?" Hawk just looked at him.

Abernathy cried out, "Oh, my God! Oh, my God, no! They're all gone. Oh, my God!" Hawk and Sophie wrapped their arms around Abernathy and they cried together. They stayed that way until Doc Bernier came in and suggested they leave so he could give Abernathy a sedative of laudanum to help him sleep. "You may come and see him in the morning."

They found a place to sleep in the backroom of a store in Oneota with a straw mattress on the floor and one chair.

"Hawk," Sophie said.

"Hmm?"

"I think this is the right time to tell you the news. It's happy news, we could all use that . . . nature has perfect timing, doesn't it?"

He leaned on one elbow and looked into her eyes. "What d'ya mean?"

"We're going to have a baby."

He stared silently for a few seconds. "A baby?"

"You know, a child? A kid? You've heard of them. Little people running around the house."

He stared. "You mean—you and me? We're going to . . ."

"Yes," Sophie said and threw her arms around his neck. He wrapped her in his arms and kissed her deeply.

After a while, as they lay in each other's arms, Sophie said. "If it's a girl I want to name her Lorraine."

"Wouldn't have it any other way," he said.

"And if it's a boy . . ."

"We're not naming him Abernathy."

In the morning they had breakfast at a cafe and walked down to the doctor's house. Doctor Bernier sat at his desk with his face buried in his hands.

"Good morning, Doctor," Sophie said.

"Good morning," the doctor said in a low tone.

"Is everything alright?"

"No. I'm very sorry to have to tell you this, but your friend passed away last night."

Sophie and Hawk looked at one another. "What happened? You said he was recovering."

"I don't know what happened. He was doing just fine last night, but this morning when I went in to check on him, he was gone. It's like he just gave up. He must have lost the will to live. It happens sometimes."

Hawk took Sophie by the hand, and without saying anything more, they turned and walked out the door. Jake and Mayhew sat outside on a bench. "Hey, Hawk," Jake said.

"Abernathy's gone," Hawk said.

"Yeah, we heard."

"That's the end of that story," Mayhew said.

"Yup," Jake said, then looked at Mayhew. "What story?"

"Abernathy was one of Hiram Berdan's sharpshooters in Tennessee during the war. One day his company was pinned down by some Confederate riflemen on a hill three hundred yards away. The Union soldiers' rifles were useless at that range, but Abernathy's Sharps was made for that kind of shooting. There were four rebel sharpshooters picking off the Union men. Abernathy killed two of them with two consecutive shots and the other two ran off. Turns out the sharpshooters were brothers. The brothers who survived swore vengeance on Abernathy and followed him for three years before they finally found him in those rocks outside of Oneota. The one Abernathy killed down by the Saint Louis River was Archer Suggs. The one Sunkist killed was his brother, Hogan."

"He sure didn't look like someone who goes around shooting people."

"Abernathy was really a gentle soul. But he was not one to mess with. He worked as Lorraine's secretary just to learn more about her. When he found that she was qualified for the mission, he manipulated her into going out to find homes for orphaned children."

"He manipulated Lorraine? He had to be pretty clever to do that. Was he as smart as Lorraine?"

"Abernathy was extremely intelligent, but not quite that smart. He took advantage of the only weakness she had—children. Lorraine would do anything for children. Well, I guess we learned how far she was willing to go."

"Can I ask you something?" Hawk said.

"Sure."

"Who were all those contacts you got your information from?"

"When men get in a whorehouse they can't keep their mouths shut about anything."

"Was Kathleen one of 'em?" Jake asked.

"Kathleen supplied me with information about some of the happenings around Crow Wing. But she was not working for the government like some of the contacts were. She's just an honest businesswoman who likes to keep a wide gap between her and the Elsa Bjorgstroms in the community."

"What about Elsa?"

"She knows everything about every person in Crow Wing County and halfway to Saint Paul."

"Was she working for you?"

"She wasn't hanging around Sunkist 'cause she thought he was so cute. When she finally figured out she wasn't going to learn anything from him, she let go. She was one of Beaulieu's people."

"And the one in Twin Lakes?"

"Common working girl."

"One more thing. Has Lorraine been in on this all along?"

"No, she was filled in when she had dinner with Sheriff Beaupre in Saint Cloud."

Hawk stood. "What d'ya think, Jake? Back to Courtland?"

"Nothing I want back there. I'm thinking about going back to Ottertail and see the farm. Might even . . ." Jake stopped talking and his eyes turned west. "Maybe I'll just go see what's on the other side of that hill."

"You don't know *where* you're going, then," Hawk stated more than asked.

"I got no one waiting for me anywhere."

"We'll be home if ye ever decide to come back to the valley," Sophie said.

They rode south to Twin Lakes where they stopped and had dinner together. "How about you, Hawk?' Jake asked. "Going back to Hawk Creek?"

"We're going down to Saint Paul and visit some friends of Sophie's. Then head home from there."

Mayhew stood, stretched, and said with a groan. "Well, I'm headin' north and find that silver."

Jake put his hand out and said, "See ye down the road, Hayes."

Hawk and Sophie rode south on the Saint Paul road and Jake took a narrow trail west and disappeared in the wilderness of northern Minnesota.

Back in Oneota, a man rowed a fishing boat up to the dock and shouted, "Get a doctor! I have an injured Indian woman in my boat!"

Doctor Bernier ran down to the dock. He brushed the hair from her face. "Dream Talker?" he said almost to himself. Her face was so swollen that her eyes were nearly closed. She had cuts and bruises on most her body and a bullet wound in her abdomen. After having some men bring the woman to his office, he worked feverishly on the wound while his helper, Kathy, washed the bruises and stitched the open cuts. When they had the woman cleaned and bandaged, they sat down next to the bed.

Morning came and Doc went into the room to check on his patient. He took her wrist to feel her pulse and she opened her dark-brown eyes and looked up at him. "*Docteur* Bernier?" she said softly with a French accent and a hint of a smile.

"Oh, my God," he said, "Lorraine Bernier!" He ran out the door yelling, hoping to catch his friends, but his voice faded away into the empty street.

A AUTHORS' NOTES

SAINT CLOUD AND THE STEARNS HOUSE

The Stearns House was built in 1857 and managed by Charles T. Stearns, the man for whom Stearns County is named. The beautiful, three-story structure was a favorite summer vacation resort for wealthy Southerners coming north to escape the heat of the Southern states. The hotel was referred to as a temperance hotel, as they served no alcoholic beverages. However, to accommodate the tastes of their Southern guests, mint juleps were served.

In 1869 the building was purchased by the State of Minnesota to become the Third State Normal School. The building that was once the Stearns House was the first building used for what is now Saint Cloud State University. The building was demolished in 1895.

· · ·

BELLE PRAIRIE AND FATHER PIERZ CHURCH

Belle Prairie is six miles north of Little Falls, Minnesota, just off of Highway 371. An historical monument marks the sight of the church Father Francis Pierz built there early in 1850.

· · ·

FORT RIPLEY 1864

Fort Ripley was called Fort Marcy in its beginnings and later took the name Fort Gaines. In 1850 it received its permanent name, Fort Ripley, in recognition of Eleazar Wheelock Ripley, a celebrated soldier of the War of 1812.

Fort Ripley was built on the approximate line dividing the territory of the Chippewa Indians and the Sioux in an effort to prevent the customary warring between the two tribes, thereby making the northern frontier less dangerous for white settlers. On April 26, 1864, the garrison at Fort Ripley was ordered to Dakota Territory to join General Sully's march against the Dakota Sioux following the conflict in the Minnesota valley in 1862. The soldiers who were unable to ride or fight were left behind to garrison the fort. This left the fort with less than one hundred men, with Lieutenant Miles Holister in command.

. . .

JOHN CAMEL'S SALOON

John Camel's saloon was one mile from Fort Ripley and a thorn in the side of the commanders there. John Camel was, himself, a brutish man who took pleasure in brawling and, in particular, beating his Indian woman. His saloon was the scene of many drunken brawls between soldier and soldier, Indian and Indian, and Indian and soldier, and frequently hosted a multicultural free-for-all.

. . .

OLD CROW WING

The town of Crow Wing was named for an island shaped like the wing of a crow that lies at the confluence of the Crow Wing and Mississippi rivers.

Crow Wing City had its beginnings early in the history of Minnesota as a fur trade center. The junction of the Mississippi and Crow Wing rivers offered an ideal place for a trading post. Red River oxcarts traveled cross-country from the Red River of the North to Crow Wing, and from there, south along the Mississippi River to Saint Paul. The ruts left by the wheels of the carts are still visible at Old Crow Wing.

Allen Morrison established a trading post there in 1823. In 1847, Clement H. Beaulieu managed the trading post for the American Fur Company and built a house for himself and his family. Recently this house was located on a farm not far from Crow Wing State Park and—thanks to the Friends of Old Crow Wing at Brainerd, Minnesota—was moved to its original location at the sight of Crow Wing City. The house stands on its original foundation atop a hill and can be viewed from an interpretive area where signs tell the history of the town. The location of the community water pump is marked with an interpretive sign, as is the sight of Clement Beaulieu's warehouse. Reverend Ottomer Cloeter was a Lutheran missionary to the Chippewa at Crow Wing City. He and Father Francis Pierz, a Catholic Priest, shared the duties of baptism and confirmation of the natives. Although they were friends, they were known to have frequent verbal battles on most any subject that came up.

You can find the sight of Old Crow Wing on the west side of Highway 371 at the Crow Wing State Park, six miles south of Brainerd, Minnesota.

. . .

HAZAEL MAYHEW JR. ALSO REFERRED TO AS: HENRY, HAZE, HAYES, OR H. MAYHEW JR.

Henry Mayhew was the single most important individual in the development of Grand Marais and Cooke County, Minnesota. He was a mineral prospector and, along with his close friend, geologist Henry Eames, took part in the ill-fated gold rush to Vermilion Lake near the North Shore of Lake Superior in 1855. He is the man who planned and built the Gunflint Trail from Grand Marais to his trading post on Rove Lake on the Canadian border.

His brother, Thomas Mayhew, was a special agent with the Union forces during the Civil War and was directly accountable to President Abraham Lincoln. Though he never enlisted, he served in the war as a surgeon's assistant for the Union Army, and as a spy against the Confederate Army. It has been stated that Thomas Mayhew was one of President Lincoln's most trusted agents.

Henry Mayhew did not serve in the Civil War, but he did enlist in Saint Paul at Fort Snelling to fight Indians after the Sioux Conflict of 1862 in southern Minnesota. He was with Henry Sibley on the march to chase the Dakota Sioux out onto the prairies of Dakota Territory in 1863. He is listed as saddler on the roster of the 1st Minnesota Cavalry.

Henry Mayhew's part in this story is fictional.

. . .

RIPLEY ESKER

An esker is an elongated, sinuous ridge of stratified sand and gravel left by rivers that flowed under or through a glacier. One of these eskers can be seen along State Highway 371 between Belle Prairie and Camp Ripley. Look to the east of the highway, across the flat farm fields, to the hills three to four hundred yards away. That is the Fort Ripley Esker. It is ten to sixty feet high, 225 to 250 feet wide, and almost seven miles long.

. . .

Saint Louis River slate beds

You can see the slate beds mentioned in this story at Jay Cooke State Park, which is located between the towns of Thompson and Fond du Lac, about twenty-five miles southwest of Duluth, Minnesota. Below the bridge where Highway 210 crosses the Saint Louis River and below the Thompson Dam are the tilted beds of slate of the Thompson formation. These beds were formed under ancient seas over two billion years ago. Directly below the bridge you will see the quartz intrusion also mentioned in the story.

Csansome, Constance. *Minnesota Underfoot: A Field Guide to Minnesota's Geology.* St. Paul, MN: Voyageur Press, 1990.

. . .

Twin Lakes

Twin Lakes was a stagecoach station along the military road from Saint Paul to Superior. The hotel, Lac La Belle, served as a trading post, general store, post office, and courthouse. It was also the Carlton County seat until about 1870. The original hotel still stands on the shore of Lac Labelle and can be seen from Carleton County Road 4 near Scotts Corner.

. . .

Fond du Lac

Fond du Lac is one of the oldest settlements in Minnesota. It has been continuously inhabited by natives and European descendents since long before Daniel Greysolon, Sieur du Lhut—for whom the city of Duluth is named—found an Indian village there when he visited the area in 1679.

John Jacob Astor set up a fur-trade post there in 1817. A historical marker is set on the sight of the post. The first treaty with the Minnesota Ojibwa was signed at Fond du Lac in 1826. Fond du Lac (end of the lakes) is southeast of Duluth, Minnesota on the Saint Louis River.

. . .

George Nettleton

By 1855, the Nettleton brothers, William and George, along with several others, had surveyed the town site of Duluth, Minnesota. William and George purchased several hundred acres of land in Duluth in 1856. George and J.B. Culver established a sawmill and a store on Minnesota Point. The

Nettletons are credited with constructing the first building in Duluth, and William is considered the city's first permanent resident.

. . .

GRAND MARAIS HARBOR

The harbor at Grand Marais, Minnesota, has been used by Indians and fur traders for hundreds of years. Two lava flows extend out into Lake Superior, forming nearly a full circle of rock that protects the harbor from the unpredictable nature of the lake.

Grand Marais was a major fur-trading port until the furs ran out and fashions in Europe changed. Due to the import of silk from the Orient, beaver fur was no longer needed for making top hats for European aristocrats. After the fur trade, the fishing industry dominated the harbor, and after that, the lumbermen took over. Today Grand Marais is a destination for vacationers as well as artists and writers looking for a quiet place to do their work. The scenery around Grand Marais is some of the most spectacular in the state. Thick, forested hills surround the town, and there is two and a half billion years of Earth history displayed in the rocks around the harbor and in the hills.

. . .

KIMBALL CREEK

In August of 1864, a survey crew was working in the area six miles northeast of Grand Marais. Charles D. Kimball—a strange sort of person— was one of the men on that crew. When the crew landed on the shore of Lake Superior, Kimball jumped out of the boat, ran into the woods, and disappeared. The next morning a search party found his clothes and shoes on the shore and barefoot tracks leading into the lake. Nothing else was ever found of him. The little stream where this happened is named Kimball Creek after Charles D. Kimball.

. . .

SILVER ON THE NORTH SHORE

On the 10th of July 1868, silver was discovered on a small island near the towns of Port Arthur and Fort William, which later merged and became the town of Thunder Bay, Ontario. Nuggets of silver "as large as hen's eggs," were reportedly found on the surface. Miners sunk a 1300-foot-deep shaft in the center of the island. During the first year of the operation, miners pulled one and a half million dollars in silver ore from the mine. A town developed on the shore of the island, with all of the amenities of a large city.

Pumps were in constant operation, keeping the seepage from Lake Superior from flooding the mine. Coal was needed to keep the steam-powered pumps running. The winter of 1884 brought disaster to the mine. The shipment of coal needed for the winter went to the bottom of Lake Superior with the ship carrying it when the drunken captain ran the ship aground. The mine flooded and was never reopened.

Raff, Willis H. *Pioneers in the Wilderness.* Grand Marais, MN: Cook County Historical Society, 1981.

. . .

MOOSE/WOLF SCENE

The incident involving the encounter between the moose and the wolves is based on a true story. It took place in one of the many deer hunting camps in Minnesota. It was told to us by Marty Dehen and edited slightly to accommodate this story.

. . .

Beaumont Boisvert is fictional.
Kathleen Marie O'Rourke is fictional.
Neena Lessard is fictional.
Anatole and the Athens Queen are fictional.
Reverend Diggs is fictional.
Abernathy Wayne is fictional.

The legend of the ghost searching for his silver is straight from the haphazard imagination of the authors.

Hawk, Jake, Sophie, Sunkist, Posey, and Lorraine were fictional at the start of this series, but now, we're not real sure.

ARVID LLOYD WILLIAMS

Arvid Lloyd Williams was born in Perham, Minnesota, and has lived in Minnesota all of his life. His appreciation for the history and geology of Minnesota prompted him to write the story of the Owen brothers, blending fictional stories with factual history. Williams shows his interest in the geology of Minnesota when describing the localities of the scenes of his stories. He is a member of the Minnesota Historical Society with books in the Minnesota Historical Society Library in Saint Paul.

BONNIE SHALLBETTER

Bonnie Shallbetter was born in Fairmont, Minnesota, and raised in Brooklyn Center. She is a graduate from the University of Minnesota where she received a Bachelor of Science degree in outdoor education. She has worked as a naturalist for the Three Rivers Park District and as an instructor for the Voyageur Outward Bound School. She also worked for the Wayzata School District as the Elementary Science Center resource manager for seventeen years. Leisure pursuits include traveling, canoeing, camping, hiking, dancing, writing, and acting.